"Shaw will someday write the big book he's always promised us, but *The Power Line* will do until that book gets here."
—Anonymous

"A romp, a thriller, a house of cards. Shaw tinkers and dodges around the edges of reality."
—Florence Marshall, founder, the Open Book Reader's Society of Lake Clear

"Frannie Germaine was a drunk and a low-life. Why would you ever write a book about that guy?"
—Old-timer in The Waterhole #3, Saranac Lake, 1991

"That Abel fellow never made it, you know. Just sayin.'" —Ben Rogers, 83, greenskeeper, Saranac Inn, 1991

The Power Line

Also by Christopher Shaw

SACRED MONKEY RIVER:
A CANOE TRIP WITH THE GODS
W.W. Norton and Co., 2000

THE POWER LINE

A NOVEL

CHRISTOPHER SHAW

Outskirts Press, Inc.
http://www.outskirtspress.com

Paperback ISBN: 978-1-9772-3213-7
Hardback ISBN: 978-1-9772-3335-6

Cover and book design by Pamela Fogg Editorial Design © 2020 Christopher Shaw. All rights reserved - used with permission.

Outskirts Press and the "OP" logo are trademarks belonging to Outskirts Press, Inc.

PRINTED IN THE UNITED STATES OF AMERICA

FOR SUE

NOTE TO THE READER

The question of what constitutes truth in the printed word is of understandable concern to the careful reader, doubly so in these truth challenged times. It goes without saying that you should bring to your reading of this regional chronicle the same healthy skepticism you would bring to reading scripture, Shakespeare, or the New York Times. The main text represents the labor of Abel St. Martin, for many years a guide, independent scholar, and businessman in the Adirondacks of northern New York State, recording and elucidating the words of a typical woodsman born around the turn of the twentieth century. Those who know the region will find numerous anomalies in its history and geography. As the Pragmatists showed us, however, the representation of reality is a very dicey proposition and bound to illuminate the character of the maker and consumer alike. We should engage it always with equanimity and a cold, hard eye.

PART ONE

Monroe's Story

[Tapes transcribed by Abel St. Martin from interviews in 1983 with Alonzo Monroe, of Lake Aurora, New York, edited and with added narrative by St. Martin.]

CHAPTER ONE

Mister H. Fucking Smith's
Power Line

"WELL, I DON'T KNOW HOW MUCH THERE IS TO SAY about Fran Germaine and how me and him met Jack Diamond and got into the bootlegging racket. It was a day I'll never forget, though, I'll tell you that."

Lonnie Monroe twisted his face up into a weird mask, the kind he made to emphasize a point. He sat across from me in a booth at the Trap Dyke taproom in Lake Aurora, New York, in the Adirondacks. His blue eyes were watery, and he hadn't shaved that morning, so his white beard prongs stuck out in all directions from his leathery face. He was otherwise well turned out in his retired-old-timer garb of pressed, tan Dickies, a felt Moose River hat, and Russell moccasins with white wool socks, rolled down. I'm doing this to make you happy, he seemed to be saying. Now let's just get it over with.

It was June of 1983. I had been pestering him for weeks to sit down and tell me about Fran Germaine and what happened at

Donnelly's Corners in the twenties, but he couldn't get used to the idea of talking into a machine, of cementing into the deep past something he clearly viewed as a living reality. Much was hinted around here about Fran Germaine, but little known. Everybody had heard fragments, but never in any coherent or very plausible form. Lonnie's versions left a lot of holes. He was a known embellisher, but he wasn't getting any younger, and I hoped to get his story down on tape while I still could.

He finally agreed because of his affection for Germaine's granddaughter, Sonja.

"He was her granddaddy, so she deserves to know," was how he put it. I hoped I could just keep him focused long enough to see if there was really anything there.

"In September of 1928," he went on, "all this country outside Saranac Lake village was just getting electrified, and me and Fran had been working for old Paul Smith and his power company since after the war, running lines. That day we had to go out and inspect the footers under them new towers on the Chateaugay line that the rain had washed out. But right before we headed out from the hotel shed, I got a message from Jimmy Mallon that the old man wanted to see me in the office. I told Fran I'd catch up with him at Bert La Fountain's, and followed Jimmy back to the office."

Here Monroe stopped to complain about how much stronger he had been back then, his health, the recent recession, and the recent air controller's strike. I was about to turn off the machine to save the expensive reel-to-reel tape when he found his way back to the thread.

Back then, he said, the newest Paul Smith's Electric Company trunk line slashed through the spruce bogs and forests of Gabriels, Bloomingdale, and Onchiota: twin forty-foot uprights of local white pine and black spruce, hundreds of them, connected by crossbars and diagonal braces, and linked by parallel cables stretched to their limit by big diesel engines. Even after they were stretched, the cables sagged in long, concave loops running northeast, until they converged in the distance and disappeared into the cut-over oblivion beyond Loon Lake.

"You shoulda seen Fran gaze down that line, with that long and empty look," Lonnie said. "After the war we'd cruised and marked every one of them trees ourselves, and he'd laid out the model on the map and sited those stanchions. Now they were up and running, with Union Falls about to start up. Never seemed to please him that much, though."

The line carried power from the dams Paul Smith had built on the Saranac River—and that drowned the falls and holes where Germaine's father, old Claude Germaine, had once caught salmon. By then so few people remembered those salmon, Lonnie said, that sometimes he and Germaine doubted their own memories and those of the older men who were starting to die off as Germaine's father had in the 1918 flu. But old Claude *had* caught salmon there. And though Lonnie and Germaine had seen industry and the railroad come and go by that time, the power line meant something different. "It was like we'd come to the end of something, but we didn't know what it was exactly. Like we'd never know the woods the way our fathers had.

"Anyway, the reason Paul'd sent for me was that he wanted me to head down to Malone to have some dealings with the bootleggers down there, get some whiskey and gin for this big shindig he had planned for investors in the new line. Well, I could do that. Everybody knew who the liquor men were, and most of them was related to people in Lake Aurora and Saranac. So I took the hotel's Model A truck down through the Nine Mile Woods Road—not as easy then as it is today—and ordered the ten cases of liquor and three of champagne, while Fran walked out the Chateaugay line."

This was in the scrub barrens and lakes of the northern

Adirondacks, where the central plateau of the High Peaks declined northward to the St. Lawrence, and glacial eskers wormed over the sand plains and spruce bogs. Germaine and Monroe had grown up in Lake Aurora, not far from the hotel. Nearby, Teddy Roosevelt, at eighteen, had identified the Swainson's thrush, the bay warbler, the ruby-crowned kinglet, and the rare spruce grouse for his *Summer Birds of the Adirondacks in Franklin County, N.Y.* A few years later, at Bay Pond, he shot one of the last moose in the Adirondacks and became a conservationist. Godfrey St. Germain, Fran Germaine's grandfather, had guided and hunted with Teddy, and they had both known men the great president had also known and asked after, and they emulated his ethos of hardihood and straightforward fairness.

That day the sky was blue as an agate marble, the light taking on an even harder edge in late afternoon. It was cool in the shade and hot in the sun, and Germaine would have put his wool-lined canvas jacket on and off a dozen times. When he reached the Loon Lake Road, he hopped a handcar that had been left there for him on the tracks, and headed back west and south, over the black bogs, the trout holes, and the sandy blueberry flats. He reached Bert La Fountain's speakeasy in Gabriels as the last light faded on the peaks to the south.

"By then I'd got back from Malone and had a beer. Around five he come in all cocky the way he did, wise-assed and swaggering, you know," Monroe said. "Acted like he owned the place. Got away with it cuzza them black eyes and hair, and because he played the fiddle like Paganini. Or so the women thought.

"'Why you no good—,' I told him.

"'Where the hell you been all day?' he says. 'I been out there twelve miles, all alone, trying to keep money flowing into Mr. H. Fucking Smith's pocket with nothing but a shovel. And where you been? You been in here.'"

"Watch yer mouth there, mister," Bert La Fountain said.

Bert and Gladys sat with Monroe in the front hall. Bert, in doublet and suspenders, pretended to run a clean house, even though sex was commonly arranged there, with Gladys's full knowledge and assistance. Her own mouth could scandalize a barracks.

"Just give me a beer," Germaine said. Bert went in back and returned with a bottle of Molson's. Germaine took it and sucked down half the bottle.

"Had to go down to Malone and back for the boss," Monroe said. "Big doin's."

"Big, huh? What's he got planned this time?"

"Party to throw the switch on Union Falls. Needed to order booze for them Albany big shots and money guys."

"Keep it to yourselves there," Bert said, ever wary of G-men and the Black Horse troop of the state police.

Coming south from Malone, it had taken Monroe two hours to get from Meacham's Lake to the hotel through the Nine Mile Woods, the road rutted and washed out in numerous places. In those days liquor flowed like spring runoff across the border, along the St. Lawrence, and south down Route 9 and Lake Champlain. But when Nine Mile Woods (now Route 30) turned icy in winter or soft in mud season, the booze ran out quickly, giving rise to a widespread and generalized thirst.

Monroe said, "Saranac Lake was like a real little city in those days. There were eight hotels and a couple of speaks downtown. Along with the usual families and mill people, you had all your lungers from all over the world, doctors, G-men, and bootleggers. The lungers couldn't get enough booze, they had so little to lose— if you get me. It wasn't part of old Doc Trudeau's treatment—and he was a teetotaler—but your average dying person is more likely to indulge in temptations. That's why so much hanky-panky went on between the patients. Oh, yeah, them cure cottages was regular cat houses. Dying people are horny."

While Monroe and Germaine talked, two bootleggers were loitering in the back room, mumbling to each other and another figure who never emerged. Eventually, the two came out. They were wearing expensive suits and had mud on their two-toned shoes. One of them was long-faced and dark; the other was smaller, more Irish looking.

"New neighbors," Bert said. "Their boss bought the place out on that island between the Flow and Clear Pond."

"Oh, yeah?" Germaine said. "Big trout in Little Loon Pond, right over that esker."

"That what?"

"Don't mind him," Bert said. "College boy."

In 1914 one of Smith's regular customers had sent Germaine to engineering school at Clarkson University, down in Potsdam, where he had lasted for two years before too many people wearing raccoon coats had compelled him to join the U.S. cavalry. The customer had recognized the lad's architectural skills in the log bridges, lean-tos, and cabins he had built on the hotel's vast forest holdings. He signed them all with a personal brand burned into the wood: a raven in silhouette, inside a capital letter G.

The men looked at Bert, then back at Germaine.

"Who am I talking to?" Germaine said.

"You can call me Basil. And this is Frank. Let's have a drink."

Basil produced a bottle of Johnny Walker Black Label and poured one for the room. An hour later the bottle was empty, and the four new friends were in Basil's Packard driving out the Oregon Plains Road to Hattie's, the real cathouse along the tracks. It had four rooms upstairs; six passably good-looking girls; Hattie, who ran the place; and ample available liquor. Hattie hired her girls from across the border in Quebec and from the reservation at Hogansburg, on the St. Lawrence—with an occasional Eastern European immigrant thrown in. Eventually, some of them married locally or became nurses in the cure cottages. As late as the sixties, the building remained standing among spruce saplings and blueberry bushes near the tracks. It was a long, two-story lodge with a low porch and sagging roof, built half of logs and half timberframe, and sided with faded green cedar shingles.

Hattie greeted them with gusto. Here were men with real money—friends, it was rumored, of Legs Diamond. Germaine and Monroe were favorites of the house.

"He was a real pepperpot, lemme tell you," Lonnie Monroe said of Germaine. "Waltzing in with his fiddle case under one arm. All bushy, black hair and eyebrows. Not more than six feet, you know, but wrapped as tight as steel strapping. After Mexico, and especially after France, he'd as soon spit in your face as say hello. No patience for anything or anybody."

They all had a drink. Then they went upstairs and got their "ashes hauled," as Monroe put it. Afterward, Germaine took out his fiddle and began to play, leaning against the doorframe between the front hall and the kitchen: "Joys of Quebec," "Soldier's Joy," "Up Jumped the Devil," "Ragtime Annie," reels and waltzes. A customer showed up who played the upright piano. Pretty soon the shades were drawn, and the floor swayed and undulated under the bouncing feet of fourteen people.

After a few songs, Basil came out of one of the upstairs rooms, knotting his silk tie, with his shoulder holster and the butt of his big service .45 sticking out. He waited till the music stopped, made a face, and said, "What the hell's all that squeaking? Sounds like a bagful of alley cats in heat. French alley cats."

The room fell silent.

"It's the sound of the bats flying out of your ass, you ugly Irish cock."

Monroe said: "Fran was looking up at Basil on the stair landing, his shoulders back and his chin sticking out. He held his fiddle like a club, his bow in the other hand with raggedy strings hanging off it. I thought, oh, mother, here it comes, and kept my eye on Frank, who was sitting on the couch with a girl who looked scared shitless. Basil just slowly knotted his tie and stared back. He looked more surprised than pissed off, like a hawk you might see being chased by a chickadee—but he was weird-looking anyway. And the butt of that big automatic was sticking right out at the room."

Hattie pushed the younger girls into the kitchen, her loyalties divided between somebody who grew up nearby and whom she had known all her life, and a new source of money, liquor, and fresh young women.

"All right, Fran Germaine. You put that fiddle down," she said.

"Hattie, I can handle this."

"I don't care who you are, or him neither. There'll be no fighting or shooting in my house."

"Fran and Basil both had that French-Irish thing, you see," Monroe said. "Now, your Quebec Frenchman and your Irishman are really one and the same. The Canadian French all came from Brittany, and the way that peninsula sticks out into the Channel, almost to Ireland—a Frenchman in Brittany is really nothing but an Irishman. That's why Irish and Canuck fiddle music sounds the same. And they both had that blackness the Canucks and Irish sometimes get, too. Not skin-black, like the colored, or even just their hair. It was scarier than that, more mental. Sometimes when you looked into Fran's eyes, you felt like it was just a big emptiness and no mercy in there. So, for a minute, things looked real dangerous."

"God damn it, Hattie," Germaine said.

Basil jutted his chin from side to side and nonchalantly seated the knot in his tie. He dropped his hands to his sides. "Don't worry, tough guy," he said. "I shouldn't a said that about French alley cats. But you gotta learn to take a joke."

One of the girls snickered, and the guy at the piano played the first notes of "Happy Days Are Here Again." Germaine dropped his hands and looked sheepish, then defiant, with his eyebrows raised in self-mockery.

"Oh you couldn't give that man an inch, nossir," Monroe said. "And they could see that in him, that he would split you from crotch to ribcage with a dull deer antler. We drank all night and he played the fiddle, and pretty soon we were thick as thieves with them boys."

In the wee hours, Basil's Packard turned off of Jones Pond Road and rolled down a double-tracked driveway through Smith's big pines and along a narrow spit of land. Soon they came to a one-lane bridge over a channel wide enough for a narrow boat to pass through. A round stone gate rose on the far side, which they passed through unchallenged. Basil parked beside a small landing. There, a beautiful sixteen-foot Hacker strained on its painters against a brand-new stone and concrete dock. Fog lay over the water like cotton batting, parting in gray rags as they passed through it.

It was a small, birch-clad island, part of a continuous low esker that paralleled the course of an ancient glacier, separated from the land on either end by narrow, stone-lined channels. On one side lay the deep waters of Clear Pond; on the other the low, weedy pike water they called The Flow. Germaine and Monroe knew the place, having camped and picnicked there often when they rowed guests out from Smith's hotel. In the middle of the island a new one-story lodge of stone and logs stood on top of a rise beneath huge pines, with a smaller guest cabin and boathouse near the shore and a big barn with brainstorm siding near the bridge—a modest outpost in comparison to the rustic summer palaces on the nearby St. Eustace and St. Regis chain lakes. They knew it had been built recently, and they knew the men who worked on it, but they never knew who owned it.

Inside, they drank French brandy and smoked Cuban cigars beside a fire in the main room of the lodge, and played Bix

Biederbecke records on the big gramophone. The sky turned gray about five thirty. Blearily, Basil told them to sleep in the guest cabin.

"We'll talk in the morning," he said.

"I was starting to feel a little strange by then, and wished like hell we'd drove the Model T," Monroe said. "But Fran, he was just right in the groove with old Basil, asking him all about who he worked for and where he come from. He knew, of course. But Basil, he just stayed cagey and hinted at very dangerous activities, filthy women, and lots of dough.

"'You'll go far, buster,' Basil told Fran. 'You're either tough or crazy—probably a little of both. I'm gonna tell Jack about you.'

"'Tell him what?'

"'Coupla tough soldier boys who could maybe help us out?'

"'We got jobs,' I said.

"'When Jack gets here in the morning, we'll see what he says about your jobs.'

"We were both supposed to be at work in about an hour and I wanted to leave, but I followed Fran down to the guest cottage beside the water. It had two rooms, one on either side of a shared bathroom. Nice porcelain fixtures, and a window that looked out of each room right onto the water below. Fran took one of the rooms, and I sat on the bed in the other. I lay down with my boots hanging over the side, too drunk and fired-up to sleep, but worried too. I had started to doze when I woke up. Fran was standing in the doorway looking down at me. He had his fiddle case under his arm wrapped in twine, and a shit-eating grin on his face.

"'Let's go,' he said.

"'Why not?' I said.

"We walked out the driveway in the gray light almost back to Jones Pond Road. But before we got to it, we climbed up to the spine of the ridge and took that narrow, snaky trail through the woods. When we cut into Smith's trails, we just stayed on them the rest of the way to the hotel. On the way we spooked a big sow bear and her cub rooting in the shallows of Osgood Pond. They splashed across the shallows into the trees in one direction, and we crashed through the woods in the other.

"'What the hell do you think Mister Legs Diamond is gonna say about us running out on his man?' I said.

"'He'll think we're pretty damn snappy, is what.'

"It felt pretty good to get away like that. Things had been going pretty smooth until then, and I hoped they'd keep going that way. That day at work we weren't very snappy, though. In fact, we were downright useless. The rest of the boys covered for us, though, and we made it through by nipping from a jug in the blacksmith shop and taking catnaps in the boathouse. We showed ourselves and looked busy every hour or so. That way nobody wondered where we were."

CHAPTER TWO

Rural Electrification

L ONNIE MONROE WAS IN HIS EARLY EIGHTIES and slowing down by the time he sat for these recordings. He lived out along the Saranac in a nice old clapboard house surrounded by piles of salvaged metal roofing, barn siding, two-by-fours and random boards, and a corral containing two Morgan bay horses. He drove a Power Wagon he'd assembled from scavenged parts, and always wore nattily pressed green slacks, a khaki work shirt, and a rakish Moose River hat. On those afternoons, we sat at the table in the bar where the old people usually kept to themselves or received the entreaties and inquiries of the young—new arrivals mostly, who were searching (as I was) for the distilled human essence of the place they had adopted and idealized. Usually they sat outside on the deck overhanging the river, played guitars on the enclosed porch or pool in the bar. For them the Trap Dyke was (as was Lake Aurora itself, and other small Adirondack towns) a grad school of authenticity, a living north woods Symposium and Agora overseen by alcoholic Solons, Diotemas, and Socrateses. Eventually old and new grew into a mutually dependent and happy, if unlikely, hybrid alliance that flourished for three or four years before the old-timers started dropping off like passenger pigeons.

Monroe had been retired for ten years. Before that, and after he and Germaine had gone their own ways, he drove teams for logging companies, managed a CCC camp, then took a job as a carpenter for the state Conservation Department, where he worked for twenty years. As long as I'd known him, he'd run a trap line, taken the odd horse-logging job, built and sold birdhouses and picnic tables, and worked odd jobs. He went to an AA meeting in the village every Wednesday, then stopped at the Trap Dyke for coffee and to trade jibes with the other old bastards. I used to think, here was this World War I vet, a smalltime bootlegger and adventurer still among us in these visibly changing Adirondacks, a nugget of meaning in the overall mess of the country.

When I started asking him about the old days, he wanted to talk, but he had a hard time remembering things. Regarding Fran Germaine, however, he was quite specific and adamant. "That Ruth Bellows oughta watch what she says about me," he said. (Ruth Bellows was for many years the tyrannical Lake Aurora town historian.) "That I made a lot of that stuff up about Hattie's, that she never ran a cat house, and other things. Well, I was a customer, and Ruth's just trying to protect people's reputations. What about mine? It wasn't bad neither, though I'm glad I met my Mary when I did." Mary had died in 1968. "Some of them girls turned into solid citizens," he added.

"Don't believe a word this guy says," said Ross Perkins from behind the bar. "He oughta get arrested, the shit he tells people."

"Oh, you know I'm telling the truth, mister. Just shut your trap and get me another Coke."

Well, he said, they never saw Basil or Frank again till the big party at the hotel. The only reason he and Germaine were there was because they had to talk to some of the men from Albany, investors who wanted to hear about the day-to-day operations of the line and the generators—not from engineers, but from the woodsmen who had planned and maintained the line. He and Germaine were supposed to be there at the cocktail hour, then vanish for dinner and the dance.

Monroe said: "It all took place in the old saloon, they called it, with the fancy wainscoting, the open-hearth fireplace, and the antler chandeliers. Big French doors opened onto the flagstone veranda looking out over the lake. It hadn't been used for anything like this since Prohibition began, really. They had some big ash logs burning and it was warm inside, right when the colors would have been the brightest if the rain hadn't blown all the leaves off.

"There were about sixty or seventy people, all big shots, dressed very grand in tuxes and fancy gowns. A few of the older wives tried to look like flappers, only more refined. There was three fiddles and one of them cellos on a stage playing Mozart or something. They were serving the punch and champagne inside the cloak room, for appearances sake, the French doors open onto the terrace, with guards posted there and at the hall entrance. But it was no kind of rowdy crowd, just experienced Protestant booze hounds with plenty of dough. People went indoors and out, men and women, and there were some real beauties, you can imagine."

There were also at least six legislators, an aide to Governor Franklin Roosevelt (Teddy's grandnephew), the director of the state commerce commission (which had supposedly cited Smith for illegally damming the Saranac), and a number of members of Albany's Fort Orange Club, where Smith also belonged. The mayors of Plattsburgh, Watertown, and Malone (which sorely needed electricity) attended, along with the directors of the Santa Clara Lumber Company, bankers from all over New York, and electrical contractors.

Germaine and Monroe drank highballs near the fireplace and accepted the fawning (if patronizing) attention of the men of substance, who idolized them as the sorts they wished they could be. Germaine would have had no sense of this, but it was a clear and still tangible memory to Lonnie Monroe.

"Good show, young man," said the president of the Hudson Valley Trust in Troy, whom Germaine had guided on a successful trout-fishing trip to the Fish Ponds in 1914. "I always knew you had it in you. How's your father, old Claude?"

"He's dead now, sir, these ten years."

A gray-haired man and his wife approached, bowing slightly, the woman displaying acres of diamond-draped bosom. "We were disappointed that you left Clarkson," the man said. "But we heard about your success in the war and working for Mr. Paul. When you're ready to move to Syracuse, you'll always find a place at the Onondaga Guaranty."

"Please call on us," the wife said.

Only two people really cared to hear about the conduct of the operation or ways to cut expenses in the field, and they were also former customers of the hotel, prominent investors in Smith's enterprise, and admirers of Germaine's log-work bridges and lean-tos from before the war. The four talked shop, the war, and the perennially dismal state of the deer herd for half an hour, almost until the party (minus Germaine and Monroe) were to be escorted into the lavishly appointed dining room.

"While them gentlemen was talking to us, I kept noticing Fran's eye roaming over toward these two females of the flapper persuasion who kept off to themselves, over by the roses and chrysanthemums, drinking champagne punch. The big one was like a Gibson girl, all legs and pedigree and finishing school. But the smaller one was a real looker, long eyelashes over huge black eyes, and black hair with a spit curl. They really stood out in that crowd. Well, that dark one, she kept looking back at Fran, too, so much that he could hardly pay attention to what the men were saying. It didn't matter, cause I kind of took over the conversational duties.

"About then, the men wandered off to join their wives, because a ceremony was about to happen where Paul was gonna throw the switch and open up the new Union Falls line and light the newly wired chandeliers. A big deal, I guess. I still considered myself a loyal employee, and I was watching the electricians getting ready. But then Fran says to me, 'What are *they* doing here?' So I turned around and there's old Basil and Frank standing over there swilling champagne punch with them two flappers. 'I don't know, but it must have to do with the booze,' I said."

They didn't wonder about it for long. Right then Paul Smith strode to the head of the room and stood in front of the fireplace. It was six, almost dark outside and getting drunk inside. The firelight shimmered on the wainscoting and the faces of the guests while Smith stood there senatorially in his old-fashioned string tie, black frock coat, and pale, wide-brimmed fedora. He appeared aged from his recent heart ailment, but he was still the imposing gentleman-woodsman, white haired and bearded and dignified. He waited quietly while the hubbub died down.

When all you could hear was the fire, he welcomed everybody with his deep and gentle-but-mannered voice. He thanked his investors and engineers, including Germaine and Lonnie, and waxed rosy on the prospect of forthcoming profits. "You could hear the women breathing, and the men's stomachs growling," Monroe said. Then Smith started counting backward from ten, and the whole party joined in. "Five, four, three, two . . ." On "one," when the switch was thrown, nothing happened. Smith looked around, confused. Then all three of the chandeliers flickered— once, and again. Finally the dozens of incandescent bulbs flashed on together and "lit up the place like Times Square," as Lonnie said. The women gasped, and the gentlemen muttered.

"Oh, goodness gracious," said Smith. He clapped, and the whole party joined in, clapping and blurting "huzzah" and "bravo" over the polite din.

Monroe said: "Of course, I heard one lady say, 'it's not as pleasant as the old gas lights, but safer I suppose.' A few weeks later the hotel started using fewer bulbs, so it didn't feel like the inside of a courthouse or an office building, but that night it just bleached all the color out of the room."

The revelry continued, however. The hubbub resumed and men returned to the punch bowl under the electrical glare. But by then Basil and Frank and the two flappers had disappeared. Germaine and Monroe looked for them in the hall, the gentlemen's parlor, and everywhere they could, with no luck. They reentered the salon just as the dining room doors opened and the party began slowly filtering in.

"We could see into the dining room, all the crystal glittering and the waiters with their towels on their arms, but we were already tired of acting polite and not so bothered that we couldn't stay. It was a short walk from there to Fran's shack on the river by Keese's Mill, and first we were going to stop at the stable for a nip with his cousin Pete. So, while everybody left the saloon, we headed down the hallway toward the door. Some ladies were crossing the hall in front of us on their way back from the powder room. Old and young, all shapes and sizes, but all very fancy and turned out.

"When we were almost in the middle of the pack, we saw the two flappers walking away with their backs to us. The smaller darker one was brushing her thigh and the fringe on her dress as she swung her right arm. After a second she turned her head real quick, looked down at her hand, and then up at us—just long enough for us to see her eyes—and then turned back like we weren't even there. Her hand opened, and a piece of pale blue paper fell to the floor."

The two men loitered for a minute, looking around. When the coast was clear Germaine sidled over, picked it off the floor, and thrust it into his pocket.

They stepped out onto the porch. The lights from the dining room cast a liquid glow through the windows, into the deepening dark. They could see their breath in the chilly air and smell the rotting vegetation—the fermenting organic matter, like cider or compost—that prefigured the long months of darkness and cold.

Germaine moved to the light of a hurricane lamp mounted on the porch. He took the note from his pocket and read it, holding it to the light and squinting.

A loon called out on the lake.

"What does it say?" Monroe said.

Germaine looked up. "Meet us at the island."

They were still standing there looking at each other when Jimmy Mallon, the night steward, put his head out the door. "Don't go nowheres," he said. "Mr. Paul wants to talk to that guy." He pointed at Germaine.

When Germaine let himself into the vast corner office on the second floor, Smith said, "Ah, François. Thank you for joining me."

"The old fart stood in front of the fireplace of round granite stones flecked with quartz, feldspar, mica, and garnet, cleaning and refilling his pipe. Above the mantel hung the mounted head of a moose—one of the last in the Adirondacks—shot by his old friend Teddy Roosevelt. Above that, a pair of crossed snowshoes, made by Mohawks in Hogansburg, on the St. Lawrence, which Smith had worn to lead his hunting party out of a remote camp near the Jordan River through three feet of fresh powder. His rifles and shotguns stood in a rack, his books in the floor-to-ceiling shelves. An ash-splint pack basket finished with mellowed oil and varnish occupied a corner near the desk, and a big map of the Adirondacks by his friend Seneca Ray Stoddard hung on the wall behind his head. 'Lovely party, what? Though we must find out why the switch malfunctioned. Did Mr. Breedlove have a chance to speak with you? He's your great admirer.'

"'Yes, sir. He wanted to know about the seasonal volume fluctuations on the Saranac.'

"'Good, good. Well you certainly know about that.' He lit his pipe and sucked on it until it got smoky. 'We've known each other a long time, François. I remember when your father worked at Bartlett's back in the eighties. He rowed, cut wood, told droll stories. Played spoons well, I recall, and had a voice like Caruso. He was a real man, he was. That grin, that rare good humor and wit, what? Hm, hm.' [Listening to Monroe 'do' Paul Smith was almost like having a news reel or recording of the man. He also mimicked Noah Rondeau's squeak—Ed.] Always admired that in a man. Never complained or turned down a job. Always on time and sober. I couldn't wait to get you, his son, working for me when you came of age. It's been a good relationship over the years, don't you think? All those structures you built. You made your mark on the north woods.'

"'Yes, sir,' Fran said.

"'I was so glad when you rejoined us after fulfilling your patriotic duty,'" Lonnie went on, in the voice of Smith.

"Thank you, Mr. Paul."

"Yes, hm. Well, we have need of your special talents again." He inserted his pipe into the corner of his mouth, and, bending forward slightly, presented his hindquarters to the fire. "A number of the men here are pushing me to expand the electric company to Malone, Lake Aurora, and Tupper Lake, though it appears that damned Dewey will control whatever occurs in Lake Placid. Well, no matter, there's no market there anyway. It's all in Tupper, with the lumber mills."

He stood erect again and turned his front to the fire, holding up the tails of his coat and showing Germaine his skinny behind. "We need to figure out how much more we can get out of Franklin and Union falls, and whether we can dam the river at High Falls.

Well, the engineers will do that, won't they. Hm."

"Yes, sir."

"And of course you know the ground so well, François." He turned around again. "You know it as well or better than I do, as well as the older guides. More importantly, you know the connections, how to get from one area to another the easiest way. We'll need a survey and men, horses, and trucks to cut out the line. I want you to run the crew."

"Well, that would be fine, sir, but what about when we talked about me taking over operations as supervisor?"

"This is a bigger job, François. I need you out on the land. We'll start immediately. Meet me at the village office in the morning, and we'll go over maps with the engineers."

Germaine just stood there.

Smith had turned toward the fire again. "What is it?" he said.

"The other job paid better, Mr. Smith. That's why I wanted it."

"You disappoint me, François. We can always talk about money. Right now, you have no family or prospects of one. If you'll handle this next problem for me at your current wage, we'll see about more later."

Germaine stood quietly for a moment, then turned toward the door.

Smith faced the fireplace. "See you in the morning," he said, as Germaine closed the door behind him.

"I COULDN'T TELL ANYTHING HAD WENT WRONG," Monroe said. "Fran walked over to the stable and through the door. I was in there drinking good Canadian with his cousin Pete LaFleur—a real nice kid, if a little wild—who grew up on Easy Street. Pete had heisted the bottle off the truck that brought it from Malone. When I asked Fran what the old man wanted, he said, 'Talked about some new power lines.' Like it didn't mean nothing. I kept prodding him, but, you know, when he clammed up you couldn't pry a nail out of him with dynamite."

"'Looks like Mr. Paul got into our hero's head,' Pete said, half drunk. 'Boss in your head, old man?' Pete was twenty to Fran's thirty. When he said hero, he really meant it. But you couldn't get to Fran by ribbing him that way, and it just made him clam up more."

They drank in the stable with Pete for an hour, then took the stable's Model T truck and Fran's fiddle and drove out Jones Pond Road along the esker. In the headlights, the fallen birch leaves and pine and tamarack needles made a dull yellow carpet over the dirt surface of the road. They turned left at the carry from Jones Pond to Rainbow Lake and wound down the unmarked and needle-carpeted dirt track through the corridor of lichenous tamarack and balsam trunks.

When they came to the bridge, the gate was closed. They stopped in the dark, Monroe getting out and walking to the gate in the glow of the headlights to open it.

"I was just about to unlatch the latch and swing open the long logs of the gate when I heard that sound—that clicking that you can't mistake for anything else—and felt the muzzle of a pistol at the back of my neck. Someone a few feet away said, 'Get out of the car,' so I knew there were two of them—and it wasn't Basil and Frank. 'Where do you boys think you're goin'?' said one of them, after Fran got out of the car. 'We're with Basil,' Fran said. 'He told us to come over after the party.'

"'He did, ay,' the guy with the shotgun said. 'Well, he ain't here. Now turn this jitney around and scram, before we got to muss you up.'

"'Just a minute,' the other guy said. 'Maybe these are the boys Basil told us about. Those tough guys. Woodsmen.'

"'Yeah, that's us,' Fran said.

"At this point all I wanted was to fly the coop," Monroe said. "The sweat was running down the inside of my shirt. Why couldn't he just keep his froggy trap shut?"

"'Maybe we oughta just keep them here till Basil gets back, make sure they're who they say they are,' the one guy said again.

"'The boss might not like it.'

"'Don't worry about the boss.'

"The guy took his pistola from my neck and told me to turn around," Monroe said. "He shined his light right in my eyes and told me to get in the truck. I didn't look right at him, but after I got in and they told us to drive and park down by the little cabin, where we'd stayed the other night, I could see he was this big guy in a striped suit, and he looked like an Italian. The other guy held a Thompson and had a little black cigar stuck in his teeth.

"We parked by the cabin and they pulled up close behind us with their lights on. Then they each opened one of the doors to take us out. In the headlights I got a look at my guy's face, and at first I thought he reminded me of the Mexicans we saw down along the border, with Pershing. But then I realized it wasn't the Mexicans he looked like at all, but the Indians.

"'Just you boys stay in here till Basil and Frank show up,' said the one with the cigar. 'Relax. Have a drink. Emile here will watch the door for you till then, all right?'

"'Wait,' said Emile (the Indian), pointing at the fiddle case under Fran's arm. 'Gimme that.' Fran stood in the headlights while the Indian took the fiddle case from under his arm.

"'Well, not so fast, I guess,' the Cigar said, pointing the Thompson at him. The Indian flipped open the latches and held the case open. The fiddle lay there on its green cushion, the glare on its burgundy finish shining like the sun, and all those loose bow hairs limp and untightened.

"'Fiddler, ay?' said the Cigar. 'All right. Can't hurt us with that, unless it's our ears. Let 'em go.'

"'Thanks,' Fran said, taking the open case back from the Indian but keeping his eyes on Cigar. 'I'll keep it low.'

"'You best do that, mister woods man. Okay, put 'em inside.'

Inside they lit oil lamps, and Germaine affected to relax, taking off his shoes, lying on the bed, and lighting a Sweet Caporal.

"Oh, well, look at you. Ain't you the man. We should of just left when they told us," I said.

"'What are you scared of?' Fran said. 'It's a nice little camp,' he added, smoothing his hand along the surface of the fancy Hudson's Bay blanket. 'Maybe we'll stay the night this time.'

"Yeah, you maybe. What if Basil and those girls never show?"

A bottle of scotch and one of gin stood on the small dresser. The men poured drinks and turned down the lamps, one of which was hanging over the table beside the window and bathing the log interior in buttery light. The moon came up over the lake. By eleven Basil had still not showed. Germaine took out his fiddle and sat at the table with the chin piece pressed into his arm, drawing the bow slowly over the strings in pensive, minor-key ruminations. Half an hour later he moved out to the porch. He leaned against the railing and played a slow reel he had heard in France, a Scots lament, a Texas polka, a Canadian waltz.

"All them songs, most of which I been along for when he picked them up in the cantina or whorehouse or what have you. It made me kinda remember that we had known each other long enough by then that we weren't kids anymore. It was the first time I'd ever had that feeling, like this was our lives, this was it. We'd damn near been killed together, in a foreign land. A coupla foreign lands. And here we were. That's when I knew something other than what he had told me had gone on in there with the old man. Even still, right then I just wanted to wring his neck.

"Standing out there with the air cool but nice, and the light on the water and that fall smell coming out of the woods. All them songs. That son of a bitch. It got me so upset I figured I'd just look out the door and maybe see which way the wind was blowing with old Emile."

CHAPTER THREE

Real Fucking Money

MONROE WENT OVER TO THE DOOR where Emile sat on a chair on the stone doorstep, smoking and staring out across the water. He wore a fedora, a wide-lapel suit, and two-toned shoes. When he saw Monroe standing there, he looked up at the door.

"I know one a them songs," Emile said. "That's 'En Roulant Ma Boule.'"

"You French?" Monroe said.

"Naw, Indian. Caughnawaga. Some French."

"Well how long we got to stay in here, anyways?"

"I don't know, but Basil's car pulled up a few minutes ago. Ask him."

"You mean wait till he comes down here and ask him."

"You got it."

They heard the sound of the electric generator—a Chrysler six—starting up in its little shack out past the bridge, followed by the low, barely audible hum of its operation. In the lodge the lights went on, the power drawn on the generator dimmed them, and then the governor kicked in and the motor and lights slowly built back up.

"That's in Montreal, ain't it?" Monroe said.

"Nope. Across the river."

Emile kept his eyes on the house, where a door had opened, projecting a bar of light out through the birches and balsams. They heard voices, and the beam diminished as the door closed. Then soft feet on the flagstone steps, and into the moonglow in front of the house stepped the small dark one, with a sort of fur cape around her shoulders and a champagne bottle in her hand.

Emile stood. "Bonsoir, mademoiselle," he said.

"Bonsoir, Emile."

She stood on her toes and, hooking an arm around his neck, kissed him. Then she turned to Monroe.

"Hello," she said. "I am Yvette."

"Good to meet you, mamzelle. Lonnie Monroe, Lake Aurora. You weren't by any chance riding with Monsieur Basil, were you?"

"Right then she saw Fran standing in the doorway behind me. You should have seen them big, black eyes of hers open up, like deep spring holes in a bog. And with that spit curl and that little cape, she looked prettier than a pinto pony."

"Basil is in the house with Wendy," Yvette said, looking straight at Germaine, who still held his fiddle in the crook of his arm and his bow in the other hand.

"Wendy, huh," Monroe said.

She turned back and faced Monroe. "Enchantée, monsieur," she said, taking his hand and dipping. "I heard music and brought champagne for the band. You won't be in here much longer, anyways, I promise. I will bring glasses."

"She sashayed right past me and Fran into the cabin. Fran leaned in the doorway and followed her with his eyes. Then he played some more of that gloomy music. Usually I liked that kind of thing, but it was just about starting to annoy me at that point."

Emile sat back down.

"Thought you said you weren't French," Monroe said.

"I speak French. Comme les habitants."

"Whatever the hell that's supposed to mean."

Emile just snorted and looked away.

"How about I go up to talk to Basil," Monroe said.

"How about you just wait right here."

"We heard a cork pop, and Yvette came back with four glasses on a round tray and handed them around. It began to feel more like we were guests than prisoners, except for big old Emile sitting there with that gat in his pocket."

"That was 'The Song of Evangeline' you were playing," Yvette said. "I love that song."

"It sounds even better on the porch," Germaine said. "Want to hear it?"

"All right. Come on, Emile."

They trooped through the cabin to the back porch, where they sipped their drinks while Germaine played all the Quebeçois and French tunes he knew. Then it was almost midnight, and they were still looking out over the water and talking about Canada, the party at the hotel, the war. Germaine switched to popular ballads, which they sang along to in low tones till a cloud covered the moon and a cold breeze blurred its reflection. That drove them back inside, where they started a fire and waited for their invitation to the house.

It came around one. The Cigar came down without his Thompson and told them to come up to the house. Yvette had fallen asleep on one of the beds, and they put a blanket over her and left her there. With Emile and the Cigar behind them, Germaine and Monroe climbed the flagstones by the light from the Cigar's flashlight and entered the house through the big wooden door that opened toward the lake. A short hall led to the great room, where four guys and two women sat around in front of a leaping fire. Shoulder holsters, pistols, and ammunition lay around on the coffee table and the arms of chairs. Basil and Frank sprawled on one of the couches, stewed, while the Cigar and Emile stood watch along the edges. On a cushy love seat closest to the fire sat a short, wiry Irishman with black, swept-back hair and a widow's peak. His shoulder holster was empty and his bow tie untied. Bix was on the gramophone, and the two women were lounging around in their garters and camisoles, with their diamonds still on, under the watchful gaze of the caribou mounted over the fireplace.

"Get outta here," the Irishman said. Emile slipped out without a word. "Throw that thing out," he told the Cigar, who nodded and threw his stogie into the fire.

"We probably shoulda been more nervous. We were being held by gangsters, but neither of us could take our eyes off them flappers. Such thighs you never seen, and them old-fashioned silk knickers, boy. I had to cross my legs, if you catch my meaning. The woman we hadn't seen before got up and lay right across the boss's lap. Himself, he looked like a real banty rooster, tight as a copper coil, more than a match for Fran in a fair fight. Suave as cold cream when he was sober, but this guy—you could tell by his eyes—was seriously loony. You wouldn't have wanted him to catch you glomming your big eyeballs on his woman. You didn't want him to catch you looking at him, neither. So we just sat there and tried to look at nothing."

"All right, everybody got a drink?" said the Irishman. He looked around at everyone, then settled his gaze on Germaine and Monroe. "Get them a drink," he said. He watched as the Cigar brought them glasses of Irish whiskey, and Germaine sipped.

"All right," he said. "Which one a you hillbillies insulted my employee in a whorehouse in front of a dozen people and whores?"

"I couldn't tell if he was just drunk or meant to do us serious harm, but he looked madder than blue blazes. Fran managed to look up and make eye contact, because, you know, it was him, not me, who done it. He didn't stick out his chin—he wasn't showing the guy up or nothing—but he didn't exactly look sorry, neither. Then it looked like he was gonna say something, but Basil beat him to it."

"Him," Basil said, pointing at Germaine.

"You know who we are, and you just go up against my man like that," the Irishman said. "In fronta all those people? Then you excape right out into the woods with no car? Jesiz." He looked around at the assembly. "That takes *guts!*" he yelled.

The women rolled their eyes and looked bored; the men nodded in somber agreement.

"I mean, where do a coupla nobodies living up here *in the middle of nowhere*"—he waved his arms as if to encompass the emptiness of the Adirondack plateau and the inadequacies of his entourage—"come by brass balls like that? You tell me."

Basil coughed. "The war, Jack," he said. (It was Jack Diamond himself, known to the papers as Legs.)

"Soldier boys, huh. God, that must have been terrible. Can you imagine. The gas, the corpses rotting in the trenches, all those horses with their guts blown out. Yuck."

It was hard to tell whom he was addressing, or the true nature of his disgust. "It depresses me to think about it. Where you boys fight, anyway?"

"First in Mexico, going after Villa, then in France," Monroe said. "Nancy, Saint-Mihiel, the Meuse. Cavalry, driving teams, some engineering."

Diamond's gaze drifted biliously, drunkenly toward Monroe. "Who asked you?" he said.

"Look, mister," said Germaine. "We're only here because we got a note from Basil inviting us over after the hotel party. I see you got the drop on us, and a lot a firepower lying around, but

I wish you'd treat my friend here with more respect. He drove a caisson and four-mule team of wounded animals across the field under enemy machine-gun fire, set up the howitzer, and took out a nest of Jerries...."

"Big heroes, huh," Diamond said, interrupting him. The party remained silent. "Get shot?"

Monroe looked at Germaine, who stood and dropped his shirt, showing the shrapnel tracks across his back, and the ragged scar where a 7mm Mauser had shattered his collar bone. He started to unbuckle his belt.

"Whoa!" the men called out in unison. The women smirked. Germaine stopped, tucked in his shirt, and re-buckled.

Diamond looked terrified. "You...You're not...?" he said.

"Naw. Bayonet wound in my thigh."

"*That* makes me feel better." He looked around and led a chorus of nods.

"Get it over with, Jack," said the woman in his lap, who rubbed her hand along his inner thigh.

"Don't the old boy's eyes roll back, and look like he was gonna pass out—or worse, like she was gonna whip it out right there on the spot and go to town. But he snapped his head up and moved her hand away."

"Look," Diamond said, "Basil here tells me about all the stuff you guys handle for that old man over there. If you're so good, then how come you got no *ambition*, huh? Tell me *that*! Hangin' around up here in these spooky woods when there's money to be made. *Women* to be made." He nuzzled the woman's neck, and, reaching his hand around her ass, goosed her.

"Jack!" She rolled over and slapped him as he looked at Monroe and Germaine with an expression of puerile complicity.

"Sounds to me like that white-haired old fuck got you fellas by the short hairs. I mean, who the fuck *is* this guy? Some kinda backwoods big shot? Place reminds me of a mausoleum or something."

He pushed the woman away and stood up, looking into the fire like it was hell itself. "God, I love a fire, don't you?" he said. He reached into the large plank woodbox and threw three big splits of seasoned black cherry onto the grates. The flames shot up the chimney and danced on his face. When he turned to speak, he stumbled clownishly.

"So, like what's the deal? You know every incha these woods and every rock in the river, or what?" he said.

"Oh, you can't know these woods like that," Monroe said. "We lived here all our lives, and—"

"Sure," said Germaine, interrupting. "We know our way around."

Diamond looked at him. "Roads through the woods the local heat or the feds don't even know about?"

Germaine and Monroe looked at each other. Monroe rolled his eyes.

"Some," Germaine said.

"Rough ones, maybe," Monroe mumbled.

"You need more?" Diamond pointed to their glasses. The Cigar poured a torrent of Jameson's into Germaine's raised glass. Monroe covered his with his hand.

"It's like Canada or something around here," Diamond said. "How do you stand it? It's so gloomy." He walked over to the fire again and stared into its innards. "Now, the Dutchman likes it up here, spends a lot of time in that town up on the border. Malone. He's got 'em all buffaloed, throwing greenbacks around like rice at a wedding. They think he's a great—whaddaya call it— philanderer."

"Woodchucks love rich people," Germaine said.

"*What?* Anyway, the feds closed down the main route through Plattsburgh. So Dutch, with all his jerk-off buddies, he's got the routes through the border between there and the Indian reservation *locked up*! We gotta be able to move west, go down through the mountains on back roads. Then make an easy shot through the farm country to Albany and the river. After that it's easy.

He waited.

"What, do I gotta spell it out for you?"

"*Ja*-ack," his woman complained.

"He wants you two to bring the booze down through the woods," Basil said.

"Only this far. We got other guys to take it from here."

"It needs to go around the Malone and Nine Mile Woods road," Basil went on.

"That's Dutch's and we don't want to go up against Dutch for it. He's got too many fucking friends around here."

"Yeah. We need friends."

Monroe looked away. Germaine looked at him, then back at Diamond. "What if we don't?" he said.

"Why wouldn't you? It's *real fucking money!*"

"You do a job, we pay you," Basil said. "Five a piece—half up front, half on delivery. Each job a day, maybe two at the most. But you got to get it here. Get my meaning?"

"Where does it come from?"

"Meyer here"—he pointed at the Cigar—"got us a cow farm down on the border near Trout River. It comes across with the cows. They're logging their woodlot, see, so you pick it up at the barn, in a log truck, and drive it up through the woods. That is, after you get it past the feds, the Black Horses, and then Dutch."

"These guys can do it, right?" Diamond said, then looked around and added, "Hey, can they even shoot?"

"What kind of a question is that?" Germaine said.

"Jack. The war."

"Wait a minute," Diamond said. "You don't scare too easy, do you, mister? What's your name again?"

Germaine told him.

"Fran-*what*?" he yelled.

"It's French," Basil said.

"French tough guy, ay? I like that. How about you?" Diamond said.

"Lonnie Monroe, Lake Aurora."

"Nothing but fucking lakes around here. Every town's named after a fucking lake. Nothing but lakes and mountains and trees. Nothing but gloom. No nice broads, like these here. No, you won't be seeing much of me around here. It's too fucking gloomy. No streetlights. No streets. No business, that's for sure. No civilized people, 'cept for a few lungers and that old man's hotel. It's like the whole place is doomed or something." He paused, looked at them both in turn. "Everything goes through Basil, see."

"Sure," Germaine said, seeing nothing.

"Back at the cabin, Fran closed his door on me and slid into bed right next to Yvette. I could hear them cooing and groaning in there while I lit a fire on my side and lay on top of the blankets trying to figure out everything that had just happened and not listen to them rutting. I kept dozing off and going over the whole scene again in my sleep, but when I opened my eyes I couldn't tell if it had really happened or I had dreamed it. That happened four or five times. When I realized it had really happened, I couldn't bring myself to think about what it meant. Especially since all I wanted to do was forget about it and walk right out and back to Paul's, like last time—by myself if I had to. But I was just too drunk. Aw, it was a real mess, lemme tell you. And I never wanted to see that Frenchman again.

"It musta been after about an hour when my door opened. I pretended to be asleep with the oil lamp on and the fire burning down, but I could smell perfume and soap. I didn't know it was Wendy, but I could hear her slipping out of her things with that swishing of her knickers and stockings. And, of course, smelling all womanish and female. Then she came over and tried to squeeze in beside me on the bed. 'Don't you want to get under?' she said. Oh, my heart was hammering. I kept imagining Basil coming in and shooting my head off, but she just unbuckled my belt and slid off my boots and trousers. Oh, I'll never forget them stockings and knickers swishing and our thighs sliding around together. After half an hour I didn't care whether Basil or Frank came in and shot my head off—especially not if they killed Fran while they were at it. My bones turned to mush, and I felt like I was sinking into a deep, soft dream."

At this point Lonnie Monroe stopped and looked straight at me.

"That's it," he said. "You got me remembering things I haven't thought of in years." He got up and put on his hat. He walked over to the doors and looked out onto the porch, where a couple of the newcomers and old Bud Warner were hammering out a passable "Jackhammer Blues" on guitar, mandolin, and fiddle.

"Reminds me of them days, to hear that fiddle." He looked at me, the porch, the door—lost. "Well, see you next week, I guess," he said, and left.

Ross walked down the bar and hovered over me as I put the recorder away. "See how upset you got him?" he said. "He takes a drink, I'm gonna blame you."

CHAPTER FOUR

The Tyranny of Silk

IN SPITE OF ITS REPUTED SMALL-TIME GLAMOUR, guiding, as I had learned over the last number of years, consisted mostly of heavy lifting, forced conviviality, twenty-four-hour responsibility, endured condescension, and lying for effect (also known as storytelling). The standard set by the great guides of history (La Malinche, Jim Bridger, Jed Smith, Sacagawea, Joe Polis) and the other frontier guides and Indians—and perpetuated in the Adirondacks by Sabattis, the Moodys and Cheney—had devolved, even by Germaine's and Monroe's time, into making sandwiches and baiting hooks, cleaning game (and sometimes killing it), and making sure customers didn't wander off and drown themselves or fall in the fire. No more journeys to the Underworld, real or implied. No more crossing untracked wastes. You rarely worked for science, or navigated unmapped territory. But you traveled by foot and small craft that you paddled and carried, still engaged in a kind of primal duet with the physical world. If you had the mentality for it, you might still be a "guide," and if you were out there long enough it might even transform you.

Right after Monroe stormed out on me, I got a call to lead a mid-week two-nighter out to the Fish Ponds for a couple of computer programmers from Boston. It was my first flat-water job of the season. I would rather have worked a few more trips on the Hudson before the run-off petered out, but these two called and asked Ollie, at Wolf Creek Outfitters, specifically for me. They brought their own sixteen-footer, and I had my forty-pound solo boat. We portaged in to Big Fish from Ochre Pond, camped at the Blagden Lean-to, caught some trout. The woman, a thirty-year-old beauty named Claire, made sketches and noted the calls and arrivals of warblers (yellow and yellowthroats, myrtles, oven birds, pine, palm, black-throated blues, et cetera), winter wrens, kinglets, and whitethroats. Her drawings and recording reminded me of Roosevelt, so that first night by the fire I told them about his years birding at Big Fish and at the other nearby ponds, where he catalogued species and wrote *The Summer Birds of the Adirondacks in Franklin County, N.Y.*—his first of eleven books—at eighteen, even as he hunted the region's last moose and wolves.

The next morning in Little Fish we ghosted along at a crawl, without splashing or bumping the gunwales, as we shadowed a bear foraging in the shallows. We got to within fifteen or twenty feet, and Claire shot pictures. Eventually the nearsighted bear winded us, stood straight up, and gazed into the blurry void offshore. When it brought us into focus it vanished, leaving the white witch-hopple blossoms shimmering chest-high in its wake.

Again that evening I told them how, by twelve, Teddy had hiked in the Alps and collected specimens in Egypt, Syria, and the Dakotas, mounting them for his own natural history museum. He read Audubon, Agassiz, and Coue; Lewis and Clark's journals; and the journey narratives of Bartram and Murray. On the way to Paul Smith's in 1869, at age eleven, he stayed at Saratoga Springs, Lake George, and Ticonderoga, visiting the ruins of the colonial forts and summer "Indian camps." (These would have been Abenaki and Mohawk from Quebec and Hogansburg, selling crafts.) From there they went fishing on the St. Regis headwaters—these very waters—with Mose Sawyer and Godfrey St. Germain (Fran Germaine's grandfather). Theodore senior read to Teddy and his brothers from *The Last of the Mohicans,* Lake George still strong in their minds. Mose told them about the time a cougar had almost attacked him. (It had really just gotten away, but Mose, according to Monroe, always exaggerated for maximum effect.) Teddy caught a ton of trout; saw moose, bear, and wolf tracks; observed and identified numerous birds and mammals by their Latin names. He rowed, paddled, swam, and ran rapids, and recorded it all in his diary.

It reminded me of how Monroe always talked about their elders having guided the future president, of having contributed to his practical education. As the radical empiricists they were (without knowing it), they claimed credit for the president's physical and philosophical hardihood. They believed they had taught him the necessity of deciding things for himself, based on observation and his own experience—as when old man Moody had set that scientist (Agassiz) straight about brook trout spawning at Follensby Pond—and of consequent action. "Of course, that was years ago," they would add regarding the affair at Follensby. Agassiz, it so happenened, was equally wrong on Darwin.

Teddy lived around those men and came to see nature through their eyes. He copied into his books their lessons on the mink, the newt, and the wolf. They loved that he could carry his own weight, shoot, ride, sing harmony, and remember all the points of a good story. Later he faced down a drunken cowboy and a grizzly in the Black Hills, led and survived an old-fashioned military charge in Cuba (whether he needed to or not), and singlehandedly reformed the New York City police and the New

York State Assembly. He knew the world *and* his home ground, as many of them did who had been to war and to sea. You could always follow a man like that, they believed, for he would never evade the obvious thing, no matter how daunting, and he would always be fair. These were sufficient criteria for character, as far as they were concerned, all else being window dressing and dependent on the most subjective judgments. A person was entitled to distinguishing characteristics, after all. And Teddy had his—oh, yes he did.

They always recognized their influence in his speeches and governance. Such practical wisdom and leadership they came to see as their due. And all the results they saw in Teddy, they fully expected later on from Germaine and Monroe and their generation. After the war, though, all that had gotten altered, scrambled, lost in the fog of bad money and bad whiskey. In those days, as Monroe insisted, besides the fact that you had to risk arrest to have a drink, things in general were seriously askew.

The whole trip, I thought of Monroe and Germaine running around out here in the old days, when Paul Smith owned most of southern Franklin County and Teddy was a Bull Moose. (They had all been Bull Mooses.) The land had passed to public use since then, or to the small college that bears old Paul's name. Now it was "wild," though essentially managed to be that way. There were unscathed pine and huge hemlock on the ridge tops, cushiony moss underfoot, dozens of ponds and lakes, and nearly a hundred thousand acres—but really, for a hundred years it had been a private park, logged scientifically and crawling with sports and nature lovers. Old Paul had gotten the most out of it, but there it was. He sold lots all over the St. Regis lakes, Lake Aurora, and Lake Clear—many of those still owned by the original families— but he had left the Seven and Nine Carries, Lower St. Eustace and the outlet, and the Fish Creek area to be a shared back yard, a fine-grained mini-wild, where all the gestures of the recently vanished frontier could be acted out. Of old there had been cabins and logging camps, and bridges, catwalks, and landings here and there, but never any permanent residence. A truck road that led into the diadem of liquid jewels surrounding Big Fish Pond was closed in the seventies, and now the lower carries and ponds were the only approaches, and motors were forbidden.

For Germaine and Monroe, the area had constituted an inheritance—a common birthright, even under Smith. They learned the ground by hearing it described over and over, even while in the womb, so when they got to a place for the first time, invited along to help and do chores at age ten or twelve, they already knew where they were and how it related to the whole. Part of that whole included Teddy and his exploits in the field and in politics. Later, to become one of the young hotel rowers and a registered guide meant ready cash, a name in the community, and a reputation among the swells (and their daughters), who might take a shine to you and render an important leg up in the world. You acquired standing, even without being Godfrey St. Germain's grandson or creating a distinctive style of log work all your own.

But your status undermined your equity in the place, your custody of it. No matter how acute your woodsmanship, or how deft your navigation of the minefields of class, you remained the help. Teddy, of course, always looked up to the woodsmen and guides, and used them as a model when picking his Rough Riders. This they knew implicitly.

At any rate, being at Fish Pond after Monroe's first long and revealing taping session, and thinking about the continuities of place and practice, made me feel connected to him in a new way, however tenuously. I had fought no war (though I had avoided one), endured no deserts, driven no teams, but on one level we had this place and its gestures and manners in common. That first night, when I finished telling the couple about Teddy, I took my solo canoe out for a paddle, alone. I felt remorse for having goaded the old guy—even as little as I had—to give up his story, and for the emotional standstill it had brought him to. Clearly the story occupied a dark room in the house of his past. Maybe in all of ours.

I always knew that I might have been recording the cloud shadows of an old man's mind, a collage of images, vignettes, and legends he'd overheard years ago and accommodated into his own history. If so, it would only have resembled the other semi-historical will o' the wisps and figments I had been chasing for years, which had evaporated into rumor, myth, and local amnesia before I could pin them down. Often the knowledge died with a person—the last one who hooked a salmon in the Saranac, the last person who knew or had seen Sabattis. But Lonnie Monroe had known Germaine, that was a fact. He wasn't the only one, but he was the only one still around. I had hoped, this time, to do what I could to get the whole thing down as he remembered it, false or not, and triangulate it with whatever other sources I could find in order to arrive at something like a complete picture.

Over the years he had dropped hints and nuggets from those days—some passed along mockingly by younger skeptics—but never in any context or spelled out where he and Germaine were concerned. At least, not in any chronological way. Nobody had ever taken him remotely seriously, in fact. But during that first session he had gone too deep, risked too much, to be making it up. His story had too much inner consistency to be a total lie. Even if he were channeling some elaborate subconscious mythology, I wanted all of it. Even if it didn't survive as fact, it might illuminate dark corners of the Adirondack psyche. I couldn't let it end there.

So, the morning after I came out of Fish Pond, I took the outboard from my cabin on Miller Pond into the village, then drove out beyond Bloomingdale to Monroe's small spread along the Saranac. The cool rain we'd had at Fish had frosted the summit of Whiteface to the east, like Fuji, and the cool air had temporarily stunned the flies. When I wheeled into his yard, Monroe was in the corral adjusting the masks on his horses' faces for when the air warmed up and the blackflies reemerged.

"Well, look who the cat dragged in," he called as I turned off the truck and got out. I stood there feeling awkward and unwelcome as he adjusted the buckle on the head of the paler of the two Morgans. "Look who's here, ladies. A visitor." The other mare ambled over to me with her mask already on and flies hovering around her eyes. I waited at the gate, rubbing her muzzle over the barbed wire while he ran the hose into their trough and spread hay around. "Pretty soon they'll have green grass," he said.

"When did you work them last?" I said. The river slid inkily out of sight downstream between ramparts of balsam and cedar.

"On a job?" He slapped the nearest mare on the flank and let himself out of the gate, closing it behind him. "Oh, couple three years, I guess. We still cut firewood, for ourselves and for old Mrs. Thomas around the bend. Mostly I just keep 'em around so somebody's left who remembers who I am. Coffee?"

I followed him through a side door in the woodshed into the kitchen—or rather, a museum of a kitchen, with low fire burning inside a coal-wood range; a small, enameled Glenwood gas range that looked lovingly restored, though it had never been out of its original use; a soapstone sink and enamel counter; a gas refrigerator; and a table covered with a red-and-white-checked oilcloth. The gray light through the kitchen windows gleamed on the polished glass and china, the lamp chimneys, and the ticking clocks as if Mary had never left.

He ground the A&P coffee beans in a hand grinder mounted on the wall, and when the pot boiled he threw in the grounds and stirred them with an enamel spoon. "How we made it in the desert," he said. "Cowboy coffee." When the grounds settled, he poured into white ceramic cups and placed one in front of me, along with a pitcher of real cream and a covered sugar bowl with a silver spoon. "I like it black," he said.

"Me, too."

We sat in silence for a minute. Then he said, "So, got your machine in the car?"

I told him I hadn't brought it, that I regretted the other day when I had upset him and he had ended the interview. "Ross worried you might drink," I said.

"What?" he said, slamming his cup on the oilcloth. "Now why does that little pissant think I would drink after twenty-five years?"

"Just the way you clammed up and left so fast."

"Oh, Jesus Christ," he said. "The memory of dames like that? How do you expect a man my age to react?" He gazed off. "All that silk," he said. He focused again. "It sure ain't enough to make me take a drink, though."

"Well, I'm glad to hear that."

"You are, huh? Here, have some more." He stood, refilled my cup from the enamel pot, and replaced the pot on the stove.

"This time of year, I just start a fire on a cool morning and let it go out," he said. "Helps the bones."

"So do I," I said.

"Anyway, gonna hitch up the girls and haul out some firewood."

"Sounds good."

We drank our coffee. Chickadees and sapsuckers came and went at the feeders outside.

"Came out of the Fish Ponds yesterday with some customers," I said.

"I haven't been there in years," he said. "Not since they closed the road."

"Paddled right up to a nice little two-year-old bear hunting frogs."

"Had one at the feeder right out there a couple of weeks ago.

Had to put a load of birdshot in his ass to make him stay away. Usually, they come around, I don't mind. But he was a feisty little bastard. Ruined two feeders. Of course, now old Ray out in Onch-eye feeds them."

"You or Germaine ever take people back there?" I said, meaning the Fish Ponds, knowing they had.

"Oh, we lived back there. Sometimes one or two from our group would go in a day early and set up camp for a big party. We'd take our time going in, then set up in a hurry, fish or hunt and drink a little whiskey, you know, until the sports showed up. We were kids, sometimes skipping school to work, especially if we knew any daughters were coming along. Most years there were tent camps left up on Big Fish and a couple of other ponds, and lean-tos and biffies to be kept up, so one or another of us would have the job of working for the remote caretaker for a couple of weeks, just going around and fixing up the landings and such. Worked a logging camp a few miles past there one winter, farther down the St. Regis West Branch, driving teams in and out on that tote road. Brought in a sled-load of girls for a whole weekend once. Snowed deep that Saturday while we were drinking and dancing. Coming out, you got a couple bad downhills, and I lost the sled at the Ochre Pond cut-off. Drunk, of course. Managed to save the team and bailed out at the last minute, but there were big, tough French girls scattered all over the woods, covered with snow and madder than hell. It took all that day to collect and re-hitch the team, haul the sled up out of the gully, keep the women from freezing. Didn't get out to the header at Green Pond 'til midnight.

"I used to go in and visit Ollie Barton's camp up there on Little Fish back before the second war. Then in the sixties all them people lost their leases when the state bought that land back there and took down the camps. Mostly I haven't been back in past St. Regis since then. I didn't know you worked in the woods," he said.

"Just canoeing and rafting. Sometimes skiing in the winter."

"Rafting? You mean rubber boats? On the Saranac?"

"The Hudson and Moose."

"Oh. Hell, we worked down there three log drives after the first war, for Finch and Pruyn, with a lot of Indians from Hogansburg." (This was news to me.) "Traded oar and pike jobs on the jam boats. Of course, we didn't have all these rubber suits and May Wests like you have now."

"Nope," I said.

"And our boats could sink. It was cold and hard. I was more scared on that river than I ever was in Belgium. That was another one of Germaine's ideas."

We downed our coffees and I followed him out to the shed, where he rigged up the harness and tack for "the girls," as he called his mares. The river curved away downstream toward Lake Champlain through a corridor of balsams. True to its name, Whiteface loomed a little to the south, and Moose Mountain to the east. Whitethroats keened. After a few minutes the three of them stood ready, more or less straight and square, if past their primes. Sunlight flooded the shed through the open doors. You could smell the citronella Lonnie had dabbed around their ears and his own hat brim. He shook the traces and the mares took off at a fast walk, with the skid chains jingling and him skipping along behind on foot. "Gee," he said, but they were already swinging wide around the corral to the right, headed for the entrance to Monroe's hundred acres of cedar, balsam, maple, yellow birch, and beech. In the woods, narrow skid tracks and foot trails branched off from the wider main track, and we took one away from the river, then another up to a low plateau through the manicured hardwoods. Up there half a dozen trees lay limbed out and cut into eight- or twelve-foot lengths, eight to ten inches thick. Sunlight penetrated the leafless hardwood canopy. Painted trilliums poked their carmine-streaked, white petals up through the sun-drenched leaf mold, and a pileated woodpecker hammered nearby. In silence he rigged a hitch of five logs, and I followed them out again, and then six more times, as they skidded out the logs without a word from Monroe, or even a grunt. Back at the woodshed I helped him rank the logs into a rough cord while the horses stood and meditated, switching their tails at the flies, which we pinched off our necks and faces. When we quit at one, before the temperature rose, we both had half a dozen tiny blood clots streaking our necks and faces, though like Monroe I rarely even raised a welt, and neither of us mentioned it.

"OKAY, TURN THAT THING ON," he said the following Thursday afternoon at the Trap Dyke.

We had not spoken again that day about either Germaine or meeting at the bar again, but only about horses, weather, the moose that had wandered in from Vermont that morning and that somebody at the post office had seen walking down the tracks out in the Bloomingdale Bog while they were fishing.

But some unspoken business had been transacted, some trust exchanged. So I drove into town again the next Thursday morning with the recorder and arrived at the Trap Dyke a half-hour early, for a bowl of chili and to read the Times in peace without anybody giving me shit about it. He came in, blinking, right on time, picked up his coffee at the bar, and set himself down in the booth looking reconciled.

I folded the paper, clicked on the machine, and adjusted the volume as he began.

"The first couple of loads went easy. The usual booze car was a souped-up sedan with the springs built up and the doors hollowed out. We drove a Ford Model TT ton-and-a-half with a ten-foot extended rack bed and ruxtell axle, and an old-looking sign on the door painted by Germaine's cousin Pete that looked like it might have said Rideau Lumber, Something Lake, New

York—like the letters was old and worn out, but you couldn't really tell. Pete dented the doors and fenders with big chunks of wood and hung skid chains, turnbuckles, peaveys, cross-cut saws, and cant hooks all over it. We couldn't make a fast get-away, but you wouldn't have suspected us, neither. The plates came from Basil, and we customized them too, so they looked all dented and rusty. We drove down to the farm on the border at Trout River, where the booze was all stored in the hay barn, and loaded thirty cases of good scotch and gin in the center of the bed and tied it down. Then we sawed logs to fit around it and look like a complete load. We dressed rough, and under the seat we carried a Remington 12-gauge pump and a .45 automatic, not because we expected any trouble or would have defended ourselves anyways, but there was always a chance somebody could squeal on us to Dutch, who owned Malone and the whole territory—or thought he did. We also had Fran's old Model 90 Winchester pump, the .22 break-down model with the octagon barrels that he always carried for good luck, because his father had given it to him for his twelfth birthday and because he could shoot the eye out of a mosquito with it at a hundred yards.

"We drove straight up the old Santa Clara Road from St. Regis Falls, and into the shed at Diamond's, as much after dark as possible, which wasn't hard that time of year. There were washouts and spring holes, but nothing we couldn't manage with the chains and that ruxtell low-range gear. The other route was up the back way through Loon Lake. That went okay, too, and we switched the routes back and forth so nobody would get suspicious. There was somebody always waiting for us at Jack's—either Frank or Emile, usually, sometimes Basil, and they paid us on the spot. Usually they loaded it right into a couple of big, hollowed-out Packards or Cadillacs and headed down the road. There wasn't a lot of traffic on the roads in those days, especially not that time of year. We heard about feds pinching Dutch's drivers along the border, but the few times we saw state Black Horse troopers on the road, and—we thought—once or twice feds, they paid us no mind. It went like that for about three weeks, five or six trips. I was nervous as a hummingbird at first but calmed down after the first few trips and the first couple of pay days.

"Days we worked clearing the line over to Tupper, like Paul wanted. Fran ran the survey crew, and me the lumbering crew. We had a hundred men, a lot of Italians from Brooklyn, the usual bums, a few Hogansburg Indians, and local kids. Fran worked his men hard, to show Paul he was the meanest and toughest son of a bitch on the payroll, and that the old man had made a big mistake, you know, not making him operations supervisor. He was a regular slave driver, and he made me one, too. We were like the officers in Europe we hated but who we followed whatever they said, no matter what, so they'd notice us. The workers, they were like us. Oh, we made a great mess outta them woods together, but we made good time. Where it would work, we ran a grapple chain between two tractors and just dragged the line clear, tearing the ground up something awful, but getting it all down to stumps in one pass. We thought it was a good thing, you know, even though you could tell it really bothered Fran. I think he felt like he was like doing it *to* Paul instead of for him, tearing up the country like that, or maybe to the Germans. But you could see it hurt him, and it made him hate himself, too, like, because it was *him* doing it, and not Paul. Anyways, on the higher and rougher ground we drew the logs to headers behind teams, then loaded them on the trucks. The slash we just used for fill in the low places, made big bonfires of, or left piled on the edge of the woods. We put in drainage ditches and culverts. A lot of the men, especially the Indians and Italians, fished in the creeks near the line when we broke for lunch, or on Sundays. Then when it got colder they carried rifles and shotguns, and got snowshoe rabbits and deer.

"As the weeks went by Fran told me what happened in the office that evening after the dinner, and I began to see how mad he was at the old man. I also began to see how, after the war and everything, that old skinflint had took advantage of us. Two nice soldier boys, woodchucks, one French, one Irish. What did we know? Well, we'd been to the city by then, lemme tell you. Fran wanted to get back at him somehow. I just wanted to make my pile and maybe go back to Texas, sneak in at the last minute before the frontier disappeared for good. Marry a Mexican girl. Work on the oil rigs or start a business. I didn't know what—some kind of a store, maybe.

"By and by the snow got deeper and the work on the line slowed down. At night, though, it seemed like the summer never ended. The speaks all had cars lined up outside, and inside people had money and spent it. Down in Plattsburgh and Glens Falls, where we went once or twice out of curiosity and because Fran wanted to play fiddle with some musicians down there, it was the same. It was a completely new feeling. To be out in your own town during hunting season, with a wad of bills in your wallet and the restaurants all full and lit up like ocean liners when it got dark out early. Booze in plentiful supply, and the most beautiful women anybody ever saw around there on your arm. Everybody else had money, too, it wasn't only us: the lungers, the workers, the bootleggers, the doctors and nurses—everybody had at least some. I never remembered a time like that before, when we felt like we lived in a real place connected to the rest of the country and the world, and that something besides just surviving might be possible. Christy Mathewson, the ball player, he was a lunger and our regular pal. Jack Dempsey came to stay at the Riverside once, where he had trained for a fight a few summers before, and we all got to pal around with him. He liked Fran's fiddle playing because he sounded like a real Irishman, he said. Most people thought we were flush from working the power line. Oh, it was high times, all right. Underneath, it felt like something was a little crazy about it, like it all might blow up any second, but it hardly ever mattered. Things just kept going along.

"Wendy and Yvette, them girls stayed out at Jack's cabin on the island. During the day they kept house for Basil and Frank, and in the afternoons made their deliveries in the village. Most nights we would stay there with them in the cabin, me and Wendy in the room on one side, and Fran and Yvette on the other. In town they dressed normal most of the time, like housekeepers or nurses, which Wendy at least had been going to school to be when she met Jack. Yvette had been a dancer and an actress in Montreal, and not of your Shakespearean variety, neither. Dancehall stuff. Frenchy vaudeville, like. She had a way about her, real friendly and sweet, and she knew a lot, like about books and history, and she spoke some other language besides French and English. I forget what, German maybe. It made you listen to her. Wendy, well, she was different. Long and leggy, daddy a doctor in Albany. She was kinda airy and far away, more like one of the fancy girls that came to the hotel, but loads of fun. I knew goddamn well, after all them girls we had guided and that we had had in Texas and France, that she was really nothing but a rich girl having her adventure before she moved home and married herself a doctor like daddy. Sowin' her wild oats, ay. And that was all right by me—I still had plenty sowin' of my own to do. She didn't expect a goddamn thing, you get me? No sense a me getting my knickers in a knot over her, especially since my own preference was for a less scrawny woman. But she had plenty to squeeze where it mattered, and the whole arrangement made things purely sublime, mostly. They were something, the two of them. And both of 'em could change into flappers in a heartbeat, like that, for the right party.

"Fran and me would meet them in town if something was going on, but we never came in or left together, so nobody would connect us that close. It was pretty obvious what was going on most of the time, anyways, but people around here were pretty tolerant about secrets, especially where me and Fran were concerned, and especially if everybody knew about it anyways. There weren't that many bootleggers right around Saranac or Aurora, but there were booze camps like Jack's and drivers like us scattered all over the territory, and a lot of families had booze money partly holding them up. Dutch had so many people on the payroll up in Malone that even today if you proposed a statue of that maniac in front of the village hall, it would pass.

"People might not of thought much about who they were, but when Yvie and Wendy got all dolled up and danced, smoking cigarettes and pounding back highballs, we four made quite a commotion. And people seen Yvie and Fran getting stuck on each other, you know. That was the main show. Them two were completely different than me and Wendy, more glued together, always mooning at each other, especially when Fran played the fiddle or they sang a song together, like 'Old Shep' or 'Silver Threads Among the Gold,' by that old guy Pettis who stayed out on Osgood Pond. Pretty soon Yvette had him speaking French and laughing at the words and accent he remembered his grandma using when he was a kid, and learning new songs she taught him, and they had a lot of private little Frenchy jokes. She made tourtiere and they argued about whether it should have potatoes in it. But she made a lot of everything that fall and winter—dumplings, roast pork and venison, lake trout, carrots and cabbage and country bread, pies and stews and soups. Always fresh coffee on the stove, and hot bread and butter. That girl could really cook. We ate a lot, and that was a good thing. We needed it.

"So that's what I was thinking about when you thought I got upset last week—them days that fall. It was like a dream for a while. Sometimes I'm not even sure myself whether it all happened or not. And of course, even though the lights were on all over town, out in the woods it was still darker 'n the inside of a coal miner's ass."

CHAPTER FIVE

Double or Nothing

IN LATE OCTOBER, on an Indian summer Sunday with the sun the color of a tangerine, the two couples filled a pack basket and a wanigan with bread, sliced cold pork, a jar of horseradish, fresh tomatoes that Emile had brought from Caughnawaga, shortbread cookies, wool blankets, a pot to boil water in, and basic utensils. Carrying a side-by-side 12-gauge L.C. Smith and a fly rod, they left from Jack Diamond's dock in Germaine's fourteen-foot guideboat, a Willard Hanmer painted black outside and pale blue inside, and a fifteen-foot green canvas canoe, a White from Maine, with brass fittings and a carved wooden yoke.

Leaving Clear Pond through the channel into Rainbow Lake, they then carried across the esker at the head of that lake a short way through the pines to Jones Pond. After following the Jones Pond outlet through a narrow, spruce-lined passage, they emerged into Osgood Pond and spread their blankets on the small beach to the right of the inlet. The reds had fallen from the early maples, the yellows were just fading on the birches, and the golds were in full crescendo on the tamaracks along shore, whose needles carpeted the small beach where they landed. For two hours they ate, talked, and drank coffee. After a brief nap the women stood in the glacial shallows amid the stalks of the hollow reeds with their skirts pulled up to their thighs, wiggling their toes in the hard, rippled sand.

The party shoved off again, the women now occupying the guideboat and the men the canoe. After rounding the point of White Pine Camp, where President Coolidge—a much lesser sport than Teddy—had recently whiled away a summer fishing and shooting, they headed down the outlet into the Osgood River. The men took turns in the bow with the shotgun, drifting soundlessly around a bend to flush the black ducks and woodies that assembled in ranks up and down the slow-moving stream, dropping them as they rose in the air. At the point where the river vanished into a tangle of alders and willow, Germaine told the party he had once seen "the big cat" when he was a boy. A mink rippled and feinted along shore.

They turned back upstream and circled Osgood Pond, the women trolling on the fly rod a Lake Clear Wabbler with a worm trailing eighteen inches behind it on a number eight hook. Brook trout, fat, bright, and full of spawn, fought over it. The women landed two fish apiece, each a half pound of vivid, orange flesh. When they reached the hotel, Pete drove them all back to Jack's in the hotel's Model T truck. Yvette barded the small ducks in salt pork and roasted them slowly with intense care, onions, and a minimum of basting. She poached the trout, and rounded out the feast with bread, potatoes, carrots and parsnips, and a pumpkin pie that Monroe insisted he had never eaten the equal of since.

Before the snow fell Monroe had bought a team of mares from a Pole down in Corinth—Morgan-Clydesdale crosses, exquisite animals famous all over the mountains. After the first large snowfall he took the team out and dragged a roller over a seventeen-mile network of old skid roads and trails up through the woods, beginning in the back lot of a sawmill down in Deer River that belonged to a friend of a friend in Lake Aurora, and ending at an abandoned header out on Paul's land near the Middle Branch. Then he went back down it with a sprinkler tank to freeze the track. The ground was mostly frozen, and they forded the unfrozen creek and another hundred yards of marshland without undue wallowing. He did that twice more before the roads closed, hardening the track in a way no G-man would ever look askance at or find suspicious. On the third trip he spent a day felling and skidding a couple of nice spruce logs for stringers and running them across a narrow creek with a soft, close bank, directly at the bottom of a short, steep drop, then nailing rough-cut, two-by-eight planks he had hauled on the sled as a bed for the fifteen-foot bridge.

After the third snow they could no longer bring the truck up the Santa Clara Road, so on the fifth of December they offloaded the booze behind the mill (after a substantial payment to the mill owner) and loaded it onto the sled, with the horses all harnessed and waiting. They let Pete drive the empty truck around to the header on the Middle Branch, chained the cases of booze on the sled, and covered it all with a tarp. Germaine rode with Monroe for safety, for company, and just to spend a few hours in the woods. The load was small for a team conditioned to full loads of saw logs, and they pulled eagerly in the six inches of fresh powder. The temperature hung in the twenties; steam poured off the horses. After a couple of miles through cut-over woods, they crossed onto an old state tract with trails running through it from when it had been a private park. Here the silence really enveloped them, except for the breathing of the animals and creak of the tackle. Low branches of spruce and balsam released big loads of powder at their approach.

"Always makes me feel empty in the deep woods," Germaine said, out of nowhere.

"When you're not full of shit, maybe," Monroe said.

"You ever give any thought to getting married, or having kids?"

Stunned, Monroe gave his old friend a dubious look and fell silent. They spoke little after that. They braced down the long hill to the new bridge, crossed it without incident, and stopped there to water the animals and have a sandwich and a shot. Thin clouds muted the light, even over the open sky of the creek bed. Snowshoe hare and deer tracks wove in and out of the cedars along shore and into the open pines.

Germaine took a second shot. "I never thought things would be this good," he said.

"Me neither," Monroe said

A mile farther on they came around a bend, the breeze in their faces. A raven croaked, and a half dozen deer stood together out on the frozen wetland, still and gray as maple bark. Germaine had his rifle up in an unthinking motion, and fired (illegally by this date) before an ear even twitched. They dressed out the old doe on the snow, and carried her out on the sled. That night Yvette cooked the heart, liver, and tenderloins.

Every month the Elks put on a dance in the grange hall in Lake Aurora. For years the postmistress, Gladys Wilson, had played piano, Roger Boudreau from Lake Clear had fiddled and called squares and reels, and a guy with a hook on his left hand from a mill accident played washtub. Germaine usually went, and often sat in or played a set of fiddle tunes with the band at some point. The hundred or so dancers feasted on a potluck buffet, accompanied by fruit punch, coffee, and cider. Despite Prohibition, booze was as present as in the earlier era called the Gilded Age, if less visible. The affair began at noon and ran until six. On this occasion Germaine and Monroe drove the Model A, and Emile brought Wendy and Yvette in the Studebaker, dressed in silk and wool like college girls for a day among the woods folk and townspeople, who were outwardly more conventional than those who patronized the speaks and whorehouses.

Outwardly, for by two the good, cheap Canadian that Monroe and Germaine had been hauling up the back way from Deer River had saturated the assembly, and a good-natured insobriety obtained. On the floor, four squares of men with women and women with women allemanded and swung their partners and corners to the pounded-out 2/4 time of "Golden Slippers" and the mesmerizing chant of Roger, who spoke the squares monotonously for long intervals and then broke into rapid rhythm, with higher pitch and volume as the music demanded, belting through a megaphone above the unelectrified pianissimo of the instruments. The floor surged, sixty-four feet shuffled and skipped, random shouts and hollers echoed through the hall. At long tables liberated from the mess hall of an abandoned logging camp, the children, non-dancers, round-cheeked grandmothers, and the crazy and feeble-minded sat and smoked; drank coffee laced with maple syrup, whiskey, or both; and ate cardboard plates of ham, baked beans with bacon, venison stew, potatoes au gratin, fried chicken, jellies and condiments, and various pies and cakes.

As soon as they arrived Germaine opened his fiddle case, mounted the stage without a word, and began to bow along in unison with Roger's less tuneful play. But Roger gave ground to Germaine's better intonation and concentrated on calling and weaving together song lyrics and instructions for the dancers. Sunlight streamed through windows in the peak of each gable and a line of windows along the western wall. A couple of gas chandeliers added their light, casting the whole Breughelian panorama in an otherworldly blaze. Yvette, reacting to a scene from her earliest memories, leaped onto the floor and began answering the calls with an invisible partner. Then a long-legged boy with a big Adam's apple, whom she pulled up from one of the

tables, turned carmine and let her twirl him in an awkward dos
à dos as he bent over to disguise the boner pushing out the front
of his wool pants. When he sat down in shame, she crouched and
shook the hem of her wool skirt, breaking into the Charleston
and drawing scattered applause.

After the band broke, Yvette addressed Roger in French.
Roger hated to look like he understood her, but he engaged her to
the extent his fluency allowed, because her beauty and animation
demanded it. When they returned to the stage he called a reel—
where the sides lined up across from each other—in English, but
with Yvette singing along in loud French harmony on the chorus.
By the end the whole crowd, even those not on the floor, joined
in on the chorus, stomping out the tune and the steps, the hall
throbbing with schmaltzy fellowship and the abstraction of the
dance.

Germaine and Yvette remained on stage. When the rustling
settled, he asked for the crowd's indulgence while playing one of
the slow, minor-key patterns that Monroe termed the "gloomy
songs"—in this case a fisherman's lament from the west coast
of Cape Breton. He played through the verse and chorus, and
then Yvette came in, calling out the verse in a quavering alto.
With the instrument in the crook of his elbow, he harmonized
underneath her for five choruses, the crowd silent when they
finished, and went straight into the old standard "The Rosary,"
in high harmony and joined by the crowd on the chorus. On
stage the couple formed a composition of varied and appealing
darknesses, she foursquare with her hands at her sides, in a
sweater, skirt, and beret; he standing just behind her shoulder
and bending to join her on the chorus or turning the f-holes of
the instrument towards the audience for volume on key phrases,
his black hair pomaded and standing up straight and falling over
in the front. In the crowd even Wendy sang along, leaning her
head on Monroe's shoulder and whispering, "My word," at the

image of their two friends on the stage.

At the break some men stood outside in the weakening sun and rotten snow of the yard, smoking and passing a large mug of spiked punch. Women in twos and threes followed each other out to one of two two-holers standing in the field. And two probable bootleggers from Malone leaned against the barn and smoked, dressed flashy but poorly in striped suits and two-toned shoes, with their frowzy girlfriends. The old-timers were examining a Remington ought-six one of them had just gotten in trade for a long-legged beagle with big feet, and he proposed they take some shots. A coffee can was quickly set up on a string and a pole a hundred paces out towards the edge of the forest, and they took turns until the hard kick and loud report wore them out. They hit it about five times out of ten.

"Hey, lemme try that," Germaine said, stepping out of the crowd. He filled a clip and rammed it into the magazine. Working the bolt fast, he made the can dance and spin on six successive shots.

"You always did shoot good, Fran," said Chester, one of the old-timers, as Germaine shot the bolt and handed the rifle back to its owner.

"I seen him spin the top off a mayonnaise jar," Monroe said.

"I'd like to see *that*," one of them said.

"Aw, that's bullshit, Lonnie," said another. "Don't bullshit an old bullshitter."

"I ain't," Monroe said.

"That right, Fran? Can you do it now?" Chester said.

"Well, I done it. I mean, maybe if the light holds. Not at a hundred yards though. I'll need three shots at fifty feet, offhand."

"Well I got five dollars that says you can't." The man stepped forward and handed a wrinkled bill to Monroe, who held it out flat in his hand toward the dozen or so men and women. "Anybody else?" he said.

One old-timer came forward and placed five ones in Monroe's hand, who then handed them over to the first guy who spoke—as close to a neutral observer as the party afforded.

"I'll make it fifty," one of the men from Malone said. He stood forward with an air of cultured nonchalance and swagger that failed for want of self-possession and native poise, and placed five tens on the stump beside the old-timer.

By then a gallon jar with a metal lid had appeared. Inside the barn, music could be heard starting up. Germaine searched his wallet and removed a wad of bills that matched the amount on the stump. While the self-appointed team of observers marked out the distance with the jar, he walked over to the Model T and stood behind it to take a leak. When he returned, he held in his hand the Winchester Model 90 with the octagon barrels.

"What's that?" the Malone guy said.

"My rifle," Germaine said.

"That's a .22," the guy said. "You didn't say nothing about no .22."

"That guy there didn't give him a chance," Monroe said. "He placed the bet before Fran could finish telling him that he could do it at fifty feet, offhand, with a .22."

"Hey, that's cheatin'."

"Just don't you worry, mister," Chester said, clutching the bills. "It still ain't no easy shot, so's you best mind your chickens. A bet's a bet. Next time handicap your horse before the race."

"Old bastard."

"Screw it on tight," Germaine called out to the neutral team now placing the jar atop a rusted-out tractor housing, at about eye level.

The men placed the jar just so and screwed on the top as tightly as they could. The sun had dropped below the clouds, its light slanted across the field and slammed against the side of the barn, the tractor, and the west-facing rock walls of the nearby small mountain. Germaine loaded a handful of .22 shorts into the magazine and brought the stock to his shoulder.

"Anybody farts, it's a forfeit," Chester said.

"Aw, shut up, you old coot."

Germaine jammed his left elbow into his hip, making a solid triangle with his arms, and sighted along the barrel, with his other elbow at right angles to his body and his finger on the trigger. He breathed, exhaled, breathed again, and the ping of the small-bore rang across the field and echoed off the rock face. It rocked the jar, but the lid stayed tight. Nobody spoke. Leaving the butt in his shoulder, Germaine pumped the action and sighted, breathed, and fired again. This time the lid spun off, and the jar remained standing.

"Gimme that rifle," said the Malone guy, while his buddy ran to the tractor and screwed the jar lid back on. Chester turned the bills over to Monroe, who counted them and handed Germaine his share. The Malone guy worked the pump, sighted the rifle, and fired, shattering the jar.

"Son of a bitch," he said.

"That's right," Chester said. "What'd you think was gonna happen?"

"Double or nothing says he can't do it again."

"Oh, he can do that all day. Why don't we just make it a little more interesting," Monroe said. He removed a deck of cards from his jacket pocket, fanned the cards, and turned up the ace of spades.

"I ain't going double on no cut of cards."

"Not asking you to. If you wanna go double, why don't you bet he can't split this card in two? Edgewise."

"They're settin' you up, Barney," the other Malone guy said.

"What? You think he can shoot that thing in two sideways?"

"Well, Fran? Can you?" Chester said.

"Might as well try. I'm ahead already."

"I'll bet he can," said the first old-timer, stepping forward with his ten-spot.

The money changed hands in both directions, betting that he could and that he couldn't. "Barney" put down a hundred on the doubtful side.

"This is stupid. I'm going back inside," the other Malone guy said, and stalked back into the barn with his girl.

About a half an hour of shootable light remained, and the neutrals rushed around preparing the target. Finally they placed the card in the end of a piece of lathe, into which a slit had been cut, with a square of cardboard mounted behind it. The light fell almost but not quite directly behind Germaine, and the card's edge could be clearly picked out.

"All right. Come on, come on," Monroe said.

"Okay, three shots, right?" Germaine said, setting himself up.

"Right," came the chorus.

He set his elbow, sighted, and breathed. The first shot nicked the front edge of the card, the bullet hole in the cardboard seeming to indicate a miss to the right.

"Jesus," said Barney.

The second shot moved the card, a clear miss to the left.

Germaine took his time. He breathed long and deep before even mounting the rifle. Then he brought it up, oozing air and tightness until his body turned motionless. He sighted. A long silence passed. Barney stared at Germaine, not bothering to even look at the target. When the shot came, finally, the card flew upward in a flurry of shredded pattern and image, and the majority of men and women watching cheered. Germaine smiled in a way that might have seemed like gloating to a loser. He looked at Barney with a grin that would have frozen a weasel.

"You sons a bitches snookered us and we won't forget it," said Barney, throwing out his drink.

"Who's we?" old Chester said. "Seems like your friend knew better."

"Who's we? Who's we? I'll show you who *we* is." He stomped inside and came out with his friend and the two women. They rushed out to a Pontiac parked in the shallow mud and snow of the lot. The others got in, but Barney fished around in the back seat of the coupe and came back toward Germaine and the others with a shotgun—no, it was a Thompson. He stopped about fifty feet away from the group of onlookers and raised it from his hip. Germaine and Monroe hit the ground. The other men scrambled inside as fast they could.

Three long bursts ripped apart the cardboard backstop and the lathe; tore apart the tractor combing, one of the two-holers (luckily no one was inside), the coffee can, and the chair the jar had sat on; and filled the air with smoke and cordite. The loud reports echoed over and over off the rock face. He emptied his clip and turned and walked back to the car, with Germaine and Monroe still face down on the ground. The first heads peered out of the barn door; the music fell silent inside. Then the Pontiac pulled out onto the road and roared away into the rapidly descending night.

CHAPTER SIX

The TB Society

THE TWELVE-FOOT BALSAM STOOD ALONE in open ground a few yards from the high, deeply undercut bank of the St. Regis River, where brook trout the size of paddle blades congregated in the summer, out of the sun—easy ambush by otters, or the clumsy but occasionally fruitful probing of flies and bait attached to threads of gut. The river cut though sand plains of glacial till, Labrador tea, blueberries, and other heaths, punctuated here and there with solitary and symmetrical evergreens, alder islands, spring holes, and small stands of taiga-like spruce and balsam. When the men came for the tree, the ground lay beneath six inches of snow, the sky a leaden matte. The trout had just returned from the smallest tributaries and gravel beds at the outlet of Lower St. Regis Lake, near Paul Smith's hotel, where they had paired off and spawned, salmon-sized in the fingerling-sized water, exposed to view to anyone peeking through the alders along shore. Just as Mart Moody had described to Louis Agassiz, the hens dug shallow depressions in the streambed with their tails and deposited strands of yellow eggs among the pebbles.

The cocks hovered beside them in the swift current, and both sexes rubbed together along their lateral lines until the males turned on their side and quivered, releasing strings of pale milt over the pebbles and the eggs. They had returned to the undercut bank only in the last few hours, exhausted and starving, while the fertile eggs divided beneath the gravel. When the men's footsteps vibrated at the lowest wavelength through the unstable earth and into the water, the trout sank in the pool on hovering fins and settled beneath the rocks, where their spots—blue, red, and yellow—faded in the murk, and they to shadows.

Now the balsam stood in Harry Rumsey's center hall, hung with baseball-sized glass spheres colored blue, red, and yellow, as well as green, silver, and gold, placed there over the last three hours by the healthier residents of the vicinity's various "sans" and private cure cottages. Other ornaments came from Norway and England, Pères Noel and crèche scenes from Quebec, gilt pine cones and other ornaments crafted locally of antler, cedar, and birch. A dozen alabaster hands laced with blue placed strands of tinfoil, delicately and singly, on each branch of the perfectly symmetrical tree, enhancing its shimmering and festive unreality. (They were under the direction of a Polish woman, an artist and onetime model of Picabia's, whose accent was redolent of smoked meat and dill.) Beneath the tinsel and woven deeply into the branches, red and blue pinpoints of light shone through, carefully insulated with gutta-percha so the bulbs wouldn't ignite the tree and burn down Rumsey's rambling manor, built in the Arts and Crafts style (with elements of Shingle) by the local architect William Distin and overlooking Lake Flower on the upper skirt of Dewey Mountain.

Besides balsam, the air smelled of cinnamon, vanilla, nutmeg and roasting meat. On the Victrola, Caruso sang "Nessun Dorma" while a hundred adult guests—primarily patients, nurses and clergy, and a smattering of school-age youths—milled and flirted, compared their illnesses, discussed the weather and the recent spate of deaths, or stood alone looking wistful. They came from the Adirondack Cottage Sanatorium ('Trudeau's), Will Rogers's (for tubercular vaudevillians), the Lakeside Rest (across Rainbow Lake from Jack Diamond's camp on Clear Pond), the Tumblehome (the rambling, many-porched-and-turreted, green-and-white structure that dominated the two-block main street of Lake Aurora), and dozens of private cottages. The patrons included various European sub-royalty, legitimate and bogus; a Russian émigré herpetologist; the director of the Halifax Philharmonic; Polish merchant seamen; pro baseball players, jockeys, and bookies; and the jugglers, clowns, burlesque queens, and magicians from Will Rogers's.

From behind a table set up for refreshments, Germaine and Monroe observed the scene, drinking eggnog. Wendy and Yvette, wearing aprons and bonnets pinned to their hair, kept them close by as they filled and refilled the trays of crêpes suzette, sugar cookies, macaroons, slices of tourtiere, breads, pies, and loaves of Yvette's grandmother's paté that they had been preparing out at Diamond's for the last three days. At each end of a long table set up in the unheated cure porch, where the host's nephew sat for eight hours of every day wrapped in a buffalo robe and playing checkers with the butler, two tuxedoed black men served unadulterated eggnog from capacious, cut crystal punch bowls.

The tree decoration had been organized under the supervision of Madeline Farrell, director of the TB Society. The tree itself had come from Lydia Smith, whose land it had stood on. Germaine and Monroe had harvested it at her request that morning. Rumsey himself had advised Madeline Farrell to request Wendy's and Yvette's assistance, since he had already hired them at Basil's recommendation for the second phase of the gala Christmas benefit.

The music stopped when the Polish artist, in an antique satin gown and with a sprig of holly pinned to her breast, stood in front of the tree and declared the decoration complete. The party clapped and resumed their conversations or brooding. Then the lead tenor of the Pittsburgh Opera stepped forward, blew on a pitch pipe, and led them in a verse and chorus of "Oh, Christmas Tree." When he stepped down, a pair of baggy-pants comics from the Lower East Side wearing elf shoes and hats walked out and stood before the Nordic pagan Tannenbaum. They pantomimed a couple of Santa's helpers, curing at Saranac Lake, who spike the eggnog at a Christmas party like this one with bootleg rum, and wind up wonking each other over the head repeatedly with rubber baguettes. As they get drunker a severe-looking doctor with mutton chops and resembling Dr. Edward Livingston Trudeau, founder of the cure and their patron saint, emerges from behind the screen, harrumphs, and calls for a nurse. Out comes Lily Knocks, pale and hollow-eyed in an elfin nurse outfit, with a Santa hat on her head, a tiny skirt just covering her tuchus, and ample cleavage out in front. She bumps once, to a bass-drum rim shot from behind the screen, and brandishes an enema bag, at which point one elf faints in ecstasy and the other escapes in terror. Amid the laughter only a few of the nurses, clergy, and stuffier of the patients showed any signs of distress.

More buskers followed. They stopped in front of the tree, juggled or made a few sleight-of-hand passes, and filtered among the crowd. Yvette and Wendy shuttled the food around; Germaine and Monroe helped and drank their (spiked) eggnog against a background of conversation punctuated by gales of relieved (if weak) laughter and song.

As always in consumptive society, the erotic energy ran high. Numerous were the large, dark eyes, the pallid complexions and angelic expressions. Couples held hands or conversed intently. After her bit, half a dozen well-dressed young men surrounded the curing Lily, most of them in a state of extreme arousal and frustration. The party went on for another hour. Finally the tenor led them in a verse of "Silent Night," and cars pulled up under Rumsey's porte cochère. The patients, wrapped in long overcoats, mufflers, and overshoes, ventured into the (presumably healing) zero-degree air to return to their houses and sans, except for half a dozen who were encouraged to walk the mile downhill together to their nearby cottage.

In the lull before the next party, Monroe and Wendy repaired to Rumsey's pantry, where Monroe ran his hand up under Wendy's apron to feel her silk underthings and the humid oasis they protected. Germaine and Yvette enacted their own amatory tableau in the alcove off the dining room. All were venting the sexual tension that had accumulated as coffins piled up four-deep at Union Station, and an aura of doom replaced the jazz-age hilarity. Sometimes it went that way this time of year—in waves, the imperative of death too compelling to resist, death following death in dominos of resignation. The medicos and all the town fathers agreed on the necessity of a bright atmosphere and ample activity through the holidays, or the losses (and illicit pregnancies) would mount, through nothing more than the powers of suggestion and futility.

Furthermore, science had discovered new agents of disease and possible routes to a drug cure. Only rapid progress on the molecular front would put an end to such seasonal losses as they were having. The TB Society had scheduled a full calendar of diversions: parties, art shows, and caroling; lectures, services, and sermons, with some of the events progressing from cottage to cottage. The larger events were planned as subtle appeals for funding, for only money—scarce even in the general affluence— allowed scientific progress. And the events themselves required funding.

Word went around through the patients, and locally through the nurses and other caregivers. That's how it came to Jack

Diamond from his brother Eddie, who had occupied the third-floor corner room and cure porch in The Tree Tops on Park Avenue for two years.

Diamond assumed (wrongly) that his brother's tuberculosis prefigured his own, and he feared the disease more than the repeal of the Volstead Act. ("Not being able to *breathe*! Are you kidding *me*?") Fear made him assure his brother's comfort and happiness. It made him sustain research at the avant-garde, and curry favor with the medical and administrative elite of North America's Magic Mountain, that enclave of healing and death, of social and cultural fusion, consumptive desire and sentiment, in the remote high forests of northern New York. He assumed—incorrectly—that he would be taking up residence there himself. As a fallback he also sent money to an institution being built in Arizona, where the sun shined more generously than in the Adirondacks.

Diamond's aversion to northern gloom—and a previous engagement in Hoboken—prevented him from attending the events. Basil handled the arrangements but kept a low profile. Nothing should raise a specter of illegitimacy, of doubt. Nothing should be allowed to disrupt the two-week collective dream, memorability and seamlessness being Jack's main goals. At some level those in charge would realize his largesse. Today's parties were only the first. Charity, for a while, would take precedence over business.

Monroe and Germaine welcomed the change. They had just finished their third transport by sled team through the woods. Their alienation from the village's daily life, their illegal sideline, their physical vigor, and their general male obliviousness had insulated them from the death wave. Wendy and Yvette, on the other hand, had picked up the first vibrations from the local women—the nurses and chambermaids who worked in the cottages where they delivered liquor and baked goods. They responded eagerly when Basil instructed them to begin food preparations for the series of parties. Their female solicitude and community spirit bore a nostalgic, non-sexual element for the men, whose mothers, sisters, and fathers—and those of their friends—had worked in the older, less posh cottages and sanitaria, and for Dr. Trudeau himself when death was commonplace and often contagious. It echoed with elements of local and personal importance, and life's impermanence. It felt familiar.

They stood on the back porch looking out over the lake, smoking, while the women prepared a second, even more sumptuous assault of food. To the south, the late afternoon sun lit the peaks of Algonquin and the Sawteeth, beyond Miller Pond. To the east, straight ahead, lenticular-clouded Whiteface and the Sentinels.

"I'll never be able to eat bacon and beans again after all this," Monroe said. "What the hell's your problem, anyways?"

"Blue balls."

They stood there in their brown wool suits, cellulose collars, and brogans, and blew plumes of mixed smoke and vapor out into the freezing air. Germaine took a drink and held out a silver flask of the sort a college kid might have used at a football game.

"Nah."

"Would you bring in the cheesecake, please?" Yvette said, sticking her head out the door. They flicked away their butts and peeled back a tarp that was under an eave. Underneath it were two large trays of bright yellow cheese-and-sugar confection. Each carried a tray inside as one of the black helpers held the door open.

Yvette stood in the center of the kitchen, surrounded by chafing dishes and tureens filled with braised wild duck, jugged hare, venison sausage, beef bourguignonne, potatoes au gratin, pumpkin and cherry pies, chocolate and angel food cakes, and various side dishes. A pair of enormous hams were almost ready to come out of the ovens. Yvette's unpinned hair flew about her head in black whorls. Her cheeks and mouth carried a high flush, and her eyes looked even larger and blacker than normal, excited and febrile. "Put them there," she said, pointing to a cleared space on the sideboard, a little giddy. They placed their trays where they were told and removed themselves again to the back porch.

"Those girls work hard," Monroe said.

"Yeah."

"Wish to hell you'd let me in on what's eating you."

"All right. I was just thinking about old Beaver Mullins," Germaine said.

Beaver had recently hemorrhaged in the basement speakeasy of the St. Regis Hotel, where he had been drinking with a handful of newly arrived nurses from Boston—flappers on their time off, who had adopted him as a quaint artifact and "safe" avuncular figure to pal around with. In his glory, surrounded by angels, he had coughed up a large gout of blood. He had once worked at Trudeau's, so they carried him up there, where he died of slow suffocation a week or so later.

"Yeah, old Beaver. Once I seen him chop down a nice ash tree and saw it into a cord of wood, split and stacked, in two hours. Guys like him, they don't make 'em anymore. Never was sick. Worked every day, or nearly, for sixty years, then just give out. His old man came here when there was nothing, just woods. He was the last one who could remember before the river was dammed. He remembered Colonel Miller and smoky whale-oil lamps. He owned the first repeating rifle in Franklin County, drank more than his share. People like that start dropping off all at once, it changes everything. Everything. You think things just go on, and new things replace old things, but they don't. It's like when Jimmy Wilkins shot the last wolf—"

"That was Myron Pierce."

"Well, now, I'm not gonna get into that old argument with

you. You know who was the bigger liar of those two. It's just that some things, when they disappear, they make everything else disappear, too. When he died he took the old days right with him."

"Oh, for Christ's sake."

"Didn't you see the looks on the faces of some of the pretty young girls inside there, dancing and talking with their beaus? Some of them ain't gonna make it. Some of them nurses and workers won't neither. Remember Eddie Lynch's sister?"

"I remember."

They smoked.

"I heard some of the older women in there saying it's because of the booze running that's going on," Germaine said.

"What? You mean all the dying? Like punishment or something?"

"Or something."

"Aw, they just don't like nobody enjoying theirselves."

"Maybe. It just makes me think of all that time we spent trying to shoot people and them trying to shoot us in places we had no business being. We were lucky. It's not like we any of us have all that much time to spend on anything, whether it's important or not."

"Well, I have no goddamn idea what you're talking about, as usual. I just hope you ain't going soft on me, not after dragging me into all this."

"Just you don't worry about me, bucky."

"You two come back here and help us move this food out onto the tables." Wendy opened the back door and delivered her message without waiting for a response. The two friends hurried inside and waited for orders. The tables had been moved from the cure porch into the great room, and now gleamed under the best crystal, silver, and china—some of it Rumsey's, the rest donated by Lydia Smith. The men wheeled in the trays and dishes and set them down wherever Wendy or Yvette indicated. A fire roared in the huge fieldstone fireplace; the electric wall sconces glowed through amber isinglass shades; the parquet gleamed around the edges of the great Shiraz. A stuffed bear—a five-hundred-pounder shot on the back side of McKenzie by Fermin Harrington in 1918—stood six feet tall at the head of the room, and a large Durand of Keene Valley after a thunderstorm hung over the mantel. Balsam greens with red ribbons rounded out the solstitial decor.

Rumsey, in a tuxedo, welcomed the first early arrivals at the far end the room, and a woman in a black dress and white apron took their coats. Rumsey's nephew, Roger, also in a tux, lay back in a reclining wheelchair with a comforter over his legs, sipping a ginger ale.

With the food laid out, the men retreated to the kitchen. They lacked specific roles, either as help or as guests. Monroe found a station in the breakfast nook off the kitchen, where he drank his eggnog while Germaine went out the back door again. The holiday idleness increased Monroe's general confusion about Germaine's maundering over the dead, the past, or whatever it was. Monroe watched Germaine out there, walking around with his hands in his pockets, kicking the woodpile, looking out over the lake and the last light on Whiteface, fifteen miles off, as if he had nowhere in the world to be. Then he disappeared into the gloom around the side of the house.

Rumsey, the Broadway agent, prided himself on entertaining lavishly and liquidly, and for the period of his nephew's cure the proximity to Canada made it easier for him; champagne flutes went around openly on trays. By six, most of the sixty guests had had at least one and had begun to move toward the food. A hired pianist played soft carols and bits of Bach and Mozart on a Steinway baby grand. Lydia and Paul Smith caused a stir when they arrived late, having been delayed by a recalcitrant starter crank, Lydia plain in a wool coat and galoshes, and Paul in a modest topcoat and Stetson that he handed off to the servant without a look. Both appeared pale and depleted by age and illness. A delegation headed by Rumsey greeted them. They were joined by Melvil Dewey, red-faced and full of bonhomie, who had developed the Decimal System and the failed Simplified Spelling, and who had founded the Lake Placid Club. He accompanied them around the room, their differences forgotten or suppressed for the moment.

Monroe watched the arrivals from a position between the buffet and the partition near the fireplace. In the crowd he recognized Dr. George Pinkton, the surgeon, who liked to fish for bullheads on warm June nights but wanted somebody else to clean them. He saw a pathologist who had drunk half a bottle of corn liquor at their campsite on Saginaw Bay, rowed off at midnight, and gotten lost. They found him the next morning, passed out in a small bay down the shore. Mrs. Hallinan, whose daughter Lois had given him a hand-job in the lean-to at Slant Rock right after he got back from France, looked younger than her fifty years and was accompanied by a man he didn't recognize.

A couple of middle-aged doctors crowded close around Jack Rabbit Johanssen, the Norwegian ski trail builder—wiry and ruddy in knickers, sweater, and toque—while he told them about his daring first ski down Marcy.

As the Smiths drew closer, squired by Dewey, Monroe turned his back so they wouldn't recognize him. They probably wouldn't have anyway, outside the context of the boathouse or stable. That's when Germaine appeared across the room standing next to the bear, drinking champagne and talking to Jacques Suzanne.

The two woodsmen couldn't have looked more outré in the cultivated surroundings—Germaine rugged if respectable in his brown wool; Suzanne clearly drunk and garbed like a coureur de bois in fox-fur boots and hat, belted Hudson's Bay jacket, and smoking a pipe. Suzanne lived on Bear Cub Road in the shadows of Street and Nye outside Placid, in a log cabin filled with traps and snowshoes, packbaskets, and knives—a dark sanctum and time machine of the wild northern frontier, lit with oil lamps and surrounded by the pens and houses of the sled dogs he raised to race and give rides to club members and tourists. Widely regarded as a mountebank, he had lived in northern Quebec and the Yukon and was one of the region's icons, despite a penchant for whiskey and fisticuffs. But his stock had risen since his adoption two years ago by a New York film studio, which had churned out a couple of two-reel melodramas set in the Klondike but filmed in Lake Placid, for which Suzanne provided dogs and sleds, props, expertise, location advice, and a kind of raffish (if histrionic) authenticity—though he could not be trusted in society.

Monroe strode over and joined the other two standing under the bear's maw. The three of them must have made quite a picture, like a delegation from the virile arts that underpinned the region's identity—or a version of it, at least. That alone would explain their welcome (and Johanssen's).

"Jacques here says he can get us in the next movie they're gonna make, Lon," said Germaine. "That right, Jacques?" Germaine was slightly drunk.

"By Jee-Chrise, you betcha," Suzanne puffed on his pipe and swizzled his mustache, glassy eyed and smelling of cheap rotgut.

"Hullo, Jacques," said Monroe. They shook hands. "That's some getup."

"Mmf."

"Good party," Germaine said, looking out over the room, grinning, and rocking on his heels.

"By Jee-Chrise, I guess so," said Suzanne.

"Where's the girls?" Germaine said.

"They took off their aprons after the food was out. They were bushed. I thought they came out here," said Monroe.

At that point Basil and his new woman-friend glided across the room.

"Who let you mugs in here?" Basil said, looking at them one at a time under his pronounced widow's peak.

"Hullo, Basil, this is Jacques," Germaine said, keeping his eyes fixed dangerously on the gowned apparition at Basil's side.

"Her name's Veronica Louise. She's an actress. Watch yourself."

"Oh, how quaint," the actress said, ignoring Germaine and stroking Suzanne's hat and coat. "Enchantée, monsieur."

"Joyeux Noel, mademoiselle," Suzanne said, with a courtly bow but stumbling slightly.

"Look, we gotta talk," Basil said. "Excuse us, Veronica. Will you be all right with Mr.—er—Jacques for a few minutes? Fine. Let's go out this way."

Monroe and Germaine followed him into the kitchen and lit cigarettes while the kitchen help kept swinging the door open and closed behind them.

"What's that guy, some kinda clown or something?" Basil said.

"He's in the movies," Germaine said.

"Movies, huh. Just looks like another Frenchy to me." He exhaled smoke. "Listen, I don't know what the hell went on at that shindig you guys shot up last week, but the boss heard all about it. He was pissed when he found out those guys you beat worked for the Dutchman. Yeah, you heard me. But then he decided he really liked what you did—that you could really shoot like that, and that you played Dutch's guy the way you did. Where'd you learn that trick, anyways?"

"Just something we worked up to entertain the troops and earn a little extra cash down in old Mexico," Monroe said.

"You still gotta hit the target, though, right?"

"Right," Germaine said.

"Right. So listen. Jack wants to use you guys a little more. He wants you to go to Montreal next week with Emile to talk to the supplier, this big-shot Jew named Feldspar. Jack's been looking for a break on the price, but the guy keeps asking him for more. He's taking heat from the Mounties, he says, who tell him they keep getting squeezed by the Feds. Our guys, G-men. You believe that? What do the Mounties care, right? Anyway, you guys gotta convince Feldspar that it's worth his while to keep his prices low for Jack, because we got a whole new territory opening in Philly, and good routes opening up, and we'll keep buying more. We're expanding all the time, see? I can't do it, because they know me up there. You guys, you're nobody to them. Jack figures you'll look like a couple of hicks going to the city for liquor and pussy. Why else does anybody go there, right? Emile'll set up the meet and let you know the details. But you gotta be ready to go when he says, get me?"

"What if the guy won't come down?" Germaine said.

"Oh, he'll come down. Anyway, we'll talk about it more later. I gotta get back to Veronica. Ain't she something?"

"Wait a minute. How'd Jack hear about that turkey shoot anyways?" Monroe said.

"You kidding? The guy sprayed a fucking square dance with a machine gun. You think that doesn't get around? Jack didn't exactly appreciate the attention it got him, but he loved that Dutch took most of it. Ha ha. Oh, yeah. And Dutch blew his stack when he heard about it. He gave that rube you screwed a royal chewing out, cut his pay in half, and made him suck his dick."

Monroe and Germaine looked at each other.

"Nah, haw haw. He's crazy enough to, though, that fucking Dutchman. But he did do something to him, I know that. The guy wasn't happy about it at all."

Basil turned to leave.

"So what do we get outta this?" Germaine said.

Basil turned back again and said, as if for the last time, "Don't worry about it. You guys handle this, Jack'll make you very happy."

"I want to know what we get, or we walk."

"What are you, crazy? Jack doesn't want no other guys. He wants you. If I tell you he'll take care a you, he'll take care a you. Now, I gotta go."

Basil turned and threw open the swinging door, knocking the tray off the shoulder of an elderly black man who was on his way in. A couple of plates that had held beef bourguignonne streaked the front of Basil's exquisite cutaway.

"Son of a bitch! Can't you watch where you're going?" he yelled.

The party fell silent; the piano stopped playing. The man looked crestfallen and sullen, and got down on one knee, picking up the scattered silverware, broken glass, and half-chewed leftovers.

"No, it's all right. Here, let me help. Sorry, sorry," Basil said, bending to the floor. "It's nothing," he said, facing the crowd and wiping his jacket with napkin. "It comes right off. All my fault. Merry Christmas."

The crowd turned back to their chatter, and the piano came in on "Toyland." Germaine and Monroe helped with the mess while Basil finished wiping off his tux. "I'll have to send this to New York to get cleaned," he said.

"Oh, honey," said Veronica, rushing over from the fireplace, pulling Jacques Suzanne by the hand. "Here, let me." She tried to grab the jacket by the shoulders to take it off, but Basil stood and shrugged her away.

"No, no. It's all right, Ronnie, darling," he said, softening his tone. "It's just an old jacket."

"Oh, Basil, guess what. Jacques is in cinema too. And he has *lots* of furs. He wants to take me to his secret pond in his dogsled, to catch fish through the ice."

By now Suzanne was cock-eyed, and openly leering down the

woman's low-cut and tremulous front. His pipe smoked intensely with cheap shag.

"Okay, that's enough." Basil turned to Germaine and Monroe and cocked his thumb at Suzanne. "Take care of this guy, will ya? Come on Ronnie, honey. Let's get back to the party. I want you to meet Mr. Dewey."

"Goodbye, Jacques," she said, pouting.

They turned and swept back into the crowd. The men steered Suzanne toward the corner by the fireplace and propped him up against the surround with a mug of hot cocoa, hoping he'd stay there for the rest of the party. He owned no motor vehicle and had ridden over with the Lake Placid contingent, so he was in no danger of driving into a snowbank and freezing to death. He kept a cheerful expression and his pipe going, while various men and women came over and paid their respects.

Monroe and Germaine were standing on the other side of the fireplace when Wendy appeared, looking lovely, if fatigued, in a different dress from the one she had cooked and served in. She wore white gloves and had her hair tucked under a Christmasy-looking cloche. They introduced her to Suzanne, who behaved impeccably. "What a fine hat," she said, stroking the burnt-orange, silver-streaked fur.

"We were upstairs resting and talking with the women from the TB Society," she said. "They loved the food, but the last few weeks have been awful, people dying who just days before had seemed to turn a corner, even some who had been thought cured and ready to go home. Everybody's so upset that it's hard for the party to get going."

"S'a great party," Suzanne said. "By Jee Chrise."

While Wendy spoke, Germaine cast his eyes around the room, bringing them to rest on Yvette. She, too, had changed into more presentable clothes, and reclined on a chaise a few feet away between the fire and the bear, talking with a group of sharply turned out men and women. Under the light from a Tiffany lamp, her eyes looked even darker than usual—ringed with darkness, in fact, her skin like parchment.

"There's Yvette," Germaine said.

"She's very tired, Fran. She'll just sit for a few more minutes, then she'll be fine."

The group of people left Yvette with their good wishes, except for one man, blonde and in his late thirties, who sat on the ottoman at her feet. He took her hand, looked at it, then at her.

Monroe had been watching Yvette, but when he shifted his gaze back to Germaine, he was struck by the look on his friend's face—one he had seen a few times in only the direst of circumstances, and always preceding violence.

"Whoa, Fran," he said, gripping Germaine's arm.

Germaine tore away and strode straight across the room, knocking shoulders with a beefy doctor in his fifties ("Really, Germaine—"). With Monroe on his heels, he came to a halt at the head of the chaise.

"Oh, Fran, I'm so happy to see you," Yvette said, offering him her unoccupied hand. "I've been feeling a little woozy, nothing serious. This is Dr. Kline. He is just taking my pulse."

Germaine softened, but remained guarded. "Pleased," he said, offering his hand, his eyebrows joined in a single, threatening furrow.

Kline put down Yvette's hand. They shook.

"Come on, Yvie. You're bushed. We'll take you back to Basil's. Give me a hand, Lon." Germaine placed a hand beneath her shoulder and began to lift.

"No, not yet. Please, Fran. The party is so interesting. The ladies of the TB Society have been so nice, and everybody's so terribly upset about what's been happening, aren't they doctor?"

Kline had stood and regarded Germaine with a tolerant expression. "It's been a difficult time," the doctor said, with a trace of accent.

He was wonderful looking, with a blonde forelock and eyes of pale steel gray. When he smiled, he flashed perfect teeth and an Old-World air.

"Well," Germaine said. "If you want."

"She should be fine for a bit longer," said Kline. "Just a touch of overwork and lack of sleep. Not to be concerned. Delighted, Herr Germaine." He bowed. "Au revoir, mademoiselle. Enchanté."

She offered him her hand again. "Merci, docteur."

He turned on his heel and joined a cluster of other youngish doctors who had gathered near the now-silent piano.

Germaine stood frozen between expressions of desperate concern and male threat.

"You feeling better, honey?" said Wendy, who had followed in Monroe's wake.

"Oui, yes. It's okay. Merci."

At that point a loud C-major chord sounded from the piano. "What's that?" Wendy said. The guests gradually lowered their voices and turned their attention toward the piano and Harry Rumsey.

"Everyone, everyone," Rumsey chanted, waving a handkerchief. When he had the room's attention he said, "I have an amazing and exciting surprise for you. Two of our favorite neighbors are here to perform for this most splendid occasion. They agreed to come from Lake Placid at the last minute, in hopes the spirit of the season and a few rounds of their magnificent music would firm up the resolution of this most excellent corps of heroic physicians to their finest work and an eventual cure for the cursed illness that built and now ravages this village. Please welcome and offer the merriest of Christmases to Miss Kate Smith and Mr. Irving Berlin."

The kitchen door swung open and out rushed a young woman—of the general size and affect of a beaming lighthouse—

in a red and green chiffon dress, followed by a black-haired cherub in a black silk suit, who sat at the piano bench and launched directly into "I Love a Parade." The stunned crowd took a few seconds to absorb the surprise before erupting in a sustained outpouring of exclamation and applause.

The chanteuse stood in front of the piano twisting a handkerchief while the guests cheered and the brief intro played out. Then she opened her mouth and her arms, and let loose with the song's opening vowel. It exploded into the room: "Ahhhhhhhhh-y, loveaparade . . ."

The piano kept up the percussive march time, adding trills and arpeggios, and the singer's voice was strong and clear. Yvette was on her feet immediately, and Germaine guided her closer to the front of the crowd near the piano, with Monroe and Wendy right behind them. She kept looking from the performers to Germaine with an expression of longing and some combination of gratitude and wonder.

When the song ended, the musicians ran quickly through lush and witty renditions of "You Made Me Love You," "Alice Blue Gown," "You're a Grand Old Flag," and then back to Berlin's own classics.

Finally, the great composer stood and joined the chanteuse, telling the audience he would play two tunes from a new show. He resumed his seat at the piano and played the vamp to "White Christmas." When it was done, the room was hushed, then the guests roared with adulation.

"Look, everyone." Again the voice was Rumsey's. He stood in front of the picture window, gesturing outside. Lake Flower and the Saranac River lay below in a gray twilight. In the distance the waxing gibbous moon rose over the peaks of Street, Nye, and Algonquin mountains—hulking shadows against a deep, purple void—with a pale nimbus encircling it and Venus a few degrees off center. The doctors and their wives shifted to the window with delighted murmurs. The great house seemed to list under their weight like a ship.

"Ring around the moon," Monroe whispered, standing with Wendy behind the other couple at the window, while Berlin comped softly on the piano.

"Snow tomorrow," Germaine said.

A collective impression filled the room, of rising above the reality of the last grim weeks.

The lights had been dimmed for Berlin's performance and the moonrise, and now they came up, along with the low conversation. To those who wished it, cognac and port were made discreetly available—just enough to put the flush back in pallid winter cheeks and inject a note of gaiety into what had begun as a dour proceeding.

That spirit reigned for half an hour, with a smiling Berlin and Smith circulating the room. But the climax had passed. The women of the TB Society began approaching Yvette and Wendy as they readied to leave, exchanging wishes for continued friendship and assistance, and an improved new year. By the third round of these visitations, Eleanor Blake, the doyenne of the squadron of nurses, told them, "Really, dears, you must get some rest after these last busy days." She turned to Germaine and said, "Please make sure that Basil gentleman takes these ladies home immediately. She looks her death."

Their faces bespoke concern rather than judgment, and Yvette and Wendy relented, despite their philosophy of seeing a party though to its bitterest dregs.

"Time to go," Germaine said.

They found their coats in the kitchen, and the women instructed the helpers in which dishes and silverware to set aside for their return in a day or two.

They reentered the main house to leave by the front door. A dozen stalwarts, including Basil and Veronica, regaled the celebrities by the fire. In a separate cluster a solicitous Rumsey helped the Smiths with their coats and hats. The four friends waited to exchange goodbyes with Basil and some of the others, when Smith noticed them and approached, leaving Lydia behind with Rumsey.

"Gentlemen. How curious to find you here," he said.

"Mr. Paul," they said.

"Lovely affair, what? Hm." He had opened his mouth to continue when a commotion began and a loud slap sounded in the alcove near the front door.

"Oh! You animal!" shouted a female voice.

"Oh, dear," said Smith.

Germaine and Monroe rushed to the alcove, where they found Jacques Suzanne stunned and chastened, eyes half opened and fox-fur hat tilted to one side, watching an attractive woman (the wife of Dr. Crawford—Elsie, by name) being sheltered in her husband's arms and weeping.

"Jesus, Jacques," said Monroe. "What the hell?"

"Get him away from her," the husband said, rushing her out the open front door and under the porte cochère.

"Come on, Jacques, let's get outta here," Germaine said. They each took an arm and began escorting him out.

"By Jee-Chrise," said Suzanne.

Rumsey and some of the others watched in shock while Dewey and Johanssen rushed to aid Monroe and Germaine.

"It's all right. We've got him," said Dewey. "It's all right everybody. Terribly sorry. Shouldn't have brought him." Turning to Suzanne he said, not without affection, "See here, Jacques. Get hold of yourself. You promised not to drink."

"Mmf," said the woodsman.

After that the chauffeur pulled up for the musicians, while Germaine and Monroe bundled their women to the Packard they had parked around back and disappeared into the dark before Smith or Basil could saddle them with any more pungent observations.

CHAPTER SEVEN

A Place in the World

FROM ACROSS THE RIVER the city looked low and sooty, lying below and about the rocky knob of the mount, and girdled by a flood two miles wide.

"Can't see much hell-raising going on from over here," Monroe said.

They stood on shore, beside a cluster of shacks on an island upstream and across the main channel from Montreal. A half dozen skiffs, wooden rowboats, and canoes—a couple of bark, but mostly cedar-canvas in varied states of repair—lined the bank, overturned or upright and making catchments for puddles of icy water. Around a bend downstream, a line of white foam and spittle ran all the way across the river, with geysers of spume exploding out if it at regular intervals, marking the head of Sault St. Louis, the Lachine rapid. And a quarter mile upstream, on a bridge under construction, steelworkers tossed red-hot rivets with tongs, others caught them in tin cans and jack-hammered them into place, and still others snaked above the maelstrom on single girders like aerialists.

"Well, it ain't Paris," said Germaine. "But it'll do."

"You men come with me."

A big Mohawk named Bernard stood behind them, half turned back toward a stone barn that leaned on one partially collapsed wall. They followed him around the barn fronting the dirt lane, where other stone and timber-frame buildings and log shacks stood. Inside, the gray light got lost in the corners, but you could read the printing on the wooden crates stacked ceiling high. Jameson's, Johnny Walker, Dewar's, Gordon's, Fleischmann's, Canadian Club.

"This is all going across before New Year," Bernard told them, "one way or the other. You'll be negotiating for next year's stock."

A couple of Indians in bad suits and hats played craps and smoked quietly inside the door.

"Everybody knows this is where the booze is, but they don't try nothing with these boys here," Bernard said.

The one closest to the door looked up and grinned through a scar eight inches wide. Just then a shadow fell across the doorway, and Emile came in.

"Feldspar says he'll talk to you tomorrow at nine, in his house on Redpath Circle. No guns. A driver will pick you up at the hotel."

"How will we know who it is?"

"Just wait in the lobby. When you get there, you do the talking." He looked at Germaine. "Don't say yes to anything. Just tell him what Jack wants and that he'll expect an answer soon, or no deal." Turning to Monroe he said, "You watch the windows, entrances, and the muscle. You get done with Feldspar, don't get in any cars. Tell him you'll walk back to the hotel, then go to this address. Your clothes from the hotel will be there." He gave them another wrinkled slip of paper. "When it's clear, we'll take you back to the mountains."

"We gotta get back right away," Monroe said.

"It'll be all right," Emile said. "Thing you have to do now is go to the city and buy clothes. Nice clothes, Basil says. No cheap woodchuck suits. Here's the place."

He handed them a wrinkled piece of paper with the name "Kleinfeld and Sons, Haberdashers, 1130 Rue St. Catherine" written on it.

"It's taken care of," Emile said.

"How do we get there?"

"In a while someone will drive you across to the hotel."

"It's a little cold," Monroe said. "Isn't there some place a little warmer to wait around in?"

Emile looked over his wide nose at the wiry Adirondacker. "This is not cold," he said, and left.

THEY WATCHED THE WATER AND THE CONSTRUCTION, walking back and forth with their hands in their pockets, smoking. Beige light softened the thinning cloud layer.

"So, explain this to me," said Germaine, the engineer, to Bernard.

"It's a bridge, ay. For cars. The railroad bridge is over there."

Barges plied the roily waters at the feet of the massive concrete piers that stretched across the channel. From the opposite shore a mirroring armature of fretted steel extended out toward mid-river, aiming—in a matter of weeks, it appeared—to meet the near side and complete the span.

"It's beautiful," Germaine said.

"That's the new way they build a lot of big things," said Bernard. "Light and strong."

"Yeah, but they need us to do it. White men, they're too clumsy to scramble around on the girders. They fall. We're more balanced. It's from always walking in a straight line." Bernard took a dozen strides toward the bridge, placing one foot in front of the other. "They found out when they hired us for the old bridge."

He pointed downstream at the railroad bridge. "Now my brother and some of his friends are working in New York. Chrysler cars is building the tallest building in the world there. But they need us."

"Maybe Indians are just cheaper," Monroe said.

Bernard looked up at the bridge, out at the water, and exhaled smoke. "Maybe," he said. "Some of us fall."

Germaine nodded toward the bridge "How many so far?" he said.

"Just two."

They walked along the bank.

"What are these boats for?" Germaine said.

"People fishing. Sometimes other things."

Germaine picked up one of the few that had been tipped over against the weather and placed it upright on the shore. It looked dry and in good repair. Inside were two hand-carved wooden paddles. He looked at Monroe. "Let's go," he said.

"What are you, nuts?"

"Not far. Come on, let's go." He slid the boat down the bank to the water's edge and paused beside it, standing a paddle on its blade with one hand. "I'm going, whether you come or not."

Monroe looked downstream at the waters of the Lachine rapid boiling and exploding like the gates of hell. Down there the channel-wide ledges in the riverbed dropped fifty feet in a mile. At this level the waves were gargantuan. Right offshore the current ran fast, but not *that* fast, and there was a large eddy where skiffs and barges tacked back and forth to the bridge piers without apparent danger.

"You'd have it coming if I let you go alone," Monroe said, helping slide the canoe stern first into a slow eddy at the river's edge.

"Don't tip," Bernard said.

They paralleled shore, moving upstream in the eddy current, Germaine astern. The eddy extended farther out than they thought, and it felt about the same as paddling in a pond. The temperature had risen into the high thirties or forties, and filtered sunlight now bathed the river's surface. As they halved the distance to the bridge, Germaine said he wanted to paddle out far enough to see what the workers were up to and examine the architecture.

He turned the bow away from shore. As soon as they crossed the soft line between the eddy and the current, the river grabbed the bow and swept it downstream, making them correct the angle with deft strokes and draw the bow back upstream. They moved back and forth upstream, the fifteen-foot craft bobbing around on a chaos of six-inch wavelets. Soon they came within fifty feet of a bridge pier and drew themselves into the eddy on its downstream side. Cables and other tackle dangled almost to the water level, and a barge slewed back and forth against the current on its safety line.

A voice called out in French, and another yelled, "Watch yerselves down there, stupid Injuns." A loud splash sounded near them and a half dozen workers laughed, "Haw haw haw."

"Fuck," said Monroe, swiveling around in the bow. "This is the goddamn stupidest thing you've gotten us into yet."

"Watch your mouth there, bucky, and get your balls outta your hat. We seen worse than this."

That was true, technically, after three springs running jam boats on the Hudson and Raquette river log drives, to say nothing of the battle for the Chevre Bridge. So far, this was nothing by comparison.

"Well, there's no point to it. I'm ready to go back."

"Just be quiet and look up for a second."

Two stone vaults swept fifty feet overhead, crowning the two nearest piers. The surfaces, tiles, and scrollwork were perfectly finished in graceful, pleasing forms—details only a boatman would ever see. The entire drainage of central North America piled against their upstream sides. Between them rose girders and scaffolds in impossible-to-decipher perspectives. Loose lines and cables swung back and forth over the water, and figures moved along the girders. Then the sun came full out and made a latticework of shadows in parallelograms, rhomboids, and multi-dimensions on the piers and the water's surface, turning the water from grayish-brown to blue.

"Jesus," Monroe said. He craned his neck, looking up from the kneeling position. It made him dizzy.

Just then Germaine said, "Hold on," and turned the bow to the right, out of the shadow of the bridge pier. When the boat moved, Monroe lost his balance. For a split second he foresaw their imminent capsize in perfect clarity. But he caught himself at the crucial instant, and his balance returned with a twinge of nausea. He grabbed his paddle and they crossed the eddy line together, riding up onto the higher tier of the current. The bow snapped downstream, a gallon of water sloshed over the upstream gunwale, and the canoe leaped from a near standstill onto a liquid conveyor plunging toward the Gulf of St. Lawrence at seven miles an hour.

"Son of a bitch," Monroe said.

They crouched and shifted their weight to stay upright. In that position they paddled hard and straightened out the canoe while the current pushed them far out into the main river. Across lay the shore of Lachine, a Montreal suburb named by fur-trade voyageurs, the best canoeists in history (possibly excepting the Polynesians), who left from the riverside chapel there en route to the center of the continent—as unspeakably distant in their minds as China itself. From Germaine's and Monroe's perspectives Lachine might as well have been China ("La Chine"), the Orkney Islands, or the Faroes, and the intervening river as broad as the North Atlantic. Beyond Lachine, the dome of St. Joseph's Oratory rose on a west-facing shoulder of the mount.

Downstream the light telescoped and magnified the lip of the great rapid, making it look closer than it was, the waves like mushroom clouds eight feet high, their white tops flashing against the blue horizon.

Working carefully, they moved the bow across the current toward the south shore and Caughnawaga. Another gallon sloshed in from the upstream side, but they finally gained a steep enough upstream angle to cross without losing too much ground against the current. But it kept pushing. Ahead, Caughnawaga slid upstream at a sickening speed: the broken-down houses and barns, the church, Emile's Ford that they had driven down from Rainbow Lake that morning parked in front of the local bar. Paddling at full strength, Monroe felt no progress. He looked downstream one more time and thought he saw an entry line in the rapid in case they missed the eddy, and paddled.

The rapid got closer, but it still looked closer than it was. Finally the thread of current they rode got sucked shoreward into a widening side channel and carried them with it. Within seconds they had pulled into the lower end of the shore eddy and begun working their way in silence back upstream to the landing, wallowing under their cargo of inboard river water.

Emile, Bernard, and the two Indian guards from inside stood on the bank, smiling.

"Crazy white bastards," Bernard said.

"You're out of your fucking mind," Monroe said. He had gotten out of the bow and stood on the frozen land, his pants soaked to his crotch, his face white with cold and fury. Germaine sat with the stern still in the water, bailing with an old Chock Full O' Nuts can. "Aw, we never got close. It just looked close because it's so big."

"You might have made it," Bernard said. "Some of our people have paddled through. One, his name was Pierre. He ran the Lachine on Christmas Day, on a bet. After that, he led the Tyrells all the way from here to the Eskimo country, by canoe. I was a kid then. You know this Tyrell?"

"Nope," Germaine said.

"Well, you might have made it, anyway."

"We never got close." He threw the can in the bottom of the canoe and flipped it over with the paddles inside.

"There just wasn't any point to it," Monroe said.

"Point?" said Germaine, taking a step toward Monroe. "Just what fucking point are you talking about?"

"Sometimes there is one, you know," Monroe said, also stepping forward. "It's not always a *completely* pointless world." He was yelling.

"Hey, you men," Emile said, stepping between them. "We gotta get you to the hotel."

Germaine stepped back. "Well, sometimes you just gotta *act* without questioning everything," he said. "Why does it always have to be spelled out, anyway?"

Monroe turned on his heel, with his hands stuffed into his jacket pockets, and headed toward the car. "Yeah, yeah. Let's just get outta here," he said. "I'm fucking freezing,"

FROM THE WINDSOR THEY TOOK A CAB a few blocks to St. Catherine's and the haberdasher's. The floor man welcomed them at the door. He directed them to a pair of pier-glass triptychs where two tailors oversaw two apprentices each. Kleinfeld, a man in his fifties, wore a vest, brushy gray moustaches, and longish bald fringe. He spoke French to his workers and English to the men, and betrayed no judgment of their relative stations, no sign that Monroe and Germaine were any less gentlemen than the insurance executives and barristers from Westmount or the importers from Halifax that he commonly served. He knew who sent them and smirked collegially at the usual low humor over the question of which side the men dressed on, and the amount of material one or the other would be charged extra to conceal its girth. He brought out bolt after bolt of fabric, and patterns of different cuts, laying them over the men's shoulders or holding them against their waists; he suggested shirts and shoes, ties, garters, and suspenders, as each of them undressed and stood in new linen before the mirrors and the apprentices measured every inch of their flesh, moving with practiced economy and exactitude. The room smelled of face powder and cologne, cedar shavings, lavender. Germaine and Monroe cherished skilled handwork and knew they were in the hands of the best. They left after two and a half hours with packages full of accessories, though still in their old wool suits.

They sat for haircuts and shaves in the lobby of the hotel, hot towels around their faces, their jackets and Monroe's new fedora on hangers in the closet. Each held a glass of brandy in one hand and a Corona in the other. The elderly barbers kept up a patter of hockey and horse gossip. Both had been to Saranac Lake, had relatives who lived near there, and knew other St. Germains. They seemed to know the kind of haircut men like Germaine and Monroe would wear—with just the vaguest hint of flash. When the men were shaved and trimmed they rose from their chairs, gleaming, both cut high and tight, but with Germaine's black shock intact and minimally formed, and Monroe's sandy top greased and slicked over to the side.

In the evening they let Jack Diamond stand them to oysters, lobster, and champagne, with coffee, brandy, and baked Alaska for dessert, amid the hotel restaurant's red plush and brass. There they chatted up the barman, an Irishman from Cork, who poured enormous shots of the best Irish whiskey. The array of legal bottles behind the bar dazzled them. As hotel experts—and therefore snobs—they read all the signs and observed that the Windsor was a bourgeois haven for well-off merchants, low-level railroad executives, stock men, and brokers. That was fine, for that was how they viewed themselves. The women, elegant enough to turn their heads and possessed of enough hauteur to ignore them, lacked the recklessness, art, and improvisational daring of women they had known in Europe, at Smith's, and from guiding. But that was all right, too.

The comparison made them think of Yvette and Wendy. And even while they considered it their prerogative to pursue any possible sexual opportunity, they knew where their loyalties lay. It made them feel loved, lonely, and free at the same time. Later they sat in the hotel lobby while the trains came in from Boston, New York, Toronto, Vancouver, Halifax, and the lobby filled up with white North Americans surrounded by leather luggage, small dogs, steamer trunks, and high fashion—the women aflame with travel and action, the men themselves expectant and flushed. They read the *Gazette* sports page in good new clothes and smoked Cuban cigars while a waiter brought them whiskies on a tray. They were soldiers and free agents—men of the world—with a place in the world, even if recently that place had begun to seem provisional and contingent.

At the barman's suggestion they took a cab east on Ste. Catherine to Rue St. Denis and the Theatre Majestique, where burlesque of a high order was performed in French, with elements of erotic music-hall performance they had seen in Paris. There were skits and musical interludes, with drinks served openly, all under the stern but tolerant eye of the largest diocese in the province. A tall, black pianist played ragtime in a tux, and the small band—banjo, trombone, guitar, violin, and clarinet, along with the pianist—played a number of Bix standards, some Jelly Roll, and a frenetic and exotic-sounding jazz style based on the fiddle and guitar that the emcee said came from French gypsies.

A mulatta, five feet tall with freckles, green eyes, a low-cut sack dress, and a voice like Lil Armstrong, sang "Fascinatin' Rhythm," "St. James Infirmary," and "Funky Butt" ("I Thought I

Heard Buddy Bolden Say") before sitting out for an instrumental on "Muskrat Ramble." In the following skit, Canadian soldiers encountered large-bosomed milkmaids in Belgium. Then came a pair of song-and-dance routines led by a willowy Québécoise in a dinner jacket and net stockings. In the production numbers, the female dancers were nude on top, and the men, shirtless in pleated pants and suspenders, showed prominent bulges. Both wore cocked derbies. In the last skit, a Pierre-and-Fifi routine, a stripper appeared totally nude but for garters and hose, her cheeks, pink nipples, and enormous red bush rouged and brushed to a high sheen and visible to all just before the blackout.

The cream of Montreal society made up the audience— Catholic, Francophone show people mixed with Protestant jazz buffs and party hounds. Germaine kept up a game front with the French waiters, though his clumsy syntax and rustic accent made him hard to understand. After the first show, he went up to the stage and talked to the pianist, who cocked his ear and listened while playing a slow drag. Germaine came back and sat, and the pianist stayed at the keyboard, sipping from a snifter while the room refilled and rearranged itself.

When the show closed at midnight, the piano player ambled over and joined them, accepting a cigar and light from Germaine and inviting them backstage. What they found in the dressing rooms resembled a Roman bath scene they had seen in a movie in Paris, but without the air of menace the scene had meant to portray. In every corner and at two central tables, costumed and half-dressed men and women sprawled and smoked, drank, kissed, and groped, all talking at the same time. In the corner the female vocalist sang the new blues from Ma Rainey, while the French guitarist backed her up with dazzling runs and chord changes. Immediately a number of women greeted them and took their arms, most in half-costume and crowns of feathers, their breasts a provocation. Someone brought glasses of brandy.

They handed around Coronas while marijuana cigarettes, which they knew of from their Mexican sojourn, kept passing through their hands.

Within minutes the piano player whispered to a bystander, and soon the band's violinist approached and opened his case on one of the few empty, flat surfaces. He tightened and rosined the bow, and played a few licks. Then he handed the instrument to Germaine, who made his way to the corner behind the musicians. At his song's end the guitarist turned around and immediately began the intro to a French street ballad. The woman began singing and Germaine came in, running up and down the scale in close, often discordant harmony with the well-known melody. His rustic style contrasted with the bluesy-French idiom. They played three more songs, then the other two sat out while Germaine dropped the instrument into the crook of his elbow and sang the minor-key Cape Breton lament Monroe had heard him play only with Yvette. A handful of voices joined him on the chorus. At the end he got an ovation and disappeared behind a screen with one of the gamines. An hour and three brandies later, Monroe himself accepted the rare treat of oral ministration from a dancer in the passage between the dressing room and the back door, while boozy Christmas carols carried outside from the dressing room, and the feathers standing up from her crown bobbed up and down against his chest.

They slept until noon, had their faces re-polished in the barber shop, and drank glasses of black stout into which the barman had broken raw eggs—a guaranteed cure, he assured them. At the barman's suggestion, they rode a cab to the Belvedere on top of the Mount. Below, the city surrounded the rocky prominence like a skirt, and spread up and down the river's broad reach: the gray stone buildings of downtown, McGill, the tiny cars on Sherbrooke and Docteur Penfield, the church steeple on the village square of La Prairie across the river, the Victoria Bridge. The river reflected the hard blue of the sky at solstice, the wind caught the smoke from their cigarettes, and their clean faces flushed in the twenty-degree air. To the south they remarked, as had Cartier and Champlain, the blue highlands of the Eastern Townships and the Green Mountains, and argued over whether Poke-O'-Moonshine or Whiteface was the Adirondack peak they could see hovering in the azure haze farther west.

Later, three of the apprentice tailors came to their room. They hung and brushed each item, and advised Germaine and Monroe as they tried on each garment and accessory. When the apprentices left, the men slept for two hours, their dreams full of animals, women, and water. They rose at five thirty and dressed slowly, self-consciously, avoiding each other's eyes. When they were finished and their hair pomaded, they stood apart and regarded each other. Germaine wore a midnight-blue, pin-striped gabardine that hugged the shoulders, and Monroe a boxier charcoal-gray with a maroon silk tie. Both suits represented the best of North America, the lapels rolled just so, the pants breaking perfectly at the shoetops. New polished shoes, dazzling white silk shirts, cashmere topcoats, leather gloves, and for Monroe an Italian felt fedora added to the effect that here were men of substance. Not gentlemen, exactly, but not gangsters or woodsmen either.

Lacking stomach for another feast, they walked around the block to a diner and ordered pea soup, tourtiere, and sausages, with coffee. They ate in silence, replaying images from the night before, with stabs of regret for their clash on the river and their sexual disloyalties.

They walked back to the hotel, Germaine smoking a Corona, where they sat in the lobby and drank coffee and brandy until 8:45, when a page approached them, bowed, and said, "Your ride is here, gentlemen."

A white-haired older man waited in the breezeway in a black silk topcoat. He bowed and led them to the curb. There a long German Benz idled, glowing under the street lamps and Christmas decorations. A younger, larger man in a Homburg sat behind the wheel, and the older man got into the front seat with him. Germaine and Monroe sat in silence in the rear for ten minutes while the car wound through the snow-covered streets with chains on the tires, past houses with candles in the windows. It climbed to the foot of the mount and Redpath Circle, an enclave of grand stone houses off Avenue des Pins, where it turned left and climbed along the face of the mount to a house overlooking the city.

The driver pulled down the short drive and under the porte cochère. When the car stopped, the older man got out and opened the door for the passengers. "This way, gentlemen," he said, leading them to the door and going straight into a center hall with carpeted stairs, gilt-framed paintings and engravings on the walls, and rooms opening on either side. He took their coats and handed them off to a woman who had joined them, patted them both down for firearms, and led them down the hall into the rear parlor through a pair of oak pocket doors, and into the library. A coal fire burned in the fireplace, and a bay window looked out over the city and the rooftop of the house directly below on Avenue des Pins.

"Please sit down. Monsieur Feldspar will be with you presently," the man said, and drew the doors closed.

Firelight played on the three twelve-foot walls of books, the engraved maps of Lower Canada, the large multicolored globe, mahogany desk and leather furniture. They sank low in the chairs, and Monroe stood up and paced while Germaine looked into the fire.

"Messieurs, I'm so sorry to leave you here," said the tall, thin man in his forties who opened the doors, turned his back, and drew them closed. "Richard Feldspar," he said, stepping forward to Monroe and taking his hand. Germaine stood.

"I'm Lonnie Monroe and this is François Germaine."

"Yes, of course. So, here you are. Monsieur Germaine, I have heard so much about you." He had turned and fixed a hawkish expression on Germaine, who returned it with gusto. "Please, let me pour you a glass of port. Or sherry, if you prefer? All right, port then."

He poured two glasses from a cut glass decanter on a sideboard and carried them over to the two men. Then he returned for one of his own and joined them before the fire.

He looked at them both and sipped from his glass. They all sipped.

"J'ai peur de ne pas pouvoir donner à Monsieur Diamond ce qu'il veut," Feldspar said.

"Ma français et très mal," Germaine said. "Je comprends, mais je ne peux parler."

"Oh, excuse me. I apologize," Feldspar said. "Your name, Germaine—I merely assumed. It is easy to forget the homogenizing influences south of the border, even in so remote a place as— Lake Aurora, was it?"

"That's right," Germaine said.

"We love Lake Aurora. So much less death-haunted than Saranac, don't you think? Many friends down there. Perhaps you know some of them. They would not have been permitted to stay at Mr. Smith's famous hotel, but they loved the woods and made do on their own, in even rougher circumstances than the opulent hotel. And now they are firmly established in the neighborhood. I'm sure you know them. When I asked, these friends spoke of you in the highest terms, except for your unfortunate association with the benighted Mr. Smith. That confuses them. Of course, I never let on the nature of my interest in you. I made it sound as if I wanted to hire you as a guide."

Germaine's expression remained hooded, except to Monroe. He shifted, his body and head angled to hear.

"But of course, the French have been established there for generations, much longer than my predecessors. Centuries. Indeed, it was New France until 1759. Plenty of time to lose the mother tongue, even the memory or pride of origin, as many families indeed have suppressed their origins in Quebec. Well, the discrimination, of course. Other families, too, remain intact and transnational. In many ways it is as if they were birds and no barrier existed. The border sometimes is meaningless, yes? Except in our little endeavor, of course."

"Of course." Germaine and Monroe sipped. Feldspar raised his eyebrows. He sipped. "You know there were St. Germains among the earliest habitants and coureurs du bois, don't you? Going back before Champlain, I believe. Here it is spelled without the e, and pronounced *Sanh Zhermenh*."

"Well, I heard just about that much," Germaine said. "But no more. Just a few old songs, and meat pie. My mémère grew up somewhere on the river and used to get visitors from there." Monroe disapproved of this thread of conversation.

Feldspar rose and went to a colonial-era map of New France that hung between the bay window and bookcase. "Here, let me show you." He waved them over and pointed to the legend. "The Jesuits made this map and sent it home to Paris in 1701," he said. "See, here is Hochelaga, now Montreal. Here are the forts running down the Richelieu and Lake Champlain, the rivers of the interior. These lakes look like the Saranacs, St. Regis, St. Eustaces, et cetera. Fairly accurate. That would be the St. Regis River, running north to the St. Laurent, and this the Oswegatchie. Here at its mouth is La Presentation, a Jesuit mission, where Ogdensburg is now. Picquet had three thousand Iroquois there at various times. And look, the name of the river almost seems to read "Os Wegatche." There even appear to be native villages marked farther up the rivers, even to the lakes, though I admit the marks are ambiguous.

"Now here," he pointed to the mouth of the Saguenay River, two hundred miles north on the St. Lawrence. "This is Tadoussac, where the first St. Germains arrived. Note the Jesuits make no distinction among tributaries flowing to the south or the north. They were equally active in either direction, though less so to the south as the English grew stronger, it's true. And they were all the way up to here by the time this map was made"—he indicated Lake Huron—"and all the way down here to the Mohawk Valley. By the time of La Verendrye, all these expeditions had French as well as Indian guides, and it is very likely that ancestors of yours would have been among them. How could they not have passed through and lived in the great wilds of the Adirondacks, eh? The Abenakis drawn north from Lake Champlain had often summered along the Saranac. So you see, Tadoussac, the upper Saranac, and the St. Regis river are connected by geography. You need a map without the distorting barrier of the border to see it. Your people may have been there almost from the dawn of settlement."

"Not all that long, really," Germaine said.

"Well, no. In historical terms, no."

Germaine stood at the bay window, looking out over the lights of the city, the village across the river, and the roof of the nearest house on the parallel street below.

"Well, thanks for that, Monsieur Feldspar," he said. He turned back from the window. "Look, I hate to be rude, sir, but we got business to talk over. With all respect, I recognize you found out a good deal about me and Lon, here, thinking it might give you some advantage. That's fair. And I'm sure I do know some of your friends. But"—he paused—"none of that affects why we're here."

"On the contrary. You're an enigma, Monsieur Germaine, from our point of view. A war hero, two years of engineering school, a great woodsman and builder. Who would have expected you to throw in your lot with a bigot and a gangster?"

Monroe, who had viewed his role as the muscle dubiously, scanned the room for possible hiding places and possible weapons in the event of an ambush. Germaine kept peering at the map. "You mean, why did he send small-timers like us?" Monroe said.

"Well, it's obvious why. You're cut from a different cloth than the usual bootlegger's henchmen, you've seen a world beyond the streets and the neighborhood bullies, looked death in the face. Anyone would want you representing them in a difficult negotiation. Though one is reluctant to credit Mr. Diamond with such wisdom."

"Well, I wouldn't place much meaning in my connection with either of them people," Monroe said. "It's purely—what do you call it when a soldier works for hire?"

"Mercenary?"

"Right. There aren't many ways to get ahead down there in the woods, and we haven't really figured out a way to just go out into the world and make our way. Have we, Lon? It doesn't appeal to us somehow. And we'll just see where our association with Mr. H. Fucking Smith leads. But right now we need to make an impression on you."

"I have already given you my answer, and as you stated, you can understand French even though you have a hard time speaking it."

"True, I did hear you say you couldn't meet Diamond's terms. But how would you know what they are?"

"It's perfectly obvious. He wants to pay less, I need to charge more. Monsieur Germaine—may I call you François? Your government has continued to pressure the Mounties to stop liquor exports to the U.S. U.S.-Canadian trade depends on U.S. business, and the fear of reprisal from raised tariffs makes government and business very nervous. It's enormously expensive to deflect such attention. The cost has already been coming out of my end for two years. Simply, it will be up to Mr. Diamond to bear some of the burden if he expects to receive the same service. Another? It's the finest Portuguese do Douro." He poured three more glasses. "It's nicer by the fire, don't you think?" he said.

They moved back toward the fire. Feldspar and Monroe sat, while Germaine remained standing. He drank.

"Well, that extra has to come out of your proceeds from Jack's purchases for the new territories in Philadelphia and Washington," Germaine said. "He'll be doubling his order over the next six weeks. Speaking as a free agent, I think you can depend on his word and his ability to sell as much as he wants. That should cut a lot of overhead."

"But it's so uncertain. No. It just is not possible. I regret it. It's been so profitable for both of us. You and I should have had a chance to know each other better, talk about our travels in wild places. My family and I have a long history in your area and on the lakes and rivers of the north. Have you ever taken a canoe all the way down through the lakes to Raquette? It's as wild as the Temagami, yet with mountains."

"Very interesting, sir. That would have been nice. But I think you're missing my point."

"Well, I don't see how you can threaten me, and if Mr. Diamond won't consider our needs and pay accordingly, we'll have to part company."

"That's what I was saying. And I wish you'd stop trying to change the subject."

"François. Listen to me," he said, gesturing with his hands and looking coolly if affectionately over his glasses. "This is no way to make a living. You have friends in Lake Aurora. Please. Look at these suits. Exquisite. But at what cost?"

"Look, mister, you and I don't know each other, and these are my last words. We been burning up the wires a little, too. Lake Ontario is opening up since Jack figured out how to reach the Coast Guard, and he talked to that guy in Toronto—what's his name? MacLean? He says he can do the same volume for about fifteen percent less than you. Of course, with the lake crossings and weather there's more risk. But it's worth it at that rate. We'd rather stay with you, but I'm not even supposed to bargain with you. I'm just gonna walk out of here and tell Jack what you said. We're ready to go to Toronto."

"Well, certainly MacLean will never be able to guarantee delivery on the amount of product that we can. It's absurd."

"You may be right, sir. I just can't say. Now, thank you for telling us that stuff about my people and everything, and for that really good glass of liquor. It would have been nice to take an expedition together. But we'd just like to get our coats and head back to the hotel."

"I'll call the car."

"That's all right. We'll walk, if you don't mind."

They rose. Monroe threw back the last of his port while Feldspar opened the doors. He led them to the front of the house, where the woman produced their coats.

"Farewell, young friend," said Feldspar, standing in the open door and offering his hand. "The real reason Diamond sent you was because he knew I would respect you more than I would him. And he was right."

Germaine took his hand. "I'm grateful," he said. "But I wish we had kept this less personal."

Feldspar shrugged. "Well, perhaps," he said. "Eh, bien. Alors. Bonne chance. We'll meet again." He shook Germaine's hand.

"Come on, Fran," Monroe said, giving him a nudge. He kept nudging him out the door and onto the drive. The door closed behind them.

"Come on, walk," Monroe said, watching behind them for the Benz and the guy in the Homburg. Germaine buttoned up his topcoat, looking distracted and about to speak.

"Don't talk yet," Monroe said. They walked to the right, east, along the snow-capped stone wall bordering the street to the next street heading downhill. They rounded the corner into the shadow of the wall that extended down the hill for another block.

"What the fuck was that all about?" Monroe said, still looking over his shoulder. "You just told that guy Jack Diamond was firing him and gave up his source. We're fucking dead men."

"Don't worry about it," Germaine said, breathing clouds of vapor and holding out his arms for balance on the icy sidewalk.

"Why shouldn't I? Tell me why?"

"Just don't worry about it. I know what I'm doing."

"Oh, you do. How come you didn't say anything to me about it? Shouldn't we at least have had a strategy? Fuck!" Monroe grabbed Germaine's arm as he lost his balance on the ice. "Fucking shoes," he said.

"I didn't think of it until he told me he wouldn't budge and started telling me all that bullshit about my ancestors."

"So that was all true about Jack and Lake Ontario?"

"Naw, I made it up. But Feldspar, he'll come down. He trusts me. Don't worry."

They had reached level ground and the corner of Sherbrooke. A few cars passed down the hill and out into the traffic, their chains ringing on the pavement. Across the street the lights of the Ritz shined on the snowbanks.

"Hey, let's try this place. I need a drink," Germaine said, and began crossing the street.

"We're supposed to go to that address that Emile gave us."

"We'll get there. Don't worry."

Germaine was halfway across the street when Monroe started walking to catch up with him. A Beefeater bowed and held open the door as they passed through the lobby and into the bar. The two barmen, both in their sixties, wore red vests. The women wore gloves, hats, and veils—and not a flapper among them, the men Savile Row. Monroe could see nothing, for his eyes watered and fogged when they stepped into the smoky warmth. He heard the swishing of satin, a soft piano. Germaine was talking about the night before. They followed a waiter to the red leather banquette in the rear of the bar. Germaine ordered two Irish whiskeys while Monroe dried his eyes with a silk handkerchief and wished like hell he'd concealed the .25 automatic on his ankle.

When Monroe's vision cleared, he saw Germaine beside him looking into a deep region of his own mind. The room held about forty people on a midweek night a few days before Christmas—diehards of whatever holiday social whirl the city afforded. The murmur was low, but animated. They overheard discussions of stocks, government, weather. People spoke Russian; others, was it Portuguese? Along with the French and English. All thoroughly adult and reserved—middle-aged, in fact. Monroe wondered how he and Germaine had even been allowed in, then remembered their new suits.

The women had noticed them, however—most of them fifteen or twenty years older than the two Adirondackers. Looking around, Monroe caught numerous sidelong glances made through exhaled cigarette smoke, the heads turned and the holder grasped between thumb and forefinger.

"Hey, where's that address?" Monroe said.

"Huh? Oh, I got it here somewhere." Germaine looked around as if he'd just come back from a long trip through open spaces. Monroe watched his eyes suddenly focus on a point behind his own head and a smile cross his lips.

"Bonsoir, messieurs," said a voice from behind Monroe. "I am Constance de Granville. May I join you?"

A tall woman in her forties, in a silk Chanel and lace shawl around her shoulders, stood over them, holding out a long-gloved hand. Germaine rose and held her fingertips in his hand.

"Bonsoir, madame," he said, sliding over on the banquette. "François Germaine and Alonzo Monroe. What do we owe this pleasant surprise to?"

"My friends and I couldn't help noticing such handsome, well-dressed young men and wonder what on earth are they doing here? I'm deputized to find out. Are you staying at the Ritz?"

"We're over at the Windsor, ma'am," Monroe said. "We should be going back there pretty soon."

"You're American. I knew it," she said, looking openly at Germaine. "After you came in the three of us—see, there they are." She waved at two women at a table of six, twenty feet away, whose husbands were locked in conversation. "We thought, hmm. Then we forgot about you. But five minutes later that gentleman there came in. He bought a drink at the bar and turned so he could observe you. Do you know who he is?" The fifty-year-old man was sitting at the bar looking at them, smoking a pipe. He had a salt-and-pepper mustache, and wore a Mackintosh and tweed cap. "Well, it's inspector Glenburnie from the RCMP. He wouldn't come in here unless he was on official business. Oh, it isn't that he isn't perfectly respectable. He just prefers a different sort of establishment."

The man had risen from his place at the bar and started over to their banquette, his drink in one hand, his pipe in the other.

"You're American bootleggers, aren't you? That's what I told them," the woman whispered. Monroe's head swam. The man bumped a knee on one of the tables, stumbled, then gathered himself and continued on, stopping beside the woman.

"Lady de Granville," he said, touching the brim of his cap. He pronounced it in the Scots way, with a burr.

"Inspector Glenburnie. How good of you to join us. I was just discussing with these gentlemen the condition of the streets. Nightmarish."

"Ah, yes. The streets. Well. I'll have a seat with you fellas if you don't mind. And you, of course, Constance."

He sat at the chair facing the banquette, but turned it outward and crossed his legs. "Well, cheers," he said, draining his glass. He placed it on the table and waved two fingers for the waiter. "Three whiskeys," he told the man. "And a glass of claret, is it, Constance?"

The men looked at him. Constance de Granville fidgeted, nervous but delighted.   "Gents, I'm Glenburnie of the RCMP, as Constance here must have told you." He flashed a shield inside his lapel, looking from one to the other. "Yanks, I gather. I thought so. I couldn't help wonderin'. See, there's been a lot of talk out on the street about some Yanks gettin' rousted, that there's formidable moneys at issue, something about bad blood south of the border. Bad blood. And then we seen youse two coming out of Feldspar's place just now. We thought you should know. Just in case, you understand."

The waiter came back with three glasses of scotch with water on the side, and one of bordeaux. "Well, here's looking up yer kilts," Glenburnie said. He threw down his drink and sipped from his water.

"Hey, we're drinking Jameson's," said Monroe, sniffing from his glass. "This is scotch."

"Jameson's! You'd drink that gutterwash when there's pure highland malt, real whiskey, to be had? And perfectly legal, at that. Not in your favor, gents. But then, yer Yanks and may be excused yer ignorance."

"Ignorance—," Monroe said.

The inspector raised a bushy eyebrow, placed his pipestem back in the corner of his mouth. He regarded them with an expression that belonged to their vocabulary of male coercion, harking back to Mexico and the War, to a lesser extent the harder-core Adirondack woodsmen's code of dominance and submission. To look at him you might at first have thought the inspector ineffectual and distracted. But now there was no mistaking his possession of all the necessary skills of human control and destruction. Doberman pincers would roll over at such a look. It combined threat with mirth and a trace of insanity, a medley that communicated itself straight to their bowels and subdued them. The men saw the lay of the land perfectly, and were grateful to know where they stood.

"Taste it, Lon. That's the good stuff. Not like the rotgut we get at home," Germaine said.

"That's right, laddie, it's the best," Glenburnie said, watching Monroe drink. "Now yer a right highlander, a regular McDougal." He reached across the table and slapped Monroe hard on the shoulder with his big red mitt. Monroe's mouth opened and exhaled a rush of malt-scented air.

Glenburnie rested his arm on the table, his mitt curled around his water glass. "What are ye, then, Infantry?" he said, with an intimation of camaraderie.

"Cavalry, sir, with Pershing. Then Engineers in France," Germaine said.

"I knew it. I could see it in the way ye carried yerselves. Black Watch, meself, but I just missed the big fight."

"You didn't miss nothing," Monroe said.

"Fought in Africky back in ought-three, though. Seen terrible things, and me but a lad."

Monroe and Germaine exchanged looks but kept quiet. Then Glenburnie leaned back in his chair and smiled at the woman, who had been listening, transfixed.

"Now, Constance, it's been dee-lightful running into you, but Roger will be ready to go to bed soon, and I'll be needing these fellas to myself."

"Oh, Inspector, I was so hoping to hear some of your exciting adventures."

"Now, now, there'll be no adventures *this* evening, Connie. Just some official conversation among old soldiers."

"Then we'll see you in church on Christmas Eve," said Lady de

Granville, rising.

"As ever, my dear. Best regards to Sir Roger."

She wobbled a little on her heels over to the far table, where Sir Roger was still in feverish conversation and her women friends greeted her with eager looks.

"We rode into Mexico after Villa, too," Monroe said.

"Well, now. I see a quality in you boys I like. I hope yer not plannin' to ride into Canady on a similar errand, though. Canadians look askance at that sort of thing, hot pursuit and what not. As a highlander, of course, one can excuse a wee border raid from time to time, but for a Canadian and a Mountie something on that order would be hard to countenance. The American War, you know."

Monroe looked at Germaine.

"Um, we're not making any raids into Canada, Inspector," Germaine said, with a suppressed chuckle. "And we have no plans to roust any of our countrymen. We're just here to do a little business and make a legitimate living like everybody else seems to be doing these days, and our fathers never had a chance to do."

"It wasn't you roustin' anybody I was worried about. It was them roustin' youse."

"Thanks, but why would anyone want to hurt us?"

He shrugged. "I ain't saying you're here to acquire contraband, but you could always be taken for bootleggers. What are ye, then, travelin' drummers?"

"You can really tell a lot about a man, Inspector. In fact, we're here to ask Mr. Feldspar to invest in our new paper pulp process, a little idea we thought up working in a mill down in Tupper Lake, New York. It's at the U.S. patent office right now."

"That so? Pulp, is it? My, that's enterprisin'. Well, everything's all right then. I'm glad we met, Mr. Germaine. You'll do right fine in the world." He held out his hand for Germaine to shake. Glenburnie and Monroe shook next, exchanging a look that said they both knew they had not introduced themselves.

"We aim to, sir," Germaine said.

"That's great. Now we gotta get going," Monroe said. "Meet that other guy."

"One more, please. On me," the Inspector said. He waved two fingers and the waiter automatically brought another round of whiskies. He held up his glass and smiled at them, a shadow of his darker look hovering behind it. He offered cheers and said, "It's almost midnight. Whom would you be meeting at this hour? Not another investor, I suppose."

"My cousin, sir," Germaine said. "He works at a club over on St. Denis and gets off at midnight. We haven't seen each other in ten years." The inspector moved to speak. "His name's Bernard Coulonge," Germaine said, giving the name of Emile's friend, the Caughnawaga Indian.

"We'll just be getting a cab and heading over there pretty soon," Monroe said. "But it's been nice talking with you, sir. We always like to meet another veteran, don't we, Fran?"

"Nonsense, gentlemen. You must let me drive you. It would honor the corps."

The lay of the land was clear, and it was useless to protest. They paid the remainder of their check and left a crisp, green U.S. ten for the waiter, who bowed to them as they put on their coats and ventured out into the night in clouds of Cuban cigar smoke and whiskey. A light snow had started and covered the ground with an inch of fresh powder. The flakes drifted down through the lamplight.

"Here's my jalopy, right here," said Glenburnie. A two-year-old Packard brougham, black all over, sat at the curb outside the lights cast by the hotel marquee, a few feet from the hotel. A man sat behind the wheel. Glenburnie opened the door and said, "You may be relieved, Jones."

"Very well, sir," said the young Mountie, emerging from

behind the wheel and stepping onto the snow-packed street. He wore a topcoat and fedora.

"I'll meet you at headquarters."

"Yes, sir." The man turned and walked away down Sherbrooke.

"Climb aboard, fellas." They opened the doors and stepped on the running boards. Monroe got in the back. "So, St. Denis is it?" Glenburnie said from behind the wheel, rhyming the name with tennis.

"That's where the club is, but we're meeting my cousin here," Germaine said, handing the inspector the slip of paper with the address scrawled on it.

"Twenty-seven St. Sulpice—my word, who'd be living down there? Well, if that's what it says, that's what it says."

The car moved slowly onto the slippery street, the wipers brushing away the flakes, the windows open and fans blowing against the windshield to keep it from fogging. Monroe put the Hudson's Bay blanket in the back seat over his legs and feet. The tire chains rang like sleigh bells and made Monroe remember getting around in winter before automobile ownership became general and changed everything forever.

They turned down Peel, moving past darkened windows where candles had burned three hours ago. The traffic had slowed to a trickle. On Ste. Catherine some of the store fronts remained lit, and couples and other holiday revelers in fur coats and hats promenaded between the taverns under the new streetlamps. The decorations in Eaton's windows and the other stores poured ambient light into the pool of winter obscurity. "It's a bonnie time of year," Glenburnie said. Then they crossed University into the eastern, Francophone side of the city, and turned right down unlit St. Laurent, moving lower and closer to the river with every block.

They entered the narrow, winding streets of the old city and rounded a corner onto the Place d'Armes. Torches lit the broad porch in front of the cathedral. The congregation for one of the many advent services leading up to the Nativity poured out the great doors and milled around, buttoning coats and exchanging greetings, the brightly candle-lit and gilt interior exposed through the open doors.

They moved lower, passing behind the cathedral into a warren of unlit medieval streets. Soot-blackened stone and cast-iron buildings crowded on either side. They turned onto St. Sulpice, within a block of the harbor.

"Well, by rights it should be right along here," Glenburnie said, pulling over to the curb. "But I can't read the numbers in the dark."

It was a block of plumbing wholesalers and machine shops, lofts, and warehouses, with the odd doorway of cut stone—now boarded over—where someone had lived or kept a shop in bygone days. He got out and shined a flashlight on the building fronts. "Here's twenty-three," he said.

An alley separated 23 St. Sulpice from the next number, 33. Glenburnie and Germaine cast about while Monroe followed the alley toward a pool of dim light that splashed onto the paving stones. It came from a four-paned window in the upper half of a heavy plank door about thirty feet in from the street. In the middle of the windowsill, the numerals two and seven had been carved in raised letters and painted black. Monroe looked around, knocked on the door (hoping to be rescued from the Mountie), and waited. He hissed to Germaine at the head of the alley, and knocked again. The inspector joined Germaine, and the three of them stood in front of the door as Monroe knocked for a third time.

"I say we go right in," Glenburnie said.

He pressed the cast-iron thumb latch and pushed. The door gave way. Inside, a short hall led into a room with cut-granite walls, in which a single oil lamp with a blackened chimney burned on a table.

"Looks like yer cousin got tired of waiting," Glenburnie said. "But the oil's still high in the lamp reservoir." He had taken a Webley revolver from a shoulder holster and held it out in front of him.

"Maybe he just stepped out. We'll be all right until he gets here, Inspector," Monroe said. Germaine had drifted off toward an alcove in the rear of the room and looked around the corner.

"Well, nothing here," he said, after a quick glance. He joined the others by the table. "I guess we might as well just walk back up to the Windsor. Maybe he's waiting for us there."

"It seems premature," Glenburnie said. "Your friend's right, maybe your cousin just stepped out for a pee. In any case, it's a dicey situation to leave you fellas in, knowing there's a scuffle brewing. I'll just check around a little more." He backed toward the alcove with his Webley held low and his sharkish expression on. He stepped around the corner, then quickly backed out. "Hul-lo!" he said. "It appears your cousin has had a run-in." He gestured for them to join him.

A body in a houndstooth jacket and pants lay prone on the blood-blackened, granite blocks. The head flopped unnaturally when Glenburnie put a hand on the shoulder and rolled it over. The neck had been nearly severed by a knife. The contorted expression on the corpse's yellow, bruised face—of unbearable terror and pain—belonged unmistakably to the guy who worked for Dutch: Barney from Malone.

He searched the man's pocket and found only a book of matches from the St. Regis Hotel, Saranac Lake, New York. "That's near Tupper Lake, ain't it?" Glenburnie said.

"That's not my cousin," Germaine said, without a glimmer of hesitation or a hitch in his voice. "We don't know this guy."

"Fuck. Fucking fuck," Monroe said.

"Now, there, laddie, it's no different than all the other corpses you seen in France." Glenburnie's face assumed its greatest degree of glower thus far. "If ya *were* in France," he said, his growl pitched to elicit fight or flight, including the sudden and involuntary evacuation of the bowels.

Monroe pushed his chest right up into Glenburnie's face. "We were there, mister!" he said. "I seen all the corpses I ever meant to see, and more besides. You got anything to say to us, you best say it now."

"There, there, bucko. I got nothin' to say." Glenburnie stood his ground but backed his face away from Monroe's. "I don't think you boys did this, not fer a minute. But ye'r foreign nationals discovered at the scene of a murder. I do have to take ye in fer a statement."

Germaine hugged Monroe around the arms from behind and walked him back away from the Mountie.

"We know, Inspector. A terrible crime has been committed, and we only want to help," he said. "We'll be happy to join you."

"Then why did you pretend you saw nothing?"

"To protect my cousin. But I see now he couldn't a done any such thing."

"Now, don't give me that cousin shite, lad. No cousin would have had ya meetin' him down here." The untrimmed lamp wick filled the room with the smell of kerosene and poured black smoke from the lamp chimney.

"I'll get that," Germaine said, bending to the lamp. He blew it out. The room went black.

"All right you two. Don't move," Glenburnie said, lighting his torch.

The door opened and Monroe rushed out. "Stand," Glenburnie called, pointing his Webley. Germaine struck him on the side of the head and knocked away the pistol. With Glenburnie struggling up from the floor, Germaine grabbed the pistol and ran out to the street after Monroe, who had started the Packard and let out the clutch. The car was rolling slowly up the block as Germaine came tearing out of the alley toward the headlights. He slipped on the snow in the middle of the street, but jumped on the running board as Monroe doused the lights and tried to speed off, the chains spinning on the snow-covered and frozen paving blocks.

The chains kept spinning as Glenburnie's whistle blew from inside the alley, and they ground down to the pavement just as he appeared in the street and began running after them, his torch bobbing in the dark. The whistle came closer, but the Packard gained traction and momentum and accelerated up the hill toward the Place d'Armes. Glenburnie fell behind. At Rue St. Jacques, Monroe turned left and Germaine swung the door wide and climbed into the front seat. Nobody followed them, but Glenburnie would reach a phone or a patrol box any minute.

They followed St. Jacques west, across University, then down through the old neighborhoods along the Lachine Canal. There they stopped long enough for Germaine to chuck the Webley into the drink. They kept the canal on their left, feeling their way around lumber and railroad wastelands, old flour mills, electrical plants, foundries, and tenements. At one of the locks, they ditched the Packard and walked back northward toward the mount, hopping on the last streetcar headed west on St. James.

They sat apart, Monroe shamming sleep in the rear, slumped against the window with his hat over his face, and Germaine in the front, with his face buried in an abandoned copy of *The Gazette*. At one stop, a constable standing among a gang of Italian streetcar workers looked briefly in the windows but stayed on the curb when the car pulled away.

The trolley ran out at Lachine, where Jews and Italians crowded in brick houses and wooden shacks near the foundries outside the village. Germaine and Monroe climbed down with the workers and asked directions to the river. They were led two blocks through the snow to a bar on the corner, across the street from the canal head and the main river. Big globes lit either side of the stoop, and one streetlamp—the only one visible—stood on the corner. New powder had mounded four inches deep on the stoop railings. The bar was called The Old Dominion.

The snow stopped; a breeze picked up. Across the street, the black water of the main current sloshed up on the skim of ice extending fifteen feet from shore. Beyond that yawned a void. A few dim lights peeked through the dark a mile away on the other side. Downstream a string of lights outlined the pilings of the unfinished highway bridge.

"Let's get a drink," Germaine said.

The Old Dominion had a long bar, a pressed-tin ceiling tobacco-stained the color of harness leather, and an enormous open room where various laborers on the canal, railway, and bridge smoked and drank beer at long tables or crowded three deep at the bar. A piano played Irish and British music-hall tunes. There wasn't a woman in sight.

"Lemme through," Germaine said, wading into the crowd at the bar and shoving men aside. "Hey, you—," one of them said, taking a swipe at him but missing. "Sorry, old man," Germaine called back. "I need to get to the bar in a hurry, so I can buy you and all your pals at the bar a round." A cheer went up.

The bill came to thirty dollars.

The men, most of them just arrived from Ireland and Cornwall, crowded around Germaine and Monroe—Yanks, and toffs by the looks of them—and talked of the war, Germany, the Reds, and the unthinkable prohibition of booze south of the border. The head man was a big guy in his forties named Mike. He introduced himself.

"And who's this comin' into the Dominion in the middle of the night, buyin' anonymous rounds fer the heathen working scum?" he said, pushing his way through the crowd.

He wore a red kerchief, the badge of union stewardship, had last shaved three days ago, and had brutish shoulders and fists like hams.

"We're U.S. inventors, Mike, coming to the city to find investors. We've invented a new process for curing wood mash into paper pulp, and we want to build a new mill, right near the border on the Chateaugay River. We're here to look for good, skilled union workers—veterans like us—to man it. They told us downtown to come here to find the best damned workforce in Canada."

"They told you right, mister, that's fer sure. Now, why union when you can get all the scab labor you want?"

"Me and my friend here, we're workers like you. It's just our good fortune that the Lord blessed us with the vision to improve our lot and share the proceeds with our working and fighting brothers."

"It is, ay? What's yer names, then?" Mike handed them cheap cigars. Then they got down to the brass tacks of available labor. There were Reds among the canal and railroad men, the Irishman said. Jews mostly, but Irish and Italians too, and they were all right. Good workers.

"That Marx feller had a lot of good ideas, ay, and it was 'bout time workers controlled their own factories. You wouldn't want a bunch a mugs like these running the whole damn country, though, would yer?"

"Haw, haw, haw," went the men.

"Well, you can have some workers in your mill, mister," Mike said, "if you accept the unions in question—oh, let's say millwrights and electricians to start—and pay the union representative an amount to be determined later."

"Why don't we just make a small down payment right now," Germaine said, slipping a Canadian hundred into Mike's watch pocket, with the numbers visible at the top.

"That's a good start, yer honor," Mike said, squinting down at the pocket stretched across his gut.

"We'll need skilled millwrights and fifty laborers. We should have our funding by the spring. And we'll take care of all the permits and provide decent housing, as well."

"Never seen the like in an owner. If you're as straight as you say you are, guv'nor, we'll get along fine. Now, tell me what I can do for you right now."

"Thanks, Mike. That's real generous of you," Germaine said. "Mike, one of the reasons I'm here is because my people are from this side. I've been trying to renew some old family ties, and I've done that so far. What are we without our ancestors, right? But these old relatives tell me we have Injun blood in us, too—like I guess a lot of people up here do. I want to find out more about that, Mike, and I heard there was an Indian reservation of some kind around here. Is that true?"

"That's right," Mike said. "But it's on the south shore. They work on the bridge, spry as squirrels they are, running back and forth along them slippery girders. White men can't do the work, they tell me. Too clumsy. It's been more than a year and only two or three have fallen in and drownded. If it wasn't fer them Injuns, that'd be four or five a my men down the drink. We got some livin' right down by the lock, don't we, Earl?"

A black-haired junior strongarm pushed deeper into the pack.

"Jamie knows one a them Injun steel workers, ay," Earl said. "I'll get 'im."

In a minute he came shoving back into the pack with a blond kid of twenty, who was pickled to his gills on strong Canadian beer.

"He's me mate, name a Eli Montour," the kid said. "Lives with his squaw down by the locks with t'other Injuns. I'll take you to him, if you like."

"You follow Jamie here, Ray," Mike said, hooking his arm

around Germaine. Then he pulled him closer and hissed in his ear, "You take care of my boy, now, won't yer, mister big shot?"

"You've nothing to fear, Mike. We'll meet again."

"Go on, then." He shoved Germaine and Monroe by the shoulders toward the door. "You be in touch, now. And thanks for the suds," he called.

The crowd parted as they followed the reeling kid out the door. The temperature had dropped, the snow ended, the sky turned clear and starry. They followed Jamie downstream a couple of blocks to a warren of laborers' and canal workers' shanties, with candles and weak lamplight visible through cracks in the shutters. Tracks in the snow led them down the unlit street. A small landing appeared on their left a hundred yards farther along, where a dozen rowboats, skiffs, and canoes lay upside down collecting snow.

Jamie kept slipping on the ice, so they had to pull him up by his armpits. "Ish right down 'ere," he said. He made it about fifty feet down the lane to the shanties before falling over in the snowbank. They got him up but couldn't get him to walk. Germaine made him point in the direction of Eli Montour's shanty. Monroe stayed behind while Germaine followed the kid's direction to a shack near the water and the snow-covered, upturned canoes.

Lamplight leaked out under the door and through the cracks in the shutters. He knocked on the planks of the door.

"Who's there?" said a voice inside.

"A friend of Emile Jacobs."

The door opened, and a man probably in his fifties stood there in a black-and-red-checked lumber shirt. "What's this about Emile Jacobs?" he said.

"Mr. Montour, we got your friend Jamie over here in a snowbank, drunk. Can we please bring him in?"

"Jamie? Wait. Who are you, mister, and what you got to say about Emile Jacobs, ay?" He looked out down the lane, where

Monroe was waiting with the kid.

"Eli, I'm Fran Germaine, and that's my friend Lon Monroe with Jamie. We're friends of Emile's from Lake Aurora. We're sorry to barge in on you, but we've just had a little misunderstanding with the Mounties downtown, and we need to get over to Caughnawaga without going over any bridges or ferries. Emile is waiting for us."

"What you gonna do, swim?" Montour said, as Monroe and the boy reached the door. He opened his door wider, draped Jamie's free arm over his shoulder in the ancient posture of alcoholic succor, and they all helped Jamie inside. The room was well lit by oil lamps on the walls and tables, the wicks trimmed and burning clean, the chimneys sparkling. A coal stove burned in the kitchen area, a clear bottle of rye stood half full on the single table, and wool blankets hung on the walls to keep out the wind. They laid the kid on a low cot against the wall.

"Fucking hump," Montour said, looking down at Jamie. "What'd he do, run into a streetcar?"

He poured the men glasses of whiskey and put water on the coal stove for coffee. When he sat back down he said, "Now, what's all this about crossing the river in the middle of the night?"

"All we need is one of the canoes over there by the landing," Germaine told him. "There's no risk to you. We'll pay."

"Might as well risk the morning ferry as drown or freeze in ice water. In the dark."

"Look, Eli, no matter how we're dressed, we're from the mountains. In canoes all our lives. If there aren't any snags or rocks we can't see in the dark, we can ferry across and land just downstream from the bridge. We'll make it."

"Wasn't nobody following you, was there? You'll need to finish those drinks and have another one. Way the temperature's dropping, you'll freeze before you get across."

He gave them leftover pan bread with honey, whiskey, and

coffee, and big buckskin shells to go over thick wool mittens. Then he led them out to the landing, with two long ash beavertail paddles in one hand and a hurricane lamp in the other. He flipped one of the largest canoes over with his toe. "You'll want this eighteen-footer. It's in better shape than mine," he said.

"Whose is it?" Monroe said.

"No matter. He'll get it back."

Montour helped them slide the boat to the verge of the skim ice, then stood while Germaine gave him fifty bucks for the boat and twenty for the kid. "And here's fifty for you," Germaine said, pressing a bill into his hand.

Montour held out his arm over the moonlit water, showing them where to paddle up the inshore eddy and strike across, aiming high on the far shore. That way they would probably come in just below the bridge. "Don't get shoved into one a them pilings," he said, "or it's Katie Bar the Door."

"We won't. Thanks."

"Wait, take this." Montour reached under another of the canoes, and then held out an empty coffee can. "And tell that Emile Jacobs I said he still don't know shit about lacrosse."

He stood at the landing with the hurricane lamp while Monroe climbed through the boat and kneeled against the bow thwart. The skim ice cracked underneath him as the canoe settled into the water. Germaine hopped in the stern and pushed off at the same time, wetting his left foot to the calf, and they chopped with the paddles while making slow progress through the ice.

Finally they reached open water and turned the canoe upstream. The moon filled the sky and covered the water, making the surface an ocean of mercury, blotting out all but the brightest stars, the far shore clearly visible but impossibly distant and remote. Paralleling Lachine's main street fifty feet offshore, they could see men leaving the Old Dominion, and the twin spires of St. Anne de Bonsecours darkening the moon sky. When the street petered out, so did the eddy, and they turned the bow away from shore into the full force of the current.

They kept the bow pointed forty-five degrees up and across, making good headway though the river pushed them hard. Ice formed on the paddle shafts and froze on their buckskin choppers. The hum of the village fell behind, replaced by the low, liquid rush of the river. Neither said a word, all speech having been obviated by the smiling gash in Barney's throat and the question of how he had come to be there. Neither disregarded the uncertainty of what might await them when they made it to Caughnawaga—*if* they made it.

The canoe bobbed on the big stream's erratic wavelets, the bow tugged back and forth by invisible pulses of current. At times they lost their point of aim a half mile upstream of the bridge pilings. After ten minutes Monroe felt the ice water seeping into the boat, soaking his shins and the tops of his feet. He paddled furiously but without strain, suddenly unbound by time, exhausted but tireless, drunk but lucid. If he squinted, he could imagine there was no boat beneath him and he was moving across the aqueous void like a ghost.

After twenty minutes the far shore looked no closer, though in fact they had reached mid-river. The moon slipped a degree or two, thin strands of cloud muting its light, but the temperature stopped falling. The water now covered Monroe's calves, and the canoe had begun to wallow, so Germaine bailed while Monroe kept the bow pointed up. They lost ground. When Germaine finished and they paddled again, they soon crossed a hundred-yard stretch of actual waves four to five inches high and relatively close together, as if over a shallow gravel bar. They shipped several gallons and had to bail again. Monroe held their place as best he could, paddling against the current, but the boat lost ground, and now the bridge pilings loomed three hundred yards downstream.

It was time to point the bow downstream. Germaine started

the slow turn across the perpendicular force of the St. Lawrence. The river pushed hard against the upstream gunwale, threatening to broach them. But they leaned downstream, then swung the bow around and toward the gulf, the city, the Sault St. Louis. Their course carried them swiftly between the two piers, which looked more massive in the moonlight—their vaults more extreme, the crosshatching of girders more abstract than before. As the closer one swept past, they angled shoreward toward the eddy behind it, drifting until the line between the opposing currents softened. A hundred more feet and they crossed the weakened eddy line, leaning into the turn and bracing, riding the reverse current upstream to the middle of the calm water behind the bridge pier.

There they rested in the piling's shadow and bailed, for the canoe had begun to wallow again. The ribs, gunwales, and paddle shafts were heavy with ice. The cold permeated them. Monroe could feel it penetrating his soaked suit and overcoat. As soon as they bailed the boat, they crossed the shoreward eddy line and repeated the move behind the last pier, entering the channel between the island and the main shore. From there they rode the eddies upstream to the bottom of the village's main street, where the cribbing for somebody's eel weir protruded above the surface.

A log circling in the eddy had gouged out the skim ice. Thoroughly numbed, they got out of the boat on auxiliary consciousness, pulling the canoe behind them up the snowy bank as far as they could in the snow and their street shoes. Their feet were blocks.

At the top of the bank, Emile and Bernard stood on the street in heavy coats, with their ears pulled into their collars.

"What the hell," Monroe said, looking at them and shivering uncontrollably.

Emile and Bernard wrapped them in blankets, put them in the car, and drove them a few blocks to a tidy brick house on a back street of the village. In the kitchen a woman in her sixties cooked and heated water on a big wood range. Beside the stove a galvanized hip bath had already been filled with steaming water and surrounded by blankets strung from a rope. The men were directed to a bedroom, where they stripped off the beautiful, ruined suits, overcoats, and shoes; dried themselves off; and put the blankets back on. Then Germaine sat with the men at the table, wrapped in a Hudson's Bay blanket, while Monroe lowered himself in the hip bath with a pewter tankard full of rye in his hand.

"Ohh," came his groan from behind the curtain.

"What?" Germaine called.

"My feet are thawing. Ouch."

Germaine looked at Emile and Bernard, who sipped their hot tea and smoked across from him. His brain, like Monroe's, was fudge.

"How did you know to meet us?" he managed to say.

"Old woman had some kind of a dream," Bernard said. "Longhouse woman."

Monroe splashed around behind the blankets. Germaine looked over his shoulder at the old lady, who removed a tin of fry bread from the stove and stirred a simmering pot that emitted ambrosial fumes.

"My mother," Emile said. "Thérèse."

"She looks nice."

"She's Catholic, not Longhouse."

"That's from olden times," Bernard said. "There's no Longhouse here, like at Onondaga or Six Nations, but some people always want things the way they used to be."

Germaine looked around. The house had an attached privy, brick, that you reached through the woodshed off the kitchen; electricity; a radio; a telephone; pictures of the Virgin and Kateri. The far-reaching blandishments of Jack Diamond's self-interested largesse.

"Nice house," Germaine said. He looked back at Emile and Bernard. They smoked. "What happened?"

"You were late at that address," Emile said.

Monroe dressed in clothes from the luggage that Emile had collected from their room at the Windsor. He came out and stood in the room, unshaved but clean and warm—and destroyed. He hobbled to the table on his numb stumps and sat on the bench beside Germaine. While the basin drained and Germaine awaited his turn, the woman brought over old crockery bowls containing a thick stew of potatoes, carrots, turnips, celery, onions, fatback, and some kind of dark and sweet game meat. There was fry bread on the side, and an enamel pot of fresh coffee.

"This is delicious, ma'am," Monroe said, attacking the food. "May I ask what's in it?"

She turned around. To Monroe her face was like a spruce cone, the same color and general topography, with a toothless hole on the middle and wrinkles as deep as crevasses.

"Mushrat," she said.

Two days later Feldspar accepted their terms.

CHAPTER EIGHT

Dirty, Evil Lies

FOR FOUR DAYS I HAD SHOVELED MONROE FULL OF COFFEE, French fries, and sandwiches while going deeper than anyone ever had into his relations with Fran Germaine. By the end he was exhausted. He rambled and maundered, got sidetracked, and snapped at me when I asked for more details about something he had said. I clicked off the machine. "Let's take two days off," I said.

"God damn right. Enough jibber-jabber. I got work to do." He looked distracted, confused. Pool balls clacked and Willie Nelson sang "Remember Me" on the jukebox. I worried I might lose him again, or that he might dissolve before my eyes. In two days, that entire pre-existing reality, that last ember of living regional memory—whether factual or partly imagined—might blink out through coronary or cerebral occlusion, orneriness, or too much coffee. I hoped he would come back as refreshed as he had the last time. I told him thanks and started packing up.

"You be here Wednesday," he said, putting on his Moose River hat. "I ain't finished with you yet." He stumbled out of the Trap Dyke into a soft, warm rain that deepened the emerging green on the higher slopes and incited the mosquitoes. He stood there on the sidewalk with his head cocked, as if he heard music playing far away. Then he got in the Power Wagon and drove out of town at about a mile an hour.

I packed up the recorder, put it in a dry bag, and drove from Lake Aurora back through the shabby remains of the once-vital village of Saranac Lake on my way to Miller Pond. The grand or at least well-built cure cottages were now cut up into substandard apartments, the Arts and Crafts moldings covered with plywood paneling, the parquets with indoor-outdoor carpeting, the architecturally singular, unheated cure porches closed off and their rows of windows covered with plywood, gaping holes in the streetscape where the old hotels had stood and burned—all that remained of the little city of the ill, where Bartok had written, and Stevenson, and Walker Percy; where Dempsey had trained and T.R. had described the state's northern avifauna. Here were the ravages of antibiotics on a village that thrived on illness, death, and recovery (and some lumber mills). Now it suffered its own wasting disease, its vitality sucked out to the lake shores, the center overseen no longer by the medical oligarchy but by a cabal of old high-school chums in their fifties: the real-estate developer, the construction contractor, the tourism director, the slum lord, the building inspector, a lawyer or two, a couple of bar owners, and the usual puppets of the town board. Where had they gone, the hotels and speaks where Monroe and Germaine had held forth; the feeling of a vital village center, remote from the world yet standing in it, surrounded by a vastness?

At the landing I called Germaine's granddaughter Sonja before heading upriver for camp, but got no answer. So I drove the boat straight out to Miller Pond in the rain. In the last few days spring had turned from a promise of moderation to a preview of summer. The bog had turned green; the first white bunchberry blossoms had clustered and arranged themselves around the roots of the pines and cedars. Moisture saturated the air. Inside, the cabin had suffered: mice had infested the enamel Hoosier cupboard and nested in the couch. The dishes lay unwashed and crawling with ants in the sink. I covered the boat and spent the long twilight cleaning up. At last I sat on the screened porch with my notebook and turned on the gas lamp. Yellow and myrtle warblers, newly arrived; hermit and olive-backed thrushes; and whitethroated sparrows sang in the dark, wet woods.

[The following is an addendum from St. Martin's journal. —C.S.]
LONNIE GRUMPY after telling me about paddling across the St. Lawrence at Christmas. Could this be true? He knows too much to be inventing. The only way he could be making it up is if he had gone there, done the research, had a plan. And that is too far-fetched. I think he's just another old-timer whose story is perhaps a little more romantic than most. His evocation of Montreal in the twenties could only come from personal experience. But if true, why had he never told anybody? Was there some other truth to the death of the bootlegger, some reason to fear retribution after so long? And if so, why tell the story now?

He's always trafficked in howlers, lies and tall tales, hackneyed old homilies about the side-hill winder, the snow snake, the hide-behind. You can hear his whole repertoire in a matter of weeks. It's not a cracker-barrel routine, but a natural outgrowth of a way of life in which the ability to sing a song and spin a good yarn— as well as stretch out a good war or hunting story—commanded respect. Necessary survival skills. He tells them like beads, along with the daily account of his troubles, his adventures, ailments, surprises, high prices, sudden memories—so often trivial and boring, yet shaped and edited. This way he keeps track of his existence in the absence of Mary. No longer is she his frame, his mirror, but the world—i.e. the Adirondacks—is. I am here, he is saying, this is what I did.

This Germaine account is driven by something even deeper, but still in his genre. If it leads anywhere (and that is always the risk) it may be significant. (*Adirondack Times* article?) But what about the historical anomalies and anachronisms? Do they invalidate it, or merely reflect the old man's imperfect memory?

Two days ago, around five, I looked up from the tape recorder and there was Sonja at the bar, watching us.

"Well, my two favorite men," she said.

"Hello, little darlin'," said the old letch. "Come over here and sit by me." He waggled his brows. Well, I couldn't blame him. After a few weeks guiding on the lakes, she had a tan so dark it had faded the facial tattoos she got on that trip we took on the Nistassinan two years ago. She wore khakis with the cuffs rolled, a tan shirt tight at the waist with plenty of buttons open, bracelets, good Italian hiking boots. I looked for the shadow of her grandparents in her face, her posture, her eyes. She wiggled into the booth next to Lonnie. "Ooh, honey," Lonnie said, mugging. "I didn't know you cared." The gross old fart.

Lonnie said, "He's had me tied down here for days. I can't get nothing done."

"Oh, you love it," Sonja said.

"Nope, he's making me tell dirty, evil lies," he said.

"Poor you. Plenty of coffee, though, I'll bet."

Her foot nudged mine—accidentally, I was supposed to think. As I sat on the opposite side of the booth, something about her nose, her eyebrows, her expression froze me. I couldn't speak. She looked, and I looked away, at the same time not wanting to seem distant or skittish. But she had a new authority that disarmed me.

Lonnie told her the outline of what he had been telling me, and then he left. Of course, I said yes when she invited me to Eagle Point. (No expectations.) We got to the boathouse around eight, still plenty of light in the sky, a half-hour till sundown. Her room and the porch upstairs looked out toward the Langfords, where the sun hovered over the notch. She had an open bottle of wine, and I accepted a glass, though I had not been drinking since I started interviewing Lonnie.

"Oh, I forgot. Should I have offered that?" she said.

"Just one," I said. "My choice."

I followed her out to the porch, where she had set up her studio. An unfinished canvas stood on an easel: amorphous swaths of yellow, green, and violet underpainting.

"It's been like this forever," she said, arms crossed, frowning at the canvas. She was scraping some paint off the corner of the canvas with a knife in one hand, her glass in the other. "Anyway, I'm interested in what you're getting out of Lonnie," she said, taking a drink. "It's significant regional knowledge, if any of it's true. If not, well, you'll do something with it, and it'll have a kind of truth of its own. Just be good to the old guy, okay? There aren't any more like him."

She scraped the dry canvas while the sun exploded behind the Langford notch and scattered fractals of light over the water. Finally she stopped, and I stood there sipping my wine, staring at the water, while she heated up some old pasta from the fridge. We ate it sitting on the shabby old couch, looking out at the lake. A few boats passed but it was relatively quiet. Downstairs her grandmother's priceless canoes and guideboats rested in their berths, and the water lapped up into the two empty boat bays underneath us. I told her what little local gossip I had heard, then she stood.

"I have to leave again in the morning, early," she said. I got up and we hugged. Our bodies still fit together. She kissed me for a long time, then backed away. "Show me the transcript when you're done," she said.

She gave me a blanket and a pillow. I lay on the couch on the porch, letting the colors of her painting swirl and morph in the late twilight. Before I closed my eyes, I looked up at the log purlins and pine boards of the ceiling. The low light reflected lines of shimmering waves against the wood. In one of the notches carved out of a beam to accept a porch post, I could see the raven silhouette, embossed within the letter G and hammered into the grain of the pine.

CHAPTER NINE

The Professor

THE TIME OFF WORKED. Monroe showed up at the Trap Dyke at noon on Wednesday, ordered coffee, and started talking.

The booze started flowing again right after New Year, he said, coming down through the woods by horse and sleigh and on the packed roads at night by log truck and custom sedan. To handle the extra volume Basil had authorized Monroe and Germaine to bring in more drivers. Pete picked up much of the slack, glad to be on the team and bringing home extra cash to his old mother and sister out on Easy Street, near Paul's. An assortment of other woodsmen, workers, and low-lifes had been recruited—for their stoicism and ability to keep quiet as much as for their proficiency with firearms, horses, or internal combustion engines.

They varied the routes as much as possible, going far out of the way to avoid detection by either the Black Horse boys or Dutch's men. Losses occurred. Running dark, two men Pete hired from Tupper went off the road between Colton and Sevey's and left the car rolled over in Bear Creek. They walked five miles in the cold and dark to Sevey's Hotel, where a state cop from Cranberry Lake was eating a chop. Hypothermic and close-mouthed, the men fell on their bowls of "mountain lamb" stew and swilled down their coffee. When the barman asked were they all right they said they'd gotten turned around putting out fox and bobcat sets, and got caught in the dark. The cop overheard the conversation, but when he left he followed the men's tracks in the snow, discovered the booze, and went back and arrested them.

Another car got hijacked by Dutch's men outside Newtonville. When it came around a bend on the road to St. Regis Falls, two black Fords rolled across and blocked its way, and another pulled up behind it. Five men got out and surrounded Diamond's guys (the McLusky brothers from Bloomingdale), aiming Winchesters and double guns in the windows. The hijackers pulled the men out, dragged them through the snow down to the frozen St. Regis River, and beat them. They got off only because one of Pete's men was related to two of the hijackers by marriage. "Tell that Jack Diamond that if we ever catch any of his men coming through here, there'll more than a beating next time." They took the booze and the car, and the men had to walk ten miles to the St. Regis Falls Hotel, where they were fortunate to find no off-duty cops.

Federal and state police roadblocks went up periodically, even on back roads. Germaine and Monroe organized convoys with clean pilot cars that scouted ahead and reported back. They sent decoys—two empty cars for every one hauling. But the demand had gone up, and it cut into production to send empty cars. In fact, on the remote bad roads and state highways in the middle of nowhere, more than ninety percent made it. For a long time, it seemed half the local economy owed a connection to booze money. Diamond absorbed the losses.

The dead kept piling up in the sanitariums and in their coffins at the Union Depot. Through the winter Yvette and Wendy kept house for Basil in the mornings. Afternoons they volunteered as cooks, and delivered food and discreet refreshment to surviving inmates of the cottages, to hotel bus boys, and to a couple of taxi-stand clients. They befriended invalid patients, as well as some of the stronger youngsters liable to recover, and visited with them once a week or so. At day's end, over glasses of Johnny Walker and wedges of Yvette's tourtiere, the women told the men what they had heard in the cottages and sans, in the kitchens and parlors: about affairs among doctors, nurses, and clients; about the clients' less savory traits; about their own semi-private transactions with various greats and near-greats of Broadway and radio. They filled the men in on political gossip and news: Coolidge would lose the primary; friends of theirs were doing well in St. Moritz; a dam broke and killed people in California. They reported patient deaths and the will-o'-the-wisp traces of intelligence regarding the strategies of law enforcement, including Captain Hamish of the Black Horses, and Shultz's minions around Malone. As far as the women could tell, and despite his occasional appearances in the village, Diamond's presence in the region was believed to be non-existent, negated by the formidable Schultz. Legs came to town, it was said, only to see his brother.

Montreal faded into memory.

The remote railbed from Utica suffered annual frost heaves and washouts. That, followed by late snow, kept the empty beds from refilling. The cure cottages and the streets fell silent. Nothing moved. The days stayed cold, dark, intolerably gloomy, despite the approach of astronomical spring. The streets were alternately frozen ice rinks or bottomless spring holes. Road transportation slowed and booze supplies shrank. Everyone huddled beside coal stoves, wood ranges, and fireplaces drinking coffee, telling lies, and husbanding their liquor. Everyone but the patients, condemned to their therapeutically cold porches and of no mind to husband anything.

Yvette's and Wendy's prices reflected the shortages. One

old-timer, whom Wendy called the Professor and Yvette called Carl, had no objection to the extra charge. A Norwegian who had explored the Southwest and old Mexico, the old man kept a library in his room at the Treetops on Park Avenue, with maps, pottery, and blankets from his travels. He told the women he had explored the Chihuahuan desert and the Sierra Madre, and visited Natives there who lived in a canyon deeper than the Grand. Once, he lay back coughing and suggested they grant a dying man his last wish.

They laughed and told him of Germaine's and Monroe's travels under Pershing, and he insisted they visit him. "It wouldn't be my last wish," he said, "but it would be a consolation."

A week later Wendy and Yvette, along with Monroe and Germaine, took the old man a bottle of bourbon and some cold roast pork and root vegetables. They built a fire in his marble fireplace and opened the porch doors to let in the raw March air. They locked the door against his housekeeper, wrapped him in a red serape from Coahuila, and propped him beside the fire with a glass in his hand. He must have been seventy, the ghost of a once-wiry frame and bone structure just visible behind the sallow mask of the disease, his hair and grizzled mustache white. He began by ignoring the men and fussing over the women. Finally they stopped returning his attentions, so he demanded the men get going and tell him their story.

"Well, we grew up in Lake Aurora driving teams, but also riding saddle horses," Monroe said. "We joined the Army to be in on the last of the western horse patrols. When Black Jack asked for volunteers to go after Villa, we were the first in line."

"Stop right there," said the Professor. "You were eager to fight, I take it."

"Yes, sir, we were," Monroe said. "We could shoot, ride, and sleep like babies on the ground. It seemed like a good way to make ourselves useful and see a bit of the world."

They crossed the border at Culberson's Ranch near Hachita in the moonlight, he went on—twelve thousand men and horses, including black "Buffalo Soldiers" from Pershing's old 10th Cavalry. They formed columns of twos, among them Monroe's company of horse artillery and Germaine's mounted engineers, with wagons and caissons in the rear.

Moving across the landscape, nobody talked. Nothing sounded but the harnesses creaking, the shuffling of the shod hooves, the doves cooing. The sierra rose dreamlike to the west, like weird thunderclouds, glowing and milky. The villages were dark. When they got to Casas Grandes they set up a headquarters at nearby Dublan.

"I knew it, Casas Grandes," the Professor said. "The ruins, the ancient tinajas still filling with sweet water. The memories residing in the earth."

There they waited for the motorized column from Columbus. It arrived in disarray, everything a mess, with numerous vehicles left behind, broken or bogged down in deep sand. The column had crossed the border in a hurry, under strict orders and anxious to surprise Villa. There was no quartermaster and no one in charge of organizing and distributing parts and equipment, or even of finding experienced drivers. Germaine's patrol under Major Brown went to dig out the quad trucks and cars that had foundered in the sand, and to improve the roads. While they were gone Monroe stayed put in Casas Grandes, forging whiffle trees out of spare wagon springs.

Except for a few old-timers and whores, the villagers had run to the mountains. Panchito was their hero.

In those days war lords for Carranza, called mapaches (raccoons), controlled the north. Villa had run them all over the desert and made fools of them. Now rumor had it that Villa was up in one of those high valleys in the mountains, a little ways south near a town called San Miguel. Old man Pershing ordered a train from Columbus to cross the border and come south down the track to Casas Grandes, carrying equipment and men to penetrate the plateau and block a rail tunnel from the west, cutting off Villa's supplies. At the same time, cavalry under Black Jack would continue south and approach the plateau from the east. If the rumors had a basis in fact, it could be an easy kill. If not, they'd be down there a while.

By the time the train arrived and the columns moved out again, Patton had shown up and taken over intelligence, and an old Indian fighter in his sixties named Dodd was looking for volunteers who could ride hard, carrying messages and orders back and forth among the scattered units. Monroe and Germaine were first in line, and the troop soon mounted up and entered the mountains.

Only one problem: nobody knew where anybody else was, and there was a lot of aimless riding around. Dodd's force ran into a squad of roaming federales under Colonel Renate, who blockaded a trail and refused to let them across the sierra. The two mounted units faced each other at the foot of a pass, both clad in khaki and leather and mounted on well-groomed animals, standing among rows of maguey with ten-foot seed stalks. The two leaders and their aides negotiated until Renate agreed to guide them over the pass himself, for a small consideration.

The company climbed for two days. The air thinned and the high ocote forests smelled of turpentine and pine duff. Snow clung to the summits. They looked down on or passed tiny Native villages lying in the hollows beside clear, cold streams.

"Yaquis, probably," the Professor said.

They all took a drink, and Yvette closed the doors to the porch. Heat flooded the room. The Professor's face glowed with the account and the whiskey. Yvette stood up and gathered the blanket closer around the old man. She looked down at him and smiled, then at Monroe, then at Germaine, and sat down. She was hearing this for the first time.

"Well, then the weather changed," Monroe said. "We camped in the snow at ten thousand feet. Renate was unsure of whether the trail would take us to the 10th or someplace we didn't even know where. Rations dried up. We shot deer and rabbits in the woods, and bought tortillas, beans, and corn from the Indians. Some of them came out in the snow in white clothes and blankets, and sold us raw cactus juice in gourds."

"That's called pulque," the old man said.

"We climbed through the driving snow, through drifts. A few men who got drunk on that cactus juice got lost or froze their feet, and we left them behind. Germaine and me knew how to get by, so Dodd made us go around and teach the southerners how to stay dry and warm. We showed them how to make beds of coals under pine-bough mattresses, and how to start fires with the inside bark of the pine trees. They were real fine horsemen, some of them, but not crazy about having us tell them what to do.

"After that Dodd promoted me to sergeant. A lot of the southerners resented us, they were so miserable—and beginning to wonder what the hell they were doing down there. Luckily it was too cold for them to hate us much. We made it over the pass and started down the other side, the trail so steep we had to lead the horses. We could barely stand ourselves on the icy rocks. A couple of pack mules pitched over the edge, bouncing off rocks with their packs tumbling around them like beach balls."

They made dark camp on a series of narrow ledges. In the morning the exhausted men and horses broke out of the clouds. Far below stretched a wide plain of new, green prairie between the mountains. Down there a squad of black 10th Cavalry men were engaged with two dozen horsemen outside a cluster of adobes. The horsemen headed for broken ground, guarding the retreat of a slightly more numerous party the gringos could see climbing out of the valley in a straggling line of horses and wagons two miles north. Puffs of smoke and dirt flew silently whenever one of the insurgents lobbed a grenade or a mortar round at the Americans as they fell back.

Dodd consulted with his aides, including the two Adirondack sergeants. The invading force had orders to avoid confronting Mexican regular army or citizens, and to confine its action to Villa and his followers. The 10th, they reasoned, must have been fired upon first or made a sufficient identification to justify hot pursuit. Dodd ordered the force to split. He, Dodd, would ride straight down in support of the 10th. Michaels, with the guide Renate and a squad of two dozen, would traverse the lower slope of the mountain on a narrow trail and cut off the lead party. "You and you," he said, pointing at Germaine and Monroe. "Go with Michaels."

The squads wheeled around, and Michaels's twenty-five horsemen set off at a fast walk, taking rapid account of water and ammunition. Soon they broke into a canter. The ground was uneven and the horses tired, but they pushed to keep the Villistas in sight through the pine and oak thickets. They all believed they were pursuing the cunning outlaw himself.

By angle and altitude they had the advantage, and soon the two courses converged. The pursuers broke onto a scree slope, and the fleeing riders spotted them. Four gunmen separated from the main body to give covering fire. They aimed their rifles upward, and for the first time in his life Monroe heard the nauseating snap and zing of bullets parting the air as they passed his ear.

They all took a drink. Yvette laid out the meal while Germaine placed a split of birch on the fire. Monroe kept talking.

The soldiers returned fire and made their way down the scree slope, trying not to shoot each other. Within a minute the rear guard turned and followed the main retreat over the rise. The gringos reached the trail at the bottom of the slope less than a half a mile behind the revolutionaries. They started after them, then held up.

The bandits had passed through a cleft in the rocks that the wind off the northern desert funneled through—a perfect ambuscado. It was noon. They found shade under pines beside a spring, watered and rested the horses and themselves. After an hour Renate took a party of three to scout on foot. They came back and reported all clear. At early evening the troops remounted, the horses barely refreshed. When no reinforcements arrived, they assumed Dodd and the 10th had captured the other party.

Michaels sent sharpshooters to the summit, and the rest charged through the cleft as a Curtiss biplane crested the rise a hundred feet overhead, wagging its wings. A half dozen of the planes had come down from Columbus on the train, Monroe said, to help scout for Villa, and it had taken that long to get them assembled and airborne. The horses squatted and shied as the shadow roared over, then the plane banked around for another pass, with the men on the ground waving it back north after the outlaws. When it flew out of sight over the next low rise, the soldiers began following the tracks of the fleeing horses.

They looked out over another valley, higher and greener than the one they had seen that morning and barred with the long shadows of peaks. The tracks led a mile into the valley, where the trail split three ways beside a creek running through deep grass and park-like spruce trees. There the tracks split, one up each fork. At the confluence two freight wagons burned and smoldered.

The party set up a perimeter and made camp. The plane roared back over, stalled, farted and reignited, and disappeared east again, coughing, the carburetor adjusted wrongly for the altitude. Later they heard the plane had seen nothing, but Monroe said it was supposedly the first time an aircraft had been used in combat.

The twilight lasted a few more minutes, then it was dark. Where the creek came down off the eastern slope, they had seen wickiups no more obvious or commodious than beaver lodges, and the acrid smell of pine cooking fires carried to them. Soon Indians in white tunics and wool serapes appeared out of the gloom carrying tortillas, goat meat, and eggs for sale, and some men shot a mule deer coming to the water to drink at last light. The gringos ate greedily and asked for liquor, so the Indians produced pulque and mezcal, and there was drinking around the fire while the soldiers traded guard duty. At dawn they split into three parties, and agreed to meet at the camp at dusk unless engaged with the enemy.

"Otomi, I suspect," the Professor said.

They mounted up as a squad from the 10th rode over the crest. Two of the prisoners they had captured from the rear guard said Villa was among the escapees. The officers, unfortunately, couldn't tell whether the prisoners might be lying to draw attention from the generalissimo's real whereabouts. The men agreed with Renate that each squad should follow a separate track and meet back there at dusk. The Buffalo Soldiers rode off in a group, while Monroe went with Renate, and Germaine with Michaels.

An hour later Monroe's squad broke over the rim and into a canyon and mountain badland. By noon they came upon a small caravan of men and burros hauling magnetite ore out of a mile-deep gorge. A turquoise ribbon wound through its center, far below. Under questioning the men said they had been much harried by the Indians of the canyon—Raramuri, they called them—but they had seen no revolutionarios. They would have been happy to, but they were just as happy to see us. Did we have any tobacco?

The squad left the caravan with a two-man guard, and Renate guided the gringos into the canyon. There were still bow-and-arrow Indians in there who resisted outside contact and missed nothing that entered their territory. Soon the soldiers sighted three white-clad, long-haired Natives fleeing across an open slope. Renate called for one of the southerners, a marksman with a Remington ought-six and an elevation sight.

Before Monroe could react, the man had dismounted, sighted across his saddle, and fired. Dust flew amid the fleeing men's feet, and two of them stumbled, but it was impossible to tell if he had hit one of them.

"Carajo!" the Professor exclaimed, erupting in a sustained, hacking cough. Wendy got up and held a handkerchief to his mouth, and Yvette took the whiskey glass from his hand. She replaced it with a tumbler of water. He gasped, expectorated skirls of crimson mucous into the water, and sagged back into the cure bed.

"We should stop," said Yvette.

"No. Go on," the old man said.

Monroe, realizing he was the squad's ranking officer, accosted Renate, who claimed he had authority to order the pursuit of insurgent Indians and give orders to invading forces. The southerners wanted to chase and shoot the rebels, but Monroe stood his ground and threatened to report them. A standoff ensued, and Renate finally relented. By then the Indians had disappeared over the rim of the canyon, and for the rest of the day they saw nothing. That was the day they came across the tiger track, he said, and the men got distracted following it, and shot deer and turkeys and tied them to their saddles. At last light they rode back into the green valley and were met by the other parties.

"That was all we did in old Mexico," Monroe said. "A lot of riding around, harassing Indians and farmers, and getting nowhere. All the tracks kept dribbling away into box canyons and wild deserts. We got nowhere and saw nothing. Soon we left for the border.

"But that evening the Indians from the wickiups brought us food and that cactus juice—whatever you called it. Michaels's squad rode in, but without Fran here. We sat around the fire and drank aguardiente and stuffed ourselves on venison and turkey. The Indians played guitars and danced. About midnight Fran rode in, fed his animal, and went to bed without saying a word."

"Never found a thing," Germaine said, shifting in his seat and taking a drink. "Like Black Jack said, Villa was everywhere and nowhere."

The Professor put down his glass and said, "Yes, well, all geographies are infinite." After a moment he added, "Of course, they knew the ground better than you ever could."

"That's right, sir," Monroe said.

"And Villa had Yaquis in his army."

"Yes, sir, he did."

"But you acquitted yourselves."

"For the most part, yes, sir. Compared to France, of course, it was just a hard camping trip."

"In any case, you're perfectly suited for your current work."

"Well, that's true what you say about geography, Professor, though it feels pretty finite around here," Germaine said, standing and leaning on the mantel. "At least we know it well enough, we should be able to avoid Dutch and the Black Horses till spring. Anybody can make a mistake, of course."

"Yes," the Professor said. "Thank you for the story and the refreshments. Now I must return the favor."

He offered a detailed account of a 1906 expedition in Copper Canyon during which, after he had won their trust, he traveled among the Raramuri, participating in an all-night peyote ceremony and joining them on a jaguar hunt the next day, the drug still in his system. His descriptions accorded with everything Monroe and Germaine had seen, and he gave the names to things they had no names for: certain cacti, tamarind trees, coatimundis, ocelots, pikas, water ouzels. They hung on his account of the hunt: the ferocity and persistence of the cat and the swiftness of the men; their accuracy with the bow; their passive resistance to the government and the church. Tears welled in the Professor's eyes.

As he tired, the women began collecting the dishes and packing them away in the baskets. Outside, the first purple twilight of approaching spring filled the sky, casting a rosy aureole over the distant Sawtooth Range. They said good night, and Wendy wheeled the old man to his sleeping porch. Then they banked the fire and made their quiet way down the back stairs, out into the street of frozen mud and ruts.

CHAPTER TEN

Monroe's Last Tape

Words of Alonzo "Lonnie" Monroe, the Trap Dyke, Lake Aurora, New York. June 9,1983, transcribed from tape:

WHERE WAS I? Well, pretty soon the news came down through Wendy and Yvette's backstairs connections that one of Dutch's men, Barney—cousin-in-law to the third-floor nurse at Sageman Cottage—had got his head chopped off in Montreal, that someone local had done it for Legs Diamond, and that a full-scale war between him and Dutch was gonna happen come spring.

We could never figure why anyone bothered to kill that useless pissant. It just ballsed things up for everybody, including Feldspar. Probably Dutch's boys just did it theirselves, he was such a stooge, and made it look like we did it, or one a them Mohawks from Caughnawaga. We went back and forth trying to figure it, but it just never made any sense. And how did he know we'd be there, anyways?

At the same time Basil kept wanting to bring down more and more booze. You couldn't carry enough. We had more cars running around than we could keep track of. The bad roads played hell with the tires, springs and axles. The feds started coming around, and oh, boy, it got hotter'n blue blazes. The cow farm at Trout River got raided and Pete had to start coming through Hogansburg until Basil could set up another crossing point, which complicated everything, wound up costing a lot, and got the Indians mad at each other.

By the *Jesus* it made me nervous, and I wanted the shit-hell out. I had ten grand wrapped in waxed cotton and stuffed in a Choc-Full-O'-Nuts can in a hollow spruce out on the Saranac River, on that land where I live now. I had just bought that whole hundred and fifty acres for three hundred bucks. I wanted to keep a few hundred to build the house and just get rid of the rest— give it to the san or throw it in the river, lay low, and go back to hauling timber after the storm passed. And Fran, you know, he just stayed as far off in his own world and as unreachable as ever. We'll get out soon, he said. Why that lying—. What are you, yellow? he said. Stuff like that.

[Monroe throws down coffee, pounds the mug on the table.]

I'd seen all the shooting I meant to see, you get me? Fran, it seemed like, had a mind to have himself one last free-for-all, for old time's sake, like he missed it or something. Then take his loot to old Mexico or someplace. Well, he didn't know shit. He just kept plunging through the mud, not talking about anything, like we had never even knew each other.

Basil, you know, told us that except for Barney, Jack had been impressed with how things had went in Montreal. You couldn't read Basil on that. Fran thought he believed that we'd had nothing to do with it, and Basil said either way, better the guy was dead. But I thought he sounded real fishy and looked even more shifty-eyed than usual.

Then it started raining. The air warmed up, and the rain turned hot. The snow up in those peaks, about ten feet of it, all came down at once. There was huge pines and outhouses just pouring down the rivers. Dead dogs, watering troughs— everything, you name it. Washouts everywhere, bridges out over the St. Regis, the Salmon, the Saranac. The woods turned into swamps and the swamps ran out all over everything. Then we lost Frank when a creek wiped out a cutbank over in E-town and took three cars and seven people along with it, including Frank and four or five cases of gin. Wasn't much of a loss, far as I could tell, but it made Basil even nervouser than before because it was so random, so little point to it. And it got even harder to get around. Even the alternate routes had washouts or flooding. People were screaming for booze, and Dutch owned Route 9. Well, we had to start sending cars down that way, so we did. But even that road had bad stretches and detours. And it rained for ten more days.

Worse than anything, we had never told neither of them women about what happened in the city. Oh, they weren't happy when they found out about Barney—oh, no. Wendy threw a conniption and a few other things. Yvette went in her room all day, and when she came out she just sat on the porch knitting a muffler. Fran and me had to make dinner, and the women turned it down. They didn't even drink. All the more reason to stick a rose up Mr. Jackson Q. Diamond's ass and drop out of sight.

Then old Professor Carl died in mid-April, right after Easter. He had been doing fine, the women said, then just up and hemorrhaged one day, and that was all she wrote. He hadn't gotten his final wish, at least I don't think he had, but he'd spent a few dozen of his last afternoons drinking good whiskey with the two prettiest damned flappers in the north country, and that must have helped him feel like all that running around in the desert was good for something.

It rained the day of the funeral. The ground had barely thawed, but the rain had driven the frost deeper than it normally would have been that time of year, and the diggers managed to sink him one of the first graves of the spring in Pine Ridge. Fran and me set up a tarp and Yvette got some wilted lilies left over from Easter at St. Luke's, and they set up the grave site as pretty as you please. The Lutheran reverend came and we took off our hats. Fran didn't know any Norwegian hymns, but he played a slow version of "Gather at the River," with little filigrees in it, you know, like he liked to do, then "Ave Maria." About ten people came, including a couple of his nurses, and Harrington the barber. The reverend said the usual words. One of Carl's compadres from old Mexico, another professor, had made the trip from Boston, and he told a story of being led over the sierra by Dr. Lummholz—that was Carl's last name. Some kind of a orchid or something down there was named after him, he said, and his travels were studied by anthropology classes at Harvard. Big deal, right? But he was all right, that Carl. Interesting. Eating that cactus shit and then hunting a jaguar with a spear? *That* takes balls.

The track had been fixed out near Floodwood and while Carl's friend made his speech, a train went by under the pines, hauling coffins. You could see the crew looking out windows in the caboose and the oil lamps glowing on their faces. We stood under the tarp, out of the rain, which was soft and warm, but clammy. Most of the ground had patches of snow, rotten and dirty and covered with dead pine needles pounded down by the rain. The air smelled like wet pine duff in spring. Those big pines on the esker loomed over everything, wet and black, like the clouds.

Finally the reverend gave the blessing and time came to tell old Carl goodbye and get a drink. Everybody threw lumps of frozen dirt on the box and moseyed over toward the cars on Pine Street, talking low about the old bird and his odd ways. Wendy and Yvette were talking to the nurse who'd found him dead, then Yvette was sitting in the grass. "She'll get soaked," Fran said.

He ran toward her, but it was kind of like he was stuck in mud. Wendy and the nurse bent over her. When I got there, she was white. The nurse slapped her hand and Wendy waved a flask in her face. But she was out.

We carried her over to Fran's Studebaker. They put her in the back with her head on Fran's lap, and I drove them and Wendy to the hospital. The nurses wheeled her into a room and called Dr. Wallace. When he showed up Fran went in with him, but he came out ten minutes later. He didn't say a word. After an hour the doctor came out. "She'll be okay," he said. "She's resting." They kept her that night. Wendy and me drove out to Clear Pond. Fran stayed behind.

We drove back in the morning. Fran had slept in the waiting room and looked bedraggled. They let him in to check on Yvette only twice, but wouldn't let him stay with her because they weren't married. Dr. Kline, that Kraut from the Christmas party, had showed up a couple of times in the night. The x-rays had found lesions on her right lung, the Kraut told him, but the cultures wouldn't be back for two weeks. She was also two months pregnant. The doctor had found a place for her in the Noyes Cottage on Helen Street, he said, where his personal nurse would look after her and she would get special treatment. There was every possibility she'd get better, and might even get cured, she was so strong. But "the effect of pregnancy must be accounted for," was how he put it.

They finally let us in to see her. She was propped on pillows, really pale, her eyes barely open, and her black hair slicked to her head. Nobody had tried to wire her family in Montreal, and she didn't want them to. She wasn't supposed to talk, so she nodded and whispered, while Fran stood near her head. Wendy and she held hands.

"You big jerk," Wendy said. "You shoulda told me you were late."

"Sorry, Wen," Yvette whispered. Wendy got her some ice and held it to her lips.

"Doc's got you in a good place. Everything's gonna be all right."

"I know, Wen," Yvette said.

We hung around drinking coffee and smoking cigarettes for an hour or so. Then Basil showed up around noon with his Broadway doxie in a big fucking fox-fur coat and a fucking fox-fur hat, just like old Jacques Suzanne. He'd just come in from New York and Albany, all snappy in his gabardine chesterfield and hair slicked back like Valentino. The floozie and Wendy kissed, and she nodded to Fran and me like we were her footmen or something. Basil had two dozen red and pink roses and a box of them chocolates in a heart-shaped box.

"How's my favorite bootlegger doll?" he says, and he bends over and gives her a kiss.

"Oh, Base, I'm sorry," she whispers, and he lays the flowers in her arms. "They're beautiful," she says.

They really smelled up the place, like another funeral or something. Then the floozie gives her a kiss and says, "You'll be all right, hon," and Basil says, "Excuse me, doll," and calls us into the hall.

"Listen, you guys," he says. "We lost more cars down on Route 9. One to feds, I don't know about the other two: maybe Dutch, maybe anybody. This fucking weather is killing us. Customers down below are dying of thirst, and Jack is getting his nuts in a knot. 'Tell those two woodchucks who handled Feldspar'—that's us—'they oughta be able to figure something out,' he tells me, 'before we all go outta business. Tell 'em to get going,' he says, 'or I'll feed 'em to the goddamn trout.' That's what he said."

Then Basil told us how much we needed to send down in the next few days and the next two weeks, and it was a lot. "Now, little missy in there is all taken care of," he said, nodding toward the room they had Yvette in, "so you don't need to worry about her.

She'll have everything the best, just like Eddie Diamond. All you gotta worry about is staying alive and making an honest girl out of her, see? The rest is busting through this damn weather and the bad roads and pleasing your employer, who pays you very well and protects your miserable woodchuck Frenchy asses."

"Hey, I ain't French," I says.

"We'll take care of it, don't you worry," Mr. Bigshot Germaine says, sticking out his chest like a fucking pigeon. "We'll get your damn liquor moving again. As for me and Yvette, you just mind your business."

"Oh, yeah? Well don't forget how you met her, my friend," Basil says, growling and twisting up his ugly mug, with that stupid rose still in his buttonhole. "If you think she belongs to anybody except your employer, you got another thing coming." Now he was yelling.

Fran looked like he was about to kill Basil, but he couldn't a killed a rat right then. So I yelled, "Yeah? So how's Jack gonna protect us when the shooting starts?"

"Listen here, Scotty. You boys don't get back to moving some serious booze, you're gonna *wish* there was a goddamn war on."

That night it snowed eight inches and went below zero. The river slid back inside its banks, leaving huge ice floes all over the fields and the roads, and everything froze solid—the dead dogs and outhouses, too. The pines and spruces around Jack's place out to Clear Pond all bent over with snow and made a tunnel over the driveway. And ice froze on the hardwood branches, so when the sun came up they looked all sparkly, like in a dream or something. The lake ice had been mushy and covered with puddles, but it stiffened up tighter 'n a bull's ass in fly season.

Fran had stayed in Keese's Mill with Pete. I lay awake all night, worrying about Basil and how to get out of the rum-running game. Next morning I came out on Jack's back porch as he pulled up in a sleigh with my two mares. They were steaming in the cold, all shaggy and farty, and frisky from being harnessed up and out in the snow.

"Let's go," he says, looking up at me from the old sleigh.

I have no idea why I went anywhere with him, ever, especially after Montreal. I threw some things in a pack basket, kissed Wendy, and climbed in next to him under the old buffalo robe. Then we tore off down the driveway and the Jones Pond Road on the slickest sledding I'd seen in years, through a tunnel of pine branches bent over by snow and ice. There were only one or two tire tracks in the snow, and we glided along under the trees with just the sound of the runners and the huffing of the mares. It made you remember the days before cars and engines, when we were kids, before all the wars and aeroplanes and telephones.

He was all cocky, but you could see he had been up all night again, and the old darkness hung all over him. He had on his service greatcoat with the wool lining, and an army hat with fur earflaps, and the buckskin choppers old Eli Montour had given us to cross the St. Lawrence. His black hair stuck out from underneath his hat. He smelled like the inside of a whiskey still and he had that black look in his eyes, like he was looking at you but nothing reflected back at him. With Yvette in the hospital and the new snow, I didn't expect to see him at all. But here he was, outwardly all sass and beans, even though you could tell something crazy was going on inside.

But I guess something crazy must have been going on with me, too—something about what happened with Basil, Montreal, the weather, and wanting to get it over with, because there I went right along with him. We were headed for Deer River to meet Pete, he said, who had already left for Hogansburg from the lumber mill in Deer River with the log truck. From Hogansburg, Emile would be flooding the roads south with cars, some loaded to get a flow moving again, but mostly decoys. At the same time, we would load the team into the trailer and haul them down to the mill, where Pete would meet us at dawn with a last load of whisky disguised by logs Emile had the Indians cut. Then we'd bring it all up from the mill on the log sled while the crust was still firm, before it warmed up and everything fell apart again. Well, all right, I thought. If it stayed cold, we might make it. On the other hand, it might be just another cockamamie, fly-by-night idea like all the others.

But if it worked, at least we would bypass Dutch's blockade of Nine Mile Woods and get as far as Jack's with as many cases of booze as twenty cars could carry. Then the decoys would circle back around to Clear Pond and we'd start sending it down the back way as soon as the roads cleared, which had to happen pretty soon. Anyways, what choice did we have?

At the stable we loaded the horses in the van and hitched them up to Fran's old Model A truck with the eighteen-inch wheels. You could take those things anywheres, almost. It was a good thing, too, because by the time we got as far as Mountain Pond the road was pure hell, all frozen ruts two feet deep, washouts, spring holes oozing ice, and three-foot frost heaves. We crawled. It's just a good thing we were going downhill. The trailer bounced off the hitch more than once, and we had to get out and reattach it and calm the horses, sometimes shovel gravel into a real bad washout. It took us all day to go seventeen miles, and we were working on a bottle of Bushmills the whole way. The snow gave out down around McCollum's, and there was a road crew from the state replacing a culvert there. We also saw Doc Stevens from Trudeau's working his way up from Malone in his Model A. He gave us a toot and a wave like it was normal day, and went on his way.

We got to the mill, put up the horses in the shed, and still had light at five o'clock to walk a little ways up the trail and look it over. The snow around the mill had all washed away, but the dirt was froze solid. I had packed down that trail pretty good in

December, and the rain had melted the new snow back down to that hard, frozen track. We walked on the frozen mud until we reached where the old track started sticking about a half mile up the trail, where the cuttings stopped and it went into the pine and hemlock shade. Here that track I'd packed was hard as concrete, but there was none of the new snow on it yet, and wouldn't be for another mile or two. But that was all right. We towed the sled and the hitch behind the truck up to where the snow began, and left it there till morning.

The mill was all shut down and the bunkhouse was locked. We let ourselves in with Fran's key, swept out the mouse nests, boiled some coffee with a splash of Bushmills, and fried a couple a steaks on the sheet-metal stove. Then when I went out and waxed the sled runners, Fran got our bedrolls out of the truck, and a blanket wrapped around a regular arms cache.

When I finished the runners, I went inside where he had laid the blanket down on the empty bed and flipped it open. A couple of .45 service automatics lay there, along with a sawed-off 12-gauge Remington pump gun, a .33 Winchester lever-action, and the old Model 90 Winchester—that .22 that caused all the trouble.

"What are you planning, a turkey shoot?" I said.

"From now on, we're always packing," he said. "No excuse to get caught with our pants down."

"Them other guys'll be packing Thompsons, and we got peashooters," I said.

"That's right, and you know they can stand by the river with one of those things and not hit the water," he said, and he was right.

We were pretty schnockered by then, but something kept us going, like when you're in a battle and just keep going for a couple of days. We sat on the bunks and fieldstripped the arms, cleaned and loaded everything.

Then he says, "Keep her honest, ay?" He reached into his pocket and pulled out an enormous rock. "Look at that," he said. "Basil wants me to make an honest girl of Yvette, does he? Well, what does that ugly puke know about honesty, that's what I'd like to know. She's ten times more honest than that dancer he keeps showing up with."

"Where'd you get that?" I said.

"Had it since Montreal. Just waiting till we were out to pop the question."

"She's a fine woman, Yvette," I said.

"She is, huh? You gonna ask Wendy?" he says.

"Ask her what?"

"What do you think, genius?" he goes.

"What, to get married? Shit, she ain't no marrying type, Fran. She'd never live on that land out along the Saranac. She'll be back down below living in a big house before she'll settle down with me, and then it'll be with a rich guy with Van in front of his name. I'm just an adventure, a detour for that girl."

"Aw, you don't know shit," he goes.

"I don't, huh? Well, when it comes to dames, I know a fuck of a lot more than you ever will."

Oh, I hated the look he gave me then. It was the second time I felt that way, like I seen how long we'd known each other, and it gave me that feeling of time slipping by. Now I feel that way all the time, but back then it scared the shit out of me. And it was the first time, even in France, where I thought time might have been running out on us.

We finished cleaning the weapons without talking. A lot of things were running through my head, like taking off for old Mexico as soon as we got out of the woods. I couldn't take much more of this.

"I'm with you as long as we need to be," I said, "then I'm out. No matter what."

"Fine."

"Fine."

"Listen, Lon," he says, looking down at me. He was drunker'n a hoot owl. "After this, after we get outta this, we'll stay friends, but we won't be like we always been. We'll go our own ways. You've been a good partner and we've seen a lot of the world together. But those days are over now."

"That's fine by me," I said. Well, I kept polishing the stock on that Winchester until it almost disappeared. There wasn't any point in arguing about it. It was time, and I wasn't in no mood to quibble about it. And we were both drunk, anyways.

"Just, I'll stick with you just as long as we need to make this thing right," I said. "But sooner it's over the better."

"We'll have each other's backs, like always," he said. And I knew that was true. Then he said, "'Look, I need some shut-eye. Wake me up at two and I'll take over."

"Who's gonna come looking for us here?" I said.

"I'm gonna be goddamn glad to be rid of you," he said. Then he flopped down on the bunk in his clothes and passed out.

I had another coffee and Bushmills and sat with the lamp off and the fire in the stove, watching the road with the Winchester across my knees. It was dark until about midnight, then the moon came out. It went down to zero again. I kept dozing off until about one thirty, then I went outside to piss. The ground was like concrete and the moon was low in the west already, a few stars and Venus up there. There was light in the sky from somewheres, and the air had that smell of flowers, like spring was on its way and had gotten about as far as Virginia or someplace. The sap would have one last shot to fill the buckets, and these days you'd be thinking of pulling out your beaver sets, but there weren't any beaver back then. I went back and tried to wake up Fran, but I couldn't budge him. I kept kicking the foot of the bunk, but he just laid there with one eye open, not seeing nothing. I gave up.

I went across the room and flopped down on the other bunk. If somebody came for us—well, that's the way it would have to be.

Well, Pete came in around five thirty and busted in the door.

"Some fine goddamn bunch of big-time bootleggers we got here," he yells.

I rared up and snapped the slide on that .45 I slept with, then I seen it was Pete and his partner, Ike Jubin from Lake Aurora.

"Put that thing away, you fucking old drunk," he says. I was only thirty, but to him that was old. I snapped out the clip, and Fran, meanwhile, just rolled over and eyeballed Pete with his one open eye. Then he gets up, takes another bottle of Bushmills out of his pack basket, and passes it around.

"Just you have a care who you're calling old," he says, taking a drink and handing Pete the bottle.

I lit the lamps and made coffee. Pete drank and handed off to Ike, who wiped the top of the bottle with his shirt, looked around, and tipped his head back. None of us was fooling around, but even I knew we had to keep our heads clear. I thoughta when Pete was a kid and used to come around begging us to let him row around in front of the boathouse, and we used to give him an unholy amount of shit. We were brutal to him, but taught him everything we knew, too. And here we were still doing it. Maybe not for the best.

I went outside to feed and water the animals while those boys passed the bottle. Well, there wasn't no point to muleskinning on an empty stomach, even without a half pint of whiskey for breakfast, so I went back in and whipped up some bacon and eggs and flapjacks. Everybody had some, including Fran, who I figured was still too drunk to have an appetite, and for a while there it was like any other time we might have been out in lumber camp or hunting camp and just having a little visit, ragging on each other, smoking and farting. Like those times, too, there was real work to be done.

We kept drinking coffee and Bushmills while we drove the truck up to the header landing, transferred the cases of booze to the sleds, and tied it all down under a huge tarp. It was just getting light, and when we were done it was piled almost as high on that log-sled as ten cords of spruce and pine—a hundred cases of rye, scotch, gin, and brandy. We had filled the sand-well with ashes from the ash heap and the water tank from the spring. We harnessed the horses, packed our baskets and shooting irons in the strong box, and climbed aboard.

Pete stayed back on the truck bed with the .33 Winchester in the crook of his arm and a Lucky dangling from his lip. He had Germaine's hair and swagger, and looked like he owned the world standing there, twenty-one, in a red wool jacket and squinting from the smoke in his eyes. He mighta been a punk if you didn't know no better. He himself *was* just about a cunt-hair shy of knowing any better, but he had brains and a good heart, and took good care of his mother and his young wife, Hilda. Well, he could crack your head, too, no doubt about it, and he shoulda known the lay of the land by that time. If we'd taught him any one thing it was to take in the ground for himself and plot his own action. That's the only thing any one of us has to go on, ever. You can't depend on nobody else's say-so. He mighta forgot about that where we was concerned, though.

"You boys get going," he said. "I'll guard your back tracks for a while, then we'll head back up the road to Paul's and meet you at the header."

"Watch yer topknots," I yelled back, and geed the horses. They dug in and skidded their shoes on the ice, but the load budged and moved out without hardly a catch. Within ten feet they'd broke the friction and hit their stride, and they leaned into the load like it was the most fun they'd had all winter. God, I loved working good horses.

Well, Fran sat up on top of the load with the ought-six across his lap and the bottle in his hand, and I stood on the dray flexing my knees over the bumps. He'd pass the bottle down to me every so often and I'd take a pull and hand it back up. The going was smooth, too smooth in some places, and we had to snub our way down some of the downhills or we would have lost the whole shebang. Good thing them horses was trained like circus ponies. We spread ashes on the downhill, Fran worked the snubbing rig, and they braced and lowered that load stiff-legged, so we made great time, crossing the old St. Regis Falls Road right around eleven.

It musta been quite a sight to see that load coming along under the hemlocks and big pines, the only sound the creak of the harness and the runners and hooves on the crust. The temperature had hit the twenties, and we peeled off our jackets and hats. We kept passing that Bushmills, and then about midday Fran got the shits and had to jump off the sled and hit the woods. He lit out across the frozen crust carrying the ought-six, with a .45 in his belt. When he got back, he climbed on and reached in the strongbox, where I'd put that bottle, and took a long pull.

"Why the by Jesus you think you got the turkey trots?" I said. "You drink any more of that gut rot, you're gonna wind up like old Roger Contois, just a wizzened-up tangle of birch bark and rawhide, with nothing left inside to hold your innards together. We got five miles to go and I need you to be able to shoot straight, we run into trouble."

"What fucking trouble? You see trouble? Nothing out here but red squirrels and chickadees."

"Well, I know the goddamn sun's getting higher, and pretty soon it's gonna get a lot sloppier trying to get this goddamn wild-west show up the hill." I took the bottle, wiped off the top, and took a pull myself. "Who's gonna help me move this contraption when it breaks through three feet of crust?"

His bushy, black hair was plastered to his head from wearing his hat and not washing in two or three days, he had three days' growth of thick, black beard, and his eyes were bloodshot. His breath smelled like low tide. Overall he looked just about like unvarnished hell, and like he weren't no kid anymore.

The wind had blown hemlock and pine needles all over the frozen snow. We started up again, and after half an hour came to the long downhill ending in that bridge I'd hammered together in the fall. The road was overhung with hemlocks and it was still cold as a whore's heart underneath. The new snow had barely filtered down through the branches. We could rough up the surface, spread ashes, and set up a snubbing rig so the load wouldn't creep up on the horses. Only problem, that creek had spread out all around the bridge in the last flood, and you couldn't tell whether the stringers I'd cut were still attached. The bridge was buried with flood-ice and snow and looked like it may have floated downstream a few inches.

We had got down to scout the hill and find some trees to lash the block to when we heard a sound behind us like a match striking. We turned around and there was Bart Harvey, the game protector, standing there on snowshoes, smoking his corn cob. He had a Winchester in the crook of his arm aimed right at us. He was wearing his trooper's hat and green wool uniform, high boots, his red wool socks pulled up and rolled over the tops, and his Sam Browne belt crossed over his chest.

"Oh, what a fine pair of outlaws like I never seen," he said.

"Jesus, Bart. Point that carbine somewheres else," I said.

"Can't. I'd be dilatory in my duties should either of you known violators be hauling anything of a contraband nature under that tarp. Deer carcasses, say, or bear galls." He motioned with his pipe stem.

"It's not game," Fran said.

"Whoo-ee. What you been drinking fer breakfast, there, Mr. Franny Germaine? Smells like mighty strong coffee, of the kind the Lord would mightily disapprove."

"Since when do you have converse with the Lord?"

"You scum-bums better be careful. Black Horses know something's going on. They're cruising the roads and poking around in the woods. I'd as soon lock ye up as tell you anymore. Just lucky fer you I used to hunt with yer pappies."

"Just cut the preaching and the bullshit, old man. Arrest us or tell us what's on your mind."

"Mighty uppity fer a man with a .44-40 aimed at his chest. Just let's have us a look under here, shall we?" He kept the carbine pointed at us while he undid the buckles holding down the tarp and whipped off a corner.

"Well, well. You're right. No ven-zin, nope, nope. But as I live and breathe, what have we here? Canadian Club, Four Roses, Old Bushmills? Music to me ears. Look at these cases and labels. That's real printing on them boxes, real quarter-sawn spruce, nice 'n clean. Like new. Let's open one of these up, bucky."

He pointed at me and I pried off the top with a cat's paw from the toolbox. He took out a bottle of VSOP, twisted off the top, and took a swig.

"Phee-ew! That's the real thing. Nothing that good around these parts, nossir. Stuff like this goes right on down the pike. Now, if it was just bad beer, you mugs'd be in trouble. But seeing as we have here a few dozen cases of the finest Canadian whiskey, scotch whiskey, gin, and brandy, perhaps we can make an exception in light of our past histories and my questionable jurisdiction. Say, delivery of five cases of this Very Superior Old Pale to my shanty on Polliwog Pond within two days? Medicinal purposes only, of course. Can you manage that? If not, I'll run ye in."

"We'll do it, you fucking old hijacker," Fran said. "But if we didn't, you'd never find us again."

"He-he-he, I been shadowing you boys all winter," he said.

"Don't worry. I know where you live. Let me add, you look like you been sucking the exhaust out of a diesel locomotive or something, Germaine. Oof. You gotta lay off this stuff until noon, anyways."

He rocked back on his heels as much as he could on snowshoes, smug and holier-than-thou like always, white stubble and shit-eating grin all over his big, red face. Well, Fran looked like he'd got whipped. Getting shanghaied by old Bart Harvey was about as humiliating as anything that could happen.

"So, what do you got for us?" Fran said, like he had the wind knocked out of him.

"You gotta guard yer whizzle-strings is what. Schultz's boys in Malone are all in a conniption about shutting down the competition and getting back at whoever chopped their boy's head off in Montreal."

"That ain't shit. We knew that already, you old fart," I said.

"Uh-huh. Well, that ain't all. The G-men are getting to Hamish and his Black Horses. They're gonna move in on Hogansburg pretty soon, shut down them damn Injuns. Ain't nothing gonna get through. And they shook down a barkeep in one of the speaks they busted in Albany, and found out a lot of the goods were moving down through the old tote roads and hunting trails. Now they've brought in a couple of ringers, trackers from Alaska. They could be on your track right now, so you better move this rig on down the hill. Of course I can't see how you're gonna get over that crick."

"Wait right here and watch," Fran said.

"And put that fucking rifle away," I said.

It was warming up all the time, and the creek bed lay under the direct sunshine. We cut a ten-inch beech and a pine about the same size, and chained them to the sled. Then we started snubbing it down the hill, with Fran trying to handle the lower end by just wrapping the line once around a sapling and bracing his foot against the trunk. The horses started off as best they could, then started to trot to get ahead of the rig. We made it down about halfway when the sled started to creep up. The horses seemed to be doing fine, but the off-lead fell on some ice the snow had hid and dragged the lead down with her, a terrible mess of legs and tackle. Then Fran slipped on the ice and lost hold of the line, and the drag logs slewed the goddamn sled off the track into the deep snow. It all happened in slow motion. Oh, what a god-awful mess. It all slid down the hill to the bottom and out onto the flood ice in a heap.

"Goddamn it! Look what you made us do, you worthless old sack of shit!" Fran yelled, turning on old man Harvey. Fran was a pretty cool character as a rule, and I never seen him so bumfuzzled. It was like he'd gone completely nuts.

"He-he-he. Oh, what a fine couple of outlaws," Bart said, like it was a big fucking joke. Then he turned all mean-looking and his big bushy eyebrows stood out like porky-pine quills. "Now, look, you fucking French drunkard. You best get all your bacon into one pack basket and fix your problem before you start threatening an officer of the law and lose your horses."

We got the mares up before their guts twisted. They shook off, none the worse for wear, I guess, just their ladylike composure shaken. But the sled leaned on its side where one runner had broken through the ice. Half a dozen cases had fallen off where Bart had left the tarp unfastened, and bottles from the open case were scattered around in the snow.

Bart Harvey leaned his rifle against a tree and pitched in to help. None of us was any too happy with the state of affairs, and I kept an eye on the top on the hill in case a bunch of Alaskan trappers and G-men all of a sudden showed up at the top.

We piled about a dozen cases off to one side, rehitched the mares, and pulled the sled up out of the ice. Underneath, the water had gone back down, but there was still a three-foot gap of hollow air between ice and frozen ground, and it was a pain in the ass pulling the sled out. But with us pushing (and sliding all around in the snow), the mares got it back up onto the froze track and we straightened it out as best we could to cross the bridge, or what was left of the bridge. Then we reloaded and balanced out the load and tied it all down again.

We fed and watered the mares, then walked out on the deck to see how it held up in the flood. I thought the whole thing had been moved by the water a half a foot or so downstream, but the corners still seemed anchored to dry land and had probably frozen solid in the mud. So after letting the girls have their snack and taking a pull of Bushmills all around, we sent old Bart on his way, watching him follow his backtrack down the crick. Then we scooted across with as much ginger as I could put in them girls' steps. We got across and just waited there for a minute, taking another pull as a reward. By the Jesus, it made me relieved to be sitting on the other side of that slough.

Things went smooth after that. It was still light when we skirted the shore of Black Pond and came up to the trailhead near Keese's Mill, a couple of miles from the hotel. It had gotten up near freezing for a while and the crust had crumbled under us here and there, but we made it, and the temperature'd started to fall again. I stayed with the mares while Fran took the pumpgun and a .45 and went ahead on snowshoes to scout the landing. According to the plan, Pete should have been waiting for us there with the log truck.

About dusk a half-hour later, Fran came back. "No Pete," he said. The mares needed food and water, and it was almost dark. We decided to pull the sled up to within a hundred yards of the road and leave Fran with the load while I rode the wiffle-tree back up to the stable at Paul's and put them up. Maybe the stable men would know what had happened to Pete.

To make a long story short, between that morning and getting to the end of that trail, our days as boss rum-runners had went sour. The men hadn't heard shit from Pete, and thought he was with us. I put up the mares and took one of the hotel trucks down to the landing, where we loaded the cases—except for five we left in the woods—in the dark. Then we drove it the three miles out to Jack's on Clear Pond. We were drunk as lords and hungrier'n skunks. There was lots to figure out, but by then there was only two things on Fran's mind: that rock in his pocket, and getting to the hospital. Didn't matter he was in no way, shape, or form to meet so much as a Bowery bum. He was a-goin'. Far as Pete was concerned, he figured his cousin could handle himself well enough that he'd had good reason not to show up, and he wouldn't get worried about it till the time came.

Well, when we got to Jack's, the place was armed to the teeth. Emile had showed up and put out guards all over the woods and a big log barricade in the driveway. It was still real snowy, with the spruce branches hanging down on either side of the drive like in a storybook. It was just like the first goddamn time we pulled in down there, only with more guns. This time the place was surrounded by Injuns. No suits, just wool and good boots, high-caliber rifles and 12-guage pump shotguns. They hadn't heard nothing about a truck like ours showing up, and they hadn't no mind to let us through, neither. We told them to get Emile, and when he showed up he let us through and started filling us in right away. Decoys had come in with cars from all over the Adirondacks, he said—guys who'd ran roadblocks for no reason when they coulda just made it through safe, and others who watched loaded cars get run down and nabbed. Now that we'd made it, they'd be able to load them up with these cases and send them out again right away, he said. Most had made it, as usual, but everybody had stories of running into state heat or G-men. Nobody'd got picked up by Dutch's men, he said. Then we told him about Pete.

"Pete don't show up soon, boss, you got to start thinking the worst," Emile said.

"Pete's fine," Fran said. "He can take care of himself."

We pulled the truck up to the barn and the men there started to unload it right into the waiting cars. When we got in the kitchen Emile said Wendy'd went to the hospital, so Fran right up and tells me to drive him back to his Studebaker over at Paul's. He's going there to see Yvette, right now.

"Boss, you look bad," Emile says. "You gotta wash up, drink some coffee."

Emile fried us some pork chops in the kitchen, and we both had another cup of coffee and a shot of Bushmills. Then we sat Fran in a tub of hot water in Jack Diamond's nice marble bathroom.

While Fran was in the tub, Emile said the trackers Bart Harvey had told us about were staying at the St. Regis. They were a couple of Frenchmen from the Laurentians who'd gone out to the Klondike to seek their fortunes, lost their shirts instead, and never come back. They'd been working as guides and trackers out of Fairbanks for twenty years, and they weren't no spring chickens.

We'd both left clothes in the lower cabins, so after half an hour Fran comes out in his old suit, shaved kind of spotty and with two or three nicks, with a tie from Basil's drawer all crooked on his neck and his hair pomaded and clean. He had put on a dab of Basil's fancy cologne, but he was still wearing his big old rubber boots. Altogether he looked more presentable, if still a little cockeyed.

I walked him outside to the truck. The moon had popped out near full, the last winter moon before the snow and ice all went to hell and the crocuses started popping.

"Wish me luck," he said, looking totally wrecked and pathetic. Oh, it was a sorry sight.

"Mind your back," I said.

With him off on his fool's errand, I cleaned my own self—I wasn't as bad off as Germaine but I wasn't far behind—and drove my old Dodge as careful as I could straight over to the Bear Cub Road outside Placid to Jacques Suzanne's cabin out there. It was a good time to catch him. He was sitting inside by lamplight, cutting raw deer hides into strips for snowshoes and dogsleds, and drinking tea. I gave him three hundred dollars—that was a lot in those days—and told him I wanted him to drop me off back at the hospital, drive down to the St. Regis, take a room, and meet these two Frenchies in the restaurant. I wanted him to chat 'em up about the old country and treat 'em to a night out at Hattie's. Once he got 'em out there I wanted him to make sure they got shit-faced and got their ashes hauled, then stayed put.

"No matter what happens," I told him, "you keep those guys getting drunk and laid."

"By Jee-Chrise," he says, "For tree hunnerd dollers I hold dem guys dere till hell freezes over."

When we got to the hospital a couple of the Sullivan boys from Tupper were sitting in the hall outside Yvette's room, obviously packing under their cheap suit jackets. They should have been home cutting pulp. They were better than nothing if somebody from Malone aimed to pick low-hanging fruit like pregnant ladies with TB who didn't do nothing but sell single bottles to lungers—but they didn't look like they could of protected a beagle. They told me Basil had put them there before he left for Albany that afternoon.

I knocked on the door and went in. Wendy was sitting in there with Fran and Dr. Hammerhead Kline, the Kraut, with his sandy hair falling over into his blue eyes and his gold watch chain across his vest. Next to him, Fran, who'd been such a stud horse in Montreal, looked like a cartoon character. Wendy's eyes were red. She immediately gave me the look-out sign, though even without it I could tell that something very strange was going on, and I hoped to hell it wasn't because Yvette had taken a bad turn. Wendy's face was red and she had deep, dark circles under eyes.

"Well, this is already far too many people in here, sir. You'll have to go back outside," the Kraut said. He was sitting in a chair on one side the bed, and Fran sat on the other side. Wendy stood near her head on the doctor's side next to a huge bouquet of roses.

"Aw, he's all right," Fran said. "That's just old Lonnie."

"She needs complete bed rest, Mr. Germaine. And if you value her health and your child's, you'll comply with her doctor's orders. Perhaps you would leave and give this gentleman your place."

"I'll do what her doctor says when we decide who her doctor's going to be," Fran said. "We're gonna take her to one of the new sans out in Colorado, aren't we, babe? Get a fresh start." He turned back to the Kraut. "And maybe *you* should leave."

Yvette rolled her eyes and gave him a sweet look, but also one like she was worried and exhausted and needed to be left alone.

"I'll just step right back out," I said. "You take care, doll," I told Yvette. Wendy followed me out the door.

I sent the Sullivan boys out into the lobby and told them I had the door for a little while. Wendy and me took their places in the two chairs there.

"How could you let him come here like that?" Wendy said.

"I'm not in charge of what he does."

It had to be my fault, I guess. Wendy'd been there all afternoon, holding Yvette's hand and consulting with the Kraut, who kept going in and out with information and tests. The Kraut had spent all night with Yvette, she said, while me and her were doing the dirty thing at Clear Pond and Fran was getting hammered over the hotel stable. Yvette was all right, though it would be a few more weeks before they could tell if she was getting any better or not. Then Wendy started bawling again.

"He just doesn't see how she loves him but can't marry him," she said, boo-hoo-hoo.

"What the—," I said.

"Oh, Lonnie. Fran came in and proposed, but he was drunk and just couldn't tell how upset it was making her. Then Dr. Kline came in and told him to leave, and it got real ugly. This is none of your business, Fran says, then Yvette said it was all right, they were talking about something important, and she asked Kline to leave. She asked me to leave, too. Kline went someplace else in the hospital and a half-hour later Fran comes out looking like he'd seen a ghost. 'She said no,' he said, and he kept saying 'No' over and over, just standing there and staring into space. It was horrible. Where *were* you?"

Well, I let her sniffles die down and tried to do what I could, but I sure didn't tell her nothing about Pete.

"It's all because of Montreal, and now the war with Dutch, because you didn't tell us the truth, and now she thinks he's going to wind up dead. She couldn't stand that. I couldn't stand that."

"Well what did you two think we were doing? Selling shoes?"

"It changes everything when there's an illness and a baby."

"And another man, I'd say. What's with this doctor, anyways?'

"He speaks good French. He has a big house on Signal Hill, in Lake Placid, and goes back to Switzerland every year. He told her weeks ago she should leave Fran because he was unreliable and liable to get arrested, or worse."

"Unreliable? Fran Germaine's as solid as that floor. Aw, that's crazy. Fran, he's—he's *nuts* about Yvette. That Kraut'd better watch out or he could wind up in the meat pie."

"Well, he isn't solid right now and nuts isn't what a woman needs at a time like this. Lon, I know you and I, we're not like those two, that you're not gonna ask me to marry you or anything. And that's all right. I'm just so sad for Yvette." She started bawling again.

After she calmed down, she told me that Fran had prowled

around in the hall like a cat after Yvette turned him down. Wendy told him to go home and come back tomorrow—that Yvette still loved him. He had to take care of himself and then come back and take care of her, she said, make sure she got settled in the Noyes Cottage all right. Instead, he went back in the room and sat by the bed talking like nothing had happened and they were gonna get married. Wendy wanted me to make him go home, but I could see there wasn't going to be no persuasion going on.

I opened the door to the room and looked in. It was a sorry scene in there, with them three sitting around looking lost and alone, Yvette especially. Fran I didn't recognize.

"Hey, I'm heading back to Clear Pond," I told him. "Don't forget we got stuff to take care of tomorrow, if you've a mind to help." Then I drove Wendy home in the Model A.

In the morning, the first thing to do was discover what became of Pete, the second to take care of Bart Harvey's goddamn cases of brandy, which we'd hid in the woods near the header. We didn't need that old pain in the ass to start blabbing to his buddies in the Black Horses. The old fart had always wanted to be a cop, always sucked up to those guys, even though he'd failed the test and never knew anybody who could give him a leg up. He was way too old and slow now anyways. But if he could make himself look good at our expense—well, he might or he might not, having known our fathers, but it wouldn't pay to push him very far.

So, before anything else, Wendy and me drove the Model A over to the header. Fran had never showed up at Jack's, and as far as I was concerned if he took a day to unscramble his brain, that would be a good idea. I knew he'd show up soon enough, and when he did it would likely be to bollocks things up.

It had been zero again overnight, but by the time we got to the header the sun was over the trees and melting the shit out of everything. The surface of the packed snow and ice was mostly still hard, but underneath it the mud was already breaking up. I backed in as far as I could until the tires started squishing around on top of the melted mud. Then I parked and we carried from there. Wendy'd put on rubber boots like me, and with her wool pants tucked in the tops and her red beret on, she looked so damn pretty in that early spring light it made me catch my breath. It makes me right now, thinking about it. We walked in fifty yards or so and she helped me carry each case and load it in the truck.

It made me a little sad because I seen she'd be shoving off soon, and she'd been a good old gal, game for anything, and mighty fine between the sheets, too, I don't mind telling you. Some of your hippie girls, now, are pretty, and tough, too, but you don't find women like Wendy and Yvette no more, except for that Sonja. I *like* that girl. She's the last one I know of around here who could hold a candle to them old-fashioned bootlegger dames. Well, of course, she's Fran's granddaughter, so it stands to reason—but that means you gotta watch her like a hawk, too.

Well, we drove the five miles to Polliwog Pond and the access road to Harvey's camp. It was all snowed in, of course. That miserable bastard had been snowshoeing in all winter, so we had to drive in on the frozen track as far as we could till it came out of the hemlocks and the sun softened it up. Turning the Model A around in that mess took some doing, as you can imagine. We had to put on the snowshoes and carry them cases in another half a mile, which we managed by lashing them to packframes and a tumpline. Oh, what a pain in the ass. I damn near ruptured myself, but old Wendy, with that load on her back and strap across her forehead, she looked like a picture out of one of them old outdoors magazines. A few months living in the mountains had turned her from a flapper into a regular Calamity Jane.

When we got there Harvey's ice shanty was sort of pulled up on the bog in front of his place, and we loaded the cases in there just like he said to. When I got back Wendy was smoking and had out her flask, and it was in the fifties. I'd loaded a snatchblock in the backseat, and it was a good thing, since we needed it on the way out when a spring hole opened underneath us and the right rear wheel disappeared out of sight and grounded the frame. I rigged the block to a tree and worked it while Wendy drove, and we got it out—but not before we had mud all over everything, including ourselves. The whole thing was a goddamn waste of time.

When we came out of there and got on the Lake Clear Road, spring was really busting out. Water was running all over the road, and you had to keep a sharp eye out where you drove. Far off you could see the sun reflecting off the slides on Whiteface, where the ice evaporated and melted and the haze starting to gather around the peaks, and there were robins and flickers in the bare, brown meadows along the power line we had started cutting last fall. We turned up north at Lake Clear and crept along, and there weren't many other cars out—there never were in those days—but a yearling bear just out of his cave and skinny as a rat ran across the road in front of us up by Upper St. Regis, and back into the woods. When we come to the crossroads at Church Pond, though—well, there were the Black Horses blocking the road. There wasn't nothing to do but just balls it out. We drove right up to them.

"Well, well. Looks like we got us some real rum-runners here, Will," the guy at the head car said. Another shithead, this one Fred Stephens from Lake Aurora, only guy from St. Ignatius who'd made it as a state cop. He was holding a 12-gauge pump with a bandolier full of shot shells across his chest, and had his trooper hat cocked forward and his chin strap under his lip like some goddamn drum major. *And* he had them goofy, high black trooper boots on.

"Whadda you want, Stinky," I said, while his partner, a G-man in a leather bomber jacket and fedora, ambled over from the other car. That's what we called him back in school, he farted so much.

He could fart on demand. I was glad as hell we didn't bother to pack any heat, you get my meaning.

"We're gonna have a look-see in your trunk, that's what," he says.

"Well, you go ahead and look, though why we'd be driving around like this in broad daylight with booze, I got no idear."

So they looked and found nothing, then they looked around under the seats just to jerk our chains.

"All right, you bum. Ma'am." The G-man bent down and tipped his hat to Wendy. "What do you know about a funny log truck we found this morning lying in the Salmon River under the Route 11 bridge? Blood all over the cab."

"Don't know shit," I said, my heart jumping around like a flea. "Officer," I added, cracking wise. Boy, I was glad them trackers were getting their hambones boiled over at Hattie's instead of out in the woods helping these tenderfeet. "What about it?" I said.

"And I suppose you don't know anything about the tracks coming out of the woods down by Smith's header when there isn't any logging going on." He nodded toward Keese's Mill, where a half dozen horsemen were coming up the road, looking in the ditches.

"Naw."

"I hear you were some kind of war hero—that right, Monroe?"

"Ain't no damn hero. Just went."

"Well, listen," he said. "It looks to us like some nice lumberjack kids with more muscle than brains got their asses handed to them by bad people from the big city, people involved with the illegal importation of alcohol for public consumption in violation of the Volstead Act, and who don't give a shit about close family ties in the backwoods. Without a body we can't prove shit. What we understand, though, is that there's bad blood over a fellow from Malone who woke up in the St. Lawrence over in Canada last Christmas with his noggin dangling by a thread. The sooner an upstanding local fellow with a fine war record like you and your friends get out of the bootlegging racket, the better it's going to be for all involved. You get me? We don't wanna be cleaning up any more hillbilly blood. By the way, anybody missing from your circle of friends?"

"I believe we're all present and accounted for, officer. Much obliged for your concern, but I ain't got the slightest idear what you're talking about."

"Okay, go tell your friends what I said," the G-man said, and let us go.

When we pulled into the stable, a couple of troopers on horseback were questioning the stablemen, Ollie and Ike Allen. The rest were out in the sugar bush. Ollie and Ike had their dumbest looks on, and had their hats on sideways. I knew that shy of having their nuts in a vise they could lie a dog off a pork chop, being guides themselves in season, and they would garble any cop's most direct questions, pretend not to understand, answer a different question than the one they were asked, and just plain make shit up. They were experts at it, and they knew where their daily dram came from, that's for sure. It looked like they'd done their work, too, because just as we pulled in the troopers were mounting up and heading back to join the others at Church Pond.

"Aw, they wanted to know was your mares out yesterday, and we tole 'em what a turble shame it was them mares hain't been worked all winter, all shaggy and fat and colicky like we said they were," Ike Allen said when we pulled up in front. "It was like fishing for suckers with dynamite," he said. "But look-y, Lon, the old man, he's not as happy as them troopers. He's spitting teeth over all these cops, and he says he ain't seen yours nor Fran's asses around here all winter. He wants to see one or both a youse at the house, pronto."

The "old man" was *really* old and sick by this time, and we had been taking for granted that nobody was paying no attention to Fran's and my whereabouts. And mostly nobody was. But spring was coming and the old bastard was getting excited about squeezing a few more drops of blood out of the landscape before he cashed his chips.

I left Wendy at the stable and hotfooted over to the house on the lower lakeshore, where Paul and Miss Lydia lived. The lake ice was gray and rotten, with puddles and honeycombs all over it. The sun reflected off the surface, making heat waves in the air. Red wings and robins, chickadees and sparrows were calling, and even a few woodies were paddling around in a patch of open water out in front of the porch where the cook had been feeding them. It wouldn't be that long before the whole gray sheet blew away and disappeared, and you'd be able to catch a big laker from shore on a rind of bacon.

I went to the back door off the kitchen and waited there for the cook to let me in. She was a new woman, Mary Hitchcock by name, and she was pretty as a speckled pup under a red wagon. She let me in and we stood there in the mudroom kind of shy while I brushed the mud off my boots in the bootjack and waited for Miss Lydia to take me in to see Paul.

"Alonzo," Miss Lydia said, when she showed around the corner from the parlor. She was stern, but gentle, too. "Paul will see you now in the library. I'll have Mary bring you coffee."

She led me through the house, over the mud rugs and into the parlor, where the old man was sitting in a rocker, smoking a seegar by the bay window and looking out over the lake.

"It'll be another two weeks," he said, still facing out. "Never varies much. One week either side of April twenty. Oh, I seen it as late as May five here, and the twelfth up at Big Fish. That's rare, and won't happen this year barring a cold snap. Sit down, Monroe. Coffee?"

"The girl's bringing some, sir."

"Good, well. Hm." He raised his eyebrows the way he did, and looked at me while he smoked that big stogie. "We have matters to discuss."

"Sir?"

"The power line, of course, hm. It's almost time to get started, wouldn't you say?"

"By the calendar, yes sir."

"By the calendar? What's that mean, sir?"

"Nothing, sir, it's time is all. When the frost's out of the ground, anyways."

"Yes, the frost."

The coffee came in and Mary put the service on the sideboard. I stood up and poured a cup for both of us, then carried it over the way he took it, sweet and black. He took a sip and looked at me over the rim of the cup.

"I'm feeling poorly, Monroe. I've been alive since well before the war between the states. I don't know how much longer I'll be here."

"A good deal longer, sir, I'm sure."

"You get a sense of your true purpose and goals when death is near. And the folly of your ways, as well."

"I seen that ugly mug a time or two, sir."

"I'm sure you have, sir. I'm sure you have. I'm close to fulfilling my vision for these parts, Alonzo. It all comes down to electrizitty and putting our rivers to work. Like harnessing the very force of life itself. Now, watching the thaw out a window puts a man in the mind of thinking he will be renewed as well. But he won't, and he only has whatever time the Lord has allotted him to carry out his plan.

"It's come to my attention that somebody from my hotel has been involved with bootleggers. Reflects poorly on our great institution, wouldn't you say? I'm a temperance man, Monroe, but in my day I enjoyed a drop, and I don't deny others the pleasure in moderation. I've had drinks with three presidents and five governors, and a good many other important men of industry and politics—scoundrels among them. I drank it up with famous old guides like Cheney, the Moodys, Sabattis before he quit. Colvin, that Democrat. Even Ned Buntline—there was a drinker, as bookish men tend to be. I had whisky and got stinking blind with Teddy Roosevelt over on Bay Pond, when he was a college boy, bird-watching, and when he shot that moose right there." He pointed to the head over the fireplace. I grew up knowing every detail about that hunt. "Last one we seen around here. That was nigh on fifty years ago. By Gadfrey, there was a real man, T.R. Soon after that he never took another drop himself. A lot of us thought his Bull Mooses and busting the trusts as going too far, but he beat them by main force and reason. Some of you men around here are still cut from that same cloth. Not that I haven't noticed a decline in grit since the Spanish War. Men who came back from Cuba and the Pacific, now, they would not have succumbed to jungle music and romantic melancholy. They had the ruthlessness to thrive on the frontier. What are we if we can't thrive in a wilderness, Alonzo? Hardly human, I'd say. Some of those soldiers did quite well for themselves in the west and South America, after the Indian question finally got settled. Teddy gave them that. They emulated him, you see. They were all 'bully.'

"Only other I knew like him was E.L. Trudeau. Now he was a Yale man, as Teddy was Harvard. Back in '88 me and him brought his family up through Nine Mile Woods from the railhead in Malone one November, snow blowing like hell'd finally froze over. He'd not been here that long, E.L., living on the lake in a tent, rowing and hunting. He wasn't even trying to restore his health yet, you see. He assumed he was a goner, and just wanted to live as fully as he could in the time he had left—as anybody would. But life in the woods made him healthy. That's how he stumbled onto the cure and started the san at Little Red on Mount Pisgah.

Made that village what it is today.

"Well, the team kept bogging down in the snow, then down around Meacham Lake it got dark. We dug a snow cave and put them old ladies and kids in there for the night. Now, the Doc himself, even though he was strong, he was never out of the woods, you know. No. But he had what it took, by the Jaysus— excuse my French. We huddled up together out in that carriage and watched over the horses—the woods still had wolves and the big cat in them—drinking from a bottle of brandy I'd brought for my own enjoyment on the trail. 'Extraordinary circumstances,' he said every time he had a nip. We talked all night. I told him how I grew up over in Vermont, looking across Champlain at these mountains, and how they drew me over to Loon Lake, then Union Falls, then here. He told me how he did his experiments at Rabbit Island, how his grandfather explored the south with that fellow Audubon. Zero outside, no food, and he couldn't have been happier. You wouldn't find that so much these days—not with these doctors—and a lot of them were in Europe, like you.

"Now, I know we do business with some gentlemen involved in the liquor trade, but I had never considered that any of my own men would become involved. I supposed a wall separated our enterprises. Well, the hotel isn't what it used to be, things are slow in the winter, and an opportunity comes along to make hard cash for your family. Very well. And perhaps in some cases the management itself must concede that it has erred in its labor dealings, out of only the most reasonable and selfless of motives. And there is always the lure of the drop itself. But I have wondered at its effects. My good old friend François Germaine comes to see me to discuss our project not once all winter. Perhaps he has cause or is otherwise occupied. He could have been a fine engineer, one of the best, but he left his education to follow you to Mexico.

"Nevertheless, you and Germaine have something these newer men don't have. I've always known it. Such men, if underused, might be the kind who would fall into the current illicit traffic. Not that you have.

"I'm getting to my point, Alonzo. You see, Albany wants me to desist with the Saranac dams. Says it has authority over navigable waterways. Fuck 'em, I say. Excuse my French. The log drives are ending. Electrizitty's where the money is—these days, at least. No money in timber anymore. The land boom's played out, hm. Ain't no more of it, with the state grabbing it all for taxes and locking it up in conservation. No, the only things we have left to make money, big money, is dams and electrizitty. It's the new frontier. The loggers got to dam them rivers whenever they damn well pleased, to run their logs to the mills. Now Albany—excuse me: downstate Jews, like we now got building their own big camps on the Saranacs—say my dams will hurt the downstream users, those same goddamn logging companies and their mills. They're bolsheviks, Alonzo, tampering with the sacred right of free enterprise, and I've paid through the nose over the years to secure my place equal to big timber. They're not saying we should take out that fraud Pliny Miller's dam in the village, are they? No, by God. Well, I aim to see my vision through to the end. And that's why I called you here.

"I need you, and I need François Germaine. He can work with men and he knows the ground better than I do myself. You tell him if it's money he wants, he can get rich if he comes back. We all can. The big woods are gone. People around here, they ain't Injuns, they don't need salmon anymore. They need jobs like real industry provides. Dams and industry—manufacturing, Alonzo—can give them that. Teddy might not have liked it, but he's long dead, God rest him, and it's a new world now. I'm gonna be dead myself soon enough, and I want them dams making power before I go. Albany and the downstate Jews can go to hell. Tell Germaine I'll pay you and him whatever you want, and give you both shares if only you'll come back and help me. Go on, now, Alonzo. Go tell him."

I left him staring out the window toward the lake, and Miss Lydia led me back out through the kitchen to the door. Mary was standing over there by the stove stirring soup, and she just managed to shoot me a glance as I made my way out. I had a lot of chances to remember that glance in the days to come.

Paul didn't even know how close he really was to the end—that he'd already hung on longer than his natural span. When I left him there staring out the window, it was almost like he was fading away in front of my eyes. It was queer to feel the earth shifting under your feet like that, like everything you'd known and believed had already survived past its time, and the world had moved on without you. The feeling stayed with me while I walked back to the barn. I couldn't take my eyes off the old hotel, with all the porches, turrets, balconies, and fancy trim. It had seen better days, and it seemed to fade and turn into a pile of dust while I watched. Ike and Ollie standing around the Model A flirting with Wendy, two as hard-bit old woods roosters as you ever saw, looked like a couple of daguerr-ee-otypes, kind of fuzzy and unfocused. Wendy saw me coming and looked at me real hard and sad from fifty feet away. Them boys jabbered away and their words starting sounding like dead people whispering. Wendy looked like *I* might a been disappearing, too, and she had wrinkles around her eyes, where she'd only been a young girl before. She turned into a grown woman sitting there, and I knew she'd be leaving soon. It all swarmed around in my head, along with Pete and the likelihood we'd never see him again, the likelihood of ugliness yet to come. And that feeling hung on for a long time.

I got in the driver's side while the boys backed away from the car and waved goodbye. Wendy and me just kept looking at each other while I started the car and headed out the gate toward Clear Pond. The G-men and Black Horses had moved on, and I hoped that old Jacques Suzanne had them trackers entertained and out of sight over at Hattie's, though the troopers might have been headed there any minute, for all I knew. Wendy put her hand on the back of my neck. We'd never been real close like that before, but we felt that way now.

"Poor Pete," she said, and if Fran Germaine had been there right then, I would have gouged his heart out with a barking spud, even though I knew I couldn't blame him for my own mistakes.

"We'll find him," I said.

Jones Pond Road was covered with meltwater, even though it was under the pines, and it was getting too soft to drive on. But we floated over the bad spots on them eighteen-inch tires, not saying anything. We didn't talk for a couple of miles, and Wendy left her hand right there on my neck skin, and it sure felt good. She asked me what Paul had said, and I told her the whole crazy story, and that I didn't have any idea what had become of my friend Fran Germaine.

We were quiet another few minutes, and then she said, "You been a good man, Lon."

"It's all right, hun. I know where this is goin'," I said. "You don't need to say nothin'."

"No," she goes. "I do."

She'd grew up at a private girl's school, she said. The only men she'd ever met were golfers and ukulele players. Running into Basil and bootlegging had seemed like the kind of real life she'd never seen. Then she met Yvette, and it was like meeting a long-lost sister or something. "First, I never met nobody like Yvette, then I never met nobody like you," she said. "Last fall and winter with you men has been something a person never gets to have," she said. "It was perfect. But it was supposed to end different." She couldn't stand to hang around and see how it might get worse.

"I know," I said.

She was going to take a room in the village, she said, until

Yvette got settled and started getting better, maybe stay until the baby came. Then she was going to move back down to Albany and go back to nursing school. That's how she could use her background, and the things she'd seen up here, to make a real life that mattered for herself and others, she said. And get rid of TB, of course. Well, I couldn't argue with that, and I was glad she did tell me.

I figured there was no point avoiding Jack's place. If it was swarming with cops, that was just how it was supposed to end. But no. We pulled on down the drive, and there were the same old Injuns guarding the gate with their deer rifles. They let us right through.

"He's in the cabin," Emile said when we found him in the kitchen. "Stewed to the gills. They found Pete's truck in Salmon River. He says it's Basil's fault, he's gonna kick his ass. But Basil said Jack's pulling his operations out of here, and you guys are on your own. Don't need no fucking peckerwoods getting nobody killed, he says. Me and my men, we're pulling out tonight, one by one, heading back to Canada and Hogansburg. We'll do fine, don't worry about us. It's your friend you got to worry about. Here," he said, and handed me a little pouch. "Burn some of this in his room."

The Studebaker was pulled up in front of the cabin where we had spent our first night at Clear Pond that fall. Peepers had started up already in the wet spots and little bits of open water, and that high, sad song the sparrows sing. I gave Wendy my keys to the Studebaker and told her to stay in town. She kissed me and left. When I knocked and opened the door, Fran was sitting on the plaid bedspread with the porch door open and the oil lamp lit, playing that whitethroat tune on the top two strings of his fiddle. Dee, dee, dee dee-dee, dee dee-dee, dee dee-dee. One a them birds would sing it, he'd play it back, and the bird would answer. That's how it seemed, anyways. Oh, it was a mournful sound, and a mournful scene, too: the peepers, the whitethroats, and the fiddle.

"How's she doing?" I said, meaning Yvette.

He looked up with bloodshot, dead-looking eyes. "She'll be all right." He looked straight ahead and scraped that bird song on his fiddle, real rough and squeaky.

"You heard about the truck," I said.

"I heard."

"I'm real sorry, Fran."

He shrugged. "Knew what he was getting into. Shouldn't a got caught."

"*That's* kind of hard."

"What do you expect me to say?"

"Well, what do you want to do?"

"I'll take care of it, don't worry."

"What the hell's *that* supposed to mean?"

"It means I'm responsible and I'll take care of it, that's what."

"Aw, don't give me that. Like what, you're gonna take on the whole Dutch Schultz gang and half the farmers and woods rats in the St. Lawrence Valley? Not if I got anything to do with it."

"Why do you gotta be in on every goddamn thing? Who the hell are you? We went our separate ways after that sleigh ride, remember? Why don't you just go play with your horses and try not to get shot or arrested?"

"Who the hell am *I*? Why I oughta—" I picked up the bottle on the nightstand and took a pull. That man could fluster the living shit out of a person.

"Pete's no relation to you," he said, still staring into space and playing along with the sparrows.

"I known him since he's a baby. I had as much to do with him getting involved as you did, and he looked up to me, just like he did you. You think I'm just gonna let you go off half-cocked, alone, on some fool's errand, you got another thing coming, mister."

"Aw, you're always whining about this and about that. It's too dangerous, you don't want to fight anymore, the money's not worth it. All right, then, have it your own way. Don't."

"Don't what?"

"Fight."

I sat on the other bed and took a second drink. He played the birdsong.

"I can fight as good as you," I said.

"I seen you."

"I just don't see the point."

"Don't have to. Just stay out of it."

I took the pouch out of my pocket.

"Look, we're out. Pete's gone. Can't bring him back—"

"Watch yourself . . ."

"And I just saw old Paul."

He stopped playing and looked at me.

"Says he wants to give us shares and pay us whatever we want to go back. No questions asked."

"He can suck my dick," Germaine said. He got his empty look back and started sawing that bird tune again, which was starting to get kind of irritating.

"We could lie low, fade into the background, move when we actually know something."

"I'm not helping that old cock squeeze one more cent out of this territory. And anyways, them Malone boys ain't waiting around for us to come looking for them."

I drank again. "Now what's *that* mean?" I said.

"I got it covered. You just go about your business and keep your head down. Might not hurt to leave the horses and go to Florida or Mexico for a while."

"I'm not going anywheres." I couldn't believe what I was saying. I thought I *wanted* to leave, right? This was the perfect chance. But nope. Pete had changed things, and I felt like if I left

Fran to his own devices, he'd just get himself killed. If there was some other reason, I couldn't say what it was.

"You stay, you do what I say, and none of your bellyaching."

"Well, I ain't gonna let you just go get yourself killed 'cause some flapper won't marry you."

"I don't aim to get killed," he said. It was one of the last times he ever gave me that look—the one that could freeze a goddamn weasel.

I laid down on that other bed with the bottle and listened to him play along with the birds and tree toads. If he was crazy then his craziness had turned hard and clear as black ice, and it made me hard and clear, too. Everything had changed in the last two days—in the last two hours, really: Pete gone, the girls gone, Jack and Basil pulled out, and the operation gone south. The fact that Fran was planning something made a kind of crazy sense I couldn't walk out on, much as I wanted to. It felt like the night before one of the big battles in Europe, when we lay around in the bunkers talking and singing songs, and whatever was gonna happen would happen. You couldn't leave, you just were. We'd been here before, and in this case nobody was lobbing howitzer rounds on our heads. It was just some farmers from Nicholville, it turned out, who wanted our nuts in a Mason jar.

In Europe I wearied of fighting as soon as we got off the boat in Dieppe, but I fought. By now we each knew the other's strengths and weaknesses, even if we drove each other crazy. We knew what the other could do. There was no reason to expect any less now—even with the amount of drinking he was doing. And on that score, I had started trying to catch up with him.

He kept scraping, and I kept nipping. Every so often he'd stop, and then the birds would stop. Outside the temperature dropped and it started cooling off inside. There was some wood stacked by the fireplace, so I threw in a few birch twigs and a nice split of maple and put my lighter to it. The room warmed up, and we left the door open a crack. He stopped playing the bird songs and started slowly bowing out little bits and pieces of those gloomy songs, the ones that sounded like bagpiper's tunes or funeral music.

The story came out slow, between the pieces of unfinished songs—nothing I hadn't heard or imagined. He'd got it from Margaret, the nurse over in Sageman House, the one who'd told the girls about her sister's friends in Malone. They'd be coming up through Nine Mile Woods, loaded, at first light, and woe betide any woodchuck who worked for Jack Diamond, especially those two hustlers from the Lake Aurora square dance—that Fran Germaine and his friend Lon Monroe—who'd slit their cuzzint's throat in Canada. He was just a kid. They knew Diamond had abandoned those two, they'd already got the truck driver and his sideman, and they meant business.

"I gather you mean for us to be ready for them," I said.

He was quiet for a long time then, and I didn't say anything. At some point I must have dozed. When I woke up, the fiddle lay on his bed and he was standing in the porch door looking at the lake and smoking. I nodded off again. When I opened my eyes a second time, he was running a cleaning rod through the barrel of the .22 Winchester pump, and the smells of gun oil and solvent filled the room. Then Emile was standing near his bed and putting down a tray on the nightstand. The smell of coffee mixed with the smell of cleaning fluids. Emile had changed from his usual suit and hat to a red wool shirt, green pants, and rubber boots.

"Wake up," he said. "You got to be sharp for morning."

"Clean that pump gun," Fran said, and he pointed at the Remington on the floor beside my bed. I swung my feet around, stood up, and went out on the balcony. I pissed a long, hard stream out onto the rotten ice. Somehow the night had slipped by, and the sky was getting gray over the big pines across the lake, even though the stars were still out. The sparrows, which had been quiet, were starting up again, and the peepers had gotten even louder. Back inside, I poured a cup from the coffee pot and sat on the bed while Emile told us he was headed back to Caughnawaga.

He said, "Where's that bag I gave you?" I took it out of my jacket pocket and handed it to him. "This'll help, if your minds are clear," he said. He dumped the ash tray out on the ice and put the herbs and tobacco in it. "There used to be things to say when you burned it, prayers, but only a few old women remember them." The smoke filled the room. He told us good luck, and left.

We didn't say anything. Fran took apart one of the .45s and cleaned it while I did the shotgun. "I know why you're sick of fighting," he said after a while. "I am too. Maybe we can do this your way." He never looked up at me, and I didn't even know what he meant by my way. We drank the coffee. When I finished cleaning the shotgun, I put it on the floor again and sank back on the bed. He did too. We lay across the room from each other, looking at the ceiling, listening to the birds. Then he told me his plan.

TWO HOURS LATER I was scouting the Jones Pond Road from under the pines on top of that low ridge that runs alongside it. It looked clear. I waved Fran ahead. The Model A rolled out of Jack Diamond's driveway onto the road. It was almost light. I climbed in, put the Remington on my lap, and we drove toward the hotel with the headlights off. At Church Pond we backed into the turnout behind the church, right across from the hotel entrance, so we wouldn't miss anyone heading south from Nine Mile Woods, whether they took the fork to Lake Clear or the one to Easy Street.

"Now don't forget," he told me for the third time. "It's like the old professor said about Pershing in Mexico. This is our territory and we have the advantage of the ground." And, "Farmers can't shoot. They'll blast away with their Thompsons and their deer rifles, and it's all for show. They can't hit shit. Just keep to the plan and don't shoot back until we've got 'em where we want 'em."

The ice on Church Pond was black and spongy, but the ground had froze solid again overnight. Lots of ice in the roadbed. Smoke coming from chimneys on the hotel grounds across the road. We sat there with one of the last bottles of Bushmills and each had a nip. We had the window open and the cold air coming in to keep us awake. Outside, the peepers and the birds made a awful racket, kind of pretty but annoying at the same time, we were so tired and hungry and nervous.

"Fran, Lon. What are you boys doin' sittin' here?"

It was old Bumpy Nelson, an old coot who'd been in the Injun wars. He lived over on Easy Street and showed up at the hotel every morning looking for work and free coffee, whether there were guests or not. He'd come up from behind us on his way to the commissary for a free cup, and stuck his head in the window. He gave us a start, I can tell you.

"Jesus, Bumpy. Get lost," Fran said. "We're tryin' to shoot some deer meat here. You'll scare 'em away."

"What deers, Fran? Ain't no d-deers gonna be crossin' that road any time soon. You're the best shot in these mountains, but not even you can hit a invisible deer. Th-th-the deer meat's gamy and tough this time of year, ennaways. You might better shoot you a nice mu-mu-mushrat. You know that, Fran. I—"

Just then a big Packard with chains on and mud all over the tires, fenders, and running boards ground across our view on the icy slop. You could see five big mugs crammed in there in their cheap gangster suits. They might as well of had the barrels of their shooting irons sticking out the windows, for all the effort they made to hide the fact they were Dutch's bootlickers. Lucky for them the Black Horses had chosen this moment to be sleeping off their hangovers.

"Sorry, Bumpy," I said. "Just remembered an appointment we have to keep." Fran put the Model A in gear and slowly pulled away. Bumpy, that real old-time woodsman, had to duck his head back out of the window so it didn't get clipped off.

"Heeeyyy," Bumpy shouted. "You're not huntin' deers, you're chasin' that car. Well, go get 'em, fellers. Hoo-ee!"

We got out on the thoroughfare just in time to see that Packard's big red taillights going around the bend down the Gabriels fork. Old man Nelson ran out in the road behind us and jumped up and down in the mud, yelling, "Hoo-ee!"

Mist hung over the wet and icy road. The sun was up behind the mist, but it was still very gray and murky at the ground level. You couldn't drive too fast for the mud, the water, and the ice, so we just ground along, getting nervouser and nervouser.

"Hold back," I said.

"I know what I'm doing," he said.

"They'll turn east in Gabriels."

"I doubt it."

We came up over the top of the hill above Easy Street on the hotel's open and broad, if rocky, dairy farm. The fog was torn and shredded up there, and the top of McKenzie kept poking through, with gold sunlight hitting the top. Then we crossed the train tracks and the power line into Gabriels, and the fog closed in again.

"They're at Bert's," Fran said.

The big Packard sat in the yard outside Bert and Gladys La Fountain's rambling frame speakeasy beside the tracks. Two of the mugs from Malone stood by it smoking, looking like real hayseeds with their farm boots and their striped suits and fedoras. They were coming up to the mountains to kick some peckerwoods' asses, were they? Well, all right. I slid down in my seat and we drove on by like nothing looked the least bit strange. That was another good thing about a Model A. You didn't stand out.

"If they hurt that old man and woman—," I started to say.

"They're in this business with both eyes open, just like everybody else," Fran said.

"It ain't whether your eyes are open, it's whether you're doing anything to hurt anybody that counts," I yelled. I was steaming.

"Well, anyway, why would they hurt those two old gasbags?" he yelled back. "They're just gonna make up some shit, like they're throwing us in, to get rid of 'em."

"What if they send them to Clear Pond?"

He hadn't thought of that.

"Where else they gonna get booze now that Jack is out, except from Dutch?" I said again.

"Well, they're gonna be switching to Dutch with no choice as of right now, so they got no reason to send those boys over to Jack's. Which they probably know is empty, anyways. They'll tell 'em they saw us heading south," he said. "And they'll be right."

We kept going on up the hill past Tucker's potato farm and pulled in behind a huge bank of bare lilac bushes at the top, at the Town of Brighton Cemetery. Both of our parents were buried there, and even though neither of us said anything about it, it felt weird to be setting up an ambush right in front of them. That, the fog, and the nerves made the whole scene very spooky, like looking out over a blasted field on a foggy morning in France. It got spookier when more of them holes started opening in the mist, so there was the blue sky overhead and nothing but pea soup over the ground. They put that cemetery right at the highest point of all them flats around Bloomingdale and Lake Clear. Pretty soon the ground fog started to lift, too. Then you could see the Sawteeth and the Sewards sticking up outta the clouds to the south, Algonquin, Whiteface, and MacKenzie, all with the sun blazing on their snowy peaks, and the surrounding dark potato fields, plowed last fall, still with patches of snow on them. It was like a curtain rising on a play, or more like just evaporating before your eyes. It gave me that same feeling I had after talking to Paul, when everything seemed to be happening in the past and the future at the same time.

"Here they come," Fran said.

That Packard with all them galoots in it had poked up out of the fog, coming south. The car was having a hard time laboring up through the icy slop with all that weight, even with the chains on—skewing back and forth, then digging in, before jerking forward a little at a time. We watched it through the screen of lilac bushes. It started leveling out and running normal about a quarter mile off. Right then Fran pulled out and turned south, ahead of the Packard.

That was it—we were out in it, just like on the log drives, when you worked your oars to line up your jam boat at the head of a rapid as best as you could. Then one moment you were just in it, and the rapid was going to have its way with you, and you could either ride it good or drown.

We drove down the road in full sunshine. With the sun spang on the white peaks and the fog still floating over the village down below, it was easy for a moment to forget that a carload of pissed-off shit-heels was on our ass. So far, they didn't know who we were, but we *wanted* them to know who we were.

"They can hit on the run up to about a hundred yards," Fran said. "After that it's all luck, and by two hundred it's a bad bet." He kept about three hundred yards ahead, and he had to crawl to do that. Those boys were still struggling along as we came over the next hill by the Harrietstown Cemetery. He pulled over to the side of the road. I didn't buy all that about the ranges of their guns, but as long as we were ahead of them and driving, I felt all right.

"Get out and take a piss," Fran said.

"You fucking get out," I said.

"You agreed." Not to bitch and argue, he meant. It seemed like a mighty tall order, but I'd gave my word.

"Fuck."

He pulled over at the top of the hill, and I got out with my Remington under my arm and pretended to unbutton and take my dick out. Well, while I was standing there like that, in the wide open with the warm sun on my back, it made me really have to piss, so I fished it out for real and let 'er rip. So there I was, highlighted against the horizon with the Packard creeping up from Rickerson Brook, with my shotgun under my arm and my dick out, looking out over the Mackenzie Range and the Bloomingdale bog down below. A little farther beyond the bog, I could see where my hundred-fifty acres lay along the river, just waiting for me to survive this latest Franny Germaine dime-novel mellerdrama and start clearing a site on that nice rise looking downstream toward Whiteface. Maybe, I thought, I'd ask that Mary from Miss Lydia's kitchen to come cook for me.

"Okay, button up and make like you've seen them coming and you want to get away fast," Fran said.

I turned around, looked back up the road and jumped, like I seen Buster Keaton do when somebody surprised him in that railroad picture. Pretty soon a Thompson stuck out the passenger side window, and a burst ripped off into the air.

"Fuck, fucking fuck," I yelled, as I dove back into the passenger side and slammed the door shut. Fran had already peeled out, as best as you could in the bad conditions, and headed down toward Donnelly's dairy farm. The Packard had gained a couple hundred yards on us and looked mighty close. It got off another burst before we put the heighth of land between them and us.

We floated right over the mud and down toward the junction with the Lake Clear road. Right before we reached it, Fran slammed on the brakes, swerved in the mud, and turned us broadside.

"Get out," he said. We crouched behind the Model A, him in

the front and me peeking around the rear fender. It was bright sunshine all around now, but the fog had risen and hung like a shining ghost, or a huge angel, about a hundred feet over the ground. You could barely see it, except as a white blur out of the corner of your eye.

The Packard came over the crest by the cemetery and immediately opened up.

"Jesus," I said, crouching lower.

"Let them shoot their damn brains out," he said. He had the ought-six, and when they got about a hundred-fifty yards out, he put his elbows on the Model A's hood, aimed, and squeezed off five quick rounds into the Packard's radiator.

Now, the Model A had been thoroughly armored in the sides, rear, and underneath by Emile's men, like all the cars used for running booze were. From the rear the only real damage you could do was aiming for the tires, which of course these boys hadn't thought of. We knew their Packard would be armored, too—but you couldn't armor the radiator. If you did, it wouldn't cool the motor, and the thing would seize up. From the front those rigs were as easy to stop as a horse and buggy.

The car had gotten close enough so we could see the radiator bleeding and steam pouring out. The shooting had slowed them down, but they kept coming with the steam in their faces, with one guy firing a sidearm out a window. That Thompson had gone silent—jammed, probably, like they always did.

When it was about a hundred yards out, Fran pumped the action on the .22 and squeezed a round into each of the Packard's front tires. It skewed around for another few yards and skidded to a stop.

While this went on, I had been leaning back against a tire, facing south and watching the hill up behind old man Donnelly's cow barn. The old man had led his herd out of the barnyard and up to the high pasture to stretch their legs in the sun and nose around in the snow patches and brown grass. It looked like old Donnelly himself was swelling up with sun and grass, and maybe visiting his booze stash, until that Packard came over the crest, guns blazing. Those first shots probably just sounded to him like the usual small explosions and gun shots country people like to set off, but when he heard that first burst out of the Thompson, he took a hitch in his stride and skittered down that hill like he had a bobsled under him.

Nothing much happened for a minute, though it was probably not even that long. I couldn't tell how long things were taking. Then the doors popped open and a couple of their men flew out either side, shooting sidearms. Fran chambered a shell, fired once from the .22, and hit a guy in the ankle who had been hiding behind the open door.

"Gaaaa! I'm hit!" the guy yelled, and fell to the ground. Nobody ran to help him, and he kept rolling around yelling, "Gaaa!"

"Fire off a couple of rounds from that pump," Fran said. I fired, pumped, fired, pumped. The buckshot loads sounded like half sticks of dynamite compared to the .22.

"All right! Listen, you limp-dick corn eaters—," Fran yelled.

"Fuck you, Germaine!"

"Why don't you get your fat lips off that Dutchman's cock for ten seconds and pay attention to some sense. We didn't kill your damn cousin in Montreal. He was dead when we got to the meeting."

"Lying frog!"

"Fucking lying peckerwood!"

"Fire again."

I shot off a round, chambered a shell, and shoved three more into the magazine.

"Listen, assholes," Fran yelled, "we seen a lot rougher customers over in Europe and old Mexico than any dozen of you shitheads. Why don't you just act smart. Your Tommy-gun's busted. Your buddy's hit. Your car's fucked. I let Monroe loose, you're gonna wish you never came south of the Town of Duane."

"Who killed him, then?"

"Dutch, for shooting up the square dance in Lake Aurora and drawing attention to the operation. Sent him up there to do us, and did him instead."

Nobody moved. A couple of bluebirds came flying in, twittering like they just showed up from Loosiana or someplace. The silence lasted forever.

"You got Pete," Fran said eventually. "Now, he knew the territory. No reason for him to be dead, but—the wages of sin, I guess. For that, you deserve to have your nuts stuffed in your mouths. However. Monroe and me, we were planning on getting out of this racket and finding a better, a more reasonable way to live—"

"Oh, ha, ha!"

"What the fuck is reasonable, you stupid French fuck?"

"What's reasonable is that we don't come over there and cut your throats right now. What's reasonable is you patch your tires, your radiator, and your buddy, and go back to Nicholville or whatever cowtown you're from, right now. What's reasonable is if I ever hear of you coming south of Meacham Lake, or if anybody I've ever known or heard of has an accident, I come down to the valley after dark and eat your livers at midnight." Fran turned to me. "Guard the flanks," he said.

I watched the side angles with the .45 in one hand and the shotgun in the other. Nothing moved.

"You gonna let us fix this jitney?" came a voice.

"Go ahead."

"You win this time, Germaine."

"Let's go," Fran said. We crawled in the passenger side door, me first. Bent over, I started the car and turned the wheel south, and we pulled away.

"Hope you get to do something more *reasonable*, you fucks. Ha, ha!"

When we sat up, I watched them in the mirror as they come out from around the doors, covering each other with guns aimed at us, and helped their man into the back seat. Two of them started working on the front tires with a jack.

"What if they don't leave?" I said.

"It'll take a while, but they'll leave."

We passed by Donnelly's and down towards Saranac Lake, leaving Dutch's minions—that's a good word, minions—to fix themselves up and limp back to their hidey-holes in the valley. There wasn't no telling what old man Donnelly would do—keep his mouth shut or report a shoot-out. All I wanted right then was a big plate of flapjacks, ham, and eggs, with good hot coffee, maple syrup, and a pile of spuds fried in butter and bacon fat, with lots of peppers and onions. But it wouldn't be that smart to show up in the restaurant of the St. Regis. Things were way too hot. As a matter of fact, it didn't feel too smart to be driving through town in broad daylight, neither.

"Where we going?" I said.

"Just drive," he said.

"Well, there ain't no sense going into Saranac," I said. "Might oughta just head over the Mt. Pisgah cutoff and make our way back along the river through Bloomingdale, then back to Keese's Mill or Lake Aurora, lay low. Hattie would put us up for a couple of days. Or haven't we thought that far ahead?"

He didn't answer. All of a sudden, instead of cocky and full of beans, he looked like a drunk old coot—like his grandfather had after a three-day binge, or one of the old Civil War vets who hung around the guide shack at the hotel, drinking rotgut and telling yarns about the war or Teddy's latest exploit. Flattened out, run over, confused. He hadn't shaved or slept in three days, his shoulders slumped, and his face looked kind of blank. No one my age at the time had ever looked that old and battered, even in the war. I probably looked just as bad, but I felt relieved. He looked like the hard part was just beginning.

"Well, where'd you get that bit about Barney?" I said.

"No place. Just nothing else made sense."

We came down the hill toward the Two Bridge Brook, where it crossed the Gabriels road. That cedar swamp was full of meltwater running in a big gray sheet across the whole thing before it squeezed through the stone culvert under the iron bridge and turned into the brook that ran down into Bloomingdale Bog.

"Pull over here," Fran said.

There was a little turn-out there on the downstream side of the bridge, where kids still fish sometimes. I pulled in and stopped. Then I craned my neck around and checked the back track. Nobody followed.

"You okay?" I said. I thought he had the shits again or something.

He got out and disappeared under the iron bridge. Then he came back out dragging a little bark canoe, with an ash paddle in the other hand. He must have stashed those things there sometime in the past. He left them on the bank, then climbed back up to the car, reached in the back, and took out his pack basket.

"What the—?" I said.

He put his face in the window, a face I hardly recognized, the eyes red as blood, gristly white prongs sticking out among the usual black whisker hairs.

"You been a good partner," he said, "and I'm glad you came along today. Nobody ever had a better man at his side. I trusted you every minute for the last twenty years. But this is where we part ways. Might be a good idear to lay low for a while. Things might not be so easy around here. You don't say nothing about me, and I won't say nothing about you."

"But—where the holy hell do you think you are going in that little boat?"

"Not even you could find me. Now, so long. And nobody come looking, hear?"

He took the .22 and stuck one of the .45s in his belt. Then he turned and trotted down the bank with his basket over one shoulder and his rifle in his hand. His pants looked kind of droopy, his shirttail was out, and he had that bad army hat with the flaps on his head. It was as sorry-ass a picture of a man as I'd ever seen.

"You're seriously shit-faced, old pal," I yelled. "This is seriously fucked up. It's been a fucked-up few weeks. I don't see no call to go off half-cocked on some *insane* excapade! Let's just get sobered up at Hattie's, let her feed us for a day or two, and think about how to get back in the race."

But he had already got in the tippy little canoe and pushed off between the bare, red shoots of the alders along shore. The high-water current of that little stream grabbed his boat and swept him around the bend out of sight, while he fended off the turn with his paddle. He never turned around, nor looked back, nor said another word to me. I never knew if he was going to live or not. The stream didn't lead nowheres except into the bog and then to the Saranac, eight miles away. Maybe he thought he was heading for Canada, I don't know. And I didn't know then that I wouldn't lay eyes on him for another five years, neither. We were never friends again, and I never got used to the way it all played out at the end. He's dead now, and I never wanted to remember any of those days in so much detail like this, not till you come along.

[Pause.]

Now turn that fucking machine off and get me a coffee.

[*End of tape.*]

Editor's Note:

ST. MARTIN'S MANUSCRIPT ENDS HERE. He stopped meeting Monroe for taping sessions. Yet the saga turned out to be a single episode in a much larger story. St. Martin never played the tapes for Sonja, he produced no follow-up work, and of the Germaine material nothing appeared in print.

He did, however, rework some of the interviews and publish them in the August and October 1983 issues of *The Adirondack Times*, under Monroe's byline. The first story featured Teddy Roosevelt shooting one of the last Adirondack moose at Bay Pond in the 1880s. This version of the story had been current in the first years of the twentieth century around the guide's quarters at Paul Smith's Hotel and the finer lodgings between there and Blue Mountain Lake. Monroe always began, "Teddy and the moose, Jesus," and shook his head. And that was how the published piece began, with no acknowledgement of St. Martin's co-authorship, and told in Monroe's unmistakable and only slightly sanitized argot. Monroe told it as if he had been there, though he had not been born yet, and he enjoyed getting the small check.

He claimed he had heard the story straight from Mart Moody about being at Follensby Pond with Emerson, Agassiz, and Stillman in 1858. This was unlikely, though the story probably did at least come down from him, only slightly altered by time and with the vulgarity intact. According to Monroe's version, Louis Agassiz, the imperious Hungarian natural scientist and Harvard academic, had misstated to the party the mating season of the brook trout, placing it in the spring along with the salmon. The wiseacres who were his guides mocked and abused him for the error. These included Cheney and Plumley, as well as Moody, son of Jacob—the 1814 Battle of Plattsburgh vet and probable deserter, and early settler of Saranac Lake.

Mart himself set the learned naturalist straight, using the

hyperbolic ridicule and disdain characteristic of the region. With raconteurial flourish and not a small bit of double entendre, Moody enacted before the campfire the mysteries of that colorful and miraculous annual ritual that took place every fall when the leaves and the trout were bright but fading, the eggs matching in color the birch leaves and tamarack needles. For his performance, the pioneer—Moody was a rather low character, even among the guides—received the nabobs' ennobling and patronizing praise. Even Emerson wrote:

Look to yourselves, ye polished gentlemen!
No city airs or arts pass current here.
Your rank is all reversed; let men of cloth
Bow to the stalwart churls in overalls:
They are the doctors of the wilderness,
And we the low-prized laymen.

Monroe's story describes the historic and fateful guideboat passage from Lower Saranac and Round lakes, over the carry where the upper lake plunged over boulders through a narrow sluice before flattening out for two hundred yards and entering Round Lake. Bartlett's Hotel stood on the flats below the falls where salmon had once been plentiful. From Bartlett's, the philosophers rowed across the southern end of Upper Saranac and portaged to Stony Creek Pond over the mile-long Indian Carry. Since time immemorial the two carries, close together and connecting three watersheds, made one of the great crossroads of northeastern canoe travel. In recent years Abenakis, and Mohawks from the St. Regis Reserve (now called by its proper Mohawk name, Akwesasne) on the St. Lawrence, still visited there in the summer to fish and hunt. At Bartlett's, many years after the hotel burned, a subsequent landowner digging a water line uncovered a cache of varied and finely wrought stone tools.

The philosophers continued down Stony Creek (where not a stone can be found) to the "Pere" Racquet River (as Emerson had called it), down that river for a mile, then up another slow, winding stream through lowland maples and into Follensby, one of the region's aquatic gems. They made camp on Eagle Point (one of many so named) beneath old-growth hemlocks and maples; sported with dog, rod, and gun; and carried out a continuous and vigorous scientific investigation and philosophic dialogue.

Monroe's yarn doesn't include this, but in Stillman's group portrait (now hanging in the Concord Massachusetts Public Library), Emerson commands center stage—slightly distracted, standing beneath the two-hundred-foot tree they termed the "mother maple," their tree of life. In the background Agassiz dissects a trout, and off to the side a group of stalwart churls and gentlemen shoot at a target. Transcendental light suffuses the camp through the canopy—partly the artist's perception, and partly just paint.

For, from then on, the idea and the reality of untrammeled nature began to fade. Civilization surrounded and penetrated wild places, instead of the reverse. A steady stream of information and mail reached the men (for they were all men) at Follensby. And, on an outing to Bog River Falls at the head of Tupper Lake, they received a messenger from Bartlett's informing them that the first transatlantic telegraph cable had been laid. The tide of history swept over them, even there. A dimension of cognitive reality—one of darkness, uncertainty and exile—vanished.

It swept over the entire region of their outing, as well. Their camp embodied all the future themes of the Adirondacks. Among these were the loss of regional identity—natural and human—through the agency of outside forces, and the union of nature-loving high-mindedness with frontier wit, self-reliance, and class resentment, setting the stage for the next century and a half of local politics and social relations.

THE TALES WRITTEN UP AND PUBLISHED under Monroe's byline achieved wide readership, more than anything St. Martin published under his own name. Monroe became in-demand as one of the earliest of the new "Adirondack storytellers" soon to be heralded as folk icons, with their own festivals and arts grants. But he died before the movement flowered, perhaps preserving in death his own dignity and that of the region's mythology before both could be diminished by mediocrity and imitation.

Of Follensby, Monroe complained that he could no longer go there himself, though it was a place central to his professional and local heritage and, therefore, his "identity" (though he would never have put it that way), and that many of the old water routes were no longer legally navigable. "It just don't feel like it used to," he said, though he might have been harking back to a day even earlier than his own.

In St. Martin's journals we often see him casting doubt on the details, if not the substance, of Monroe's narrative. Sometimes Monroe may have been pulling his callow interlocutor's leg, as tribal informants are prone to do with anthropologists. What frustrated St. Martin, however, was not so much that Monroe mixed his memories with invention, but that he had not indicated which was which. "I should have seen it coming," St. Martin wrote in his journal. "He never stopped being a guide." Eventually, he rejected using Monroe as the main source for a Germaine/Donnelly's Corners project. It was a blow, as he had already corresponded with Syracuse University Press on the possibility of a book.

A little before the time these tapes were recorded, I met Abel St. Martin when we both guided raft trips on the Moose River and the upper Hudson River gorge. I worked for one of the new, local outfits based in North River, New York; he for his old company from up on the Ottawa River. He had lured them down to his home ground in the Adirondacks soon after the amnesty for draft resisters, and made one of the original companies on the Hudson. I joined up about '79.

I had spent two years in Toronto with a phony 4-F draft deferment, as a sympathizer and pretending to be a student. He had emigrated and guided in the Ottawa Valley. He had a few years on me, and a knack I never acquired for making or otherwise getting money at any given moment. In the early eighties we both met Sonja Germaine, also a guide on the Hudson. They became lovers.

St. Martin and I stayed close for years, though a gap in our ages and experience always separated us. Later, when I edited a regional magazine, he was rarely around—often in the Arctic or Latin America, and deeply involved in various projects I knew little about and which bore little fruit. The exceptions were his remarkable Sabattis study and the award-winning essay on the ambiguous taxonomy of wild canids.

We went our ways, but kept meeting occasionally to discuss organizing a paying raft trip on one of the tropical rivers he was scouting. It never happened. But four or five times a year I visited his camp on Miller Pond, paddling out from the village to stay a night or two and hear of his latest trips. He also gave me a key, and I sometimes stayed there while he was away.

So when I heard he had disappeared on the Brazilian trip in 2000, I went straight out to check on the camp on Miller Pond, paddling across the lake and up the inlet through the bog. His dock among the cedars and balsams was empty. I pulled my canoe out onto the dock, climbed the hill, and let myself in with my key. Inside, the cabin was pristine except for the usual signs of varmint invasion. I opened the curtains and the windows. The bookshelf held all the titles I had grown familiar with and read over twenty years; the lamp chimneys all gleamed; the gas refrigerator was empty, defrosted, and spotless. I brought up my own pack from the landing and put some food in the warm refrigerator and closed the door. Then I went around outside to look over the grounds.

Birch limbs had come down from the blow in April, but otherwise everything looked normal. The tree swallows were nesting in the shed rafters as always, the babies' heads poking up over the sides. Phoebes flew in and out of their place under the porch eaves, alarmed or excited by the human activity—probably the first since November. Some bear had left a big, muddy paw print on one of the kitchen windows, probably also back in April, but it must have realized the caloric payoff of breaking into an empty larder was slim, and desisted.

It was about five in the afternoon. I picked up a bunch of the downed birch and made a little stack of it in the fireplace, which I then doused with kerosene from the shed. I lit it, added dry wood, and went back inside.

By that time we knew only the vaguest details of Abel's disappearance on the Javari River in remote western Brazil. The expedition was underfunded and underprovisioned, as his always were, the waters remoter and severer than expected. The party of two canoes and one raft had not emerged thirty days after their estimated arrival at Iquitos. A week of flying over the rivers produced nothing besides the usual garimperos, gold prospectors, and visual contact with a rarely sighted tribe. The disappearance could not be explained, except by the infinitude and absolute indifference of the geography, even as the new road to Peru penetrated it mile by mile. The whole point of the place seemed to be that it would swallow you, if not by one route than by any number of others. People disappeared out there all the time. Abel was good in the woods, but the trip was a stretch even for him, and he hadn't been getting any younger.

Over the fire I heated a can of chili I had brought with me, and I sat outside as the first whitethroats started calling. Abel would have liked being swallowed that way, I thought. I tried to imagine the various scenarios of his death: kidnapping, torture, and execution; snakebite; an arrow through the throat; a bad hydraulic in an unscoutable canyon; coke traffickers; blackwater fever. What else? How had he been at the end—the end we all have coming, the end he had foreordained? That he reached the advanced of age of fifty-seven at all had been lucky.

It was a week shy of solstice, and the light held on forever. Before it faded I went back inside to light an oil lamp and fetch my bug dope and headlamp. In the office, which I had avoided and where I sometimes slept on the couch when the place was full, I noticed one of his notebooks on the desk—but when I turned my gaze more directly, I saw that it was a *stack* of notebooks, with two more boxes of them on the floor. Beside the stack of notebooks stood a box full of typescripts and legal pads, with two more of those under the table—all material I had never seen before. I picked up one of the typescripts and carried it outside by the fire. The light lasted until ten. I went inside at midnight, having finished four of the more than forty journals. Those four contained the story you have just read.

Abel's will left the cabin and its contents to Sonja Germain, who would have published the story of her grandfather's adventures and phlegmatic character, except for concerns about Monroe's veracity. Then in late 2004, after her mother had died and left Sonja the rambling old camp at Eagle Point, another notebook was found behind the wainscoting during a long-needed renovation.

It was the lost journal, dating from the late twenties until her death in 1936, of the political theorist and social critic Rosalyn Orloff, whose husband, the early American psychoanalyst Arnold Orloff—a friend of George and Bob Marshall's and a student of Freud's and Ferenczi's—had built Eagle Point on Lake Aurora. Ms. Orloff had studied with William James at Radcliffe, where she had also known Gertrude Stein.

A version of the journal follows, with material not relevant to our purposes excised, excepting perhaps the passage on her traverse of The Range in Keene Valley with Carl Jung during his fateful visit there with Freud in 1909. This is included as a glimpse into one of the many lost connections in the Adirondack story. The entire journal has been placed in the Orloff collection at the Adirondack Museum, where it may be perused by scholars. We think it clarifies and amplifies the Monroe account, and offers a measure of clairity to a still-murky past.

PART TWO

Rosalyn's Story

From the diaries of Rosalyn Orloff, 1884-1936, Central Park West, and Lake Aurora, Franklin County, New York.

April 22, 1929. Letter from Vivien, London. She is "studying" with that painter, reputedly Sargent's former student. He implies they were lovers, and she *believes* him. She sends news clippings outlining the fascist groundswell on the continent, the fluctuating dollar. (Here the papers ignore anything that questions the stock market bubble and U.S. monetary policies). She smokes cigars and attends party rallies and suffrage demonstrations, and alludes to unheard-of sex practices with goateed matinee idols and white-flannelled tennis players. Her canvases have improved, though she thinks she will pass on showing them to Stieglitz for the time being. "The series needs more time," she says. She is ready to move to Paris, however, where the food is so much better and she can go to the bars where women dance together and wear men's clothes. You should see me in my waistcoat and gabardines, she writes, with my hair brilliantined and my Havana Corona.

Was there ever a bigger dilettante? I fended off frustration with a pot of strong coffee, and put on my Malone pants. Nietzche, seeing me lacing my boots, began capering and nipping at the laces until I let him out the door. With the lake ice rotting we had been unable to make our daily crossing to the Moody Islands. Before then the weather had been stormy and changeable, and I had been busy finishing the Mercury review. But this morning broke clear and cool, the snow crust firm.

I sat on the porch and put on my snowshoes, with Nietzche absolutely beside himself. The resident red squirrel chattered and diverted his attention. I buckled on my harnesses while the dog gave chase, and the squirrel, well-practiced by this time, dashed up one of the pines to the stable roof—a tableau enacted hundreds of times in the last three years. Nietzche, as usual, skidded to a halt at the base of the tree in a spray of snowy granules.

We headed down the trail under the hemlocks on frozen snow. Dead needles darkened the way, but the sun filtered through the trees with a rounded spectrum it had lacked for weeks. Nietzche raced ahead no more than thirty yards, as he was trained to do, quartering the field like a real retriever, pushing his nose into every squirrel hole and deer track. We came out into the open birches along the outlet and followed the old tote road for a mile toward the confluence. Here the sun had softened what snow remained, and it stuck to the rawhide snowshoe laces. The ice had gone out of the outlet and the black current ran like melted obsidian. At the mouth of Moose Creek we turned upstream on the old lumber-camp trail.

I had packed a basket with coffee, water, and sandwiches, hoping to make it to Black Bog and the new beaver ponds at the headwaters in time for a snack, and then home while the weather held. I wore my beret and Malone pants, my Johnson mackinaw, and rubber boots. But the temperature rose quickly, and I had to take off the hat and mackinaw and put them in the basket along with my gloves.

After an hour we came out of the thick balsams onto the open flats where Moose Creek ran fast, spreading out into the dead, brown grass and almost flooding the trail. Nietzche had by now settled down and kept a steady pace a few feet in front of me, casting a look back every few seconds. In the sun, the tops of the pines and spruces on Steuben Mountain shone like the copper roofs of Quebec, and the osiers along the creek were red with sap. Wood ducks flushed from the slough, setting off Nietzche; redwings and wrens flitted in the dry reeds, and everything had that smell of thawing mud and leaf matter, rot, ferment.

By now I had the snowshoes off and strapped to the outside of my pack basket, and I walked through the slushy remnants on the bare ground and slippery mud. We hiked up through the hardwoods, the creek cascading over boulders and ledges, crossed onto state land, then broke out in the upper meadows. Nietzche ran ahead and disappeared into the dry sedges along the shore of one of the new beaver dams. I was about to call for him when a dozen geese rose and lifted up over the pines, their honking and flapping startling me, then fading and leaving behind the silence of the breeze and the water running over the dam.

The state brought in the beavers from the Rockies a couple of years ago, planted them here and thirty miles away in St. Lawrence County—the first east of the Mississippi since at least the eighteenth century. Nobody expected them to make it, but they have thrived. Robert calls it one of the little successes that can lead to bigger ones. "If you can have the beaver back, you can have the wolf, the cougar, and the moose, too," he says (with the optimism of the young), as long as you keep the habitat. It's a matter of time, money, public education, and making sure those species survive elsewhere. It pains him, he says, running around in the big country south of Cranberry Lake to talk to the old men he so respects as woodsmen and who so recently trapped wolves and hunted moose and cougar, to walk where the animals walked in our lifetimes, then to visit Idaho and Montana, where the people are hell bent on eradicating them there. Conservation must be viewed as a social benefit as necessary as a minimum wage and labor laws, his book will argue, and a national strategy must be outlined.

Last summer Robert considered the upper meadows and Black Bog his favorite spots, though he insists the old lumber camp must be torn down: "Industrial remnants detract from a place's beauty, making it gloomy and undistinguished."

Nietzche waded in after the geese and stood in the icy water up to his chest, biting and gulping at the surface. He growled, and I saw the brown head and wake of a beaver twenty yards off. Nietzche growled louder. The beaver arched its back, accelerated, and slapped its tail in an explosion of water and spray. Then it came up and splashed four more times, to Nietzche's initial delight but rising concern.

When the beaver stayed submerged, Nietzche kept growling and looking across the meadow, where the old lumber camp stood like an ancient ruin on a rise amid young slash pines and berry cane. I remembered coming up in the winters before the war, when it still operated and Arnie was alive, the skid roads iced and the teams hauling the last of the big hemlock and pine off the far ridge of Steuben. It was already the second time around for most of those woods, and when the war emptied the camp it was no longer economical to go back for the twigs, so it was abandoned. Steuben is green again and absorbed into the Forest Preserve, but I loved the boys and men of the camp and the wood road, and the women of the camp: the cook, Eveline, who eventually came and worked for us, and Flo the laundry girl. The men sang for an hour after the communal meal—Swedes, French Canadians, Irishmen and a few Indians—songs from the railroad, "Rackets Around Blue Mountain Lake" and "A' Lumberin' I Will Go." There were tough customers among them, injuries and deaths, some prostitution and violence, but for the most part the camp operated as a unit, and any kind of deviation was frowned upon.

Toward the end Czechs and Italians came. It had the feeling of a vanishing culture even back then, and you mourned its disappearance even before it disappeared, for you knew it would be gone when the woods were gone.

We crossed the meadow, Nietzche with his head low and growling intermittently. I assumed a raccoon or other animal had been occupying the ruin, and he smelled it. The buildings seemed shrunken and closer together than they had formerly, the space between them once paved with bark and sawdust, now grown up to dead grass and raspberries. The zinc roofed bunkhouse and commissary were in reasonable repair, the creosoted planks gray and weathered, the grain raised into sharp ridges. It looked out over the swale where the beavers had taken advantage of the broken-down cribwork dam that had historically flooded the meadow and flooded it once again. The old porcelain doorknobs, the grass rugs, the enamel stove were intact, and tableware left in the cupboards as if nobody had ever left.

Above the bunkhouse stood the soaring pine the lumbermen had preserved as a kind of totem, and for which they had concocted an elaborate legend that outlined the consequences should it ever be cut down. Canada would conquer the U.S. and everyone would speak French. Black flies would grow big as crows. There were more but I couldn't remember them, nor the tree's equally fabulous origin story, and I regretted not writing them down back then.

To the camp clung ghosts of a legitimate and honorable labor, whatever else you thought about it, when reality looked and sounded differently than it does now and our memories harbored fewer nightmares. Something about ruins, the feeling of raw life and tragedy that clings to them from the days before the trenches and the mustard gas. I agreed with Robert, yet I hated to lose such a powerful talisman of that reality.

The dog now faced the bunkhouse on point. His growl grew louder as I advanced toward the building and opened the door, hoping not to surprise a bear just out of hibernation. The large room was empty and smelled strongly of bat, mouse, and porcupine urine. Someone had left a pack basket in the back beside a bunk stuffed with balsam tips, on which rested a book of Robert Service poems and an army blanket. In the middle of the room, the big barrel stove with the rusty pipe felt warm to the hand.

I closed the door and circled the building. Under the pine on the south side, facing the pond, a table had been built out of sticks lashed together with strips of bark. A line had been strung between two trees, holding an enamel cup and pot. There was a red chair from inside, a tin box, a fireplace of rocks (cold, but with finger and wrist sized sticks stacked beside it), and a stick pot gantry stretched over the fire pit.

The dog held his head low and faced the corner of the building. His lip curled back and he barked, spraying saliva.

—Nietzche! I called.

—All right, you: sit! came a voice.

Nietzche's hindquarters slammed into the earth and his ears pricked up.

—Now stay, the voice said.

The voice was calm and firm. Nietzche's eyes froze on the corner of the building, his head cocked to one side.

A man stepped out from around the corner of the building, with a rifle in one hand and two trout dangling from a stick in the other. I recognized him from the villages, and from the TB Society Christmas benefit I had attended with George Hathaway. The man had worn a brown suit that night and spent a good part of the evening with an outlandish Frenchman from Lake Placid, the one who has the sled dogs. There was a row over something, and he'd had to rescue the man from an angry husband. His woman friend, a dark-haired Canadian girl, had catered the affair. I had heard he was a veteran and involved in the rum trade, along with half the people in the region, and they had both seemed impossibly dashing and young.

His black hair stood up straight in the front and flopped over to one side, just as I remembered it. He was clean shaven, but his clothes were covered with pine pitch and ash, and he wore the haunted look of a refugee.

—He doesn't usually answer to men, I said.

—Aw, he's a good boy, he said, facing Nietzsche, then glancing upward at me.

Nietzsche got up and started squatting and wagging his rump like a bitch—a pathetic display. The man rubbed him behind the ears and kneeled to receive a tongue wash.

—We didn't expect to find anyone here. He was only trying to protect me.

—My father used to work here, he said, standing again. I like to come up in the spring to fish.

—But you have no fishing rod, I said.

—I brought a line and hooks, and I busted up a rotten log down there in the hollow and pulled out six fat white grubs.

—So, you wouldn't call that sport fishing, exactly.

—No, ma'am. Well, there is sport to it. I just like to come up and start the spring off close to the elements.

—Of course, I said, seeing that he was lying. He affected a devil-may-care manner that belied the lost look in his eyes. I stepped forward.

—Rosalyn Orloff.

—Pleased, ma'am. That would be Eagle Point, I take it.

—That's right. You know it?

—Well, I knew people who worked on the main house, back before the war, and I guided plenty of fishermen past it.

—You're from Lake Aurora.

—Born and bred.

—Were you hunting, too?

—No, ma'am, I'm not a game violator, oh, no. This time of year, though, you never know when you might stumble on a lady bear with cubs.

—But that's a .22. Would that work against a bear?

—You have to aim for the eyeball, he said, and by then both of us knew we were enacting a charade.

He hung the trout on the line and knelt before the fireplace.

He made a stack of bark and twigs in the fire bed and lit it with a brass lighter such as soldiers used. The flame crackled to life, bursting with the scents of birch and balsam. He took the lid off a galvanized bucket and, with the dipper inside, filled the coffee pot he had just lifted from its wire hook.

—I'll be having some coffee, Mrs. Orloff, he said, if you and your boy here would care to join me.

I sat on the red-painted chair while Nietzche turned around twice and curled up in the dirt at my feet. The man hung the pot off the gantry and added bigger sticks to the fire. Out over the pond, clouds blew across the sky on a breeze straight down from James Bay.

In a minute the water boiled and he lifted the pot with a stick, placing it on one of the flat fireplace stones. He opened the pot lid, and from the tin box poured in a measure of coffee, which he stirred with a long enamel spoon. The breeze was cool, but with the fire and the high sun the air grew warm under the pine boughs. He got up and took off his worn canvas jacket, turning his back to hang it on a nail and exposing the leather strap that held his holster under his left shoulder. It was hardly unusual at any time of year to meet men in the woods carrying firearms.

While the grounds settled, he slit the gullets of the trout, stripped out their viscera, and split them expertly down the spine. He walked down the slope toward the pond and placed the guts on a stump close to the water. Then he strode back up to the fire and sat on a log, where he ladled out the coffee into tin cups.

—You have to take advantage of weather like this, he said, handing a cup across to me. I hope you like it black. When he extended his arm, his hand shook and some of the liquid sloshed on the fire. Smell of burned coffee.

—Thank you.

We drank. I nodded at the butt of the pistol handle that jutted forward from his armpit.

—Bears? I said.

—Excuse me, he said.

He took out the pistol, pressed a button on the side, and ejected a magazine full of bullets into his hand. It made a mechanical zing that jarred against the wind-driven pine needles and the plunging of the beavers, who were still alarmed by our proximity a hundred yards away. He placed the magazine in his pocket and the pistol on the table.

—My husband used to bring me here, I said. Sometimes in the winter when the camp was operating.

—Your husband was a fine man, he said. He knew the territory.

—You knew him?

—Knew of him.

The man said he had come here often as a child, as well, and asked if I had a cigarette. I told him no.

He got up again, poured himself a second cup, and started piercing the two sides of the splayed trout onto green, forked sticks. He propped the sticks about ten inches above the fire, then he leaned over and took my cup to refill it. When he tried to hand it back, his hand shook so badly he had to hold it with the other. So much splashed out he had to refill it.

We sat and looked out over the water while the trout cooked. He turned them two or three times, until the skin curled and they were brown or charred all over but still moist, then he lifted the sticks and placed one of the fish on an enamel plate.

—Had some bacon and hard tack, but it ran out, he said. Hope you can eat it this way. He handed me an enamel spoon and the plate holding the charred and flaking trout.

He used his fingers while I used the plate and spoon. The grilled trout tasted dark and primal, like cedar. The scene recapitulated the stark sensory archetypes I had absorbed in my first years with Arnie: fire sawing in the breeze, smoke in one's eyes, black coffee, taste of trout and smell of pine, the racing clouds, the mud, pale light, patches of snow, and distant loon call. For Arnie it all had extra-literal, metaphysical overtones.

—Delicious, I said, placing my plate on the ground for Nietzsche. This is second nature to you, isn't it, Mr.—.

—Germaine, ma'am. François Germaine.

—Were you also in the military, François?

I remembered the old French Canadian Claude Germaine, who worked on the house, and who died in the flu epidemic.

—Yes, ma'am, in old Mexico and France with Black Jack Pershing. More like first nature, really.

—And what do you do now?

—The last few years I've worked for Mr. Paul's son, Phelps, at the hotel and the power company. But I'm thinking about heading west, maybe Alaska, trying my hand out there.

—It's a little late for that, isn't it?

—Late, ma'am?

—Well, they say the frontier is closed. The Klondike has been played out for twenty-five years, hasn't it? There are the oil fields, but not the opportunities there once were. Nor the romance.

—There's plenty of timber left to cut, I'm good with my hands, and a man who wants to work can always make a living.

—You're not married, then.

—No, he said.

The alders near the beaver pond moved, and a raccoon stepped into the open, scanning the air with its snout. It stepped out farther, identified the direction of the fish guts, and followed it, waddling then trotting forward and putting its front paws on the stump.

—Stay, Nietzsche, I said, as he huffed and raised his hackles. Some consider them vermin, I added. Would you shoot a raccoon, Mr. Germaine?

—There aren't too many things I really feel like shooting any more.

The raccoon twisted its neck so it could lay its head to one side, nipped one set of guts in its teeth, then the other, and dragged both back to the alders.

—She's got a litter back in there. I feed her on that stump so she won't come around the bunkhouse so much.

I had spent an hour with him, and had an hour walk ahead of me. We sat for another few minutes and finished the pot of coffee. Then I rose to leave, taking the sandwich out of my pack and placing it on the table of sticks.

—Thank you for the trout and coffee. How long do you think you'll stay? I said.

—Not too much longer. The work season will start pretty soon, and I'll need to get to wherever I'm going to get a jump on it.

I said goodbye and he said he enjoyed chatting with me.

I walked home with my sleeves rolled up, overheated, the coffee surging in my head.

April 24. Return letter to Vivian. Suggested she concentrate on work and health, try to spend less money. Paris is cheaper than London, I reminded her, and she might have more luck with dealers there. She should leave Sargent's ex-lover in London, however, etc.

Lake ice a day or two from going out. Consulted with Oly on the boats–the Fay & Bowen's new drive shaft, what color to paint the Hanmer. Spent an hour on the new Mercury article (Veblen), then walked to the lumber ruin with more sandwiches, coffee, cheese.

Nietzche led the way, tail high and his face stretched back in a canine grin. It was the third fine day running, a record for this time of year. The mud had softened and deepened along Moose Creek, making it slow going. I'd worn rubber boots, but Nietzche was covered. When we arrived the outdoor fireplace was cold, the tin box and other implements unused. I opened the bunkhouse door to the odor of mingled animals' piss, hoping to leave a note inviting François Germaine to hike to Eagle Point for lunch some day before he left. If he hadn't left already.

The oil-drum stove was cold. I began to write a note. Then Nietzche started whimpering and pushing his nose in the darkened rear of the building. The bunk back there stirred, and a husky voice whispered.

—Good boy, it said, then, Ohh.

—François? I said.

—Mrs. Orloff. Oof. I guess you caught me a little under the weather.

—You've no liquor, have you? Is it serious?

I had stepped closer to the bunk, not wanting to catch him undressed, just so I could see him in the shadows. Nietzche had squatted beside the bunk and watched it ecstatically.

—Just a touch of fever I picked up down in Mexico. It'll pass.

—May I come over? I brought food.

—It's all right. I'll get up.

After a minute he stirred again, and I could see his bare legs and feet swing out onto the floor. I turned around. In a minute he had walked out to the center of the room in his canvas pants, bare feet, and his long-sleeved undershirt, bloodshot-eyed and sweating.

—You're a sight for sore eyes, he said. And a man can see some pretty peculiar things alone in the woods.

—You look terrible. Have you eaten?

—I don't really know. I don't think so.

—What sort of fever is it?

—Unhh.

He sat on the filthy mattress on one of the closer bunks, then lay flat. I sat beside him and took the canteen out of my pack basket.

—Drink, I said.

—No.

—Yes. Come.

He pushed his head up and tried to prop himself on an elbow. I held the canteen to his lips. He took it himself, and when he started to drink he took so much I had to make him stop.

—Let's go.

I got him up and led him outside to the red chair.

—Sit, I said.

—I could really use a smoke.

I had thrown a pack of Lucky Strikes into the basket, and I dug them out. He unwrapped the cellophane, tapped out a cigarette, and lit it with the brass lighter from his pocket. While he smoked I made a stack of birch bark and twigs. Then I took the lighter from his hand, lit it, and built up the fire. There was water in the bucket. I filled the pot and hung it over the fire as I had seen him do. While it boiled I took out the sandwiches and cheese, put them on the plate, and placed them on his lap.

—Can't eat, he said.

—You must.

He sat on the chair, with half a corned beef sandwich on pumpernickel with mustard and pickles in one hand and a cigarette in the other. He took one bite, then another. I gave him the canteen again and he drank.

In a minute the water boiled, and I prepared the coffee. He alternately smoked and took a bite of the sandwich. His gaze remained unfocused, and from time to time his head jerked one way or another as if he were watching a tennis match.

—What's that? he said.

—What, François?"

—Well, that might not have been real. But what's real is that I have to get out of here before Bart Harvey catches up to me.

I knew very well that Harvey, the old game protector, was nearing retirement and of no mind to go out in the woods and get himself shot by any drunken deerjacker or rum runner.

—Now, when were you planning on going out?

—No plan.

—Where do you live?

—Can't go back there.

I poured the coffee and placed the pot on the flat rock. We drank it while I pondered the nature of his fever. He had said it would pass. I assumed he spoke from experience.

—Gotta leave, he said. Bart Harvey's gonna find me.

—You're in no condition to leave, I said. How long does the fever usually last?

—Not long.

—When did it start?

—Don't know. Maybe yesterday.

He was shivering. He threw his cigarette butt into the fireplace and finished the sandwich.

—That was good.

I gave him the other half. When he finished it, he stood up on his own power and poured himself a second cup. I resisted the impulse to introduce reason into the exchange by asking why Bart Harvey was after him, if he wasn't a game violator—an "outlaw," in local parlance.

—Come on, he said, lurching away from the fireplace, barefoot, cup in hand. I followed him down the hill toward the pond, and through the alders to the pond's edge. There, a beaver's house of sticks was pressed up against the high, undercut bank.

—Listen. Can you hear that? he said.

For a minute I couldn't. Then came the far-away whimpering, like geese, of the beaver pups deep inside their mud-and-stick dome.

—I hear it, I said.

—Thank god, he said.

In a matter of seconds one of the mature beavers emerged

from the house and began plunging and splashing its tail. He watched the beaver, then looked at me.

—It's hard to tell what's real when the world is so strange, he said.

—These are the first beavers here in two hundred years.

—Strange, he said. It's strange here.

—Where?

—Everywhere.

—Yes, it is. Will you be all right, François, if I leave?

—Tomorrow, all better. Have to leave tomorrow. Please, don't worry about me, Mrs. Orloff. You go. Thanks for the Luckies.

—You have to promise to eat this other sandwich and cheese. And tomorrow you may walk out by way of Eagle Point, if you'd like, eat a real meal with me before you go west to seek your fortune. I won't let Officer Harvey on the property, I promise.

He made a face of alarm, then caught himself and relaxed. If anything kept him away it would not likely be the spectral Harvey. I put the leftover food on the table of sticks.

—When you go inside, don't leave it out here for the raccoon. Take care, François. Please don't leave without saying good-bye.

—I won't.

I left him sitting on the red chair, smoking another Lucky Strike and looking distracted.

May 12. Today FG moved into the annex. Legal? Unclear, though morally legitimate, and not to be learned of by Vivian.

One surprises oneself so seldom. Yet, unpredictability and the capacity to exhibit new behaviors distinguish us from non-humans. These abilities easily atrophy with the acceptance of convention, the drive to succeed, to raise children—to belong. The common difficulties may occlude them altogether. Thus, when the capacity asserts itself, the effect can be terrifying, and it can be liberating. It may enlighten or destroy, and the choice whether to yield or suppress depends on many variables.

I made the decision in a second. Anecdotal history, scripture, myth, and literature abound with impulsive acts, disastrous or redemptive, with neither outcome favored. The best strategy is to neither yield nor suppress, but to study, compare, practice, listen to the deep ethical sense that resides in the heart, and act. It is chimerical to imagine we can outwit fate through reason, and ultimately we are driven back on our own sense of justice.

The decision to harbor FG seemed, on the available evidence, not only morally and practically justifiable, but necessary as well.

Two days after my second visit to the lumber camp, he came to the house, sweating and delusional, claiming that someone from Malone who worked for the gangster Dutch Schultz had found him in the night. He had sensed the man's approach, surprised him, held him at gunpoint, and bound him to the big pine with rope. He put a burning stick from the fire to the man's eye and forced him to reveal that his missing cousin, Pete, had been thrown into a grain elevator and buried alive.

—You go back and tell whoever it was who sent you to come themselves next time, he told the man, and see what I got waiting for them. And tell whoever threw my cousin into the hopper that if they want to keep their nuts in their sack, they better make tracks for some place far, far away, like the Sahara Desert, maybe, or Mongolia. (This is my closest approximation of his typical speech, using the twang and profanity of the regional dialect, and its violence, but without its diphthongs and glottal stops.)

He cut the man's bonds and stood back.

—Now make tracks and don't look back until you get to that miserable little town with the rest of the cow fuckers.

The man turned to leave, then spun and attacked F. with the frying pan that had been suspended from the wire. F. shot him, twice in the throat with the service automatic, and buried the body under the floorboards of the commissary. Then he replaced the boards so that nobody would notice they had been removed.

He had his pack basket with him, but had somehow misplaced his firearms and canvas jacket. Later he said he threw them into the beaver pond.

I won't deny it thrilled me in a way I had never felt, hearing him tell his tale. His glazed look could have betokened shock or madness. He may have killed a man, though I would never dig up the boards to find out. Nevertheless, I let him in. He looked around and asked for coffee and a cigarette. I found another pack of Luckies in the pantry, which I kept for guests, and asked Eveline to make coffee.

—We'll have Mr. Germaine for dinner, I said.

He was in no condition to go west, nor to do much of anything, recovering as he was not from an obscure tropical fever but from a severe and extended bout of drinking. And I realized, after hearing the merest outline of his recent history, that not only his military past but also his bootlegging activity and professional disappointments had left a profound and indelible mark on him.

Still, after he was installed (with a good deal of fruitless resistance on his part), I underwent the usual crises of doubt, and investigated.

The villagers, except for the most abstemious and puritanical, considered him a good neighbor. The commonplace observations were that he was a hard worker, a war hero, an expert (if hardly law-abiding) hunter, the best marksman in the Adirondacks, a bit wild, a hard but fair boss (of non-union labor—there are as yet few unions in the north), honest, good looking, a first-rate fiddler, and a master builder in the rustic style. It was harder to discern his less obvious, more abstract qualities. A few said he was hard to know, standoffish, cold.

Nobody called him a drunk, though he must have been. Those who surely knew of his bootlegging declined to report it. None mentioned anything the least suspect from the point of view of deviousness, personal weakness, disloyalty, or criminality.

Yet, criminals are often wildly popular, shielded, even revered in their own communities, never mind the mayhem and discord they sow elsewhere. And despite the bland encomiums of the villagers, here he was in hiding—if not from the law, then from other bootleggers and some self-generated ogre of his own psyche.

Technically, then, I am harboring a criminal and in theoretical danger from vengeful, unnamed smugglers from Malone, though I could find no evidence that he is wanted for anything, or even that law enforcement knows of his illegal activities.

After William's practice of not allowing any element not directly experienced to corrupt my perceptions, nor to ignore anything experienced, I had found him enigmatic but hardly a criminal. His capacity for violence, the norm in the area, seemed tempered by a high ethical curiosity and integrity, and a generally benign disposition toward society and nature. He had gone to engineering school for two years, and acquired there (or possessed already) an acute reasoning mind. Yet, his crises are complicated.

Along with alcohol withdrawal, he is in a state of acute melancholia precipitated by the rejection of his marriage proposal by the dark-haired Canadian, Yvette Landry. His mother died when he was twelve, from tuberculosis contracted after working for years at the Tumblehome sanitarium in Lake Aurora. Afterwards, his father drank until he died in the Spanish flu, and F. began supporting himself as a guide and a trail worker at Paul Smith's hotel. He showed independence early, developing a style of rustic log construction that drew the attention of sponsors who sent him to Clarkson. There he lasted for two years before he joined the cavalry and left for Mexico and Europe. Since the war, he had worked as a crew boss for the electric company. His sympathies seem to be with labor, but his own ambition is toward something grander, though devoid of pretension or Veblen's "conspicuous consumption." He has the temperament of an artificer, a visionary.

None of this recommends him as a lodger, and I can easily predict the objections and suspicions of various neighbors, village busybodies, and Vivien (hypocritically). So be it.

May 19. F. grows steadier by the day. For the past week he has stayed in the annex, with its high casement windows overlooking the lake, keeping the fireplace lit when the weather turned inevitably cold and dark after those two weeks of sunshine and Canadian high pressure. He sleeps, and browses in the library, ignoring the long shelves of political and psycho-analytical texts, and reading for the duration of his limited concentration from Adams's Mont St. Michel and Chartres, Colvin's "Reports" to the Legislature, and an oversized facsimile edition of Vetruvius that Arnold had collected in London. They lie open on the library table when I take him coffee and fruit, or eggs and bread when he has the appetite, or when he has perhaps stepped onto the balcony to smoke, for he has determined not to smoke inside, he says. The high windows and bookshelves remind him of a gallery or sanctuary. Nietzche goes straight to the annex door when I let him out in the morning, sleeping for hours curled on the hearth rug beside F.

The story emerges in little nuggets. On the fifth day, I was drinking coffee and writing letters at the round oak table in the kitchen when he entered from the covered walkway, pale but rested and unagitated, in the old clothes of Arnold's I had left for him in the annex closet: the worn, moleskin corduroys and Scots plaid flannel shirt, with his own well-greased moccasin boots. He had washed and shaved. He stood in the doorway while I introduced him to Eveline, who was baking for the week, and asked her to bring us more coffee and scones.

—I ran into Officer Harvey in Charlie Green's market in Saranac Lake yesterday, I said. His retirement had come through. He said he was looking forward to spending the summer at his camp on Polliwog Pond, fishing and having nothing to do with game violators. He hoped he had a few more years like that before he couldn't get around anymore.

F. sipped his coffee from the green-striped stoneware mug.

—Oh, he'll get around, all right, he said with a rueful smile, the most benign and moderate expression he had shown me since we met at the Santa Clara lumber camp.

Eveline placed the plate of scones on the table—a little roughly, I thought, for an employee. When she had gone down to the laundry room, I looked at him.

—I didn't tell him you were here, I said. But why do you think he's looking for you?

—I don't really remember now. He's retired, you say?

—Yes.

—Old bastard. It's about time.

—What does he mean to you?

—I've known old Bart all my life.

—Yes, but what do you think of when you think of him?

—My father, I guess. They were the same age.

—That was Claude?

—Yeah, that was him. Old Claude.

—Up on Moose Creek, you were afraid Bart Harvey was coming after you.

—I might have been confusing some things for others a few days ago, he said.

—Had anything happened recently? Was he connected somehow to the bootleggers you told me about?

Then he related how, on the last run of liquor he had made, up an old tote road through Madawaska by horse team during the big snow a month ago, Bart Harvey had surprised him and his partner from Lake Aurora, one Alonzo Monroe. The old man had come out of the woods and held them by gunpoint while he extorted a case of brandy.

—He's a hard and rough man of a frontier mien. He represents a former way of being.

—Well, I'm not sure what you mean by a former way of being, F. said. But when he got the drop on us like that, it showed me that the booze had dulled my edge. I'd lost my judgment. If that old coot could ambush me, then worse things were coming.

—And were they?

—When he had us out there, he told us Schultz's Malone gang had gotten my cousin Pete LaFleur, one of our drivers. Pete was going to take over when me and Lon got out.

He was looking at the floor, breathing heavily.

—Pete was wild and he shouldn't of got caught.

—And you never got out. Not until now.

—This ain't out, he said.

He is twelve years my junior, but in the meeting of our eyes in that moment, you could see the shadow of his ancestors, the remainder of his days stretching out ahead of him, and the burden of his generations.

—Mrs. Orloff, you've been awful good to me. I'm real grateful. I don't know how much longer this arrangement might last, but it would be best if you kept my being here a secret for the time being.

—Of course, François. It goes without saying.

—Thank you, ma'am. Now, right now I'd just like permission to take one of your guideboats out for a row on the lake.

Without meaning to, I hesitated.

—Don't worry, Mrs. Orloff. I'm not going anywhere. Not yet, anyway.

I told him to take the 16-footer. He left by the kitchen door and walked into the boathouse with Nietzche at his heels. I watched as he rowed the blue boat out into the bay in a gentle breeze. Soon I heard Nietzche barking wildly inside the boathouse as the guideboat moved swiftly toward the Moody Islands in mid-lake. The dog ran out of the boat house, back and forth along shore in front of the lodge, then out to the point, where he leapt six feet off the rock into the forty-degree water.

—Nietzche! I called from the porch door.

But he kept on swimming, with his upper body half out of the water, in a desperate attempt to catch the boat. I was about to start the Hacker to see if I could rescue him. Then the guideboat slowed, turned parallel to the shore about a quarter mile off, and waited until the dog caught up. F. reached over the side and pulled the dripping dog into the boat. Then he shielded himself with his hands as Nietzche sent a fine mist spiraling off his body.

June 3. I had written Robert and told him I had a visitor, a local man—a veteran and woodsman—with an interesting background in forest industry. I suggested he might enjoy meeting him and exchanging local knowledge of the woods and mountains.

He came up from New York earlier than I had thought he would, and sent a note from Knollwood on Lower Saranac. Louis was still busy with court matters and would come up later in the summer. He would be a few days directing the staff at opening up, and he would come to visit at the earliest convenience.

I forgot about it and finished the Kropotkin piece. In the annex F. had finished with Adams and Vetruvius, and taken up Cadwallader Colden, Lewis Henry Morgan, and the banker and historian Donaldson, whom he had once rowed around one of Smith's lakes fishing. For a local man, Donaldson was high-handed with the guides, which didn't go over well with the men. He was also a well-known fish hog.

A week before F. was to take him out, he had shot a raccoon and left it in the sun on a shed roof to rot.

—The day before I took him out, I rowed that stinky thing out to a spring hole we tried to keep for ourselves and tied that 'coon to a big rock and sank it in the spring hole. I hammered a wabbler out of an old nickel and rigged it up with a big gob of white grubs like the ones I used at the lumber camp. They looked like great big, white maggots in the water. I rowed him over that spring hole and he caught one four-pounder, then its mate, a female with big red spots, on the next pass. I killed both and we stopped for tea. After that I avoided the exact spot, and we caught and let go only two twelve-inchers the rest of the day. He was happy, but he never asked for me again, and he only got away with those two big speckles.

F. had also begun helping around the camp, painting the stable and barn, repairing rotted logs on the annex. In all this time he had not left the point except to hike back to the Santa Clara camp or to row on the lake when he thought no one who would recognize him would be out. So, yesterday he appeared in the door of my study after cleaning the paint off his hands.

—You can't sit inside on a day like today, he said.

I changed and followed him and Nietzsche into the boathouse, where we took down the 16-foot Hanmer from the rack. I sat in the stern working the sneak oar, with Nietzsche amidships, as F. rowed in the bow. This opposition created an awkward but pleasant effect. I had worn my khaki skirt and canoe moccasins, a long-sleeved silk blouse, and my wide-brimmed hat with the bug veil. It occurred to me only then that we might have been considered scandalous to a certain kind of local observation. You thought of the romantic scenes depicted in canoes and row boats on the covers of film magazines and sheet music, and that the builders in Peterborough and Canton exploited in their specialty "courting" canoes, with the removable center thwart and cane lounge seat to ease the promised consummation.

He reached forward with his hands crossed and feathered the

oars. The blades reached backward the length of the boat and dipped into the water. He pulled and repeated the movement. Beyond the point the prevailing northwesterly blew away the flies, and I lifted my veil. Where he had been able to speak directly to me with the veil on, he now avoided my eyes, and I, I found to my surprise, his.

—You could paddle from here all the way to Montreal, with a few carries, he said.

—Would you like to do that, François?

—I'd like to, but I'm in bad odor in Canada, he said.

—Well, if you could paddle as far as Montreal, you could paddle almost anywhere in the world. Weather permitting.

—I suppose that's true.

I looked over toward the Sentinel and Langford ranges in the east and north, and he turned his gaze from one side to the other as he rowed. The dog whimpered, sensing some confusion between us, some emanation. The moment passed. As we neared the islands Nietzsche stood to watch the approach over F.'s shoulder, crowding up in front of F.'s face as he rowed, pawing F.'s privates with his front feet, as if to make a point between male animals. I said his name and tugged his tail to make him sit until we landed.

The boat cruised into a narrow channel that separated the sun-warmed rocks in mid-lake. The ripples projected waves of sunlight on the stones five feet down. We pulled into the pocket-like bay among the cluster of four islands, none more than six feet high or an acre in size, and drifted.

—I used to catch crayfish in these rocks, he said.

Sheep laurel bloomed in patches of moss on the rock shore, along with the odd arbutus and clusters of bunchberries, partridge berries as they call them here, the stunted, wind-sculpted red pines and balsams like Japanese bonsai.

He shot the oars and the boat skidded across the bay, suspended over the rocks, and with a dip of the right oar swung to beside a low granite bench six inches high. We disembarked and lifted the boat out onto a bed of moss and lichen. Before us stretched a geography of miniature continents, the islands in their interesting alignments and variegated forms, their aesthetically pure if accidental proportions, oppositions and complementarities, as if some meaning were contained there—something more than the pure randomness of geology and weather. (What more meaning should there be?) They were dry except for what water collected in the little glacial kettle holes gouged in the rock.

We wandered and explored the microcosm separately. After a few minutes I took a seat near a fire ring of weathered rocks someone had built there years ago. Now moss sprouted over the charred ashes.

Over the water, swallows—dozens of them—feasted on mayflies. Blackflies hovered, but not enough to lower the veil. Soon I felt the dog's nose in my neck and heard the scuff of F.'s moccasins. He sat five feet away on the rock, with the dog between us, looking across toward the western shore. A new opening had appeared in the shoreline forest over there, where Roger Johnson in the village had just sold another lot.

—I'm sorry I brought no picnic, I said.

—That's all right. Shouldn't stay long anyway, he said.

—I love how the islands echo each other's shapes, but inexactly. It would be interesting to inhabit them in some different proportion.

—But not so small that you'd always have to think about hawks.

—It's good to be here at any size. Thanks for thinking of it.

My girlishness alarmed me. The first thing anyone would think, anybody watching, was that I was mesmerized by his beauty, his danger, and the thrill of possibility. They would be right. Nothing beyond that occurs to me, at least not in the form of visual cognitions, as William would have called them. Or not yet. But I still look forward to seeing him in the course of a day, and when it comes time for him to leave, I won't like it.

—That little island right off the inner point in Eagle Bay sure is pretty, all right, he said.

—I call that Arnie's Island.

—Nice place to watch the sunset. I thought I'd like to build a log footbridge over to it. Like the ones I used to make for Paul, but a little different. If you'd like.

—Do you think a structure should be added to that sufficiently lovely spot?

—I'd try to make it fit in. I'm pretty good at it. It's all right if you don't want me to.

—Can you make something that long that will hold up to the wind and the ice?

—It's pretty sheltered right there.

—It's too much to ask.

—I've been feeling better and thinking I shouldn't take any more advantage of your hospitality. It's about time to move on. I'd like to do it as thanks for your attention and kindness.

—That would be very considerate. I'll have to think about it.

I had pulled off my socks and soaked my feet in the shallows. The water was no longer glacial and it felt wonderful, though it was terrifically bold of me, and I could tell he noticed. He tried not to look, but his eyes kept flicking toward them as we talked, then back to my face. Oh, to hell with it, I thought. The sun, the rock, the water and its yeasty smell. There was an extra-erotic connection between us that had as its model something less contorted.

The dog put a paw in my lap and tried to lick my face.

—Nietzche, stop.

—Here, boy.

The dog obeyed, and I took the chance to get up and brush off my skirt.

We rowed back in silence.

In the boathouse Nietzche leaped out. I left F. to stow the boat and followed the overeager dog onto the porch and into the living room.

—So, that's your visitor, is it?

Robert stood in the living room, where he had been looking out the bay window. Nietzche wagged his tail. Robert's face showed his impish and irritating side, and an implication of shenanigans on my part.

—My visitor, yes. And that's all.

—Don't worry, Ros, he said.

—Oh, Robert. Don't be ridiculous. How are you? Here, let me hug you. You look hale and fit, if a bit rubiginous.

—I know him, he said when we parted.

—François?

—Yeah. He works for the power company, manages the crew on the Tupper line, cutting the woods around Saranac Inn and Deer Pond. A real tough boss and a right-hand man of the Smiths.

—All right, but I think you'll find him more complex than that. He was living in the old Santa Clara camp on Moose Creek when I found him, hiding from bootleggers and the law. You can't tell anyone he's here.

—You're entitled to a private life, he said. Just don't make me have to worry about you.

But he would believe what he believed. Just then F. walked in. He stopped quite suddenly, and as quickly moved forward with his hand extended.

—Fran Germaine, he said, looking into the center of Robert's eyes like a friendly but unreliable predator.

Robert rose to the occasion, like a bantam fighting cock afraid of nothing. He offered back his hand and big, smiling moonface.

—Bob Marshall. Ros is the only one who calls me Robert.

—Rice's friend.

—Oh, I'd be honored to be so considered.

—I heard about you.

—And I you. Your war record and employment with the Smiths.

—Well, I'm on my own now. I'm here to build a bridge over to Arnie's Island, if Mrs. Orloff and I can agree to terms. Then I'll move on.

—A contractor.

—Nope. Just a worker.

—Ros is an old friend of mine. Her husband knew the woods better than anybody around here.

—He was a good fellow, that's for sure.

—Rice tells me you're good as well.

—Me? He looked amused, but coiled to strike.

—In the woods. On the trail.

—Aw, I don't know anything. But I've been around.

I left them and went to the kitchen to order coffee and sandwiches. When I came back ten minutes later, they had moved out to the porch and looked out over the bay. F. held his arm and hand before him, stretching toward the island, drawing in the air as if to fill in the landscape with a picture of the bridge. Robert cupped his chin, nodded his head up and down while he listened, then back and forth when he realized what it would mean.

—My friend's ashes are buried on that island, he said. It's sacred ground, inviolable.

—This won't be anything that won't fit there, like a railroad bridge or something. Just log and rock. It'll look like part of the land. When the weather whittles it down and takes it away, there won't be nothing left.

—Oh, an artist, ay?

—Hell no. The only thing I know about is how to put logs together.

—And which you'll have to cut and peel. They'll take a year to dry.

—There are enough stacked in the barn left over from when Dr. Orloff built the guest house.

The exchange went on, with rising and falling levels of heat. I called them in and we stayed on the couches by the fireplace, drinking coffee and talking, until dinner time. I asked Robert to stay, but he had to leave to work on his forests book.

F. kept talking all the way through dinner. Robert had needled him, and he liked it.

July 8. Today to Saranac for appt. with Claridge. When I return, the first pine logs run from either shore to the two log cribs filled with stone and set in the water. F. floats in the White canoe, kneeling and working on one of the stringers while Robert watches from shore, talking and gesturing.

Last week F. took a day and accompanied Robert and Mr. Rice on a bushwhack of the Sewards, all three summits, none with trails. They came in at midnight, laughing and arguing. In the morning F. was still covered with bites and scratches.

—Never saw anybody walk like that man, he said. Wore me right down. He wouldn't stop no matter what, *had* to make all three peaks in one day, damn the darkness. Then he complained the view from the top of Seymour disappointed him. And he talked every inch of the way.

—That's Robert, I said.

I stand at the living room windows watching them. When I turn around I see, lying on the library table, a plan for the bridge F. has drawn on Arnold's watercolor paper. It is to scale, with views from various angles and a rendering of the setting that uses color washes and egg tempura to emphasize exact details. The larger background is rendered in delicate line. In the lower-right corner it is signed with a small cartouche that looks like a crow or raven inside a capital letter G. It is striking, and looking at it, then out at the piers and stringers, I can see for the first time how the bridge will continue the flow of the shore's contours to the answering contour of the island. I roll and store the drawing in a tube for framing later.

At dinner the phrase "people's forests" arises, which we tell F. means conservation as much for wilderness and human well-being as for industrial resources. And all in public ownership, including the national forests as well as the state Forest Preserve.

F. rejects the idea at first, except that he cannot see any reason why the current model of loggers and miners exploiting and abandoning public or private land should be any better—and we know he has both suffered and participated in such practices. We explained that with new scientific logging practices such as Gifford Pinchot had developed on Jock Whitney's woods (and Gifford was great friends with F.'s hero T.R.), the public can derive the greatest value from the nation's wild underpinning. Removing market incentives from forestry is the only way to make this happen. In the last fifty or sixty years the Adirondacks have suffered the disaster of unchecked capital: the naked ranges, dammed and polluted rivers, the shrunken water table, the railroad fires. Pinchot's techniques, if followed, would keep the resource intact. Had T.R. survived the aftermath of his Brazilian adventure, he would be our powerful ally. Without him, we are forced to imagine his arguments.

F. stays remote, probably imagining we have a Bolshevik land grab in mind. But what about the people, he wonders. Strong, independent local economies, we respond, connected by existing roads, no more.

—This isn't going to last much longer, says Robert, meaning the stock market bubble. Five years, ten. It'll be a gift to workers and to the future.

The subject changes to Babe Ruth and the Yankees, both of

whom Robert worships. I excuse myself, weary of advocating.

An hour later I wake to the sound of a violin. F. has found the instruments left over from Arnold's fantasy of a string quartet.

July 29. The twilights are long and full, day after day like the last. Calm, warm mornings. In the afternoon clouds, perhaps a shower. Humid evenings, a breeze and light like hammered brass on the water. Swamp maples on the low shores showing the first bloody swatches.

Lately the camps all full, the water by day a slowly shifting composition of sails and guideboats broken only by the odd motor launch or runabout. Afternoons, unannounced visits by boat or canoe. It is a gay atmosphere: too much food and a good deal of contraband drink. Young people in bathing costumes, drinking, flirting, and spooning. This traffic, delightful as it is, drives F. underground.

Mornings he manages to work on the bridge. It is nearly finished, a thumbnail of articulated wood and stone, a bridge of bridges, its joints fitted with pegs or held together by their natural tension, the railings naturally curved cedar logs with the bark still on, unvarnished and raw-looking. It has minimal ornamentation, yet a great sense of the materials and their textures. In the forge he hammered out a brand of his cartouche, which this afternoon he burned into the southern onshore corner post.

Evenings he comes out after the late diners leave, and eats the leftovers. Then he takes a lantern and a guideboat, or the 15-foot White, his favorite canoe in the boathouse, and paddles out into the near dark. I follow the movement of the light as he circles the lake, stops to fish or smoke a cigarette. He comes back after I have stopped watching and have drifted off on the upstairs sleeping porch, trying to absorb as much of the soft air and long light as possible. (Summer is short.) By six in the morning he is frying bullheads in batter, with fresh eggs, pancakes, maple syrup, and coffee.

Earlier tonight he emerged after the Rinzlers and the Morbachs left. I was sitting in the kitchen with the door open, listening to the bull frogs, hermit thrushes, whitethroats. He had been working at the drafting table he had set up in the annex and become distracted, unfocused. He eyed a bottle of Canadian beer someone had left on the kitchen table. I made him coffee and a plate of leftover chicken and dumplings, and took the beer down to the cool-cellar, out of sight.

He wolfed down the food, washed his dish in the sink, and headed for the boathouse. I followed him down the walk and stood at the boathouse door as he took down the White from the rack and placed it in the dark water.

—Care for a passenger? I said.

He turned with a start, his face losing its vague distance and springing into focus.

—Dee-lighted, he said.

We paddled toward the islands in the dark and drifted over the shallows into the sheltered inner bay. I faced the stern, sitting on the canoe seat on the floor planks. He lit a cigarette and baited a line.

—Watch out for that lantern, he said.

In a minute he had boated three ten-inchers and put them in the wire basket over the side. The next thing I remember is waking in mid-lake, disoriented, with the Milky Way streaming overhead and my equilibrium confused. At the other end I saw the glow of his cigarette in the dark, felt the rocking of the canoe, and smelled the faint odor of fermenting lake water and fish.

—I fell asleep.

—Two hours ago.

—Where are we?

—Widest part of the lake, a hundred feet deep.

A minute of silence passed.

—Nothing better than being in a small boat in big water, he

said. Want to hear a story?

—Please.

He told me of an escape from Montreal last Christmas, when he and his partner had canoed across the St. Lawrence to the Indian village on the south shore in the moonlight, with the air temperature around ten or fifteen degrees and the water temperature not much higher. It sounded treacherous, foolhardy, but he claimed he never felt anything but the highest spirits while they were out there. It was the first detailed account of his past he had volunteered to tell me. I considered it a breakthrough, but there were pieces missing, and I filed it away for later as he paddled us slowly back to camp with the stars overhead and the darkness full of night sounds.

Aug 10. Claridge has ordered tests. I told him I feel fine and will give it due consideration.

Last week we inaugurated Arnold's Bridge. A little audience arrived by car and boat: Louis and Robert, Peggy, the Rinzlers and Morebachs, Rockwell, Meyer Elman, from Tupper. Oly, now retired, rode over from Lake Clear with his buckboard and team. The Petty girls brought a picnic.

Robert stood on the bare rock where it sloped to the summer-clear water, and near the two shore-side posts. F. had tied across the entry a garland of woven cedar roots, peeled up out of the shallow duff like ribbons. A small, hand-lettered sign in birchbark and set in a twig frame read, "In Memory of A. O.: Husband, Woodsman, and Friend."

—Friends, said Robert. We are here in fellowship and love to dedicate this bridge in the name of our husband, mentor, colleague, trail companion, and friend, Arnold Orloff. You all remember how the principle of avoiding harm guided his decisions. To have altered the character of Eagle Point would have demanded from him the highest contemplation of the historical, natural, and aesthetic consequences. To find the proper guidance he would have consulted arcane texts and the most astute local experts. But he could not have found a better architect and builder than Lake Aurora's Ray Balzac (the pseudonym we had created for F.), or one more agreeable with his belief in human and natural harmony. This bridge of wood and stone, held together by its own tension and perfectly carved joints, stands as a monument to our dear friend and to the impermanence of human designs. It draws no attention to itself except in its beauty and the modestly placed artist's signature: a sign, rather than a name. It hews to the shore, the water, the background, and the island from every view, and resembles at times a blowdown, a logjam, a sculpture. But it is a functional sculpture, built with indigenous materials, and when we are gone, or the current historical period ends, it will go back to its origins in wood and rock. It is a model for how to mesh the human and the wild here in the Adirondacks and in the national forests and other wild areas. Let us see it as a bridge to the new era of beauty, wilderness, fairness, equality, and prosperity.

Or words to that effect.

He turned and cut the garland with a pair of nippers. We applauded and processed across the bridge to the island, in no particular order and in a cheerful frame of mind. When we reached the middle, moving slowly to admire the joinery and running our hands over the magical wood, the sound of a violin carried over the water from the island. F. stepped out from behind the big boulder that balances on its crest. He played a sorrowful French-Canadian folk song in a minor key. I had long since given up on the conscious afterlife, where we persist in our beings. But right then I felt Arnold's presence imbuing the surroundings in a way I never imagined.

The sky stayed blue, with a breeze and gentle waves on the lakeward rocks. We ate roast chicken and potato salad, and lamented the recent lynchings in Georgia. The girls swam. Ray

Balzac was the whimsical name we had bestowed on F. prior to the ceremony, to preserve a semblance of anonymity. Nobody recognized him, though Meyer looked at him long and hard. F. wore clean work clothes of Arnold's. He played "Garryowen" and two other tunes called "Eglise de Sherbrooke," and "Soldier's Joy," a kind of a jig. (The names of the tunes were beautiful, and I had him write them down for me later). Then he ate some chicken, received compliments, and exited after fifteen minutes.

I avoided questions, though I twice allowed the implication that he was a new caretaker to stand uncorrected.

Aug 12. Last night in the lakehouse with a fire against the chill, he appeared at nine. I hadn't seen him all day.

—Remember when I told you about crossing the river?

—Of course.

—Can I tell you another one?

—I wish you would.

In '16 he left Clarkson and enlisted. Within weeks he was across the border with Pershing to catch Villa, who had raided Columbus, N.M. His company was deep in the sierra, closing on its quarry, when the fugitive band split into three parts. He was nineteen. He had made sergeant in the field, and went in command of a squad that included a Carranza captain trying to ingratiate himself with the Americans. They followed one of the tracks out of the valley and into a canyon maze inhabited by an unconverted, recalcitrant tribe. At one point they caught sight of the party in flight, and one of the aides with field glasses insisted he had seen Villa on horseback. They crossed a knife-edge after him and ran into a wall of fire from their flank. Naked Indians with long hair and headbands ran away. F. saw machetes, but no firearms. They gave chase briefly, but left off when the Indians disappeared.

They returned to the main chase. Rounding a bend, they met

a barrier of boulders. Furious, the southerners refused F.'s order to dismantle the barrier. He attempted to win them over, but the Arkansan roused the other southerners to follow him after the Indians instead. They went back and climbed through the rocks to the high bench the Indians had fired from. From there tracks led across a green height of land. The Arkansan spurred the gringos on, but F. hung back to scout among the rocks. Soon he found the bodies of two Villistas with U.S. Springfields at their sides, in khaki, their heads and throats slashed. They had been guarding the backtrack and firing on the gringos, he reasoned, and had been murdered opportunistically. The Indians would have taken the arms, had our soldiers not fired on them. F. spurred his mount across the height of land, more than a half-hour behind. It led into a box canyon drained by a creek. The ground was torn by hooves, but he could also see the odd footprint and moccasin track.

He heard the firing ten minutes before he came upon it, the thud of grenades and semiautomatic rifle fire. He rode under a high overhang that sheltered lodges of wattle and adobe, like an ancient pueblo. Then their roofs were on fire, and children ran past him headed out of the canyon. The mayhem took place on the flats below the adobe lodges, out from under the ledge, and it was mostly over by the time he got there. He counted thirty bodies before he came upon two Tennesseans getting ready to carve a woman cowering against the inside of a clay oven, her baby in her arms. He wanted to shoot them but instead ordered them to ground their arms, and he turned on the Arkansan, whom he told about the two dead Villistas guarding the retreat. These Indians wanted to kill you, the man said. They aren't even men. He waved his arms toward the carnage, the burning lodges, the blood-spattered soldiers. We've won a great victory. You've won an arrest, if I have anything to do with it, F. said. We'll see, the man said, spurring his mount. Let's go, he called, and waved the Americans out of the canyon.

F. hung back, but more than once he heard threats murmured in his direction. The men had found bottles of the native liquor in the lodges and passed them back and forth. When it got dark and they were still an hour from the rendezvous, he fell even farther behind, pausing by a spring along the way to let it get darker. He had demonstrated his marksmanship in contests for money. Usually he won. If they meant to ambush him it would probably take more than one of them, but he meant to take no chances.

Eventually he saw the fires of the rendezvous from the rim of the valley. When he drew near, he hung outside the firelight long enough to see that the other squads had returned and he would be safe. He rode up in silence, ate beans and venison from among the leftovers, and curled up in his bedroll without speaking. This memory had spurred him in European combat, he said. That he never spoke of it to a commanding officer haunts him.

—Have you dreamed of it?

—It's going on even while I'm awake.

I had seen him wearing a towel after using the outside shower, the starburst scars of entry on his shoulder and back, the jagged tracks of shrapnel across his chest.

"Soldier's Joy."

Aug 29. The long days falling off toward winter, the wind backing into the north, bringing hard blue skies after thick morning fog. The creeks are trickles of tinsel among the dry rocks. The loons fledged, warblers off already to unknown climes, young deer turning from red to gray.

Robert and F. have left for Cranberry Lake and beyond for three weeks. Loneliness, and the news from Claridge. So, off to the Lake Placid Sinfonietta with Charles, to whom F. is "Ray," the new caretaker. He is so kind, and good company. He wants more but is patient and tolerant. Strange to join him at the Club's annual swan song, with Dewey's anti-Semitism still a driving force—the sleek, satisfied patricians in their straw-boaters and silk cocktail dresses, with the resting place of the Harper's Ferry martyr Brown just outside of town a striking contrast, and old man Epps, the last of the Timbuctoo settlers, recently dead. Fortunately, Lake Aurora is remote enough that few recognize me. The program was Offenbach, Gilbert and Sullivan, visitor Herbert, and, in the second violins, a grossly out-of-tune instrument. The conductor was too drunk to notice, but the finale was gay and bright, the fireworks delightful. It was there at the reception, sipping a fruit punch, that I overheard the news about the young Canadian singer and her newborn, eight-and-a-half-pound, out-of-wedlock son, with his dark hair and eyes so unlike those of Dr. Kline, a resident at Trudeau's.

September 13. The men returned at midnight, and I joined them at the round oak table in the kitchen while they drank coffee and told me of their journey. They had retraced sections of Colvin's 1873 circuit of the vast, mostly private area west of Long Lake. Whitney's, Low's, Webb's, etc. had granted Robert permission based on vague promises to evaluate standing timber and existing levels of fire destruction and insect infestation, etc. They went in by Bog River, and at Low's dam had to carry over into the reservoir. F. feared the caretaker, one of the Frenettes from Tupper Lake, would recognize him, so he circled through the woods. Robert carried over the dam and met him a mile down the southern shore. On the way he spent an hour chewing the fat with the man—on the possibility of fires, the condition of the woods, various recent game violations and smuggling arrests, the fitness of the deer.

They carried the canoe into Big Deer Pond, Colvin's "Lost Lake." Robert rated it modestly beautiful and confirmed the gloomy aspect of the area that early writers had described. F.

said, rather, that it had "a good feeling to it." In the morning they left the canoe and a cache of food and visited the monument marking the "great" corner of Hamilton, Herkimer, and St. Lawrence counties—"the most hell-and-gone place" F. had ever seen outside old Mexico (as he insists on calling it)—and hiked another three miles to the upper Oswegatchie, leaving behind the burn line and attaining the edge of the virgin forest. They spent the rest of the day on the Oswegatchie, while F. teased big trout out of the water on a hand line.

I gather Robert kept up a steady patter. He was indefatigable as ever, to F.'s dismay. F. had no problem keeping up, but had more curiosity about each bog, creek, and ledge they stumbled across, and wanted to investigate. In the morning they traced a compass line cross-country to the Five Ponds, and soon entered a gallery of two-hundred-foot pines that they never emerged from that day. It reminded F. of stories he had heard about the woods when his father was a boy, that he'd never seen. Robert said he felt the hovering spirits of the last wolves and cougars, who had held out in the region. At Five Ponds, they stayed three days at a hunting camp and explored separate ponds and glacial ridges. Robert added notes and details for his guidebook.

On the second night an old man arrived, getting ready to open for hunting season. It was Bige Clark, from Cranberry, who had known Claude. He also had fresh corn liquor. They got drunk and told stories, and in the morning all three had hangovers. F. went into a funk that lasted for three days. Robert kept talking as they walked south on the remnants of the Red Horse Trail, and they almost came to blows far off in the remotest part of the state. But they observed silence for an hour, and soon began making neutral observations and comments. By the time they reached Beaver River, the storm had passed. There they spent the night in the hotel, which was full of flappers who had come up after a wedding in Utica.

They turned back east on the railbed, upriver, where the blueberries grew thick and fat, and from the neutral shadows observed the passing of one of Webb's last private rail cars.

—The railbed changes the shape of the land in your mind, Robert said. It is no longer itself, but some other thing.

They traversed moonscapes, where the dried logging slash had burned the soil to the rocks, and the blackened corpses of burned giants reached skyward like a prophecy.

—That all this should be private, Robert kept lamenting, the organic basis of our national identity.

They reached a vague area south of Partlow Lake.

—Around here Colvin shot a cougar, Robert said.

—I saw one as a lad, F. said, jumping across Osgood's River.

—Impossible, Robert said.

—Well, I saw it, F. said.

Robert said he believed extirpated animals still inhabited the collective mind.

—I don't know if Jung recognizes that subcategory, I said.

—It wasn't in my mind, F. said, I saw it.

They made their way across Whitney's, through cut and burned lands, and the ponds that George Washington Sears had visited in the eighties, zigzagged over to Lake Lila, on Webb's, then back over to Big Deer Pond and the canoe. It took them ten days. It took Colvin a month. They could have done it in five, Robert said, but there was enough country out there to stretch it out to three weeks.

—It's a half-million acres with no roads, he said. Someday it will belong to the people again.

We drank the last of many coffees, and Robert left to walk fifteen miles to Knollwood in the moonlight.

—He'll get there before dawn, F. said, after Robert walked out the door and left us at the table.

Rather than let the subject fester, I decided to tell F. the news.

First I got up and put a stick on the wood range. Oh, Arnold, I thought. Would this person have come into our lives were you alive? Am I terribly deluded?

I sat and looked at him. Something had altered him in the woods.

—You have a son, I said.

He turned inward as if exploring the untraveled quarters in there, and gazed around the kitchen. I became acutely aware of the hour, the coffee, the nature of the moment, and the unusual life that sustained us. Nietzche stretched at our feet under the table.

—How did you hear?

I told him.

—She isn't married, I said.

He mused.

—She can live on her own if she wants to, he said.

I told him she was staying at a private rooming house on Park Avenue, where cured TB patients sometimes moved before returning to normal life down below. He said how the night before he left for the lumber camp, after she had refused his proposal, he had driven over to Lake Placid from the hospital and visited one of the local bankers at his home. There he gave the man all his money, a sizeable savings, and told him to set up an account in Yvette's name, and to let her know about it, discreetly, as soon as possible. He had reserved a sizeable bribe for the banker's pocket.

—She might marry the doctor, he said, but I know Yvette. She'll keep her money to herself. What did they name him?

—Bartholomew, I said. Bartholomew Francis Germaine.

October 10. Central Park West. F. now on the payroll as Ray Balzac. Last month when I told him about Bartholomew, he still meant to leave. The subject hadn't come up for a while, and at that point it seemed unlikely he would be setting off for the west or Mexico anytime soon. That's when I took the initiative and induced him to stay. He is officially "employed," though his role in our lives cannot be so classified.

A week later I contacted Yvette Landry and met her in the living room at her house. The house mother hovered in the kitchen holding the baby. I could easily imagine F.'s pain at losing her black eyes, her spit curl, her trace of a Quebec accent and compact figure, now with full and leaking maternal bust. She apologized for her not-unpleasant perfume of milk and vomit. She had improved, she said, though she and the baby were under close observation. She listened, agreed to keep F.'s whereabouts confidential, acknowledged his fatherhood and her sizeable bank account. She regretted their separation and began to explain, but I told her not to. We agreed to speak once a month, until it became safe for the child and the father to meet.

A few days ago, for the train to New York, F. dressed in one of Arnold's charcoal pinstripes, homburg, and chesterfield. He might have been any Jewish banker en route to his Manhattan townhouse.

We got in at ten. My appointment was at ten the next morning. I put him in the guest room, to Mrs. Murphy's distress. She threw up her hands.

—You're a grown woman, Missus, but I hate to think what Mr. Arnold would say.

We took a cab to Logan's office on East 63rd. The exam took an hour. F. waited in the anteroom. Logan decided to put me in the hospital and remove the breast that night. I agreed, not for fear of death, but for the absolute necessity of finishing my work and finding out what happens next.

I am writing this on the fifth floor of Beth Israel, drugged, with a view up Irving Place toward Gramercy.

November 12 (?). Off morphine, with consequent sleeplessness, irritability, tears. But also improved bowels and clarity of mind.

Last week F. took the train north to winterize the house and annex and keep them open. Murphy now accepts him as an employee and an equal, if one with special privileges. She dotes on me, makes certain to change the sheets daily, though I only ask for twice a week, changes the dressing, makes tea, scones, curry, shepherd's pie. Every night a new apple or cherry pie. But the operation and the almost immediately ensuing market crash have thrown her into a brown study.

—All will be well, Missus. The Lord's will be done.

—We are in this together, Murphy, and nothing will make us let you go. We'll need to be frugal but we're perfectly secure. Now please take a walk and gather yourself. See what you can find us in the way of fresh meat or eggs, and bring home someone you know who needs a dinner.

The wound heals steadily and begins to itch. The "noble" oozing has stopped, the scab forms. Yesterday, stood before the mirror with the bandage off, naked above the waist. Wept for the first time, feeling foolish and vain.

Nov 16. Various institutional visits: the banker, the editors, the party meeting. The bank is weakened, yet private sources of good, conservative gold have been tapped to shore it up. It has closed—a "holiday," until conditions improve. In the meantime, the cash reserve at West 73rd and Central Park W. suffices.

Donald will keep publishing no matter what. As long as paper and the postal service survive, the magazine shall be published forth, he says. After half a day I limp home, exhausted.

The party meeting packed, rousing, festive, angry, triumphant: that strange political phenomenon of reveling in the doom your side predicted. But fractures are forming, the cracks of ancient and inscrutable origin. To one so aware of death, the conformism and hair-splitting grate.

Here reference to William's concepts and particulars bears scrutiny.

The male leadership spins its wheels, overwhelmed by good fortune. There will be character attacks, expulsions, dithering, before useful work takes place. Labor will be fertile, but the Soviet model won't work. Much can, and must, be accomplished outside its constricting orbit. One turns back to earlier templates of thought and practice.

As always, I hear Arnold's voice, and William's, and duty falls heavily.

Even with the crash, the knowledge of one's cancer predisposes people in one's favor, if it doesn't turn them away. TB has mythic resonance in the collective mind. This is something darker, lacking a redemptive theme. The general anxiety increases people's reaction, however. I ask for large favors, and they are granted without question. Note: make a list of all favors to request—activist, editorial, personal—before the novelty wears off.

Telegram from Vivien, who arrives on the Queen Mary in three weeks.

Nov 15. Letter from F., who prepared the buildings, then spent ten days at Cold River hunting with Rondeau. The hermit isolates himself partly to avoid drink, so when not hunting they drank tea and passed Rondeau's squeaky fiddle back and forth in the low-roofed cabin. F. shot a six-pointer and Rondeau a spike horn. They ate venison stews and meat pies, hot cakes, and potatoes. Rondeau knew of his bootlegging and would never talk.

On day six a couple of hikers from the Adirondack Mountain Club climbed over Ouluska Pass and pitched their tent in the clearing—a woman doctor and an engineer from Schenectady, who had both visited Rondeau before. Each carried a pint of rotgut rye, enough to make Rondeau dance around his clearing on one leg, sawing on his fiddle and giggling while the other three dos-à-dosed each other with an imaginary fourth to make a square.

Somehow the recent upheaval bypassed these men, for whom meaning depends so little on economy. Sufficiency is within their grasp, money a luxury or plaything—but only so long as their *habitat* survives. Their culture of solitude—or of minimal interdependence, based on pre-industrial skills—relies on meaningful expanses of forested geography lacking roads (and usually a sustaining woman somewhere in the wings.) By all rights, it is they who should be its chief defenders. But they will sell it out in the spirit of cheap resources when given the chance.

I speak generally, and not of F. or Rondeau specifically. What either might do should economic emergency force a destruction of the forest is unknown, but F. has proven himself capable of action. Rondeau's retreat from society may include the capacity to resist. What I might do, should it come to that point, remains a matter of conjecture.

On day ten, F. put the remaining venison quarter in his pack basket, wrapped in waxed paper, and carried it out via Corey's in a steady, light snowfall. It will cure in the cool cellar until I return.

Nov 30. Poring over old letters—from William, primarily, but also from Carl and Arnold. To read them in the aftermath of the war, the stock-market boom, and the recent crash makes their abstractions and posturing sound dated and specious. Yet, I respond to them with the same concrete emotions as of old, and I see nuances I missed when I first read them as an ambitious and callow postgraduate.

William, at Rye, 1909 (twenty years back): "That I write again so soon after the last letter only emphasizes how good it was to hear from you, and how much there is to tell. Yesterday I was rushed by an appt. with Chesterton, so mailed that last brief note. How much more I wanted to say! Your recent Rome letter sent me into a flurry of nostalgia. I remembered visiting Henry there when you were in Florence, when we met to discuss the new psychology out of Austria and the fires burning near St. Hubert's. You pushed me so on the pluralism talks. Grazie. We have had a decade-long colloquy and deepening bond. Your charm and grace inform every word I write. I no longer have a thought without referring it to your judgment in some way. Yet I feel I have failed your expectations. Well, I have tried and gotten as far as I will likely get. One is satisfied with the state of the work, however much remains to be done.

The summer has been alternately Englishy glum and humid, yet Sussex at least is colored with flowers and soft breezes, and peopled by yeomen and husbandmen speaking with mediaeval accents. Their ancient practices enliven and structure the landscape, the design of their husbandry expresses their lives through the shapes of the land. The very stuff of our heritage lies scattered about the landscape like geology itself, and with Conrad living right down the road. The roundedness of everything, the ancient pushing through the pavement into the immediate present so unlike our rawness, newness, our close-to-the-bone weathers. Darwin prevails in "New" England, and Canterbury still in Olde.

H. works all day. Alice and Peg cavort in Switzerland while here I dither and correspond with all manner of philosophical disputants and sycophants. But the soft evenings mean social engagements and the fellowship of Chesterton and Welles. The English have such manners and decency, despite their reserve, and are so wholesome as a race, far more than the half of our people who are ragged and deprived. Yet still I have felt cut off from my own desk and books, and the good companionship of the Shanty and our friends in Keene Valley.

You mentioned reactions to the truth book. There are questions, as you know. What I have emphasized over and over, as we discussed that evening in the Stoop, is that to recognize something as real, you cannot freeze it in time. It exists as a kind of potentiality until unfolding action frees it to be actualized. So you may only see it as part of the flux of concrete experience, which is the only reality we can speak of. This is the answer to Kant, and toward the dynamism of Bergson (a man of depth, wit, and kindness, as I discovered this summer).

This was the phrase that occurred to me during our tramp over the range that day eight years ago, when I was still a reasonably able pedestrian. The place has always freed my mind and stimulated my intellect, and it was only there that I began to see what Bergson meant by the elan. Something in the special character of the air and light. It makes you think how places have influenced the thinking that has come out of them, and how the very ideas themselves are embodied in geography.

It always reminds me of old Phelps and his ilk, who guided us when Putnam first bought the place. They were the truest radical empiricists, sweeping away cant and reliance on essences in their perception of the real. Likewise, they accepted the mystical as part of ordinary experience—if sometimes rather credulously. I first understood this when working on the religion lectures that fateful summer. We must emulate their view, their directness.

The Lake District was diverting, the mountains bare as the Altai, and the waters as limpid and expansive as ours. England is beautiful in its soft, round-edged way, and paradise for trampers. Alas, I am no longer able to see it on foot, which is how one needs to see it, and I doubt I shall return. So smooth and old compared to the Adirondacks and New Hampshire. We are so far behind it. We ourselves are in process, but I don't know if we shall ever catch up.

Dear, dearest Ros, Enjoy the rest of your stay in Rome. Remember me atop the Belvedere. Looking forward to our rendezvous at the Shanty in September, when the Europeans arrive with all their promising ideas and old-world neuroses.

Yours in fellowship and affection, WJ."

His heart was going, and he foresaw the end. The collegial praise—no doubt unfeigned—masks the flirtatious tone, the failing organism testing the residual sexual impulse. He was dead by fall.

January 2, 1930. The lake groans and booms in the night—"making ice," F. says. A smear of stars obscures the void. After venison on New Year's Eve (backstrap roasted with apples, potatoes, onions, and parsnips, and glazed with maple and brandy), walked across snow ridges all the way to the islands: F., Vivien, Rockwells Sr. and Jr., Nietzche sliding on the ice where the wind had swept it clean. Temp in high teens. Once or twice I fell behind, but the wind had died, making it seem mild, and the party waited for me.

Pressure cracks ran under our feet. Nietzche ran ahead into the dark. I worried he had fallen through, but he always came back, skidding and panting across the glazed surface. F. and Rockwell insisted the ice was safe. On the islands they built a fire of sticks and driftwood, and we toasted, from the bottle of champagne Rockwell had procured, the new decade and hopes for world.

F., Rockwell, and Viv lit cigarettes. Rockwell's dairy operation suffers continuous vandalism, he said: milk bottles broken, cows let loose, truck tires slashed. He fears poisoning or worse, and blames the local grange. He and Viv spoke of Kropotkin's autonomous local communities held together in a self-reliant mutual aid, and he marveled how easily the principle should translate for remote, rural communities exploited by capital—colonies of the south, in effect. The ideal sounds so typical of rural and frontier America, a kind of Arcadian essence completely nonexistent in reality. The colonized identifying with the colonizer.

F. listens, respectful yet alert. You wonder what he's thinking, but he was Bull Moose as a boy, and he pays attention.

New Year's Day, Rockwell and the boy ate breakfast and drove back to Asgaard, temp about 8 with hazy sunshine. At noon Viv emerged, and at 1:30 she and F. skated to the islands, where the ice was clear enough to see the bass and trout finning under their feet. I watched from the daybed in the upstairs lounge. They flew across the windswept surface with their arms wide, Viv wearing her absurd sheepskin greatcoat and stocking cap, and circled each other in wide figure-eights.

Viv staying upstairs in the Balsam Room, though in the night I thought she had gone downstairs. There had been a short exchange when she arrived in mid-December, along these lines:

—The caretaker, Ros? That's so Lawrentian.

—We aren't lovers.

—He looks like Valentino.

—Nonsense. He's not what you think he is.

—I'll have to find that out for myself.

—No doubt.

Part of me appreciated her assumption that illness and surgery had not blunted my drives. We're not so different after all.

On New Year's Eve they stayed up late, talking in the living room. I heard her come upstairs, and after an interval go back down.

So when she drank her coffee and disappeared outside, I knew it was to find F. The outcome was inevitable as soon as she wired her arrival from Europe. Nevertheless, when it happened, and then watching them on the ice, I felt a betrayal. I shall not let it disrupt the household, and I am prepared to deal roughly with them should either make it necessary.

March 18. The cab arrived from Saranac Lake at noon as planned. F. came out of the annex in new wool shirt and dress trousers, his hair combed back, his brogans polished. Arnold's gold watch chain crossed his chest. (Vivien and I watched from the upstairs lounge.) The cab door opened and Yvette's silk-stockinged legs swung around while he held open the door, then bent to receive from her the squirming plaid bundle that was his son. He cradled it awkwardly and stood back while she rose, accepted the bundle back, and followed him into the annex in her cloche and veil, her stylish wool coat. The cabbie sat in the kitchen and drank coffee for an hour. Then the annex door opened, and the parents and their child emerged into the warm sun. F. carried the boy, and the cabbie opened the door for Yvette. She climbed in and accepted the boy from his father.

The cabbie closed the door. F. watched as they headed down the driveway between the high snow banks.

—She's beautiful, Vivien said.

—Next time we can hold him, I said.

April 12. Stranded by mud. Full melt on lake and land, spring holes in the driveway, a washout around the culvert where beavers dammed the creek. F. says he can trap them alive and move them, but they found their way here from oblivion, and we will just have to accommodate them.

Along with his duties, F. is designing the boathouse he will build for the Morbachs this summer. Vivien has found her muse and produced strong work. The lovers are in full creative cry, whereas I am blocked and unproductive, dulled somehow in the mind but not in the passions.

We finished Sunday breakfast alone, the dog asleep under the table after a run, his legs twitching and a fire snapping in the wood range. F. was in the annex at his drafting table.

—I've come between you, she said.

—Don't be absurd. The question is what you intend for each other.

—He told me his name. He told me how you found him. He says he killed a man at the lumber camp and buried him under the floor.

—He shouldn't have told you that. It's uncertain. He has a reckless streak.

—You saved him.

—You can't save anybody. The dog liked him.

She leaves for San Francisco tomorrow, then returns in August.

July 19. Bread lines in New York, Albany, Montreal, Syracuse. Strikes on the New York Central; the B&M men laid off from the mills in Tupper and Fine gather near the railheads in Faust and Conifer. More men than ever are available to fight summer fires, more living off the land, poaching. In Saranac, more women supporting families with sanitarium jobs.

A small settlement has formed at the lumber ruin, which F. discovered when he hiked in to fish the beaver pond. They snare rabbits, trap trout, jack deer, bait bears. You wish they wouldn't, but it's hard to deny them. F. goes back every few days with a pack basket of bread, canned fruit and beans, coffee, sugar, tobacco, bacon. He also takes Arnold's violin. One of the men has a harmonica, and another a "Jew's" harp. Every man knows a song.

One cool evening when the flies were manageable, I followed F. and Nietzche to the camp. There was a fire outside under the pine, and smaller fires and lean-tos scattered around the clearing and down toward the water. About thirty men sat around outside, though others may have been nearby in the dark. There were a couple of women and scrawny youngsters. They started singing and drinking mixed, leftover liquor around 5, just about when we got there. Their pine-duff smudges stung the eyes and nose, and carried strange memories and associations. F. rosined his bow and played something slow in a minor key, then ran together a few jigs and schottisches. Somebody started playing spoons, and a couple of men whirled each other. The tune ended on a crescendo, with a great cheer. Then the man with the harmonica played songs he had learned in Texas, and F. harmonized behind him, and they collaborated on two polkas with the Jew's-harpist trying gamely to keep up. Around nine the tone changed. It wasn't a hymn-singing crowd, but it fell to the same level of nostalgia and bathos, and ended on a few slow, popular ballads from the nineties.

F. had started to pack up the violin by the firelight when a man came up to him, a man with ravaged teeth, a gaunt face, and white whiskers. His pants were held up and boot soles tied together with twine, and he wore a smoke-and-pitch-stained jacket.

—Hey, I know you, he said. Ain't you Fran Germaine, used to run the power line crew out of Lake Clear for Smith? I heard you was dead from the bootleggers, or down in old Mexico hiding from John Law. We all thought you was a shit-heel and a company man, but you don't seem so bad now.

—I'm Ray Balzac, F. said. Lots of people get us confused, but I'm right here and he's in Mexico, or dead, just like you say.

—Okay, Fran—I mean Ray. I get the picture.

I had never seen him flare so ferociously. He grabbed the man by his jacket front and picked his feet off the ground. Nietzsche barked and worried the man's trouser leg.

—There's no picture to get, mister, see? I'm Ray Balzac and that guy you were talking about is dead.

—Okay, okay, the man said and tried to rip his jacket away. But F. threw him back into a cluster of men sitting on the ground, who scuttled away with a rattle of tin cups.

We left by the light of F.'s lantern, Nietzsche with the low growl in his chest, and a strange thrill of horror in mine. We heard angry voices, then loud laughter. I worried the group would do the man more violence, but F. said they would merely mock him, then shun him, and he would probably wander off soon.

—He was a good worker, F. said. I hated to rough him up, but

I had to.

—In accord with your reputation.

I was sharp with him, but tolerant inside. His outburst at first seemed like rage, as if the man he insisted had died still inhabited the Belgian trenches and the Mexican canyons of his mind. I couldn't have accepted that. But on reflection I saw it was measured and cold, theatrical. I had known no one with this ability to slip in and out of personae since Carl. Any regret on F's part, you felt, came as much from the regression it represented as the violence. For he never lost control of his emotions. He used them with cunning to achieve a predictable outcome, and he knew his man. It was a useful skill.

We had reached the flats along Moose Creek when we heard Stephen Foster, in four-part harmony, carrying through the woods like a choir. "Hard Times Come Again No More." The phantom under the floor boards must have shivered.

Over the next two years, Orloff's journal mentions Legs Diamond's assassination and the repeal of the Volstead Act, the Winter Olympics in Lake Placid, her growing dissatisfaction with the Stalinist left, and support of the New Deal—but the entries lack the previous years' narrative energy. That energy probably went into her short book, Politics and Pragmatism, now the work she is chiefly known for, and her political activism. The novelty of Germaine had worn off. She seldom mentions him, and when she does it is to report on the completion of one of his new camps on Lake Aurora, or his journey with Bob Marshall to the Brooks Range, where he shot moose and caribou and spent a winter among Gwich'in Indians in the south-slope village of Wiseman. Orloff herself traveled in Europe, alone and later with Vivien, whose eccentricity had mellowed with her continued (if intermittent) relationship with Germaine. In the south of France, the two women helped establish a way station for refugees from the growing Spanish fascism, and came home to assist in the organization and funding of the Abraham Lincoln Brigade. The journal resumes in Lake Aurora in 1935, with some of its old vigor and with references to Germaine.

May 15, 1935. Eagle Point. Three weeks for the inner life to enter the old rhythm, for the world to fall away. Three years of prolonged *outward* direction, and you crave the momentariness of life lived day to day, especially here. (Freud's *Psychopathology of Everyday Life* one of literature's great titles.) Enough for the loon to call, the wind to shift, the first swallows to announce their arrival by wheeling around the bay before nesting in the boathouse rafters, and for the inner voice to cease.

F. is always there, fusing intention and action, except for the odd times when his demons rise. At any rate, the place now hews to his mental rhythm, the maintenance proceeding at an orderly, seasonal pace with sufficient outside assistance—the ice cut and covered with sawdust in the ice house, the boats painted, varnished, and protected in their exquisite new house, the "controlled" logging operation well established. We are a small, non-union jobs program, and much of F.'s time is taken managing the stream of job seekers walking a mile down the driveway from the state highway. There is a new bunkhouse out behind the barn near the creek, and a stream of itinerant workers and laborers come and go. Most will move on soon to WPA jobs nearby or in the south. Next week a photographer will come to document their situations. F. keeps them busy, and their comings and goings barely affect the peace. Arnold's ghost no longer haunts me with its expectations. It has become the place he always hoped it would be.

June 3. Saturday. Yesterday odd, like a window opening on one of those magic-box dioramas. The flies thick by 10, the air and water still, mist rising from the glassy surface. The herons, the eagles on the point, the loons—so evident in the first weeks after ice-out—all on their nests now, out of sight. Each year it is a kind of temporary abandonment, until they emerge again in late July with their young.

Viv, back from New York at the end of May, sat with me on the porch drinking too much coffee while F. managed a crew cutting firewood behind the barn. We heard their laughter, the zing of the cross-cut, the thunk of the maul opening the splits, then a motor coming down the driveway. Soon an old Model A truck, painted green and with its wooden side racks covered by a canvas tarp, rolled into the yard and came to a halt. A man stepped out and looked around. He wore a short ponytail, his black hair streaked with gray, denim overalls, and a green slouch hat. A job seeker, I thought. But there was a woman sitting in the cab with a child in her arms, and few of the men looking for work arrived in trucks.

Viv took her mug and went down to greet and talk to the man, who had ambled down to the water's edge and looked out over the bay with his hands in his back pockets. She spoke to him, and he turned and answered. In a moment he held out his hand, and they shook. They walked back to the truck. He leaned on a fender, she put a foot on the running board, and they talked. She looked in the window and said something. Then the man led Viv around to the back of the truck and threw open the tarp, revealing ten or twelve stacks of nesting pack and laundry baskets, all of ash splints, some with intricate sweetgrass details. I learned of the details later, but I could see the baskets from the porch, gleaming patterns of wood and air, beautiful and useful circumscriptions of space.

The man leaned on the fender with his arms folded while Viv climbed the stairs onto the porch.

—He's going around selling baskets to the hardware stores and tourist shops. He heard we were logging and wants to know if we have any black ash trees he can buy. He needs them straight, fifty to sixty feet, high crowns.

—Ask François.

—His wife's pretty. There's something about him.

Her expression was quizzical, and she returned to the car with her hands in the back pockets of her slacks, as his had been. They talked, then she led the way around the other side of the barn.

Nothing happened. Eventually I went down to the truck and looked in the open window. The woman looked back at me with an open, untroubled face. The girl in her lap holding a wooden rattle wore the same expression.

—I'm Ros, I said.

—Hi Ros. I'm Glenda.

—Would you like to come up for some coffee?

—All right.

The child entertained herself with her rattle and Nietzche while Glenda drank coffee and looked at the water. She wore a cotton summer dress and no shoes, smoked two or three cigarettes, and said little except when I asked her something. She was from Hogansburg, she said. She wasn't married to Emile yet, but he was a good man. You seldom thought about the Iroquois still living on both sides of the St. Lawrence and scattered around the mountains, though every northern trade included a few, and some French Indians from Quebec. She looked Indian, around thirty. The girl looked Indian, too.

Vivien came back alone, shaking her head. She gave the sign and I joined her in the kitchen.

—They know each other from before. He was a bootlegger, a Canadian.

—Emile, I said, remembering the name from F.'s accounts.

—Right. I told Fran to take him up to the porch, but he told the men to break for lunch and took Emile out to look at trees.

From the kitchen we watched them come in an hour later. They stopped at the truck. Emile took down a stack of baskets and they held them up to the light, turning them over to examine the bottom weave. Emile then pointed out the intricate cross-weave of the rim. Other men gathered and stood watching, their hands in their pockets or smoking. Emile reached inside the bed of the truck and extracted a darker basket, wider at the waist and taller, and with a heavy, hand-stitched, green canvas harness. It had a rich, oiled finish and brass nameplates, and was interwoven with sweetgrass designs. One of the men went to the bunkhouse and came back with a small rifle (a single-shot 7 mm Remington, as F. told me later). He turned a screw on the side, broke it into two parts and stood it inside the finished basket. The men nodded in admiration. The man reached in his pocket, handed Emile some bills, and took one of the unfinished baskets. More palaver ensued. Emile gave the finished basket to F., who first demurred and then accepted, at Emile's insistence.

F. stalled on the kitchen porch before he came in. Finally, he opened the door and entered, rubbing his hands on his pants and looking around. He waved Emile in behind him.

—I see you all met, he said.

I stood.

—Hello. Ros Orloff, I said, extending my hand.

—Emile Jacobs, he said. This is for you, he said, placing one of the big, round laundry baskets on the floor.

They all took seats and Fran poured coffee. Four good, solid black ash trees had been found and blazed, F. said. If we didn't mind, Emile would come back after he sold all his baskets and drag out some eight-foot lengths.

—They make the best baskets, Emile said. Strong and light. I'll come back in the fall with more, and snowshoes too. I'll bring you some.

After that he would move to Brooklyn for the winter, and work riveting steel girders high on the (aptly named) "Empire" State Building.

By then it was midafternoon. Work had vanished from the day's agenda. We switched from coffee to iced tea. Glenda put the girl down for a nap on the living room couch and lay down beside her. Soon she was snoring prodigiously.

When I walked back into the kitchen, a bottle of homemade peach brandy had appeared. Both the men and Viv had small snifters before them on the table. Emile was telling F. how he'd come to Eagle Point.

—I knew you were here, he said. Old woman told me.

—Another old woman, F. said.

—No, same one. She told me I'd find ash here, but also that I'd find the man who came out of the river in winter. That's her daughter with the girl in there. She's Longhouse, Bear clan. Real powerful. They don't like drinking, but I grew up Catholic.

—Don't do it much myself these days, F. said, taking a nip.

—Lots of people died from it, Emile said, looking down and drinking to their memories.

Neither of them drank much after that, but their tongues loosened. I drank one and Viv had a second and a third. Tipsy and forward, she asked him to explain how the woman was powerful, and what he meant by the Longhouse.

—They're like old times, he said. Not Christians. Though some of them go to church. The women are the clan bosses and tell the men what to do. Husbands take the women's names. They follow the seasons and organize the secret societies. Some of it's from back in the days of the feather Indians, some goes back to Handsome Lake, the prophet from Onondaga. He was in the Revolution, with England. That was a very bad time for Iroquois people. After it, Handsome Lake had a vision and saved the old ways. These Longhouse women tell the future from dreams. It was that same woman told me about that guy who died in Montreal.

—What? F. said.

—Yeah. He didn't die because of anything to do with liquor. It was a Mohawk girl from Hogansburg, fourteen. She worked on his cousin's dairy farm, and that guy—Barney, his name was—kept raping her. Warrior society heard about it, then the old woman dreamed about him in that place on St. Sulpice Street. The warriors sent a veteran like you, a real hard guy, to take care of him. We figured it was all right, since the only reason Barney would be there was to rub you out. But I guess that's why she dreamed of you crossing the river, and why she sent me here now. Because of your cousin, and because you should know.

F. didn't move. He didn't say a thing. His expression never changed. He got up very slowly, turned, and walked out onto the porch. There he lit a cigarette and followed the path down to the dock.

Glenda and the baby slept until three. Emile and Viv kept talking like nothing had happened. I, disturbed, walked around looking for F.—in the boathouse, the barn, the bunkhouse, the Stoop, the cold cellar. It was unlike him to behave like a wounded animal. I followed the trail along the ledges and out to the point, where the arbutus and sheep-laurel blossoms bloomed alongshore, and partridge berry under the balsams. Something about the encounter had put me in the mind of mortality: mine, Arnold's, the men of F.'s and my generation. William and Carl.

The day had turned dull and sultry, the swallows scooping big, dark mayfly drakes off the bug-littered surface. I had not felt so doom-ridden since F. had arrived, even when I heard my diagnosis. Those two occasions had non-mortal outcomes thus far (disregarding the lumber-camp phantom), so I persuaded myself this time would be the same.

I came to the bridge and followed it over the water. Stepping from the wood planks onto the lichenous granite on the far side, I felt my rational underpinnings slipping and the field of consciousness warping and shifting. I remembered how William had called his crisis on Marcy, while writing the religion lectures, a "Walpurgisnacht." Mine was a feeling unaccompanied by panic or fear of death, but rather a slow upwelling of dread—not of the void, but of the possibility that nothing had been effected, that one's time had been ill spent. Of having skated along the surface as on a frozen lake, despite strenuous efforts to know the world, to effect change and make right. A vain exercise to inject meaning into an illusion.

The feeling persisted while I sat on the stone bench that looked out toward the islands and Whiteface in the distance. The swallows wheeled faster over the water, which lapped the sloping granite shore. Here was our landscape at its dourest, the greens lost in the humid murk, the sky like dishwater. I couldn't trace the feeling or identify its seed, though I had felt its first twinges while regarding the past circling back on F. like swallows after bugs, through the vehicle of an old woman's dream. This was not one of Freud's dreams. It was more like one of Carl's, or all of ours. It was death calling out to him from the future. I felt our stories flowing together, and the irrevocability of our deeds.

The obsessive concerns of my student years and of my exchanges with William and Carl rose up again, which I had regarded as abstractions to be made concrete through action. Right then I would have grasped at any of them with all the ardor of the converted—the homing instinct of the apostate nearing the end, returning to the fold.

I heard Williams say, "The immediate flow of sensible experience is our only experience of reality and a constantly changing much-at-once." At that instant I felt a stay let go like a mainsheet in a gale. I too had received my notice, and I knew I must discover what I most needed to effect in the time remaining

In a moment the feeling had gone. The scene became a muted but lovely late spring day, the lake and its environs pulsating with life. I knew I had glimpsed a world beyond the veil, but that the field of common reality held sufficient interest for the moment, and for the completion of my days.

Back in the kitchen F. sat with Emile, drinking coffee. Viv had gone upstairs to nap. Glenda and the child sat on the dock playing with Nietzche. Eveline had started roasting a pork loin and making pies. When I asked where he went, F. said he had gone out to check on the men.

Emile and the woman stayed late, then overnight, and finally left, after endless talking and coffee, at about eleven this morning.

Young Bartholomew Germaine attended the new Northwoods School in Lake Placid and visited his father at Eagle Point on a regular basis, becoming close to both his "aunts," Viv and Ros. His stepfather acquired poliomyelitis from a patient and died in 1936. Orloff's cancer also returned in 1936, after she developed a pain in her left hip. She was hospitalized in Saranac Lake and, on recovering, returned to Eagle Point. Most of her accounts of her decline are brief and to the point.

Bob Marshall had moved to Washington, D.C., and started the Wilderness Society, of which both Orloff and Germaine were founding members. Marshall died in 1939.

While not central to her relationship to Germaine, the long entry on her meeting Carl Jung, the Swiss psychoanalyst, is included for the light it sheds on the intellectual history of the Adirondacks— or rather intellectual history in the Adirondacks. Few traces of "bully" Roosevelt-ism, pragmatism, or Jungian psychology persist in the regional mind, or even in the founding legislation of the Adirondack Park. You may argue that the "sacred grove" archetype somehow stands behind the concept of conservation, and certainly any pragmatic examination of the pros and cons of the current structure would necessitate a conservationist conclusion—with perhaps a more elevated awareness and attention to the human environment. At some level, Marshall and Orloff's vision had an impact, and here Orloff's notion of interlocking, self-reliant communities protecting the common resource would have been a better model than the current bureaucratic hodgepodge.

Those are tenuous arguments, however. Jung merely dropped in and did no work there, and while James's connection was much deeper and he often mentioned the ways place and mind interacted, neither his name nor his work is remembered. Neither is the region's abolitionist history anywhere evident; it exists as an abstraction and artifact of the distant frontier. Steiglitz and O'Keeffe in Lake George, and David Smith in Bolton Landing caused not a blip, made no impression on the regional consciousness—except as local eccentrics. Rockwell Kent was reviled in Ausable Forks. Nobody grows up Transcendentalist in the Adirondacks just because Emerson spent a couple of weeks there.

Yet, their presences resonate down the decades. The place changed those who stayed there—and changed their work in many cases. In the current cultural moment, you might say the Adirondacks have no intellectual character, except that of sentimental distortion and kitsch—and the worship of wealth. Even the language and written expressions of conservation have become degraded and one-dimensional. It makes the place feel protected and beautiful, if brain-dead.

May 17, 1937. So it is decided. We remain at Eagle Point for the duration, all together except for Murphy, who has chosen to remain in New York. Claridge is happy to come whenever required. When it is over, I will join Arnold on the island.

F. has hired Wendy Featherstone, a nurse, to live with us and help. She is delightful (if rather patrician), expert, and matter-of-fact, qualities we need around here for the moment. She belonged to the bootlegging gang of old, it seems. Viv has got hold of herself at last, and manages to work in her studio over the barn most days, drinking coffee and smoking.

The boy is entering that age of male perfection in the run-up to adolescence. He couldn't be happier, except that everybody's worried about Aunt Ros. Still, here we are, ice-out just past, a sense of promise in the air. It is the strangest sense of festivity when you forget what's going on, which we all do for hours at a time. He will be out of school next week and here for the summer, when he will have friends, sail the guideboat with his sailing rig, and go hiking with Robert, his father, and Aunt Viv.

F. has made a cane of stout spruce, with a ferrule and handle of raw deer hide. I depend on it on my daily walk along the ledges, out to the island, down the driveway and back along the outlet, with Nietzche flopping gamely along on his bandy hips. Most days I can go, but not all.

The *Life* article: Orloff's widow publishes book on mentor, suggests his philosophy drive economic policy. Typical Luce(ifer). But the pictures show the place to good effect, the women in their white tulle on the porch, rowing the Hanmer, and even Nietzche. There I am on the green at Radcliffe with Gertrude, and there on the Queen Mary with Arnold. Robert and F. (unidentified) in their high boots atop Marcy, with wide grins and sunburns. Rich Jews at their leisure, with nothing better to do than plot against property. On the next page William and me at the Shanty in 1902, he alone at Chocorua. Shots of worker bunkhouse, logging, trail system and F.'s lean-to on the point, concluding with a full page of me standing on the island near Arnold's marker with Martha R., whose book was last year's hit.

Later on the 17th. The dissolution not hard to imagine and anticipate, but impossible to prepare for.

Letter from Carl: "I have found that subjects with strong beliefs or notions of an afterlife, and who pay attention to preparing for it, do better at the end. Regard it with equanimity. Death is always coming."

To maintain equanimity in pain? Fear is not my concern, though I am afraid, yes. I have no particular framework other than that spirit of inquiry and exploratory psychology we thought we were inventing thirty years ago. It encompassed religion and philosophy and showed us their origins (or the differences between "fruits and roots"). In the way of process, much of what emerged so swiftly in the exchanges between Cambridge and Vienna, then among the people around Putnam, Davidson, and James, has been borne out in history, to the worst possible effect. But the matrix of those ideas, I am convinced, contains access to truth.

What I can depend on is the certainty of Arnold's presence when it comes; the knowledge of the invisible reality that William, despite his inability to believe, always accepted.

Carl goes on: "You have made of pragmatism what it never got to be before the war, that Dewey and James could never body forth on their own. It needed to steep and be tempered in the collective psyche these last difficult years. It makes me see where North America was heading back then, and got sidetracked from. For you, good—good work that will last. A sense of wrapping up and passing it on. So much came from James, whom I came to admire and feel affection for. His theories of types and association laid the foundation for our work."

He will come in October and prays I will last. In the meantime, he stays alone in his tower up Lake Zurich, writing the incomprehensible *Mysterium*. Back in Zurich it is still his ménage with those hard-bitten Protestant women, but the summer seminars are all smart young American and British girls, and he dallies when he can. They sustain him.

June 2. Slow walk with Nietzche. We are pathetic. Muted sun glinting on rocks and gunmetal water surface. The gnawing in hip and thigh. Nevertheless . . . still here.

Flies? Hello sister Black Fly, I welcome thee in all thy spectacular particularity. None of the creatures embodies more meaning than thee.

Only now and nothing else, all at once. Bird song, wildflower, fluid surroundings of all.

Stop to rest by lean-to on the point. The dog pants in the dirt. After five minutes I notice the half dozen snapping turtles lying like rocks over their nests in the sandy duff at the top of the rise. They gaze with profound detachment toward the lake, utterly gravid, the size of truck tires. Then they kick to cover their eggs and wallow exhausted over the lichens to the water, where they drift on the surface like jellyfish till their strength returns.

July 7. Rain and cold. F. starts a fire downstairs and we have a meeting, F., Viv, and I. I tell them how I want it. Claridge would allow no discussion of it, but when he left, there on the mantle was a paper with the necessary words.

I tell them that if it comes to that, I want F. to do the job. Viv is weeping, F. dark and quiet, but I keep it as straightforward as possible. It is not my preferred course.

The weather makes me want it sooner rather than later.

July 28. Occasionally a day like this, a respite in the succession of systemic failures. Today all is possible, Hitler will fail, dinner will be excellent, the wine the finest we ever drank. Toasts all around the kitchen table, to me, to F. and his survival, to Viv and her new pictures, to death. Then more, the infinity of deserving people and concepts, and we are all laughing and inebriated, and fall away from each other at last—Wendy and I to the porch bed; the others to the lake, the studio, the annex.

August 29. 11 a.m. Wendy leaves with the syringe. Oh, the blessing of it. An hour of delightful oblivion, then sometimes of clarity before the agony resumes.

The leg will not set, Claridge says, but it is a hairline fracture. I may still hobble, carefully, though with the wrong pressure it could snap at any time. So I am confined to the daybed on the porch.

Today old photos—the oldest, Arnold's mother at sixteen on a village street in the Pale, taken by an itinerant portraitist, her eyes and posture Arnold's. I, at the same age, in tennis whites, then in old-fashioned hiking skirt and bloomers on the hitch-up-Matildas at Avalanche Lake, with a party from the Shanty. Then with Ferenczi and Carl at the Shanty in '09.

William's absence that day hung over everything. Though Putnam had invited Ferenczi, it was supposed to be as much William's occasion. For Helen and me it was purely a gay interlude. The old bourgeoises, we felt, had generalized their bowel complaints and affairs with young servants into a dogma, ascribing to them the appearance of scientific rigor. The bodily processes they openly discussed shocked the lesser attendees, for whom psychoanalysis and its emphasis on childhood sexuality were only beginning to sink in. They idolized Freud, though when the details of his system were discussed, they blinked and harrumphed in embarrassment.

In our beds in the farmhouse, we laughed over the men's and women's bathing pools in the creek—separate but close enough together that "accidental" sightings of nude bathers were common and handled with a kind of supremely benign indifference and politesse. Oh, how titillating and Bohemian! Across the road on the lower lake, the club members regarded us as a haven of nymphs and satyrs to be tolerated for the fame and probity of James and Putnam—but also to be avoided.

Heraldic shields, crafted by Dr. Emerson, the philosopher's son, of secret hiking and woodcraft societies hung around the dining quarters attached to the rear of the old farmhouse. At dinner we felt ourselves admitted to something like the secrets of a new continent from which Freud and Boas were bringing home reports of unexplored geographies of meaning and understanding that were our chief interests as graduate aesthetes. While we were there to represent the female principle, we told ourselves we were not mere window dressing. Our own interest was in the older men's intellectual vigor and freedom, the daring and outré element of it that men our own age lacked, obsessed as they were with rowing, archery, and their genealogies.

At dinner on the night of the guests' arrival, Helen was seated beside Ferenzci and I beside Jung, who seemed to swell and take it as an honor, or perhaps as the kind of exotic hospitality Eskimos or Tahitians might extend. I made clear immediately my reading of Freud's *Civilization*, and my long connection with William and his thought. Ah, he said, in his drawling Schweizerduetsch, a lady pragmatist, and a Jewess. An attractive if unusual combination. We must discuss it.

With that, he ignored me and continued his conversations with the gentlemen, often in German and with reference to Bergson, Wagner and the Niebelungen, Mahler's Lied von Der Erde, the Sacred Grove of Zeus, the incest taboo, experiments with schizophrenics on both sides of the Atlantic. Freud sulked and excused himself, citing his intestinal discomfort and the wretched boiled food. The guests rose and bid him good evening with excruciating awkwardness. The courses of boiled and roasted meat, boiled potatoes and vegetables rolled on, the conversation avoiding any mention of William's absence and illness, or the controversy surrounding Freud and Jung.

When the time arrived for dessert and cordials in The Stoop (the small pavilion beside the creek), Jung invited Helen and me to come along. Perhaps we would honor them with an American folk song. At the Stoop a huge fire had been laid in the fireplace against the September chill, coffee and cigars handed out, and a bottle of brandy opened. In William's absence no one stood forth to guide the conversation, leaving it open to the strongest egos, which in this case belonged to Jung and Ferenczi, Freud having surrendered the field. I accepted a cigar and pretended to smoke it, while also drinking coffee and a cordial, then another; and given the opening by Ferenczi, held forth drunkenly on Ethical Culture in the context of Emersonian idealism, all of my callow student's observations received with grave mock seriousness by the gentlemen.

Toward midnight Putnam conferred with Jung on the hike planned for Haystack the next day. Jung turned to me and said, You'll join us, I hope, and Miss Liebling, as well.

At the time, I was fit from tennis and riding. In summers past I had hiked the Range among the parties William organized and led, so I was familiar enough with the ground to be included as a way finder. Of course we accepted. We were both drunk, and it was late. The men stood, and we excused ourselves to our beds in the farmhouse, having escaped the duty to perform "Go Tell Aunt Rhody" or "Oh, Susannah."

In the morning we left at dawn. I wore heavy boots and linen trousers. It was assumed we would complete the entire seventeen miles and six peaks, beginning on Rooster Tail, making our way along the ridgetops and the five aligned summits of the Wolfjaws, Gothics, Basin, and Haystack, with its precipitous drop into Panther Gorge, and back by way of the lower lake. Dinner would be held for us, as we would not likely return until after dark.

Almost immediately Helen paired off with Ferenczi's young assistant, Arnold Orloff, and I with Jung, who wore lederhosen and fine heavy hiking brogues with his socks pulled to this knees. On his head he had a Tyrolean cap with a brush of chamois hair sewn into the brim. Hattie Shaw, the cook, had given us a picnic, which Putnam carried in his rucksack, and canteens of spring water for each—five in all. In addition, Jung carried in his leather rucksack a rawhide wineskin, his meerschaum, and pouch of tobacco.

Within an hour we had risen above the morning fog and hardwoods and into the krummholz. Around us rose the steepest and sharpest Adirondacks, in jagged array. The blueberries and other low heaths above timberline had turned russet. Autumn reds, oranges, and yellows formed a belt of color from just below our altitude down to about fifteen hundred feet, where the first signs of chlorophyllic decay could be seen amid the deep green hardwood canopy. The valley and the lakes reposed under a layer of fog, and the raw slides and cliffs bore dark streaks of condensing fog and dew.

—Extraordinary, Jung said at intervals, gazing about. No sign of husbandry, a shepherd's shack, nor so much as a hay meadow. Just raw, untended forest.

Gradually we moved ahead of and above the others as the trail climbed toward Gothics. Jung took the lead on his well-muscled, blond-haired thighs, and with some burst of second wind I sailed along on his heels. On a craggy lookout just below the summit, with the rest of the party lagging, he paused and opened his throat in an Alpine yodel he called the "Haying Prayer." Herdsmen delivered it in call-and-response across yawning chasms, he said, in thanks for bountiful grain and fecund herds, the echoes crossing back and forth over each other in a wild cacophony. Normally it was sung in two parts, one answering the other, but he sang both, with the echoes seeming to take half a minute to return from the opposing face of Gothics until they met and passed through each other in vibrating oscillations that unhinged the mind. In that instant he was a pre-Christian tribesman and nomad, the uber-mensch he aspired to be in his writings and in his complex relations with colleagues.

Within half an hour we had dashed across the top of Gothics, down the saddle to the top of Basin, where we awaited the others. On the summit we drank from our canteens. Carl loaded and lit his pipe, cupping the match to shield it from the wind. He took the wineskin from his rucksack, showing me how to hold it above the mouth and squeeze it like an udder to catch the gleaming stream. Inevitably the stream splashed my face and dribbled on my blouse, causing him to grab it from me to avoid waste. Nevertheless, I managed a few deep gulps, and on top of the exertion and the early hour, the effect was immediate.

—So, he said, admiring the cliffs on nearby Gothics, you've been a student of James, and absorbed the philosophy of pragmatism and the healthy mind. It sounds as much a product of New England as baked beans and boiled cabbage. Please tell me what it is.

The request shocked me. Was it a taunt rather than an authentic query?

—It merely describes a technique for arriving at a truth, I said, and not a philosophy. The healthy-mind movement was a thread of American thought James had identified, not developed.

I realized, as I gave it, how unsystematic and jury-rigged the whole thing sounded.

—Good. Your grasp is strong. True, it has the virtue of originality, despite its homage to Hegel and the Scottish mystics, and Bergson of course. And what a mind, James's. Brilliant, catholic, promiscuous in the best sense. That is the necessary condition to approach the unconscious. He is correct to throw off the yoke of Kant and Descartes and admit the ubiquity and unexceptional nature of the nonrational, the mysterious, the random. He has not accepted the correctness of psychoanalysis, alas, despite his openness to its principles. It is somewhat patronizing, yes, and puzzling too, except for the fact of his youthful psychosis. The fear, you see; his father, et cetera. He has afflictions about the heart and bowels, and the very philosophy itself sounds constipated and unfocused, an attempt to force these disparate forces of his unconscious into a system, to rationalize and synthesize Christianity and science. As interesting as it is in itself, it is neither, as you say, philosophy nor psychology. It reflects James's mind rather than the collective mind.

—Psychoanalysis, on the other hand, goes to the very core of that mind. The flare-up of his heart condition that keeps him from joining us derives, I am sure, from his terror of Freud, who as you know is suffering incontinence from my resistance to the seduction theory. Well, it is part of the process. We are enacting the origin myth of our discipline, that is all. James must submit to analysis for his work to be made palatable, though he is terrified to look inside. As well he might be, I would add. He must do this before he dies, or his work will lapse into obscurity. And what can we say about Bergson, really? It is all sensation and no thought.

He held up the wineskin and opened his mouth to drink from the stream. The air hummed with light, the hard-as-blue-ice sky, the sun on rock. He swallowed, passed me the wineskin. When I took it he wiped his mouth, drew on his pipe, and looked around at the slides on Gothics, Basin, Noonmark, the lakes in their deep cleft.

—You expect to see mountain goats, he said. Chamois, or something. Are there goats? No? Pity. At any rate, Freud makes James see the template of the intellectual future, and it terrifies him. It aggravates his father hatred. These experiments of his with mediums, scopolamine, cannabis, they show him the outlines of consciousness and the collective mind, but they are not leading him to the resolution of his thought and psyche that he needs to make. They lead him away from the necessary confrontation with the self. It is this look inside we place at the center of all self-knowledge. For you, too, it goes without saying. Beyond that, in the emphasis on intuition, the rejection of logic, he avoids making—I say, here's Putnam.

Indeed, the other four appeared over the rim of the summit and found us eviscerating my mentor, or so was my semi-addled impression at the time. Mr. Putnam looked confused as he approached us, surprised, I suspect, to find a celebrated European scholar drinking wine on a mountain top with an unmarried Jewish female.

—We were discussing James and his philosophy, Carl told him. Wonderful chap, too bad he couldn't be here. I would have loved to have shared all this—he made a sweeping motion with his hand—with him.

—Yes, yes, of course. Old James, Putnam said. He loves this tramp. Let's have a snack, shall we?

He smeared bacon grease on pieces of rough camp bread and placed strips of bacon and cheese on them. In the international spirit I accepted one, and at that altitude and in the flush of exertion and wine, it tasted magnificent. We washed it down with spring water from our canteens.

Putnam was a bit short with Carl, having appointed himself Freud's chief exponent in the U.S. He fully blamed Jung not only for Freud's "inflamed appendix," but for William's illness as well. In fact, it was the beginning of William's decline and death, in a few months' time.

—Wasn't it here he wrote the religion lectures? Carl said, finishing his bacon and relighting his meerschaum.

—Well, here and New Hampshire, yes, Putnam said.

—They're his best, don't you think? He looked from Putnam to the others, to me.

—Of course they're brilliant, Putnam sniffed. But pure research. I prefer the essays on radical empiricism.

—Really? Tell me what they say.

—Simply that experience is the sole measure of reality. One state of mind follows another. Beyond that it is hard to draw a sharp distinction between the subject and the object, the outer and the inner.

Putnam waved an arm as if to encompass the Range, Giant,

Dix, the whole corrugated and multi-hued field of perception.

—Yes, of course. He would say that. I'll have to read it.

Within another half-hour we had again pulled ahead of the party. On a small knob below the summit of Basin, we stood and drank again from the wineskin. The hour approached noon and the temperature had climbed. He lowered his suspenders, pulled his shirt over his head, and stuffed it into his rucksack. Then he pulled the suspenders back over his shoulders.

—This is how we do it in the Alps, he said, turning and leading over the bare rock and tundra, from rock cairn to rock cairn marking the route across the naked granite.

As I write, the force of this memory strikes me like a punch. Who was this odd and rare man who seemed so conventional and outrageous at the same time? I recognized hidden blockages in my self-definition—objections, judgments I had rationally rejected but still unconsciously held. To climb into a sphere where mind and sense could coexist, and to see them embodied in such an eccentric genius, flooded me with unusual responses and associations—sensual ones, certainly. I felt a sympathy and attraction for the sun and stone, rock clefts and glacial erratics, a synesthesia brought on by nothing more than sunlight, glassy air, exertion, and three glugs of claret.

It needed to be embraced and tempered. Perhaps that was the emancipated female role. To embrace but clarify opposing principles. It forced on me a piercing attention. Here was the enactment of something I had been imagining and intellectualizing for five years. It existed, but I distrusted the reality of it when it was before me.

On Haystack, the trail steepened over bare rock in the last five hundred feet. Carl often climbed directly above my head. Looking up into the darkness where his thigh and lederhosen met, I saw that he wore no underclothes. His great ballocks dangled and swung like Swiss cowbells. We climbed log ladders and pulled ourselves over the steep pitches, he finally slowing and I beginning to flag. Looking ahead at the summit, I felt I could just make it at our current pace. Below, the other four made their slow way across an open knob, at least half an hour behind. We reached the top an hour past midday, six hours after we had left the Shanty. It would be at least three going back, down the south face of Basin and along the lakes. We threw off our packs. Carl dropped his staff, and sprawled across the rocks. I took off my boots and hose and opened my feet to the air and the bare rock. The lubricity of it all was delicious.

I drank from my canteen, saving half for the way back. Carl loaded his pipe and I knew the wineskin would follow. It did. I had pulled my pant legs up to my knees. He noticed as he lit and pulled on his pipe.

—You have strong calves, he said. Delightful. Like that chasm below.

—Panther Gorge, I said. That's Marcy on the far side.

—Beautiful, all of it. I think you are avoiding my eyes because you are attracted to me.

I resolved to remain detached. I looked up straight into his eyes.

—And you to me, Herr doktor.

—I could come to you in the night.

—I would rather not confuse my admiration with something else.

He moved closer. I felt his breath. Below, an eagle disappeared over the gorge's rim.

—We have time now.

—I have prized our time together, sir. What you are suggesting is impossible.

He drew back. I looked at him again. His lip curled over the stem of his pipe. His eyes squinted and his face focused into concentration.

—You missed an opportunity, he said. It could have been

such a Jamesian moment, to have entered the flux of concrete experience, what?

—The point is that you know reality by what occurs out of a number of possibilities. Choice can be the determining factor of truth.

—Oh, pish and twaddle. You Americans have lost the connection of Eros and nature, that's all. It's still raw in Europe. Freud sees it everywhere, perhaps, but in my conversations with James, his sex seemed completely bottled up, constricted, inaccessible. I hope you don't get that from him: it is the beginning of neurosis. It starts with your Puritans, naturally, for whom the primeval forest harbored everything unbridled. The devil lurked there, and witches held their covens in forest clearings. But I blame the Concord transcendentalists, Emerson and Thoreau, for etherializing nature in order to redeem your vast resource of wild beauty from the perception of evil. They needn't have castrated it, too. The Puritan Hawthorne certainly didn't, nor the New Yorker, Whitman, for whom all of North America was a phallic projection. The transcendentalist projection, on the other hand, was sentimental, chaste. Their intellectual heir and your mentor, James, suffers, I think, from erotic repressions he looks to nature in order to sublimate. All this manly tromping, covered in wool even in the warmest weather, acting out his neuroses on the wild frontier. But he never removes his shirt, never lets the phallic energy of the sun caress him. Europe, so relatively poor in landscapes like this, has kept alive the erotic undercurrent of the classical era. Even in my repressed country we are closer to the elementary forces than your frontiersmen and rustic thinkers. As a Jew, of course, you have easier access to the classical memory, and I had thought you more emancipated in the modern fashion. Well, all right. You speak from a place of self-knowledge I admire, and I'm certain we will remain in touch. (And I hope you'll let me analyze you when we return. I did Freud in a taxicab.) But here you must redeem nature from the sentimentalized vision, return the archetype of erotic nature to your conscious awareness. You may find god on the mountain summits, on the plains and in the tall forests, but you must also accept the primordial phallic energy.

EXHAUSTION. REGRET. I lower my pen, Carl still visible, the past present, the images scrolling like a newsreel.

Sunset. Voices on the water. Car doors. Distance.

F. a phantom, fading, inchoate. The death agent we welcomed and love. He arrives at dusk on the porch, sitting in the Morris chair. Wordless. Arnold was no James, and goatish in sex. We stopped at nothing, and the memory had been strong enough to sustain me in the hard hours. Who else could have lived up to such animal intimacy? How late for desire to rise, when it has been dormant so long.

Later, pale night. Wendy again. She retreats and F. still here. Closer, I tell him. He shifts the chair to my side. Give me your hand. He places it in mine and I place it on my existing breast. No, he says, and sobs. He bends his head on top of our hands as the tears come. No, he says, louder. I place the hand under the blanket, there, and press him to me. The head stays on my chest, powerless to rise, and the tears flood quietly like a slow river, soaking everything, mine and his, the years, the errors and losses all mingling in the salt. My love. I know you will deliver me.

September 10, 1938. So much, and enough. All remain watchful. It is well.

Afterword

Lonnie Monroe died in spring 1983. According to *Adirondack Daily Enterprise*, Monroe's neighbor, Jim Reynolds, found him in the sugar bush a half-mile behind his house, lying under a dead maple limb. Reynolds had become concerned when he saw Monroe's team of Morgans (the "girls") standing in the yard wearing their hitch. Monroe's chainsaw lay a few feet from his body, and the maple he had felled made a perfect line between two larger trees.

In 1929, according to St. Martin's notes and the *Enterprise*, Monroe had gone to Texas after the encounter at Donnelly's with Schultz's Nicholville irregulars. There he worked on an oil rig for six months before coming back, building his house on the Saranac River, and marrying Mary Hitchcock. While still flush from smuggling, he managed the CCC camp at Duck Hole for two years. Until World War II he traded horses around northern New York and Canada, and ran a trapline in the Adirondacks and the Laurentians. During the war he trained horses at the Army Cavalry training camp at Fort Bliss, Oklahoma. Finally, in 1949, he joined the New York State Conservation Department as a carpenter, and worked out of the Region 5 shop in Lake Clear for twenty years. He quit drinking in 1958.

Beginning in the thirties, Monroe kept a tent camp on state land at Fish Pond, where he fished for lake trout and hunted deer and snowshoe hare. His was one of hundreds of such camps dotted around state-owned lakeshores, which lease-holders could occupy for decades for a small fee. The temporary camps were limited to platforms with no foundations, small square-footages, canvas roofs, and outhouses. Nevertheless, the lease holders— prize-winners in a lottery that was often locally rigged—became attached to their modest retreats. In 1971, when the new state land master plan of the Adirondack Park Agency cancelled the leases, Monroe abandoned his reluctantly and with mixed feelings. He recognized the importance of protecting the area when Paul Smith's estate donated it to the state Forest Preserve, and of the public having access to its own land. He also reasoned that he already lived in a nice place in the woods. But he never returned to Fish Pond. "If Myron was more interested in it, I'd of said something," he said, "but he only cared about cars and girls at that point, and he hated going cause he couldn't watch TV there. Well — I never really knew what Myron wanted." A loyal state employee, Monroe always hunted and fished legally, but he disliked the austere tone of state regulators regarding local concerns.

To St. Martin, who never knew Germaine, Monroe represented the last gasp of an earlier reality, a former way of viewing the world and the Adirondacks. In his journal St. Martin relates how it pained him when he went with Sonja Germaine to the old rascal's funeral, at Fortune's in Saranac Lake. After the service, Myron Monroe accosted the pair at the reception and blamed them for the mess that had become of the Adirondacks, his home, and called them "tree-hugging commie faggots" for supporting the park agency (though both had objections to details and thought the agency could have worked better). This was shortly before the couple's important journey in Quebec and Labrador, forthcoming in this series.

In later years, Myron used his father's house on the river as a weekend retreat from his prison-guard job at Dannemora, and as a hunting and snowmobiling camp. In 1990, he helped organize and lead a massive traffic slow-down on Interstate 87, protesting new land-use regulations to be added to existing ones. Hundreds of cars backed up for miles on the Adirondack Northway, from Plattsburg to Albany, going thirty miles an hour. When the cavalcade of pick-ups and low-riders reached its destination late that afternoon, it circled the state capitol like a Mongol horde, honking horns and waving banners of class anger and bile. After an hour everybody parked and assembled before the capitol, where they aired their grievances in incoherent diatribes delivered over a cheap megaphone. You couldn't understand the words, but the point was clear: any new standards, laws, or zoning in the Adirondacks would come at a cost.

The Mario Cuomo administration swept the recommendations under the rug, and the ever-complacent, bureaucratic environmentalists never recovered their philosophical bearings. One night in February, 2004, Myron Monroe left a bar in Lake Clear, headed home to Bloomingdale on his snowmobile. Somewhere in the boggy flats along "Negro" Brook (one of many places so named after the fugitive slaves who once lived there), he ran at high speed off the locally maintained trail system and into one of the log stanchions of the old power line. He lived for a month, but his neck was broken, and he died in March.

AFTER JACK "LEGS" DIAMOND WAS SHOT IN 1932, Basil Hare disappeared into the tenderloins of northern and central New York: Oswego, Syracuse, Herkimer. He emerged in the late thirties as the proprietor of the Gold Shade Restaurant and the Dream Street Newsstand in Glens Falls. The newsstand grew into a company that still controlled magazine and newspaper distribution around northern New York and Vermont. Through the 1990s, it was also the center of a bookmaking operation for thirty years.

While Hare maintained his underworld ties, he cut a dashing local figure and polished his public persona as a civic-minded businessman. In the 1950s he developed much of the west side of Lake George below Bolton Landing, and a number of housing developments in Queensbury. He served as Queensbury town supervisor for ten years, and, during his term as chairman of the Warren County Board of Supervisors, got pretty much whatever he wanted. In later years he waxed nostalgic over golf at the Glens Falls Country Club, and at the Saratoga race track every August, about his past as a bootlegger and ladies' man. Many people between Saranac Lake and the Catskills boasted about how well they knew Legs Diamond, but Hare was one of the few who weren't whistling out their ass. He died of cancer in 1962.

JACK DIAMOND'S CAMP AND OUTBUILDINGS BURNED in the late thirties, and now the island belongs to the New York State Forest Preserve. Pines and birches shade the crest of the esker, and the concrete landing and stone channel remain. Paul Smith's Hotel also burned in the thirties. The fire, in an old building that had survived multiple woodstoves, fireplaces, and gas lamps, was caused by faulty wiring.

EMILE JACOBS MOVED TO AKWESASNE (Hogansburg) from Kanewake (Caughnawaga) in the thirties, and soon became known as one of the best craftsmen on the reserve. He married Glenda Michaels in 1939, when he was forty and she was twenty-five. Jacobs joined the traditional Longhouse then being restored on the reserve after a long eclipse, and began learning the Mohawk language from Glenda's mother and grandmother. In

1947 he represented a crew of Mohawk boatmen going against the Finch-Pruyn Lumber Company over payment for one of the last pulp-wood drives on the upper Hudson. The crew claimed the company had promised them ten dollars per man per day, but when they arrived at the North River barracks, they were told it would be five dollars. The boatmen voted to stay put in North River and not continue downriver until the company agreed to pay. These were not the same people it had been so easy to exploit in the thirties. Most had been airborne during World War II, and had parachuted into Sicily and Normandy. The state police surrounded the barracks, but by then supplies of booze and beef had been laid in, and musicians and women from North Creek procured. A three-day revel began. At the end of the second day the state police, fearing a riot, withdrew. The next night, with a hundred Mohawk boatmen and locals watching, the barracks burned, and the revelers drifted off, unpaid. The pulp drives came to an end.

In later years, Jacobs lived in Brooklyn and Schenectady, and in the seventies he supported the Moss Lake takeover. He was among the founders of a school on the reserve that taught the Mohawk language and the religion of Handsome Lake. He died before the flare-up of hostilities at Akwesasne in the 1980s, over gambling.

HATTIE GILMAN CLOSED HER PLACE IN ONCHIOTA IN 1932 and started a rooming house for nurses in Saranac Lake. Many of her residents were former employees. During the Depression she acquired land and a reputation for sharp dealings around Lower Saranac Lake and lakes Colby, Aurora, and Clear, and developed cottage communities that became popular resorts in the forties and fifties. In the early fifties she started the Woodlands Real Estate Agency and transformed many of the village's grand cure cottages into inexpensive rental units. She always denied being the Hattie of the Onchiota brothel, but a dozen or so former customers kept the memory of her singular establishment alive. She died of emphysema in 1958.

VIVIEN GOLD SOLD EAGLE POINT IN 1939 and moved to Taos, New Mexico, where she joined the circle surrounding Mabel Dodge Luhan. Her paintings owed much to the visionary art of Rockwell Kent, and were widely admired and collected. In 1980, after being diagnosed with pancreatic cancer, she killed herself with an overdose of Valium. The Adirondack Museum mounted a display of her early Eagle Point paintings in 1979. "Caretaker, Lake Aurora, 1930" (now in Sonja Germaine's possession) depicts a nude male with bullet and shrapnel scars on left shoulder and buttock. He stands in a green canoe, facing away from the painter, with one foot in front of the other and the blade of a long beavertail canoe paddle in the water. A red sunset streaks the sky over the low mountains, and trout, pike, turtles, and salamanders sport and copulate in the green depths under his feet.

WENDY FEATHERSTONE CORNING GRADUATED with an advanced nursing degree from Russell Sage College, in Troy, in 1935. When Rosalyn Orloff declined in her last days, Germaine hired Featherstone — through Yvette Landry — to assist him and Vivien in her care. Wendy had remained close to Yvette Landry all her life, and often stayed at the Lake Placid Club, but Sonja had lost touch with her when Yvette died. In World War II Corning had been a colonel in an Army Air Corps WAAC unit, and saw combat in Africa and Italy. After the war she married her commanding officer, Colonel William Corning, M.D., and moved with him to Saratoga Springs. As a reservist she helped redesign the structure and operation of combat MASH units in the late forties, and became the chief of nursing at Albany Medical College. She also used her experience and love of skiing to advance the standards of the National Ski Patrol. In the mid-nineties, Sonja Germaine found her old Aunt Wendy still living in Jupiter, Florida.

YVETTE LANDRY RECOVERED FROM TUBERCULOSIS, married Dr. Hans Kline, and moved into the rambling Shingle-style house on Signal Hill in Lake Placid that she occupied until she died in 1984. She never remarried after Kline died from polio in 1936. She often traveled to Europe and the Caribbean, and maintained an apartment near her mother in Montreal's Square St. Louis. She promoted performances of classical and folk music there and in Lake Placid. Her longtime association with Charles Norton, the Lake Placid lawyer, lasted until his death in 1974, though they only lived together openly after Bartholomew Germaine went to graduate school at Columbia in 1953. She reigned over the local arts community and the Olympic Committee, and was known for her couture and dinner parties that combined colorful local characters with visiting dignitaries.

Landry and Fran Germaine remained close. Her son kept his name. People knew she and Germaine had been "wild" in the twenties, when everybody was. Yet somehow their past never stained her reputation. Her invitation to Lake Placid of the Sicilian contralto Aiella Brindisi in the fifties led to Bartholomew's marriage and the Italian's purchase of Eagle Point in 1958, after years of neglect by the failed Boston banker who had bought it from Vivien Gold.

FRANÇOIS GERMAINE LEFT EAGLE POINT AFTER THE WAR and moved back to his own modest frame house in Keese's Mill, on the narrow headwaters of the St. Regis River's Middle Branch. In 1946 he was invited by friends of Marjorie Merriweather Post, his neighbor on Upper St. Regis Lake, to build a fifteen-room log camp on the Snake River near Jackson, Wyoming. He spent the summer and fall of 1946 there, building his masterpiece, "Tioga." That led to a job in Lake Tahoe, and in the following years he built log and rustic structures in Jackson, Wyoming; Sitka, Alaska; New York City (a celebrated interior in an Upper East Side brownstone); Saratoga; Lake George; and all over the Saranac Lake/Lake Aurora area.

After Bob Marshall's untimely death in 1939, Fran became an honorary trustee of the Wilderness Society, and in 1949 published a memoir in *Wilderness Magazine* about his hikes and travels with Marshall. In 1948 Germaine joined the Schenectady conservationist Paul Schaefer to defeat the Ball Mountain dam proposal, on the Moose River near Old Forge.

In 1952 he appeared on the Arthur Godfrey show with Noah John Rondeau—billed as the "Adirondack Hermit." Rondeau answered questions and told indecipherable hunting stories in his squeaky voice and French-Canadian accent. Germaine played "Devil's Dream" and "Joys of Quebec" on the fiddle, and sang "A-Lum'brin' I Will Go." After that he was more in demand as a fiddler for square dances, but performed only occasionally. He preferred playing for special occasions like friends' weddings or pig roasts, where he would jam for an hour or so with the band and have a single glass of brandy, then go on his way.

People always assumed his cousin Pete LaFleur had run away from bad debts and his wife, Hilda. Germaine never let on what really happened, except to say he missed his cousin and hoped he was all right wherever he'd gone.

He never married, but had three long-term relationships. The longest was twelve years with Josephine Williams, who owned the Tumblehome Inn in Lake Aurora (formerly the sanitarium). In 1958 she sold and moved to California. Germaine stayed behind to be close to his son and daughter-in-law, and his new grandchild, Sonja.

Over the years he spoke out, in a quiet but reasoned way,

about conservation. He tried unsuccessfully to convince the state to enforce an old decision against Paul Smith and remove the Franklin and Union Falls dams on the Saranac River, where his father had once caught salmon. Laurence Rockefeller consulted him in 1956 when he was considering proposing an Adirondack National Park for the High Peaks region, but Germaine helped him understand that a state structure protecting the entire Adirondacks would work immeasurably better, and protect more wild land. Immediately afterward, Laurence's brother and state governor Nelson's Temporary Study Commission, which ultimately outlined the goals and structure of the Adirondack Park Agency, consulted him on a regular basis, and he became a kind of sentimental father-figure to many of the young environmental wizards on the staff. Privately, he said they were all nice boys, "but you wouldn't want to spend much time in the woods with any of them." In the mid-sixties he wrote a famous letter to the *Albany Times-Union* supporting the establishment of a "Park with People," administered by local appointees and trained staff, which would guide not only development in the back-country, but the villages as well. When Rockefeller pushed through a differently-modeled APA Act over Christmas break in 1969, the letter turned many against Germaine. But he had always remained aloof from the villages and had never really been all that close to the business community, either.

IN 1973, ARTHUR J. PRATT, JR., OF STONY CREEK, near Lake George—a transplanted Hunkpapa Lakota from Standing Rock, North Dakota, and a musician and proprietor of the Stony Creek Inn—bought ten gallons of hard-to-find gas from a logging contractor and drove his '61 Mercedes north to Lake Aurora, looking for "some crazy Frenchman named Germaine" he had heard about in a Glens Falls bar, possibly the Gold Shade. Pratt had owned the inn, a loggers' and sportsmen's hotel in the remote crossroads hamlet, for three years and needed to attract business from Saratoga and Lake George during the first gas crisis and the subsequent economic slowdown — severe in the rest of the nation and doubly so in the Adirondacks. He had planned a fiddler's jamboree and invited musicians from the southeastern Adirondacks and Glens Falls/Saratoga region, and advertised extensively on the radio and in newspapers as far away as Troy.

The event was scheduled for Sunday, July 25. Pratt left on the 22nd, determined to find the mythical fiddler of the north for his grand experiment. When Pratt failed to return to call the squares on Saturday night, the 24th, a sense of inevitability fell over the regulars, the old-timers, the twitchy Nam vets, and the long-haired young newcomers—all the outcasts of circumstance for whom the place had served as a kind of combined social center and church.

Pratt had left the preparations to the wait staff and bartenders, who carried out their duties cleaning up after the Saturday night square dance—decorating, prepping the food, and laying in beer and liquor. Nobody really believed Pratt or the public would show up. Nobody ever came to Stony Creek, supposedly, unless they were lost. The musicians began arriving at 11:00 a.m., tuning their instruments and having a first beer. The temperature rose into the nineties. Customers started showing up at noon. Somebody decided that Smokey Greene, the local radio star and country-western band leader, would officiate in the event Pratt failed to appear. Karen Jones of Lake George tended bar in jeans and a low-cut maroon leotard. Some of the musicians of the Stony Creek Band, the country-rock group that had just moved to the town, sat on the porch with their friends, recovering from last night's gig in Lake George and watching for Pratt's arrival. The lead guitarist, Hank Soto, was showing the young Chan Goodnow, his future banjo and mandolin player, how to finger a D chord. A car pulled up carrying four women from one of the nearby dude ranches, who were wearing halter tops and cowboy hats. They sashayed into the bar ignoring the men, and the men watched them sashay in and looked at each other. The afternoon went on that way, the cars pulling in carrying more and more resort trash, more woods folk, more music hounds, more dudes from the dude ranches. Inside, Smokey Greene and his band ran a sound check and began a set, Greene covering ably for the absent Pratt. By then cars were parked up and down the road for half a mile, the tables inside full.

Revelers were three deep at the bar, the high windows open, when the Mercedes rolled down the hill from the direction of South Johnsburg. Couples were already necking on the windowsills and smoking joints on the second-floor porch. Pratt looked around at the cars and said, "Oh, Jesus Christ." The tails of his snap-button western shirt were out. He was unshaven and disheveled, his eyes bloodshot. But he got out and looked up as he readied himself to pass indoors, his fiddle case under one arm and the guitar case that carried his Gibson Hummingbird with the sunburst top in his opposite hand. He stopped on the top step, framed by Baldhead and Moose mountains in the distance, and looked at the porch sitters. "I got him," he said, just as a 1954 Willy's station wagon with wood panels and a roof rack rolled into the four corners. "I got Fran Germaine. Hey, Fran," he yelled. "I got you, you old rascal."

The driver of the station wagon waved, smiled, then pulled into a spot that had opened across the street next to the Roaring Branch. He got out. The door opened on the passenger side, and a girl of fourteen climbed down wearing a sleeveless blue summer dress and huaraches. Her hair was long and black and wiry with humidity. The old man rummaged in the back of the station wagon and came out with a bag and a fiddle case. He looked around, made sure the girl was behind him, and started toward the inn.

By now Pratt could be heard onstage inside, slurring his way through a long-winded greeting and account of his delay and discovery of Germaine in the diner of the Tumblehome Inn in Lake Aurora "a hundred miles north, almost to Canada," his pitchman's delivery embroidered and upholstered over thirty years of mountebankery.

(Pratt's father, Arthur Sr., had gone to Carlysle and come East to drive teams pulling the last big pine and hemlock out of West Stony Creek. Pratt Jr. was a crack horseman, as well, and had wrangled for the earliest local dude ranches. Later he drove modified race cars around California and the Southwest with A.J. Foyt and Parnelli Jones, and played grange-hall dances and lumbermen's bars around the Adirondacks with his brother Bernard, "Beanie", who died by his own hand and an old Navy Colt in the sixties because of love gone wrong. When the rescue squad arrived at the homestead on Wolf Pond Road, the old man was in full ceremonial dress and singing the death song over his son.)

Germaine mounted the steps in khakis with the cuffs rolled, wearing Russell moccasins, no socks, and a white, short-sleeved cotton shirt. His black hair, streaked with white, stood straight up on his head. His eyes were brown as root beer, his face as creased as the Mexican canyons he had ridden of old. He looked into the hot, crowded hotel, nodded to the porch sitters, then bent and whispered something to the girl. The old man placed his hand on her shoulder and walked into the bar. "There he is, everybody, there's Fran Germaine," came Pratt's voice over the P.A. The crowd, wound by now to a lather, exploded, and Jimmy Hamblin from South Glens Falls launched into "Foggy Mountain Breakdown."

Jimmy Hamblin had a deformed hand, arm, and leg, and usually sat in a wheelchair or leaned on a crutch as he played, gripping his bow in his claw and fingering with his good right hand. Weeknights, he played organ at a sixties-style restaurant in South Glens Falls, an after-the-track hangout, and brought a goofy lounge-lizard showmanship to the act, playing crowd-pleaser novelty songs along with his blistering bluegrass.

Ken Bonner from Thurman played next, all old-time songs, then an old boy from Ticonderoga named Rollie Swinton, and another from Minerva. The band stayed on stage, substituting members from among the local musicians and the Stony Creek Band. Pratt called a break at around four to let the crowd sort itself and sell as much booze as he could. New arrivals filled the porches and flowed into the street. He recruited extra waitresses and bartenders from the crowd to help with the overflow. He stopped collecting at the door, but kept a waitress busy outside serving the milling crowd. Across the street at the Stony Creek Lodge, owned by Ethel O'Neill of Schenectady, the mid-day contingent of retired soldiers, old lumbermen, superannuated cops, and ne'ers-do-well had opened the bar door, and stood outside listening with their drinks in their hands.

The musicians, who by then were loosening up, went outside to smoke. Germaine drank coffee at his table. He took out Arnold Orloff's violin at Sonja's suggestion, tuned it, and bounced the bow across the strings. Pratt joined him and they discussed the next set: Germaine would play after Smokey Greene sang "Hello Walls" and "Crazy." While they were talking, One-Eyed Jackie Bonner, Ken Bonner's son, burst in, drunk, wearing an eye patch and cowboy hat, and yelled: "I'm a stock-car driver, a rodeo rider, a nicotine fiend and a lovin' machine! I like all sizes and breeds and most livestock. Hee-ahh!"

After Greene had opened the set, Pratt got up and introduced Germaine as the main event, the "best old-time fiddle player in northern New York and New England. Some people say he was a bootlegger back in the Prohibition and that he worked for Legs Diamond, but he won't say and I don't know. He's a fine horseman, I know that much, a rifleman and a woodsman, and a great builder, too. Why, he's one hell of an old hoot owl, aren't you Fran, you old hoot owl. Hoo-eee!"

They started off playing a duet on "Joys of Quebec" in a much slower, less jazzy pace than the version Pratt himself played. Pratt could hardly follow Germaine's timing and became lost when Germaine launched into a third section Pratt didn't know. But they circled back around to the main theme and bowed through the whole thing again, with a repeat and a coda that left Pratt out of breath and loose strings flying off his bow, and both of them hopping on one leg while they played. Pratt finally left the stage, and Germaine continued the forty-minute set, alternating traditional tunes from Quebec and the Adirondacks, like "Maple Sugar" and "Petronella," with Tin Pan Alley and Appalachian melodies now part of the universal musical vocabulary. The band, thoroughly drunk and under his spell, drove the music forward, pushed him, and he pushed back. If you had spent much of the last fifteen years listening to pallid folk music, bar bands, and industrial-grade country-and-western singers, the effect was electrifying.

The jamboree lasted until seven, when all ten fiddlers got on stage for an endless rendition of "Orange Blossom Special," each solo outdoing the last. Germaine and Jimmy Hamblin improvised a call-and-response exchange that drove the stoned-out, liquored-up, hyped-up old-timers, woodchucks, hippies, and tourists nuts. It exhausted everybody, and when the cheering ended, the silence came as a relief. A long break ensued, with orders of burgers, fries, and strip steaks flying out of the kitchen, and people going outside to throw up, smoke joints, do lines, and grope each other.

With the crowd reduced by half, the Stony Creek Band played a long set to clear the crowd's musical palate. Then they stayed onstage backing up other musicians who had songs or tunes to perform. Annie Goodnow sang "Springtime in the Rockies" with Pratt on harmony. Smokey Greene joined them and all three sang "Waltz Across Texas." This second, slower part of the day lasted until ten, when Germaine played a half dozen slow chanteys and reels from Cape Breton. He ended holding the fiddle against his chest and singing "Las Golondrinas," which he had learned in Mexico, while John Strong backed him up on bass and Hank Soto noodled on guitar underneath the melody. When the last note faded, it felt like a full minute of silence preceded the ovation.

The hardest core of musicians moved across the street to O'Neill's: Soto, Strong, Pratt, Germaine, and a few stragglers, all drunk but Germaine, who was on his twentieth cup of coffee. At the bar sat Grant Richards, George Arndt, and Moe West, all in their seventies like Germaine, and other retirees and freelance alcoholics. Ethel O'Neill sat smoking and smiling at the end of the bar. Her twin chihuahuas attacked the party, barking and scrabbling their nails on the parquet floor. She tried calling them off in her gravelly voice, to no avail. Her husband Randy Knowlton, a descendant of the original Stony Creek settler Randall Combs, got off his chair to call off the dogs, then opened his shirt and revealed inside the squirming, wrinkled, hairless skin and grimace of a micro-chihuahua. "Look at my kiiiiid," he intoned through his goggle-eyed glasses, leering and screwing up his face like a gargoyle.

The Buddhist geographer Jan Whipple was in there with her partner Ed Carlton, a retired IBM engineer, as were Tom and George, the gay and oddly accepted couple from Albany, who kept horses at their weekend house up on the Kenyon Road cut-off. Jon Cody was down from his cabin "over the mountain"; Todd Kelsey; Gail Stern; Cindi Muratori; the photographer Vincent Wooley; Slim Waddell and his wife Doris, who drove drunk down to Ethel's every morning and spent the day spouting non-sequiturs of painful truth and relevance, then drove home;

Dobber Atwell from Corinth; and Joe Clark, a union carpenter originally from Nogales, Arizona, who had been a merchant seaman and a Wobbly.

Ethel's son John O'Neill, later the town supervisor, brought out his Martin D-35 and played country standards à la Ernest Tubbs and Waylon Jennings, with Clark on chromatic harp and various others on backup guitar or fiddle. Then each of the old men, in quavery tenors, led a ballad from their youth or a World War I tear jerker, the tears wetting their cheeks in defiance of their maudlin smiles.

Many of these men and women had characters you would not recommend as models. Yet tonight, nobody fell down or got swinish and crude. The only bad note occurred when Roger Baker from Warrensburg found out Germaine was the same Fran Germaine—that Rockefeller toady—who wrote that letter to the *Times-Union* about "the APAs."

"Who does he think he is to speak in the names of us Adirondackers?" Baker said, while being restrained by Joe Clark and Pratt. "Them Albany big shots drove that fucking bill through on Friday night over Christmas. Ya know why? Cause they knew the town supervisors were against it, that's why!"

This was a new concept. Before then, nobody who lived in the "north woods" thought of being part of the greater region. People lived in Tupper Lake, or North Creek, but never in "the Adirondacks." Certainly not the Adirondack "Park." Baker lunged at Germaine, who regarded the fiasco with cool detachment from a safe distance. Other pairs of hands grabbed Baker, and Clark led him politely but firmly outside and let him know in no uncertain terms that he would be unwise to go back inside and to renew his line of inquiry with Mr. Germaine, who everybody knew had worked for Legs Diamond. In his argument, Clark employed a length of two-by-four in one hand and a Buck knife in the other.

So the day ended on a high note. Around 1:00 a.m. Hank

Soto led a sing-along on "Wild Mountain Thyme," in twelve-
or thirteen-part disharmony. Then Germaine gathered up his
sleeping granddaughter, put her with his fiddle case back in the
Willy's, and drove into the night, straight north. A small group
followed him out the door and stood in the street, watching.
Overhead arched the brightest show of northern lights they had
ever seen.

Two nights later Germaine went bullheading on Lake Aurora
on his seventy-sixth birthday. He drove the station wagon to Eagle
Point from his house in Keese's Mill and took Bart's lapstrake
Lyman across the lake to Moon Bay. When Bart rose the next
morning, he noticed the station wagon in the driveway near the
boathouse and the boat gone from its bay. He took down the new
lightweight canoe, made by a company across Lake Champlain
in Vermont, and paddled across to his father's favorite spot. He
found the Lyman anchored over the sand-and-mud bottom in
water ten feet deep, a few yards off the mouth of Grass Creek.
Germaine was slumped over in the seat, his rod still in his hand,
a nice fish on the line and four more in the wire basket over the
side. His Luckies were in his pocket and his thermos of coffee
half full, but the railroad lantern had blackened its chimney and
burned out.

They buried his ashes on the island beside Arnold and
Rosalyn (and Nietzche), and sprinkled a few on the waves for
good measure. Yvette insisted on a mass, though he hadn't been
to St. Ignatius in fifty years, except for the odd funeral. Bart and
Sonja talked her out of it, and she came to the simple ceremony
in a black dress and veil, along with Wendy, Emile (walking with
the help of two canes), and Sonja's mother, Aiella.

All this I got from Sonja Germaine years later. That night of
the fiddlers' jamboree, she and her grandfather had driven the
back roads home through North Creek, she told me, then up
Route 30 through Blue Mountain and Tupper Lake. Oh, that

was deserted country. The sky vibrated ahead of them all the way, the summer air filling the station wagon and the gas gauge drawing dangerously low while her grandfather talked of her grandmother, about the St. Germains of Quebec and Brittany, about logging and hunting, and about characters like Rondeau and Ma Schaefer. He had always hoped her father would be a doctor like his stepfather, rather than a stock broker, and work to cure a disease like cancer or TB—and live in Lake Aurora year-round like when he was a boy. She had a sense of herself that night that she had never had before. When she woke up a few mornings later, he was gone.

I remember the northern lights of that night, too, for I was among the porch sitters who watched Pratt and Germaine arrive that day. I heard Germaine play ten years before I met Abel St. Martin and the adult Sonja Germaine on the Hudson River gorge. I always knew I would write about it. It was in the days of fuel depletion leading to a half-decade of Adirondack cold and poverty, before Vietnam faded entirely from the screen and we drifted into our deep national sleep. For a little while two realities leaked into each other, one, stretching back to Teddy Roosevelt, of hard life, easy violence, and unforgiving judgment; the other of an evolving land ethic, nostalgia, and the feeling of something lost. After that the crack widened, the realities grew apart. By the 1980s the men and women who sat at the bar that night trading war stories and corny songs were all dead, and the living mental images of that world died with them. The true Adirondacks became an idealized, incompletely imagined version of itself, a collage with gaping holes, and not until Abel St. Martin died did I begin to understand everything I'd seen, and learned to see its shape.

—*Christopher Shaw, Miller Pond, September, 2004*

CPSIA information can be obtained
at www.ICGtesting.com
Printed in the USA
LVHW031047180421
684819LV00004B/21

9 781977 232 1